Twilight's Last Gleaming

A CAUTIONARY TALE

David J. Aiello

ISBN: 1519402090
ISBN 13: 9781519402097
Library of Congress Control Number: 2016907780
CreateSpace Independent Publishing Platform
North Charleston, South Carolina

NOV – – 2018

All characters and events in this book are fictional. Any resemblance to persons living or dead and events depicted are coincidental.

"Those who would sacrifice liberty for security deserve neither, and may lose both."
Paraphrase attributed to Benjamin Franklin

The Prince of Darkness

GREEN SMOKE FROM the flares curled upward, dancing erratically from the turbulence of the slowly rotating blades of the Apache helicopters. The blood-orange sun was just becoming visible over the mountains in the distant horizon. An AWAC aircraft, flying at fifty thousand feet, was monitoring air traffic. In Langley, several operations officers were observing and recording the activities in the area with the aid of a satellite. A dozen soldiers from a Special Forces marine unit had secured the perimeter of the landing zone on the Pakistan-Afghanistan border and were awaiting further orders. The men in the unit were combat-hardened, seasoned veterans. They had become accustomed, almost desensitized, to the everyday violence, carnage, and death, but none of them had ever witnessed violence carried out to this degree. The desert winds howling through the mountains sounded like a ghostly dirge casting an eerie mood over the landscape.

The men tried to remain detached as they observed the aftermath of the massacre. Flies and other insects were buzzing around the dismembered bodies of what appeared to have been Taliban and Al-Qaeda soldiers, possibly from the Pashtun tribes. A few of the soldiers had tied their khaki handkerchiefs over their noses to avoid breathing in the stench. The unit was ordered not to enter two makeshift tents that appeared to contain two dead American soldiers and an unidentified corpse. As the shadows moved with the rising sun, the area took on a surreal air as more of the hacked body parts and the blood-soaked desert sand became visible. Gray and white smoke was still pouring out from several still-smoldering camouflaged vehicles. All distinguishing features identifying the Humvees as American had been removed.

An enemy pickup truck with an M-60 machine gun mounted in the back was riddled with minigun fire and still smoldering, along with the burned and charred bodies of its occupants.

A transport helicopter landed, and several soldiers began unloading body bags on gurneys. They unzipped the body bags and quickly and methodically began placing the bodies strategically throughout the site. The bodies had been dressed and outfitted with weaponry to appear to have been allied resistant fighters. Two of the bodies were placed in one of the Humvees and doused with an accelerant. Then one of the soldiers unstrapped a Russian-made AK-47 assault rifle, shot each corpse several times, and then placed the weapon next to one of the bodies.

Another soldier was scouring the site, looking for anything that could be identified as American. He came across a corpse with an eighteen-inch black sais sword deeply embedded in his neck. He took a few pictures. Then he placed his foot on the corpse's chest, pulled out the weapon, and placed it into a green plastic bag.

A sergeant with the Special Forces unit who was assigned to secure the perimeter walked over to his lieutenant. "What the fuck happened here, sir? What's this all about?"

The lieutenant heard the rotors of a helicopter in the distance and looked up at the approaching Black Hawk. "I don't know, Sergeant, and I don't want to know!"

Colonel Bishop, who had arrived earlier in the transport helicopter, walked out slowly and surveyed the landscape. He put one of his hands up, blocking the sun as he tried to get a better look at the approaching Black Hawk. He was a career soldier. Although he was in his early fifties, he looked much younger. His light-brown hair was cropped short with only a few gray areas near his ears. His well-built six-foot-two frame and bold, chiseled features gave him a commanding presence.

The colonel had served in both Iraq wars, and the numerous medals he wore were a testament to his conquests. The men under his command never questioned his orders or actions. They knew him to be a vengeful officer, sadistic and meanspirited. All of the men knew that if you crossed Bishop, he would make your stay in Afghanistan a living hell.

By all accounts, the colonel was a rising star in the Far East theater. He knew this incident would be an indelible blemish on an otherwise stellar career. He also knew who was in the approaching Black Hawk. For the first time since he was transferred to the region, he felt anxiety and a sense of impending dread and trepidation—emotions he was not accustomed to experiencing.

The sun, along with the temperature and humidity, was rising quickly. The heat was making the stench from the rotting bodies unbearable. One of the soldiers turned around, crouched, and vomited.

The Black Hawk landed, and two men dressed in civilian clothing exited. One of the men, who had a video recorder slung over his shoulder, began taping the slaughter. He moved around and about the bodies carefully, positioning his camera to get the best angles. As he saw something of particular military significance, he paused, focusing in on the event for emphasis. The other man was taking notes and talking into a voice recorder.

The third man exited the Black Hawk as if he was taking a stroll in a park. He seemed oblivious and indifferent to the surroundings and the events that had taken place. He held his head erect, with perfect posture. His graceful gait gave him an air of superiority and arrogance. He wore a loose-fitting beige shirt and a matching pair of Dockers. His shoes were highly polished, dark-brown leather Cordovans. He took out his beige handkerchief and wiped the dust off his brown teardrop sunglasses and replaced them over his eyes.

Although the blades of the helicopter were still rotating slowly, producing a downward draft, every strand of his dark-brown hair stood perfectly in place. He adjusted an ear mic that was digitally connected to his phone. He was not using the device to talk to other CIA agents. He was listening to an eclectic collection of popular music. He listened until the chorus of his signature song, "Sympathy for the Devil," by the Rolling Stones, ended: "Pleased to meet you. Hope you guess my name, but what's puzzling you is the nature of my game." Then he took off his mic and placed it into his top pocket.

"Jesus Christ!" the lieutenant said to the sergeant in a voice slightly above a whisper. "What the fuck's he doing here?"

"Who?"

"The Prince of fucking Darkness! Not just a—spook. He's *the* spook."

"The spook?" the sergeant asked, bewildered. "What's his name…his rank?

"I never met anyone who knows his real name, but I know it's him. I saw him once before in Riyadh. He's the head of CIA operations Far East division. Those other guys that came before him are a CIA cleaning crew. If you really want to know his name, go ask him."

"Not me!"

"All I know is that if he's here, someone's in deep shit, and I hope it's that asshole Bishop!"

One of the aides to the Prince of Darkness was recording an oral description of the surroundings and taking notes as he walked. He came within hearing distance of the sergeant.

"What happened here?" the sergeant asked him.

"I'm sorry"—the aide looked up from his clipboard to see the rank of the soldier asking the question—"Sergeant. I'm not at liberty to say."

Colonel Bishop and the Prince of Darkness were talking out of hearing distance of the men. As they walked toward the makeshift tents, the Prince of Darkness motioned for the videographer and several other soldiers to come into one of the tents. Two American soldiers were tied and hanging from a metal bar wedged into the top of the tent. There were several sets of ropes with dried blood on them that had been cut.

"Document what happened here," the Prince of Darkness said. "When he's through, cut down these dead American soldiers, put them in body bags, and take them back to Bishop's base," he said to the two other soldiers. "Leave the third man on the ground."

One of the dead American soldiers had cigarette burns on his hands and face. His throat had been cut. The other soldier had his hands tied in front of him with black cable ties. Several of his fingers had been cut off and lay on the ground underneath him. He had been gutted, and his intestines and other internal organs were either on the ground or still dangling from his body. There was a pool of dried and coagulated blood under the soldier. It appeared as black as ink and didn't look real.

The other aide to the Prince of Darkness stuck his head into the tent and looked down at his clipboard. "Excuse me, sir. Line fifteen under the category as to—"

"Terminated with extreme prejudice," the Prince of Darkness said, interrupting him.

"Thank you, sir," he said, taking a glimpse at the dead American soldiers and quickly backing his way out of the tent.

After the men had finished and left the tent, the Prince of Darkness walked over to the remaining corpse, placed his foot under the man, and turned him over. He had a gaping hole in his chest. The front of the light-brown hemp garment was soaked with dried blood. His throat had been cut from ear to ear, and he had been stabbed multiple times.

"This piece of shit was your contact—Sihar Labuti," the Prince of Darkness said in disgust. "You got some bad intel, Bishop."

"I get twenty reports a day. This contact is suspect. That agent might be a mole. Here's bin Laden. Now he's there. How do I plan my missions? All I know is our contact," he said, motioning to the dead man on the ground, "was going to lead our men to an Al-Qaeda base camp."

"Lambs to the slaughter. Didn't you read *my* report? Confidence was high that Labuti was Al-Qaeda."

"There's so much misinformation. What am I to believe? Which leads do I follow?"

"Listen, Bishop," the Prince of Darkness, said trying to suppress his anger, "and never forget! When I say something is the way it is, it's the bible!"

Colonel Bishop and the Prince of Darkness made their way back toward the helicopters. "Bishop, how many of your men made it out?"

"Five, maybe six, depending if one of the soldiers survives."

"Well, let's see. We brought in six bodies, and there were already a dozen dead Al-Qaeda here and only two dead Americans. Not a bad ratio," he said, talking to himself but out loud. Then he turned toward Bishop. "You know that Langley is looking at us right now and that we're almost twenty miles into Pakistan. Were you trying to create an international incident? You know those towelheads don't trust us!"

"I know, but Labuti didn't exactly give us the precise coordinates of the camp."

"I'm going to have to interview the extraction team."

"Extraction team, sir?"

"The rescue team! Who rescued your men?"

"He disobeyed a direct order. Command did not yet authorize a—"

"You mean to tell me," the Prince of Darkness said, cutting off Bishop mid-sentence, "that one soldier is responsible for all this carnage, and the rescue of all your men. One! One man?"

To the best of anyone's recollection, no one had ever seen what even resembled a smirk, much less a smile, on the Prince of Darkness's face. A barely noticeable smile, a Cheshire cat grin, appeared on his face, which he quickly suppressed. He was looking upward, grasping, and trying to formulate a cover story out of thin air.

"It would appear so, but it's doubtful if he's going to make it. He's the one that was wounded. When I left the base, he was in the OR prep, unconscious, stable, but in critical condition."

"Yes," he said to himself, not paying attention to Bishop. Then he turned to Bishop. "Yes. I'll put a nice spin on this. Damage control. One of your men went rogue. Contravened a direct order. Cost two American soldiers their lives."

"That's not too far from the truth, all but the last part."

"Good, Bishop. You stick to that story, all but the *last* part. I'm going to cover your ass on this one, and one day, I'll call in the marker. Do we have an understanding?"

"Yes, sir."

The green flares had all gone out. They were collected along with any other evidence that Americans had been present. Several charges were set on both Humvees and at strategic locations on short timers. As the helicopters flew away, low, resounding thumps echoed, followed by orange flames and black billowing smoke, which contrasted against the brownish-gray mountains in the distance. As Colonel Bishop returned to his base, he became apprehensive, and he could find no solace as he came to the realization that in order to salvage his career, he had just sold his soul to the Prince of Darkness.

Blu Vineyards

Two years, three months later. The day after tomorrow.

IN SOUTHERN CALIFORNIA, Silver Verde Valley was one of the most productive agricultural areas in the region due to its rich soil, perfect climate, and abundance of water. The Silver Verde River meandered through the mountains and across the valley and emptied into the expansive Silver Verde Lake.

The Blu estate was a 450-acre vineyard that bordered the lake. It was located ten miles southwest of the small, quaint town of Silver Verde. Since their father's death, fraternal twins Raymond "Junior" Blu and William "Billy Ray" Blu owned and operated the vineyard. Junior was the elder of the brothers by six minutes. There had always been twins in the Blu ancestry, going back at least three generations. Junior was in his late thirties, tall and handsome, and he had an outgoing, happy-go-lucky, upbeat personality. Billy Ray resembled his brother physically, but that's where the similarity ended.

It was the first week in October. Blu Vineyards was hosting their annual harvest festival, celebrating another bountiful year. The grapes had been harvested and pressed and were fermenting in one-thousand-gallon stainless-steel tanks and oak wine barrels. The Blu family's generations of wine-making expertise had produced some of the most highly regarded and award-winning wines in the world.

The Blu estate featured a sprawling Spanish-style stucco ranch with an open courtyard and steep-pitched roof of red California-clay tiles. It was set on one of the highest elevations on the Blu estate. The courtyard and rear of the estate had been set up with banquet tables, decorations, and potted plants. The rear of the home had an outdoor kitchen, with flooring of interlocking brown pavers. A colorful donkey piñata filled with sweets, nuts, and fruit was hanging from party lights that had been strung above. Intertwined on a pergola that encompassed the entire rear of the home were bougainvillea vines splashed with hot-pink, scarlet-red, and fuchsia flowers. The area was landscaped with tall pink pampas grass, yuccas in flower, large steel-blue agave, various shapes and sizes of cacti, and succulents. A large American flag was flapping in the gentle breeze that cascaded on top of a tall white fiberglass pole with a bronze eagle sitting on the summit. The slight wind blowing through the coleus perfumed the air with a pleasant, subtle fragrance.

The farmhands, mostly Mexicans, Cubans, and a few Guatemalans, began arriving with their wives and children. Several chefs had been hired for the annual event and were cooking various succulent meats on large charcoal and wood-fired grills. Rotating slowly over a large open fire pit was a whole side of beef that one of the cooks was basting with a small culinary mop.

As Jenny walked through the courtyard, everyone's eyes gravitated toward her. Electricity filled the air. She carried a large bowl of fresh avocadoes picked from her farm that morning. She was wearing a floral-print sundress. The after-noon sun glistened on the lightly tanned, sinewy muscles of her arms and legs and her long, flowing brown hair. As she walked, with a slow cadence in her gait, it was as if a cool, refreshing breeze followed in her wake.

Junior was standing near the banquet tables talking and joking with Father Patrick "Pat" O'Keefe, the local Irish parish priest. As Jenny passed by Junior, she leaned over and placed a soft kiss on his cheek. Then she placed the bowl of avocados on the outdoor-kitchen prep area and began making guacamole for the celebration.

Strangers would stop in midstride, trying to preserve her image into their memory. Everyone was drawn toward her, held spellbound by her aura and the hypnotic quality of her voice. With her striking beauty and storybook-like quali-ties, one would expect that she had a demure personality. However, she was a strong-willed, outspoken woman with unwavering convictions and principles, never afraid to express her opinions.

Jenny Haas was born in Alberta, Canada. Her family moved to California when she was a child after her father inherited the small farm from her late uncle.

Their small forty-acre avocado farm bordered the Blu estate to the north. Two gray granite columns and a wrought-iron archway adorned the entrance to her farm. The letters in bold iron inside the circle of the arch announced the name of the farm, Four Strong Winds. She named the avocado farm after one of her favorite songs by Neil Young.

Jenny graduated from Los Angeles City College with a degree in English literature. In between her duties at the farm, she donated her time at the local library, reading to young children at story hour. As she would read to the children, she envisioned that one day she would be reading fairy tales to her own children. No one could ever detect the inner sadness and quiet desperation she hid so well. Now in her midthirties, she felt that life was passing her by. Her biological clock was ticking, and something was missing to make her life whole. Regrets began to take the place of the dreams she feared would never be realized. Today, she prayed, that would all change.

"Jenny, where's my brother?" Junior asked.

"Where else? He's up there," she said, nodding in the direction of the high ridge in the distance.

"Do me a favor, honey. Take the Jeep and tell him we would appreciate the pleasure of his company...before the day is over."

Billy Ray had been up since five working in the production area of the winery, preparing for the most important business meeting in the history of Blu Vineyards. About midday, he made his way to his private sanctuary on Blu Ridge, a high bluff overlooking the entire region for miles. The road leading up to the summit was steep. On top of the ridge were huge brown boulders, scrub pines, wild yuccas, and eucalyptus trees, which gave off an aromatic fragrance in the wind.

He had left the vineyard abruptly some years ago. After his tour of duty was finished in Afghanistan, with his good business sense and hard work, Billy Ray had led Blu Vineyard to more profit in one year than the previous decade.

Before he left, he was more like his brother: sociable and outgoing, with a good-natured but somewhat satirical sense of humor. At times, his eyes were like the blue expanse of the California sky on a lazy Sunday afternoon—calm and pleasing with the reassurance that he was in harmony and at peace with everyone and everything. But there were other times when his eyes transformed into cold, rolled blue steel, piercing, calculating, and disturbing to anyone who caught a momentary glimpse into his dark side.

He sat down on a chair with wooden slats and leaned backward. Two wooden wine crates were set up as makeshift tables. On the tables were several laptops, a bottle of Blu Chardonnay, a half-filled glass of wine, and some fresh figs in a small white-and-blue porcelain bowl.

He took comfort in the thought that, from this remote location and vantage point, he was safe, at peace, and the master of all he surveyed. In the distance, where his property merged into the mountains, he could see the remnants and tailings of the old Blu Silver mine that had been played out years ago and closed after the tremors of an earthquake had caved it in.

It was a calm day, and the sun shimmering on the lake made the water look like a bluish-white sheet of glass. Several groups of large birds, maybe turkey vultures or osprey, soared slowly on updrafts across the sky.

On two of the laptops were various chess games in progress. On the first screen, he was playing speed chess with a short time limit. He took a sip of wine and navigated from player to player, making each move in less than thirty seconds. On the other laptop, he played chess masters with screen names like Chess King, KGB, and Black Knight. His screen name was Big Blu. He would beat most of the players, but the best he had ever done against Black Knight was a draw.

Billy Ray turned around abruptly as he heard a vehicle heading up the incline. Jenny got out of the Jeep and paused briefly to take in the panoramic view.

"I will say one thing, Billy. It is breathtaking up here," she said, still looking over the horizon.

The afternoon sun was behind Jenny, casting the silhouette of her body through the sundress. As she turned toward Billy Ray, the sun danced off her face. He never took her beauty for granted, but today she looked exceptional. "My God," he thought, "she's so beautiful."

Billy Ray closed the laptops, stood up, and stretched his arms. "My brother sent you up here to fetch me."

"Almost everyone is already there. We...he thought you weren't coming."

Jenny looked down and saw the new fencing around the southwest part of the vineyard.

"What is it with all these fences, Billy? What is it that you are walling out?"

"Or walling in, Miss Librarian," Billy said jokingly, knowing that they both made a reference to Robert Frost's poem, "Mending Fences."

"I knew I would eventually get you to smile," Jenny said.

"The fences are to protect the new grapevines from the deer."

Jenny paused and looked into Billy Ray's eyes. He could see she was struggling to find the right words. "I...we...wanted you to be the first to know... before it is announced at the celebration...Your brother and I are announcing our engagement."

"Congratulations," he said, after an awkward silence. Looking away, he began to gather up his things to leave.

"And that's all you have to say?"

Billy Ray stopped packing. He put his arms around her and gave her a hug and a kiss on her cheek. He could feel the warmth of her body and drank in her fragrance like a parched man given a small ration of water in the desert. Old feelings surfaced that were simultaneously the source of his greatest joy and his greatest anguish.

Billy Ray pulled away slightly and looked into her eyes. "I know my brother loves you very much. I wish you both all the happiness you deserve."

It wasn't the answer she hoped for, but the one she expected. "Well, hurry up," she said, putting on a false smile, "before all of the food is gone."

After Jenny left, Billy Ray gulped down the rest of the wine in his glass. The last thing he packed was a tattered copy of *The Art of Violence*, by Tsiang Kieun. After the reign of the Samurai had ended in Japan, the book was banned. Japanese immigrants had taken copies throughout the world, and it had been translated into many languages.

Although every line of the book had been engrained and committed to memory, occasionally Billy Ray would reread passages to bring back the memory of his late mentor, Leong Mei. On the way down the steep slope of the ridge leading home, he reminisced. He had just entered high school the day Leong had given him a new copy. Ghi and Leong Mei operated a grocery store in town.

They also sold herbal remedies and operated a small martial-arts school. Ghi's family had been in the United States for many generations, while Leong's family only arrived on the mainland in the early fifties. Billy Ray's face had been bruised from an altercation, and he'd had a black eye.

"Wife tell me you to be pupil in school, maybe," Leong said. "Hardworking, honest, respectful, the Blu family. Friend to the Japanese people even during World War. Wife's grandfather work for your grandfather after no more work on the railroad. Work many years in silver mine and on grape farm. And now young Blu, learn self-defense, yes?" Leong asked as he pushed Billy Ray's face from side to side looking at his bruises.

Billy Ray's voice cracked as he spoke. It was partly out of respect and fear of the master. He cleared his throat. "Yes."

"When wife tell me young Blu wish to learn self-defense, check with nuns at catholic school you go. Tell me you enigma. You know this word *enigma*?"

Billy Ray nodded.

"Then you smart boy. I not know this enigma. Have to look up meaning in book. It say you a puzzle. Nuns say not know why you smartest boy in school then go outside and beat McFarlane boys with piece of fence for ganging up on Junior. You use the fence for defense." Leong smiled at his own pun.

Billy Ray grinned and then quickly suppressed the expression.

"You want learn for what reason? Hurt people maybe?"

"No," Billy Ray said. "That's not the reason."

"Good answer, grasshopper," Leong said, laughing as he made a reference to the popular movie. "Cause I no teach you that. Not like other dojos in big city. Teach for defense only." Leong took a new copy of the *The Art of Violence* and gave it to Billy Ray. "You read. If you smart as nuns say, no problem understanding. In book lesson more important than what I teach. Then maybe, if worthy, you begin learn."

When Billy Ray arrived at the celebration, Father Pat chastised him. Father Pat was the type of priest every priest aspired to become. He was in his early seventies but kept in shape and looked much younger. Although he had been the parish priest of the small congregation of Saint Mary's for as long as anyone could remember, he still spoke with a distinct Irish brogue. God only knew how this Irish Catholic priest ended up in distant California, far from his humble beginnings in Ireland.

"Mr. William Blu, most everyone has already eaten, and I have yet to say grace and make the announcement, and I haven't seen you at service the past two weeks."

"Harvest time, Father. I promise I'll be there Sunday."

As Father Pat called for everyone's attention, the music was turned down. He motioned for one of the guests who was filling the toast glasses to fill his. "We thank thee, oh Lord, for these bountiful gifts...good food...good friends... and for you sending down one of your angels to watch over us," he said jokingly as he motioned in Jenny's direction. Everyone clapped and cheered, which made Jenny embarrassed.

"Father, please," Jenny said, blushing.

"Have you ever seen a more beautiful of God's creatures?" he said, holding her hand. "I truly mean it."

"I think you've had too much wine, Father." Jenny said.

"I also want to bless Junior and Jenny, who announced the engagement of their plans to enter the holy right of matrimony. Bow your heads in prayer, and raise your glass in a toast to their health and happiness." After a moment of silence, he said, "Cheers."

As everyone cheered and clapped, Father Pat shook Junior's hand and kissed Jenny on her cheek. After the crowd calmed down, Billy Ray filled a plate with food and sat at the end of the table with one of the Spanish farm employees, Juan Sanchez. Everyone called Juan "Ocho" because of his muscular build and his six-foot-eight height. Ocho was Billy Ray's right-hand man at the vineyard. He could operate all the equipment and was a hardworking and trusted employee. They had a mutual respect and a shared love of horticulture. Billy Ray and Ocho were discussing upcoming vineyard developments while they ate. Ocho's voice was deep and low. When he spoke it echoed as if it were coming from a deep canyon.

Father Pat, Junior, Jenny, and Mayor Paul White came to the end of the table where Billy Ray was eating. The mayor had moved to the region a decade ago. He was a young, educated, and energetic politician. He spoke English and Spanish and was well liked by everyone, in part because he always put the concerns and welfare of the people above his own.

"Billy we wanted your opinion on a rumor that's been circulating in the next county," the mayor said. "Have you seen all the land surveyors in the area?"

"Can't say that I have," Billy Ray said, slicing through a piece of steak.

"I saw two on the way up here with their surveying tripods set up," Father Pat said.

"What's the rumor, Mayor?" Junior asked.

"Rumor is that California Power and Light wants to put a hydroelectric dam in the valley and seize all the land necessary to build it, with the power of eminent domain."

"Could they really do that?" Jenny asked the mayor.

"Yes, I'm afraid they could. If they could secure the permits."

"I'm sure Senator Bryant would never stand for that," Father Pat said. "He and I go way back. As a matter of fact, I performed his wedding ceremony. He carries a lot of weight in Washington. He's one of us. A good man."

"Is he, Father?" Billy Ray asked not looking up at him. He resumed eating. He didn't seem overly concerned.

"I do know something is up," the mayor said. "Senator Bryant's office called me this week and wants to set up a town meeting at the village green in two weeks."

"We'll fight them down to the last man," Junior said, raising up his hands in mock warfare, slurring his words in a joking manner. He had too much to drink and was mildly intoxicated.

"What's your take on this, Billy?" the mayor asked.

Billy Ray swallowed what he was eating and took a sip of wine. "There's no way they could build anything like that for miles in any direction."

"How could you be so sure?" Jenny asked.

"They could never build a dam that close to a fault line," he said emphatically.

"Yes, I forgot about that," Father Pat said.

"I don't understand," the mayor said, with a bewildered look on his face.

"Before you moved into the area, in the early nineties, there was an earthquake, and it was a pretty big one. The aftershocks caved in our silver mine. We never fully opened it up again. It's all on record. My father had a report from the county records office outlining the fault. They can't get a permit to build a dam near a fault. Never happen."

"Hopefully you're right, Billy," the mayor said. "We'll have to bring that fact to the senator's attention at the meeting."

It was late afternoon. The sun was low on the horizon and casted a soft orange light through the haze. Jenny put on a CD of her favorite songs. She turned up the volume, and most everyone got up to dance. Jenny gave Junior a kiss, led him to the courtyard, and began to dance. A short while later, Father Pat bowed, cut in, and began dancing with Jenny. As the song ended and another began, he walked to the end of the banquet table, took Billy Ray's hand, and led him, reluctantly, to dance with Jenny. The song playing was "I'm Yours," by Jason Mraz. As they began dancing, Billy Ray stopped, looked up above Jenny's head, and smiled.

"What?" Jenny asked. "What's the matter?"

"I was just looking for your halo," he said in a playful manner.

"Please," she said as she grazed the back of her hand on his arm. "I'm never going to live that down."

Billy Ray could feel Jenny's heart beat faster as they danced close together. Junior, who was talking with the mayor, took more than a casual interest in their dancing.

Well open up your mind and see like me,
Open up your plans and, damn, you're free
Look into your heart and you'll find love, love, love, love.

A late-model silver Mercedes Benz sedan pulled up in the rear of the house. As Mr. Phillip Renard got out of the vehicle, Billy Ray called out to Junior to come to the dance area. Junior motioned to him that he would be there in a minute.

"Sorry, Jenny. Business calls."

"It figures. Even today, it's always business with you." As Billy Ray went to meet Mr. Renard, Jenny was left momentarily alone, listening to the lyrics as the song ended.

Phillip Renard lived in Paris. He was part owner and the US broker and representative of an international consortium of wine merchants. He was tall and slender and approaching his middle sixties. He had thick black-framed glasses, black hair, and a pencil-thin mustache. He spoke with a thick French accent and had effeminate mannerisms.

"Mr. Renard," Billy Ray said, shaking his hand. "Would you like something to eat?"

"No, no, no, Mr. Blu. But thank you for the offer. I am truly sorry to interrupt the festivities, but as I told you a week ago, I'm only in the States for another few days. I am very excited to tell you of our findings."

Mr. Renard removed two small suitcases from the trunk of the Mercedes.

As he and Billy Ray made their way down the path to the production plant, Jenny, who was still dancing with Junior, watched them until they disappeared around the corner.

The Blu production plant was a two-story building with an artfully crafted sign above the entrance, with dark-blue lettering surrounded by gold leaf that stated, "Blu Vineyards, Est. 1893. The trademarked logo on the sign and on every bottle of wine was a small, cobalt-blue bluebird. The rear of the building had been carved into a steep hillside, with limestone walls reinforced with concrete. These walls provided a cool, stable, year-round temperature to process and store their wine. Against the back wall were countless thousand-gallon, stainless-steel tanks and hundreds of oak wine barrels.

Mr. Renard placed both suitcases on a large oak table. He opened one and took out a bottle of wine, two glasses, a pocketknife, and a corkscrew. He opened the bottle, stroking it gently, as if he were caressing a women's leg, and poured Billy Ray and himself a glass. Before Renard took a drink, he swished the wine around in the glass and held it under his nose. Then he took a small sip and waved his free hand in the air, savoring the moment. The label on the bottle read "Domaine Romanee Conti."

"Ah," he said, "nectar of the gods. The holy grail of wines. The most rarefied." He took another small sip. "I'm sure you know what this is, Mr. Blu."

Billy Ray took a sip and nodded his head. "It's the best and one of the most expensive wines in production."

"Up until now, if the experts are correct, Mr. Blu, up until now. We think we know most of the story why your wine is equal to DRC wine, but there are too many pieces of the puzzle missing as to how you arrived at the lot of wine you gave me on my last visit. The climate and the southwest-sloping topography are almost identical to Vosne, Romanne, in Burgundy, France. But many vineyards have tried to duplicate the conditions and have failed to produce a wine equal or superior to DRC. How did you do it? What are we missing?"

Billy Ray took a sip of DRC wine and smiled. "We did amend the soil in an attempt to duplicate the composition of soil in Burgundy, and as for the climate, we can only thank the Almighty for that. But the cultivar of grape is quite a different story."

"Yes," Renard said with growing enthusiasm. "Tell me about the grape."

"About six years ago, I purchased hundreds of scions of the Pinot Noir grape from a grower in Burgundy. I grafted the scions on California understock. The following year I cross hybridized the French grape with the California grape, maximizing all the desired traits but keeping in our resistance to disease and pests. The cross resulted in an almost identical profile and brix level to the Pinot Noir grape from France."

"Ha! That's the missing piece of the puzzle," Renard said, nodding as he quickly analyzed and understood what Billy Ray had told him. "But we will keep that little secret among ourselves, *oui*?"

Renard took another bottle of wine from his suitcase. He opened a bottle of the wine and poured two glasses. They both drank some wine, and Phillip held the wine in his mouth, swishing it around to savor and evaluate the taste. "What's your honest opinion, Mr. Blu?"

"Honestly, it's not as good as DRC."

"How close?"

"Very close," Billy Ray said, taking another sip.

"You have an objective pallet. You see Mr. Blu, this bottle of DRC is twenty years old," he said, holding up the bottle, "and your wine is only five. Your wine is still about two years away from full maturity. Given the fact that your wine reaches full maturation in only a third of the time of DRC, when it matures it will be equal in taste to DRC. That fact would make Mr. deVillaine and Mr. Leroy, the owners of DRC, envious."

Phillip opened the other suitcase on the oak table. "If everything is in order, we would like to take shipment of your entire allotment of your first vintage. I believe you said there were nine hundred cases at the agreed price of six hundred dollars per case, which totals five hundred forty thousand," Renard said, turning the suitcase toward Billy Ray. The suitcase was full of neatly stacked, bank-wrapped one-hundred-dollar bills.

"Thank you, Mr. Renard. That's more than generous."

"No, thank you, Mr. Blu. In all the years I have been in the wine business, this is my greatest moment. We are all going to become very wealthy men with your wine. Just one bit of advice, and it's good advice. Increase production. In a very short while, I assure you, demand will exhaust supply."

Billy Ray nodded in acknowledgment of what Mr. Renard said. In his heart he always knew this day would come. "I wish my father was alive to see this. He never had any faith in my vision."

"In any event," Phillip said, extending his hand, "my partners and I are looking forward to a long, prosperous, and pardon my pun, fruitful relationship."

Main Street

LATER THAT EVENING, Billy Ray left the Main Street Coffee House, where he could be found most evenings. The coffee house was a gathering place for college students for socializing, surfing the web, or doing their homework on laptop computers.

He thought how fortunate he was to live in a town like Silver Verde. It was a town where you never had to lock the doors to your house or car. A town without the crime of the big cities. Everyone knew everyone by first names and helped each other. You could still get a root beer float at the local five-and-dime for under a dollar. Where you could get the local gossip along with your haircut at the barber shop with an old-fashioned red-and-white barber's pole spinning day and night. In the window of Maggie's Beauty Salon was the hokey sign, "If you're not becoming to him, you should be coming to us."

Dr. Horton still made house calls, carrying his little black leather bag and wearing a stethoscope around his neck. It was an easy, predictable, and vanishing way of life. Main Street was an era frozen in time, as if it were taken from one of Norman Rockwell's *Saturday Evening Post* covers. It was as wholesome as Mom and apple pie, and as they were about learn, Senator Bryant knew this town was ripe for the picking.

On his way home, he drove slowly down the dimly lit Main Street. As he passed by Sparkey's Pool Hall, he saw the McFarlane brothers' pickup trucks outside the bar. The brothers never forgot the beating Billy Ray had given them after school that day and swore that someday they would get even. The brothers had grown up to become the town derelicts, always looking for confrontations. Billy Ray never frequented the pool hall, always remembering the philosophy of *The Art of Violence*, which postulated: "The Warrior must avoid situations and environments where violence may occur. To engage in casual violence for petty transgressions, or for sport, diminishes the nobility of the Warrior."

On the outskirts of town, a woman stood alone under a streetlight. Billy Ray recognized her. It was Carla, a high-school classmate. She was still very attractive but overdressed for Main Street. She wore too much makeup, which barely hid the hard life and hardship in her life. She survived an abusive marriage, and after the divorce, she could be found late in the evening selling the only commodity she had left, along with her pride, to support herself and her two children. As Billy Ray stopped at the intersection, Carla walked over slowly. She knew he wasn't a potential customer. She just wanted to see her old friend.

"Billy Ray," Carla said, smiling. "Every time I see you, it reminds me of the good old days."

"You look great, Carla. As pretty as ever."

"You're being kind; we're not kids anymore. All the girls in school had a crush on you and your brother, including me. Remember when we danced at senior night?"

"How could I forget? You were the life of the party."

"Oh please, Billy. I remember Jenny got real jealous when we danced. She didn't talk to me for weeks. What ever happened between you and Jenny? Everyone thought that you'd marry her when you got back."

"Sometimes things don't work out the way we plan."

She looked away from him momentarily as a bad memory surfaced. "I know what you mean. Someday, Billy, when you get lonely, like I always am, you'll know where to find me."

Billy Ray reached into his pocket and pulled out several hundred-dollar bills. As he tried to hand them to Carla, she walked away, shaking her head. "I can't take that, Billy."

"Think of it as a deposit on…someday," he said as they both laughed.

"I'll hold you to that promise…someday," she said, smiling through the sadness. "Oh Billy, Billy, Billy Ray, how you bring back the memories."

As Billy Ray pulled away, he remembered the song "Main Street," by Bob Seger. As the lyrics and melody echoed in his memory, he couldn't help thinking that it played every day on every Main Street for lonely people like himself and Carla.

When Billy returned home, he could see Junior and Jenny in the courtyard. They were lying on lounge chairs, keeping warm by the slow-burning embers smoldering in the fire pit. He went up to his room, turned on the light, and prepared for bed.

"What did my brother say when you told him of our engagement?" Junior asked in a voice slightly above a whisper.

"Not much. You know your brother. He never tells anyone what he's really thinking or feeling."

"Are you hiding something from me?" Junior asked jokingly. "I mean you and he have a...history."

"No," she said, nudging her elbow into his side.

"You're hurting me," Junior said as he put his arms around her and kissed her on the nape of her neck. "Did he sound surprised?"

"If you must know, he said congratulations and wished us the best."

"Really. I told him about our engagement a week ago, and he said it was about time I made an honest woman out of you."

A cool breeze swept up the valley. As Junior and Jenny embraced to keep warm, she kept looking up at the light in Billy Ray's room until it went out.

Senator William Wadsworth Bryant

As CHAIRMAN OF the Senate Banking Committee, Senator William Wadsworth Bryant was one of the most powerful and influential men in the United States. His senatorial district encompassed most of Southern California. He was middle-aged, handsome, and stately in appearance. He had a charismatic personality, was independently wealthy, and had been born to parents with old money. His in-laws were extremely wealthy and influential members of Newport society. He stayed at their Bellevue Avenue mansion while he earned his undergraduate and master's degrees in political science at Brown University. Above all his political attributes was his gift for oratory. He was an eloquent speaker who had an encyclopedic knowledge of the English language and literary references. Whenever he wanted to make even the most shallow or superficial statement seem profound, he would break up the words into lingering syllables, emphasizing the point he was making.

He had the typical vices available to elite politicians in his position. He was arrogant, self-absorbed, and self-serving, but his public-relations staff had done an exemplary job of convincing the public that he was a man of the people, a public benefactor. Although he dined regularly on the delicacies of the Washington banquet table of excess and privilege, his insatiable appetite for power and prestige was never satisfied.

The senator sat in his plush California office polishing and cleaning a commemorative silver-plated nine-millimeter handgun, humming the song "Hail to the Chief." He was confident and had aspirations that one day that song would be playing for him. The state capitol building could be seen in the distance through a large window decorated with custom beige drapery. The walls were highly polished rich mahogany and dark-cherry wood wainscoting. Adorning the walls of his office were many framed photographs of him with several presidents, celebrities from the entertainment industry, sports figures, and foreign dignitaries.

In his outer office, the Prince of Darkness sat waiting patiently for an unscheduled appointment. He was wearing a black pinstripe Armani suit, white cotton shirt, red, white, and dark-blue tie, and a highly polished pair of black leather Cordovan shoes. He was growing impatient, and when the senator's secretary left the room, he entered his office.

"Excuse me. You're not allowed in here," the senator said, startled as he reached under his desk for the security alarm.

"I wouldn't press the alarm, Senator," the Prince of Darkness said, handing him his card.

Senator Bryant looked at the card and then up at the visitor. "Speak of the devil," he said, fumbling as he put the gun and cleaning paraphernalia in the top right-hand drawer of his desk.

"I'm surprised our paths have never crossed...until now."

"We travel in different circles. Do you have a permit for that gun, Senator?"

"It was a gift from my constituents."

The Prince of Darkness had come to the senator's office on a fishing expedition. He also wanted to see how he would react under pressure and adversity. How far he could push him. Test his character and resolve under duress. He would use misdirection, cunning and guile to extract from, inform, and evaluate him. Whatever information he came to impart or extract, no matter how serious or benign, his demeanor would be calm, with an even keel, without raising the tone or altering the inflection in his voice.

With this tactic, he thought could elicit the opposite reaction from the senator.

"If you would be so kind to tell me why I have been graced with your presence," the senator said with indifference, "we can get on with this intrusion."

"This is going to be the most important meeting you've had in quite some time, Senator. I've come here to, metaphorically speaking, slap some sense into you, and in the process teach you a little humility."

"I beg your pardon," the senator said with indignation.

"When our meeting is over, you will receive my pardon and beg for my unwavering loyalty and all the magic and sleight of hand that would accompany our new friendship."

All the red buttons on the senator's phone were blinking. His secretary beeped in on the intercom. "Excuse me, Senator. Senator Mann from Appropriations said he needs two minutes of your time."

"Cynthia, tell the senator that I'll get back to him shortly, and hold my calls."

Senator Bryant wrote down a few notes and then looked up at the Prince of Darkness. "There is a saying that would be apropos in this situation: 'Beware of Greeks bearing gifts,'" the senator said, with an expression of growing skepticism on his face. "What stars aligned that would make me the recipient of your magnanimous generosity?"

"We can speak frankly here, Senator. Save your lofty speeches and gravitas for the floor of the Senate. In about four years, the conventional wisdom in DC is that you're at the top of a very short list of candidates for the vice-presidential nomination. I'm here to offer my services and guidance to make sure you don't make any…mistakes. The board also wants to know if they're backing the right horse."

"What an honor," the senator said sarcastically. I still don't understand your interest in my activities. My responsibilities are domestic, while yours are foreign."

"Let me bring you up to speed. I was getting bored and distracted with all the bureaucratic red tape in our foreign policy. So when the powers that be decided that the American public would be best served if my…unique talents were used domestically, who am I to question their decision? I'm to head up the Big Brother program under the new ISS; the Internal Security and Surveillance division, unofficially, of course. I will have complete control and jurisdiction. We will be monitoring the activities of subversive and un-American activities."

"How Orwellian."

"Precisely."

"I have heard of this new task unit, but why haven't I been informed of your appointment?"

"You won't."

The senator had an expression of doubt on his face. The Prince of Darkness saw the skepticism and elaborated. "When you were young, Senator, do you remember seeing *The Wizard of Oz?*

"Where are you going with this?" the senator asked, growing impatient.

"Humor me. Do you remember when the wizard said, 'Pay no attention to the man behind the curtain'? Well, that's me. I'm the man behind the man behind the men. All smoke and mirrors, so to speak. Take, for example, Colonel Bishop. Do you know of him?"

"I heard something to the effect that he was in line for a promotion."

"The colonel will be promoted to the rank of general. He owed me a favor, and I reciprocated. A few strings pulled here, some arms twisted there, and quid pro quo, the colonel becomes a general. On my recommendation, he's going to be the new director of the ISS. You know how it works in DC?"

"All too well, and that's what puzzles me about your visit. What did he have to give you in return, a pound of flesh?"

"Actually, much more than that. How jaded, Senator."

"Comes from the years of experience of dealing with men like you. And once again I have to ask, what does all this have to do with me?"

"I'm getting to that in my own convoluted way. First, you're going to have to be a little more discrete with your...indiscretions."

"To what are you alluding?"

"Senator, Senator, Senator. I'm in the intelligence business. I know everything there is to know about anyone of importance that could possibly be an asset or a liability for me and the government I serve. Intel is a commodity, like currency. I invest it. Watch it grow. Use it frugally. Loan it out upon occasion. Use it like a debit card. When my investment matures and shows a nice return, I cash it in. And today, you're going to give me a hefty line of credit."

"Are you going to come to the point?"

The senator had been spoiled and coddled all his life and was not accustomed to being chastised. As the Prince of Darkness looked out the window at the capitol building, his plan to rattle the senator began. "You've been letting your little head think for your big head. Do you think your constituents can envision this picture? I certainly can. Late at night. The senator in his office. Hard at work. Doing the people's business. Pants down around his knees. Your pretty young secretary—what's her name—Cynthia bent over on your desk right here."

The Prince of Darkness reached over and began slapping the side of the senator's desk rhythmically. He could see that the senator was growing agitated. "'Oh, Senator,' I can hear Cynthia saying, 'you've got my vote!' Make a nice sound bite on CNN, don't you think!"

The senator did not respond. There was an awkward silence in the room.

"What, no glib remarks from the silver-tongued senator? Actually, Senator, I don't give a rat's ass who you're fucking, including the public—but the public, and let's not leave out your wife and kids, might. But I digress; we have more important issues to discuss."

The Prince of Darkness believed in the pugilistic philosophy of discourse, which postulated that if you were going to hit an opponent, make sure he stays down. With that in mind, and while he had the senator off balance and on the ropes, he hit him with another blow. "This nation is a tinderbox with so many little fires of discontent smoldering all over this country. One of the mandates I was assigned was to make sure that all these small fires don't merge into one out-of-control wildfire of anarchy and civil disobedience."

"What are you talking about?"

"Remember the radical hippies of the sixties? Well, those baby boomers are now respectable members of the establishment. It wouldn't take much to ignite and awaken the dormant rebellious spirit that brought this country to its knees back then."

"Never happen. Different time. Different attitude. Altogether different country. It's all under control."

"Is it? People whose opinions I trust advise me that things are actually much worse than we're letting on. We may be on the brink, the precipice."

"I've heard this all before."

"Well, next time, pay attention! The GNP is in the toilet. The national deficit is incomprehensible. Some economists predict the dollar may collapse within a decade. Terrorists and illegal immigrants enter and exit this country at will. The rate of foreclosure and unemployment is the highest since the Depression. Wall Street is a crapshoot. Many sectors of our economy are unstable. Health care is in shambles. People can't afford to stay healthy. The Middle East is falling apart."

"Are you blaming me and the rest of Congress for the state of the economy and all of the ills of society?" he asked, feigning indignation. "I don't have to answer to you!"

"And I'm not asking you to. But if you really have political aspirations, you're going to have to answer to the people. The baby boomers are just now entering the AARP. Someday, they'll hold someone responsible, and that someone may be you."

"Your vitriolic accusations are misdirected."

"It was on your watch, in your committee, that Brooksley Born warned you that the failure of the OTC derivatives and the credit default swaps would cause a systemic breakdown of the entire financial system. You failed to act on reliable information."

"The financial crisis *was* averted."

"Not by you, and some think it hasn't been averted but delayed. You and the boys on the hill were more concerned about the political contributions from your pals on Wall Street and the special interests groups representing the banking industry than you were about the welfare of this nation."

"That's not what the historians will write. Very few people knew this country's financial system was in such a crisis."

"Of course they didn't. Ignorance *is* bliss. If the people were told, it would have created panic. Maybe there would have been a run on every bank. There are those who believe that this country is heading toward the twilight's last gleaming, going to hell in a handbasket."

"In that case, you'd be right at home," the senator said in a smug, condescending manner.

He looked at Bryant with his piercing eyes and a disconcerted smile. "Is that off-handed remark a reference to the name I am called in the field? Actually I'm flattered by the reference. It keeps assholes and ballbusters like you from wondering what I've done and what I'm capable of doing to have earned that pseudonym. If anyone is going to have testicular fortitude in DC, it would be me. And when I bust balls, it's with a sledgehammer or in a vise. And *now* I'll tell you the primary reason for my visit."

"And all this up until now has been what, foreplay?"

"You can save that for Cynthia, Senator.

"Who's busting whose balls now?"

"You are on the advisory board of California Power and Light. And don't you own millions of dollars of stock and stock options in that company?"

"Jesus, is this the Inquisition! I know what you're driving at. Yes, I do. And the ethics commission saw no conflict of interest."

"I'm sure. The foxes watching the hen house."

"What possible interest would that be of yours?"

"Aren't you about to throw your constituents under the bus in Silver Verde when California Power and Light takes their land by the power of eminent domain for the hydroelectric project?"

"Ve-hic-u-lar homicide. And they'll never see it coming. Nothing short of divine intervention can stop that project now. Big money and big business are behind it."

"And all of the geological, environmental, and seismological permits are in order?"

"Absolutely," he said looking away.

"Really?" the Prince of Darkness said, doubting the senator's response. "You and your partners stand to make millions, no tens of millions. Then would it be fair to say that what you are about to do to the residents of Sliver Verde is the same thing you've been doing to Cynthia for the past year or so?"

"And you have a problem with that?"

"There's a key piece of land that will have to be acquired for the project to proceed. Could present a problem. One of those small fires I was telling you about."

"We'll have no problems with those yokels."

"You're attending a town meeting in about a week. Quid pro quo, Senator. I'm going to do you a favor and give you a little added security, and General Bishop will get to introduce the new ISS to the American public."

"Jesus, I want to keep this simple."

"You'll never know we were there. Better to err on the side of caution."

"All right, I'll play your game, even if I haven't figured out yet what it is. You think I have time for lunch before Armageddon?" the senator asked rhetorically.

The Prince of Darkness headed toward the door to leave. "I think our meeting went rather well, don't you, Senator?"

"Wonderful! Like a protracted visit to the dentist for multiple extractions, without Novocain. And next time make an appointment."

"You still don't get it, Senator. I was never here, and at no time in the future will I ever be here."

"Sure, sure, sure," the senator said, looking down at the papers on his desk, waving his hand in the air as if shooing away a bothersome pest.

If there wasn't going to be a conflict in Silver Verde, the Prince of Darkness could easily manufacture one, a small fire, that could easily be extinguished, he thought. In the process, the senator would "get with the program," and he would have him exactly where he wanted him—by the balls. Then he would squeeze him and turn him into a puppet, an asset he could manipulate with the dangling of a few strings.

You Can't Get There from Here

BILLY RAY AROSE at five the Saturday morning of the town meeting in the village green. He wanted to pick up a copy of the seismology charts from the county records office, which closed on Saturdays at noon. It was a long ride, and he wanted to be back in Silver Verde in time for the meeting. It was still dark when he made his way down Main Street. Barely visible in the dimly lit village green, he could see a decorated band stand that had been set up for the senator's arrival. Above the white gazebo next to the stage, he could make out the words on a banner tied between two pine trees that read, "Welcome Senator Bryant."

A mile out of town, Billy Ray smiled as he saw a billboard with a large picture of his old friend, who was ironically called Handsome Butch. He owned the largest firework factory and retail store in California, and under his picture was the slogan "Come in and see Handsome Butch. You'll get a bang out of him."

Before Billy Ray got on the interstate, he made a stop at the cemetery to visit his parents' gravesite. The white diffused light from the rising sun glistened off the polished dark-mahogany gravestone and the metal urns with dried flowers on each side. Deeply carved into the face of the stone was "Rest in Peace, Adeline Fiorenzano Blu, Raymond William Blu, Beloved and Sadly Missed," and the dates.

The early-morning sun and the cool breeze blowing reminded him of when he and his brother were fifteen years old accompanying their father on a Saturday morning to the Blu silver mine. The mine had been played out years earlier, making commercial production no longer worth the effort. On a good day, Raymond Blu and his boys would extract only a few hundred dollars' worth of ore. For their father, it was more of a hobby and to teach the boys some of life's lessons, such as brotherhood, a sense of family, and the ethic that hard work equaled success, values that he hoped would be part of their character after he was gone. Adeline would pack a basket of food and thermos bottles filled with either homemade chicken soup or beef stew for her husband and boys.

One morning, as they drove up the steep incline leading to the mine, they noticed an old F-150 pickup truck parked near the entrance of the mine. A makeshift camp had been set up, and a blackened metal coffee pot was suspended over a small smoldering fire, with steam pouring out of the spout. Their father looked into the bed of the truck and noticed that it was loaded down with silver ore. Two men came out of the mine. One of the men had a pickax and shovel in his hand. He was tall and thin and had a long scar on the side of his face from his earlobe to his chin. The other man pushed a wheelbarrow filled with silver ore and was short and overweight. His face was pockmarked, and he wore a red bandanna on his head. They were both unshaven, disheveled, and covered with gray dust from the mine.

"Excuse me," Raymond said, startling the men, "but you're trespassing on our land."

"Is that right, amigo?" the man with the scarred face said. "We didn't see any signs, so if you just get the fuck out of our way, we'll be on ours."

"Not before you empty that truck, *amigo*," Raymond said, mimicking the man.

When the scar-faced man raised his shovel, Junior looked around the area, trying to locate something to defend his brother and father. Billy Ray stood paralyzed, not knowing what to do.

"No problem," the short man said, dumping his wheelbarrow as he winked to his partner.

The scarred man reached into the open window of the pickup truck, pulled out a hickory ax handle, and hit Raymond with the butt end in his stomach, doubling him over. Junior grabbed the man, and the pockmarked man shook him off, punching and kicking him. Billy Ray punched the man in the face. He shook it off, laughing, and hit him repeatedly until he was nearly unconscious. Raymond, Junior, and Billy Ray lay on the ground, writhing in pain.

"We'll be on our way now," the scarred man said, laughing to his partner. As they were about to get into their truck, the pockmarked man reached into

Raymond's truck and took out the basket of food and the thermos bottles. He looked inside the basket and smiled. "You be sure to thank the missus for these fine vittles," he said as made his way to his truck. "Adios, motherfuckers," he said, bringing up some phlegm and spitting on Billy Ray as he got into his truck.

No one could have foreseen the impact that incident would have on Billy Ray's life. It would define the man he would become and became a blessing and a curse the rest of his life. On that day, he had decided that he would never again be a victim, defenseless, and at the mercy of evil men. The next day, eye blackened and badly bruised, he had gone to see Master Leong Mei to learn how to protect and defend himself. In the months that followed, he would sneak away after his chores to receive his training. When his father had found out, he was outraged.

On the way out of the cemetery, Billy Ray visited the gravesite of his friend and mentor, Master Leong Mei. He had a few private moments and left, driving to the interstate that led to the county records office. He passed the time on the long ride reminiscing about the day he began his training with martial-arts weaponry. He had been in training for nearly two years. His mastery of the martial-arts disciplines was far superior to any of Leong's former students, in the United States or in Japan. Although the master was most impressed by Billy Ray's ability to channel and combine his speed, motion, and strength into an almost mystical force, he seldom praised his protégé. He didn't want Billy Ray to become complacent.

Billy Ray had arrived earlier than usual. After warming up, he stood mesmerized, staring at a wall displaying martial-arts weaponry. He was particularly interested in two eighteen-inch highly polished, black steel sais swords.

"Maybe think time learn to use weapons of the samurai?" Leong asked, with his hands clasped behind his back, walking about the room.

"Yes," Billy Ray said.

"No," Leong said, shaking his head. "Not ready. First you learn special training."

"When do we begin?"

"Tomorrow. Daughter teach."

"Your daughter?"

"You in for surprise," he said, smiling a devious smile.

The next day, Leong introduced Billy Ray to his daughter, Christine. She was demure, only five feet tall, and a couple of years older than him. Her long black hair was fashioned on top of her head in a tight bun. She had a very light complexion, like Chinese porcelain, which contrasted sharply with her large, bluish-green, almond-shaped eyes. She wore a white karate gi, with a black sash tied about her waist. She opened a black case and handed Billy Ray two majorette batons and kept two for herself.

"What are these for?"

"Have to learn crawl before walk, yes? Daughter majorette in high school. I no like this, but mother side with daughter. One day you learn most valuable lesson in life: that all wives boss of house, but not from Leong," he said, winking at his daughter.

Christine demonstrated the proper technique, at first slowly and then with succeeding revolutions increasing the speed until they were a blurring image.

"Now you can try," Christine said to Billy Ray.

Billy Ray was becoming frustrated as he tried to twirl the batons. He kept hitting his forearms and eventually dropped them on the floor.

"I don't see the point."

"No question. Do. Something like wax on, wax off. You know this saying from karate movie?

Billy nodded.

"Me not see movie. Daughter tell me about it. Now, no more questions. You learn from daughter."

"When will I be able to use the sais swords?"

Leong and his daughter laughed. "First you learn twirl. Then you practice with rubber sais. No cut off arms this way. Maybe six months uses real sais."

⋄⊨◉ ◉⊨⋄

When Billy Ray entered the county records office, he walked upstairs and told a secretary the information he was requesting and was given several forms to fill out. As he filled out the forms, other people entered the office. When the secretary handed the head clerk, Mr. Cook, the request forms, an odd, almost alarming expression appeared on his face, which he quickly suppressed. The clerk was a middle-aged weasel of a man, balding, with a slight nervous twitch on the left side of his face. He wore horned-rimmed glasses and a gray pinstripe suit, twenty years out of style, a white cotton shirt, and a small black bowtie.

"Mr....Blu," he said, looking for his name on the forms. "The information you requested is in the vault room. I'll be back in a minute."

When the clerk reentered the office, he only had Billy Ray's forms in his hand. "I'm sorry, Mr. Blu. You've come all the way from Silver Verde, but the information you requested is not in the vault. It is under review."

"What does that mean, Mr. Cook?"

"What it means is that from time to time, records and maps are updated with the most current information. The charts are now in the capital city, where the adjustments are being made.

"If you give me the address, I'll go to the capital and pick them up."

"You can't get there from here."

Billy Ray looked at him, puzzled by his remark. "What's that supposed to mean?"

"Well..." The clerk fumbled for words. "Let me rephrase that. What I meant to say is that the records are there, and you can go there, but the records are not there...for you...to be seen."

"What?"

The left side of the clerk's face was now twitching uncontrollably. "After they are updated, they'll be sent back here. Then they will be here...for you...to be seen. I have your name and number. As soon as the information you requested returns, I'll give you a call. And once again, I apologize for the inconvenience."

After Billy Ray left, the clerk went into his office, closed the door behind him, and looked for a phone number in his desk. He dialed the number and was transferred several times before he was connected to Senator Bryant's private line.

"Excuse me, Senator," Mr. Cook said. "Someone from your office said to notify you if anyone came in requesting certain information about Silver Verde."

"And what did you tell them?"

"Exactly what I was told to say, that the records were under review."

"Excellent. And do you have a name of the person making the request?"

"Yes, a Mr....William Blu," he said, looking down at the forms.

All Senator Bryant knew about the Blu estate was that it was a key piece of property for his plan to go forward. He wondered if that was the same piece of property that the Prince of Darkness said could present a problem. "Very good. Keep up the good work."

"You won't forget about me, Senator. You know what we spoke about. My son will be graduating college this spring and is looking for a state job."

"Just let me know when he's available, and the job is as good as his."

In the meantime, a late-model Crown Victoria was traveling at a high rate of speed down the interstate. The Prince of Darkness put a disk into his CD player. The song playing was "Hotel California," by the Eagles. He turned up the volume and adjusted his worn and tattered copy of *The Art of Violence* on the passenger's seat to keep it from falling. He hit his turn signal as he approached the sign post that read: Silver Verde—Next Exit.

Eminent Domain

WHEN BILLY RAY arrived in Silver Verde, he had to park at the end of town because Main Street was lined with cars. Families were walking toward the village green. Some of the small children had balloons tied to their wrists; others were eating treats bought from the street vendors. In the distance he heard the high-school band playing. He stopped, bought a bag of freshly popped kettle corn, and walked on.

The closer he got to the village green, the louder the music became. As he approached the white clapboard church, he saw that the parishioners were holding a bake sale with tables of baked goods set up on the sidewalk. Behind the church was Saint Mary's school, the Catholic school he attended when he was young. Father Pat was greeting the townsfolk as they passed.

"Good morning, Father," Billy Ray said.

"Top of the morning, William. Your brother said you went to the county records office. Did you find what you were looking for?"

"Oddly enough, Father, I didn't. They said the records were under review and that they would contact me when they were available."

"I wouldn't worry too much about this eminent domain. Senator Bryant and many of the congregation attended a special mass this morning. He assured me personally that he would intercede on our behalf."

The village green had been transferred into a carnival atmosphere. The sun was shining brightly, and the humidity was low. The American flag affixed to a tall flagpole in the center of the green was flapping in a slight breeze. The residents were holding posters attached to three-foot pieces of furring that the citizens' committee had made with Jenny in the town library. The signs read: Senator Bryant Save Our Farms.

The high-school marching band was playing the song "American Pie," and the majorettes, wearing attractive powder-blue-and-white uniforms, were twirling their batons. The smell of fresh-cut grass, roasting nuts, and cotton candy filled the air. Occasionally a child would lose his balloon, and it would go sailing into the air. Senator Bryant and members of his staff, along with Mayor White and members of the town government, were talking on stage. A town worker was testing and adjusting the microphone on the podium.

Billy Ray saw Jenny standing near the stage, talking to several women and holding a sign by her side. As he walked over to her, their eyes met, and they both laughed because they were both wearing dark jeans and identical red-and-black checkered cotton shirts. About two dozen security soldiers with the ISS came marching through the green and took their positions around the stage. They were wearing blue-and-gray camouflage field uniforms with matching berets tipped to the right and highly polished black boots. On their armbands were their ranks and an ISS patch with the slogan underneath: To Protect and to Serve. Billy Ray looked at the type of lettering in the ISS patch and thought it looked inappropriate. To him, the lettering resembled Nazi swastikas. The only weapons the ISS soldiers carried were two-foot-long, black wooden batons in a side holster and canisters of pepper gas. They were standing at attention, stoic, displaying no signs of emotion.

Billy Ray walked up to Jenny and offered her some kettle corn. "You look pretty today, Jenny," he said as she scooped up a handful and shuffled a few into her mouth. "Where's my brother?"

"He's around here somewhere," she said, looking for him in the crowd.

Carla walked by with her two boys tagging along behind her. They were eating mounds of lime-green cotton candy. "Hi, Jenny, and hi, Billy Ray," she said, flirting with him.

After Carla had passed, Jenny leaned close to Billy Ray. Gossip traveled fast in a small town, and Jenny had heard the rumors about Carla's nocturnal activities. "Another member of your fan club?" she asked in a quiet voice, smiling.

Billy Ray smiled. "Have some more popcorn," he said, changing the subject.

Junior made his way through the crowd and snuck up behind Jenny and gave her a kiss on the back of her neck. When he saw that his brother and

Jenny were wearing identical clothing, he stopped and held up his hands. "And I thought that Billy and I were the only twins in town. Was this planned?" he asked, laughing.

"I had no idea what your brother would be wearing," she said as they all laughed.

Ocho came walking through the crowd with his wife. He towered over everyone. They were an odd-looking couple, with Ocho being a giant and his wife barely five feet tall. He saw Billy Ray, and they acknowledged each other with a simple nod, and then he stood a short distance away.

As Billy Ray looked around the crowd, an uneasy feeling overcame him. What his brother had just said about Jenny and him dressing alike was fresh in his memory. His facial expression changed, and his pupils became dilated. His senses became astutely keen and razor sharp, and his observations became vivid. As his awareness heightened, he had a premonition; his instincts told him that something ominous was about to happen. Men in the crowd, who he didn't recognize, were all dressed too similarly. They were wearing various-colored flannel shirts, dungarees, baseball caps, and sunglasses. The more they tried to blend in, he thought, the more it set them apart. Then he noticed that several of the men were wearing earphones. Upon occasion, he saw some of them talking into the lapels on their jackets. All these strangers had a white-and-red button fixed on their left shirt collar. The strangers were carrying signs that appeared to have been made in a print shop, with identical colors and lettering. Billy Ray observed a man standing far from the crowd with a video camera slung over his shoulder filming the events. He spotted a man looking through binoculars in the church tower. Two more men were observing the events, one from the rooftop of Sparkey's Pool Hall across the street, and another from the rooftop of the town hall. He knew from his military training that the high ground was the preferred strategic location for forward observers and snipers.

The mayor stood up and asked the residents to quiet down. As the mayor was giving a short speech, Billy Ray observed a stranger from the corner of his eye who was slowly moving closer to him. The stranger looked familiar, but he couldn't recognize him. An LA Dodgers baseball cap and sunglasses were obscuring his facial features. He kept watching the stranger as he moved closer to him in a slow, deliberate manner, like a predator stalking its prey. As the stranger moved about twenty feet away, Billy Ray recognized him. He knew it was the Prince of Darkness. As his apprehension grew and a sense of impending danger became the center of his consciousness, his adrenaline level, heart rate, and strength increased dramatically. He knew it was time to leave, as one of the cardinal rules from *The Art of Violence* echoed in his memory: "The warrior must avoid situations, people, and places where violence may occur."

When the mayor finished his speech, he introduced the main speaker, Senator Bryant. As the senator approached the podium and adjusted the height of the microphone, several residents cried out, "Help us, Senator. Save our farms."

"That's why I'm here," he responded.

Billy Ray turned toward Jenny and Junior. "We should be leaving," he said, keeping a watchful eye on the Prince of Darkness. "Something here isn't right."

"Jesus," Junior said. "You're always so paranoid! Can't you just enjoy yourself for once?"

"At least stay until we hear what Senator Bryant has to say," Jenny said.

"Junior, do me a favor. Look up at the church bell tower and on top of the town hall, and the roof of Sparkey's. Who are those men?"

Junior looked up, trying to placate his brother. Then he spotted the men. "I see them. Yeah, I see them. What do you think they are doing up there?"

"Jenny, you see those men over there?" Billy Ray motioned in the direction near the stage. "Do you recognize those men? Look at their signs. Did you make those signs?"

"No. I don't know who those men are. Those are not the signs we made."

"I'm leaving," he said as he turned away.

"Billy," Jenny said as she reached out for his hand, pleading with him. "Please stay."

"Po-wer-ful men," the senator said in lingering syllables, "are plotting against us. Are we going to let them destroy our community?" Senator Bryant paused and waited for the response.

"No," the crowd shouted.

"Are we going to let them take away our livelihoods?"

"No," the crown responded once again.

"Rest assured. I'm going to use all of my energy. All of my power. The full weight of my office…to stop this evil…and protect my friends in Silver Verde."

The crowd clapped and whistled as they gave the senator a thunderous ovation.

"It won't be easy, but with your support and the help of the Almighty," he said, looking up toward the heavens, "we will per-se-vere! Together, we will stop these ty-rants!"

⋯⊷⊜ ⊜⊶⋯

The Prince of Darkness could see that Senator Bryant was almost through. "What a piece of work," he thought, laughing inwardly. "Almost had me convinced." Then he said aloud, talking into the microphone on his shirt collar, "OK, boys, time to take one for the team."

One of the strangers pushed an ISS soldier to the side and ran up to the stage waving his sign. "Liar!" he shouted. "How are you going to help us when you're on the board of California Power and Light?"

Senator Bryant was speechless. He backed away from the podium, looking at one of his aides.

Another one of the strangers was waving his sign and pointing at the senator. "You're not here to help us. You're one of them!"

All the strangers were screaming at Senator Bryant, trying to rally the crowd behind them. Then one of them took a grapefruit from under his jacket and heaved it at the senator, striking him in the arm.

The Prince of Darkness talked to the commander of the ISS soldiers. He smiled with glee as the conflict escalated. "Use your batons for crowd control," he said to the commander.

Pandemonium broke out as the ISS began pushing the crowd back from the stage. One of the strangers began hitting one of the soldiers with his sign. Another hit a soldier in the head, breaking the sign post in half. The residents scattered, with panic and terror on their faces as the ISS soldiers drew their batons and began hitting everyone in their path. Jenny raised her sign to protect herself from the onslaught of the soldiers. One of the soldiers swung at her upraised sign, breaking it into pieces. As the soldier raised his baton to strike at her again, Billy grabbed it out of his hand just as it was about to strike her.

"Stand down, soldier," Billy Ray shouted. "You're better than this."

Billy Ray could see that several soldiers were coming toward him to aid their comrade. They were smashing residents with their batons as they cleared a path toward him. Once again the teachings from *The Art of Violence* came into his mind. "When confronted with a nonlethal act of violence, the warrior must engage the opposition with an equal, opposite, and measured response. No more. No less."

In one swift decisive motion, Billy Ray swept the legs out from underneath the soldier with the baton and hit his solar plexus with an open palm, knocking him unconscious in an eye blink. Another soldier came from behind him and hit him squarely on his shoulder. Billy Ray spun and placed the heel of his boot on the side of the soldier's leg, breaking it at the kneecap. Jenny had been knocked to the ground and was crying. Billy Ray picked her up and looked through the crowd for his brother.

"Jenny, where's Junior?"

"He was standing right next to me."

Junior was lying on the ground near the side of the stage. He had been hit with a baton on the side of his head and was dazed. Blood was pouring out of a deep gash behind his ear. Billy Ray pushed Jenny away from a soldier who was rushing toward them.

"Run, Jenny," he shouted. "Don't stop. I'll be right behind you."

As Jenny ran down the street, Billy Ray turned and looked through the chaos for his brother, but he couldn't see him. Then he walked out of the village green in the direction of where he last saw Jenny. As he walked down the street, he saw a half dozen ISS soldiers down the street, blocking his path. Two majorettes were sitting on the street curb, crying. One of them was holding her leg. He walked over to them, still keeping a watchful eye on the soldiers. The girl holding her leg was Dr. Horton's daughter. He knelt down next to the two girls.

"Are you all right?" he asked.

"It's my leg," she said, shaking, trying to wipe the tears from her eyes.

"Let me see that," he said. "It's only a scrape. Help your friend up and take her to her father's office. You girls don't mind if I borrow these for a little while?" Billy Ray asked rhetorically, picking up the girls' majorette batons.

Billy Ray watched Dr. Horton's daughter hobbling down the street until she was a safe distance away. From his years of training, his instincts began to take over, but he was having a difficult time controlling his rage. He placed one of the batons against the inside part of his forearm. As he began spinning the other baton, Master Mai's laughter and words echoed in his memory: "Like wax on, wax off."

As he moved closer to the soldiers, he dissected and planned his moves as succinctly as if he were mapping out a quick resolution to a chess match. One of the soldiers broke ranks and charged him. With one of his batons still tucked firmly under his forearm, he clotheslined the soldier under his chin using his forward momentum to knock him off his legs. The inertia caused the soldier to rise several feet off the ground. In one swift, decisive motion, he slammed the soldier to the pavement. Then he began spinning the batons with such speed and force that they were barely visible to the naked eye. He charged the middle of the soldiers, changing direction at the last possible moment. He rose several feet off the ground, striking the soldiers on either side of him and instantly sending them reeling backward. He spun and hit the remaining soldiers with such force and speed that they were rendered unconscious upon contact.

The Prince of Darkness stood on the perimeter of the village green paralyzed with awe, only moving once to make sure the videographer had his camera focused in on Billy Ray. He had seen countless films of violent confrontations. He had been involved in training exercises with soldiers in mock hand-to-hand combat. He had witnessed the aftermath of the carnage of violence, but he had never seen anyone dispose of their opposition with such ease, precision, and skill in real time. Billy Ray's movements seemed choreographed, as if staged, slowing down and speeding up at random. It didn't seem real, but he knew it was all too real. It gave him an exhilarating sense of joy and horror simultaneously.

The three McFarlane brothers had been in Sparky's Pool Hall drinking whiskey and were mildly intoxicated. When they heard the screaming and shouting, they ran out of the bar to see what was causing the commotion. The door of the pool hall remained opened, and the Bob Seger song "Still the Same" was blaring on Main Street.

In keeping with their nature, the McFarlane brothers bravely turned their tails and ran across the street, backing up against the wall of the town hall for protection. They stood aghast, mouths open, as they watched their old nemesis take out one soldier after another. All the soldiers lay on the pavement either writhing in pain or unconscious. Billy Ray turned around and continued walking down Main Street. The village green was almost empty except for a few residents trying to recover from their injuries. When the remaining ISS soldiers saw the men in their unit lying on the payment, they came running, double time, down the middle of Main Street. As Billy Ray continued on, he saw Carla hiding in the doorway of the malt shop, huddled around her boys.

The deputy sheriff, a young man in his early twenties, came running down the street and stood in the doorway next to Carla. He drew his revolver nervously, and called out to Billy Ray. "Billy, what should I do?"

Billy Ray motioned to him with a baton to lower his weapon. "Put that away, and take Carla and her boys inside."

"Do you need any help?"

"Don't worry about me," he said, looking behind him at the oncoming soldiers. "I'll be OK."

The deputy sheriff opened the door quickly and escorted Carla and her boys inside. As the soldiers were nearly upon him, Billy Ray turned and faced them. He gripped his batons tightly and placed them by his side.

"Put your weapons down, and get down on the ground, face first!" the ranking officer shouted at him.

Billy Ray's eyes glazed over as his rage grew. A side of him, which he wished no one would ever have to see, began to surface. "Such brave men," he said to the soldiers, mocking them. "Are you proud of what you've done to old men, women, and children?"

"I said lay down your weapons. Get down on the ground. Now!"

"It's your move, "Billy Ray said as he turned away and began walking down the street.

One of the soldiers attempted to spray him with pepper gas. As the soldiers rushed him, Billy Ray spun his batons, but this time he added additional speed and force, breaking arms, legs, and ribs in the matter of a few seconds. He broke the nose of the ranking soldier. Blood was pouring from his nose and mouth.

The Prince of Darkness was still so mesmerized, savoring the spectacle Billy Ray was displaying, that he didn't realize that the small fire had escalated into a firestorm and an embarrassment for the ISS. The sniper in the bell tower, who had been repeatedly calling out to him, snapped him out of his trance.

"Sir, should I take the subject out? Sir, respond."

"What's in your jacket?"

"As instructed, sir. Rubber bullets."

"Take him out. All shots below the waist. Do you understand?"

"Affirmative, sir."

Several shots rang out. Anyone in or near the village green was alarmed and dove to the ground. Billy Ray was hit twice, once in his thigh and once in his calf, sending him kneeling to the pavement. Two ISS soldiers picked up their batons and hobbled over to him. They placed both hands on the batons and swung them like baseball bats, striking Billy Ray repeatedly on his shoulders and lower back until he collapsed to the ground. Suddenly a shadow overcame the soldiers as if a dark cloud was blocking out the sun. A huge hand reached out and grabbed one of the soldiers by the back of his belt, picked him up high in the air, and threw him through the windshield of a parked car. Several shots rang out, striking him in the back. It didn't seem to have any effect on him. He picked up the other soldier, shook him like a rag doll, and flung him against a metal lamppost. As the soldier collapsed, several more shots rang out, and Ocho fell to the ground. Several ISS soldiers hobbled over, handcuffed both men, and dragged them away.

→►═◉ ◉═◄←

Father Pat was kneeling down on the grass in the village green comforting an elderly woman and young child. He had hit his head on the side of a park bench after being trampled. Dried blood covered the side of his face. He looked up to the heavens as if to ask the Almighty why. Several children who had been separated from their parents were crying. Senator Bryant and his aides had been whisked away by ISS soldiers when the violence began to a waiting black stretch limousine. Their driver was traveling at a high rate of speed and was just entering the interstate highway.

And as the flames climbed high into the night
To light the sacrificial rite,
I saw Satan laughing with delight
The day the music died.

—Don McLean, "American Pie"

The Prince of Darkness was standing outside his Crown Victoria looking at the aftermath in the village green. "Give me a secure line to Senator Bryant's private phone," he said to the operator at Langley.

When Senator Bryant answered the phone, his hands were trembling. He and his staff were disheveled and visibly shaken. "What the hell happened?" he shouted into the phone.

"I hate always being right, Senator."

"Jesus Christ. What a fiasco. The press will have a field day with this!"

"No, they won't. I have a cover story already in the pipeline. It's being leaked to the press as we speak. Actually, you'll be portrayed as a hero. Victimized at the hands of some malcontents while you were trying to help your constituents in Silver Verde."

"I hope so. I could have been injured or killed."

"I don't detect any gratitude on your part. Come on, Senator; you can say it."

Bryant hesitated. "OK, you were right. Thank you."

"Never thought I'd hear that coming from you. You're going to have to learn to trust me. I'm your new guardian angel. When I tell you something is the way it is, it's the bible. We'll be in touch, Senator."

When the Prince of Darkness closed his phone, he got in his Crown Victoria and drove down Main Street. He knew he had the senator exactly where he wanted him. Now, he thought, as he smiled a cat-ate-the-canary grin, he would try to conceive a plan to bring Billy Ray into the fold.

Later that evening, Jenny was at home with her parents, watching the news stations who were all reporting the story. Junior walked in wearing a bandage wrapped around his head. He gave Jenny and her mother kisses on their cheeks.

Jenny's mother embraced him and moved his head to get a better look at his injuries. "Oh, Junior, are you all right?"

"Fifteen stitches. There's a line outside Doc Horton's office. Everyone's getting patched up."

"Where's Billy?" Jenny's father asked.

"No one knows. There's a rumor he's been taken to a federal prison. Another rumor says that he and Ocho are in the county hospital, and another that," he said, pausing, "he was shot and might be…dead."

Tears were flowing down Jenny's face. "He knew something wasn't right. He wanted to leave, and I asked him to stay."

"I should have listened to him," Junior said. "It was a setup."

"Don't worry, Jenny," her mother said, trying to comfort her. "I'm sure he's all right. Billy is indestructible. Everyone knows that."

Jenny's father switched the station to CNN. Breaking News was flashing across the screen. "This is Wolf Blitzer from the Situation Room. CNN reporter Ron Clark is live in Silver Verde, Southern California. Violence broke out today in this normally peaceful town at a rally where Senator Bryant was taking questions from the residents about their concerns over the prospect of their farmland being taken by eminent domain for the proposed California Power and Light's hydroelectric facility. We go live to Silver Verde, Ron."

The CNN reporter was standing in front of yellow caution tape. "Wolf, what you see behind me is the aftermath of a riot that broke out as Senator Bryant was talking on the platform behind me to the residents about the possible loss of their farms and homes for the proposed hydroelectric plant," he said as the camera panned to the area behind him, displaying banners, posters, vendor carts, and other debris littering the grounds. The flagpole had snapped in half and the gazebo was in shambles. Musical instruments lay strewn on the ground after the band members had made a hasty retreat.

"Wolf, I talked with Mayor White of Silver Verde earlier, and he asked Governor Maxwell's office to assist the local sheriff's department in catching the outside agitators who he believed are responsible for starting the riot. He also asked the governor to investigate the use of unwarranted force by the ISS soldiers against the residents of Silver Verde. At this time the federal authorities have two Silver Verde residents in custody who were injured and will be charged with...as of yet undetermined offences. Back to you, Wolf."

Everyone's Entitled to Their Opinion

ALONG WITH THE other property owners whose land had been taken by eminent domain several days after the incident when lawyers representing California Power and Light filed papers with the state and local district courts taking nearly all of the land south of the center of town for the hydroelectric facility, Junior received a registered letter outlining the procedure and timeframe when they would have to surrender their land. Sheriff Roy called him and said that his brother and Ocho had been treated for minor injuries in the county hospital and transferred to the infirmary at Tywater Federal Penitentiary, located in Southern California.

Mayor White, Father Pat—still sporting a large purple contusion on the side of his face—and Sheriff Roy traveled to the capital to meet with Governor Anthony Maxwell. They thought it wise for Junior not to attend the meeting but assured him that his brother's interests would be represented. The meeting had been set up in a conference room. When they arrived, they were greeted by two members of the governor's legal staff. In the conference room, graphs and charts displayed various aspects of California's economy.

When Governor Maxwell entered the conference room, everyone stood up out of respect. He had his suit jacket slung over his arm, which he placed on the back of a chair at the head of the table. He was a large, distinguished-looking man, and his six-foot-five, 250-pound frame gave him an imposing presence. He wore gray slacks, a white cotton shirt, and a dark-blue tie with matching power suspenders. After the introductions, the governor's legal staff took out pads and began jotting down notes. A secretary and an assistant came in with a silver urn filled with hot coffee and a tray of pastries.

"Sit, gentlemen. I'm sorry to have kept you waiting. I was in the State Legislature, where I just got an earful from both sides on the immigration reform issue, and our status as a sanctuary state. I'll tell you, between the wild fires, earthquakes, mudslides, and the illegal aliens creating a burden on social services and not paying their taxes, our state is heading for disaster. But let's face it, men; we need the spick vote to remain in power," he said in jest, which did not mask that he believed in his policy as a sanctuary state. "Now, what can I do for you men?"

The governor had granted an audience with Mayor White on short notice out of respect of his office. As the meeting continued, it was obvious to everyone present that Governor Maxwell was polite and civil but annoyed with the topic. "Mayor White, I have been briefed as to your concerns, but I really can't see what I can do to help. It's a question of federal jurisdiction."

"There are several related issues, Governor. We're not disputing the utility's right to have taken nearly half or our county for the hydroelectric facility, but was it wise and prudent to have taken some of the most productive farmland in California and place a dam in an area prone to seismic activity?"

"I have been assured that extensive research has been conducted in picking the site. All of the necessary permits are in order, and due diligence has been performed. And as far as it decimating Silver Verde, I'd like to quote what an actor friend of mine once said in one of his movies: 'The needs of the many outweigh the needs of the few, or the one,'" he said, raising his eyebrows.

"My other concern is how the ISS soldiers overacted and used excessive force resulting in damage to our town and injuries to our people."

"My sources paint quite a different picture."

"I was on stage seated three feet from Senator Bryant. All of the gentlemen here with me and other citizens witnessed what really happened. I can tell you categorically that William Blu did not initiate the altercation. One of the sheriff's deputies did witness Billy Ray defending himself and others from the baton-wielding ISS. I'll stake my office and reputation on that, Governor!"

"And you probably will," the governor said indignantly. "Reliable sources have confirmed that William Blu orchestrated the protest that led to the riot, the attack upon Senator Bryant, and the ISS soldiers. He's going to be charged with some pretty serious offences."

"That's why we're here, Governor. We were hoping for you to intercede in this matter, or at least help us with the investigation. Everyone involved intends to testify on his behalf."

"That's your prerogative, but some of the ISS soldiers received serious injuries, and they positively identified William Blu as the culprit. Assault on federal officers carries a mandatory sentence upon conviction. I don't see what evidence could be produced to exonerate him. Is that a fair assessment?" he asked, turning toward his legal staff.

They nodded in agreement.

"We're trying to find the person who videotaped the event and subpoena the tape," Sheriff Roy said.

"What tape?" the governor asked, holding out his hands. "Prior to our meeting, I was briefed by my legal staff that you believe there is this *mystery tape*. No one seems to know anything about this tape."

"What happened in Silver Verde doesn't add up," the mayor said. "It seemed staged. The question is, who taped the event? Why was he taping the event? And why has this key piece of evidence disappeared? That's the opinion I will voice in court."

The governor did not immediately respond. He took a sip of coffee. As he took a pastry from the tray, some icing got on his hands. He walked over to the wet bar and washed his hands. "Everyone's entitled to their opinion. That what the courts are for and why they're backlogged. And why we pay these men," he said, nodding in the direction of his lawyers, "so much money. Since the charges are federal, it's really out of my hands," he said, folding the bar towel and placing it on the rack. As the governor turned, he noticed the bruise on the side of Father Pat's face. "Are you here for moral support, Father?" the governor asked.

"Of course, Governor, and to say a prayer that justice is served."

"In all due respect, Father, I don't think even the pope could help William Blu," he said, looking at his wristwatch. "I'm running late, gentlemen. But if there's anything I or my legal staff can do to help, within the confines of my office, give me a call. Good day."

After they left the conference room, the governor opened a closet and removed a small putting green, his favorite putter, and several orange golf balls. Then he opened a cherrywood humidor and removed a large hand-rolled Cuban cigar. He placed the unlit cigar into his mouth and began practicing his putting.

"Until three days ago, I never even heard of Silver Verde," he said to his legal staff, "or knew that a town that small even had a mayor. He has an opinion, an opinion. You know what they say about opinions," the governor said, head down, lining up a putt as he chewed on his cigar.

"No, sir."

"They're like assholes! Everyone has one!"

"Should I make that last statement part of the official transcript?" the attorney asked in jest.

"By all means," the governor said, clenching his hand as he made the putt. "Submit it along with your resignation." He chuckled. "What makes that nothing mayor from that nowhere hick town think I'm going to raise a finger to help him? I talked with Bryant. He wants this Blu put away for a long time. We're playing golf next week. That reminds me. Have my secretary block out next Wednesday morning for our golf match."

"Yes, sir. What do you think really happened in Silver Verde, Governor?"

"An opportunity," he said, looking down as he lined up his next putt. "An opportunity."

⇥⊙ ⊙⇤

On the four-hour ride back to Silver Verde, the three men discussed the disappointing meeting with Governor Maxwell.

"What's our next move?" Father Pat asked the mayor.

"It's obvious that we'll get no help from the governor. He patronized us. It's what he didn't say that speaks volumes. Someone with power is pulling the strings, and we don't have the political clout to fight it. You know one thing that keeps bothering me? It's what one of those outside agitators said. I remember someone saying something to the effect that Senator Bryant was on the board of California Power and Light. If he has something to hide, maybe it's something we'll have to look into."

"Sheriff, do you think Attorney Lawton is capable of representing Billy Ray?" Father Pat asked.

"No way. He's a country bumpkin. Perhaps he can refer a good criminal attorney to represent Billy Ray and Ocho. Junior said there were snipers on the rooftops and that Billy pointed out the men who instigated the riot. Someone thinks they pulled the wool over our eyes. They were not from Silver Verde. I'm just a small-town sheriff, but I agree with the governor. Without some type of miracle, or the tape, those charges are going to stick."

"Even if we testify on his behalf?" the mayor said.

"I'm afraid so," Sheriff Roy said. "Whoever represents them would have to establish that the ISS soldiers overacted and used excessive force. The prosecution will claim that they used reasonable force to quell the disturbance, especially with a senator of Bryant's status. Without the tape, Billy Ray and Ocho will be convicted. I'll talk to Junior and Lawton when we get back to get a good law firm to represent them. They're going to need all the help they can get."

When they returned to Silver Verde, Sheriff Roy met with local attorney Bill Lawton and Junior. He referred Junior to the Los Angeles law firm of Coyle, Mitchell, Goldman, and Sharp. They were a highly regarded firm and had been involved in many high-profile criminal cases.

Senior partner Frank Coyle asked for a $25,000 retainer and began working on the arraignment. He visited Billy Ray and Ocho at Tywater Federal Penitentiary to gather information and to discuss their pleas.

A few days later, Ocho was arraigned under his legal name, Juan Sanchez. He was charged with two counts of assault upon federal officers and resisting arrest. Frank Coyle entered a plea of not guilty. Federal judge Arthur Tores denied him bail and remanded him to Tywater Penitentiary to await trial.

On the fifth of November, Billy Ray was escorted into the courtroom under heavy guard by the California State Sheriff Department. He had a separate arraignment because of the media attention. He wore leg and wrist shackles and an orange Tywater Penitentiary jumpsuit. He was walking with a limp from the injuries he received at the village green. He appeared gaunt and weary, as if he hadn't slept or eaten for days. Junior, Jenny, Father Pat, Mayor White, and many other residents attended the arraignment. As he was led up to the front of the courtroom, he glanced at Jenny and the others and acknowledged them by nodding his head in their direction. The arraignment only lasted five minutes.

"Mr. William Raymond Blu, alias Billy Ray Blu," the state prosecutor said, looking in Billy Ray's direction, "is charged with fifteen counts of felony assault upon Federal ISS Officers while in the performance of their duties. Fifteen counts of felony assault upon same with a deadly weapon. Carrying a weapon while committing a crime of violence. Inciting a riot resulting in bodily harm. Felony assault upon a government official, Senator William Wadsworth Bryant. And resisting arrest. Due to the seriousness of the charges, and his years in the military, where William Blu was trained in escape and evasion techniques, the state believes that he is a flight risk. The state recommends that bail should be denied."

Much to everyone's disappointment, Frank Coyle did not mount a persuasive argument to have Billy Ray released on bail. He entered a plea of not guilty, and Judge Tores denied him bail and remanded him back to federal prison to await trial. As Billy Ray was led from the courtroom, he looked at Jenny. His smile was a thin disguise for the embarrassment, hopelessness, and despair he was feeling. As their eyes met, her spirit sank, feeling and seeing the sadness and desperation in his eyes, emotions she had never seen him display.

Outside, on the cascading gray granite steps of the federal courthouse, dozens of network camera crews were interviewing government officials and the state prosecutor and reporting on Judge Tores's decision. It was a media circus. Junior, Jenny, and other residents of Silver Verde stood on the steps as Mayor White gave the media his account of the incident.

→→=◎ ◎=←←

It was a crisp November morning. The white light from the early-morning sun was burning through the light fog, giving way to a beautiful day. The dew on the grass had not yet lifted. It was an ideal day for a round of golf at the exclusive Bella Vista Country Club in central California. Governor Maxwell and Senator Bryant were partners. They would be playing against their invited guests, Judge Arthur Tores and attorney Frank Coyle. The only sounds on the golf course were the clinking of the sprinkler system in the distance, and the cackling and flapping of Canadian geese as they were startled by the approaching golfers.

"I see you have a guardian angel," Governor Maxwell said to Senator Bryant as he sunk a putt for par.

"It's a dog-and-pony show," the senator said. "After Silver Verde, a security detail has been assigned to me twenty-four seven…just for precaution," he said, taking his putter out of his bag.

"Is there something you're not telling me about this Silver Verde deal, Bill?"

"Why, have you heard something?" Bryant said, head down, lining up his putt.

"No. It's just that you've been calling in a lot of markers to bury this town and that Blu."

"I don't know why you'd think that, Tony," Bryant said.

"Because I know you, Bill. The fox that bit your ass died. I just hope what you're hiding doesn't come back to bite all of us in the ass. And what is all this shit Mayor White keeps talking about with this mystery tape?"

"It's much ado about nothing. Trust me. It will never see the light of day."

"We've both come a long way, Bill, and I could always tell when you were lying, but not this time. Sometimes a lie is more revealing than the truth. We have a judge and an attorney present. Let's ask them if your statement would pass close examination," he said jokingly.

"Trust me. The tape will never surface!" Senator Bryant said adamantly.

"If you tell me the fix is in, I'm OK with that."

The Prince of Darkness had assigned a detail to protect Senator Bryant after the incident at Silver Verde. The secret service agent was dressed in leisure clothing so as not to stand out. He had a Nike bag slung over his shoulder. Little did the men in the foursome know that all of their activities were being recorded with a small parabolic eavesdropping device hidden in the valise, and a video recorder. The Prince of Darkness had his own agenda. He could not have devised a better scenario to have these prominent men interacting at the same location. He saw this situation as a perfect opportunity to gather intel for future reference and leverage.

Judge Tores teed off on the eighteenth hole. As his ball sliced and headed toward the rough, he tipped his head, trying to will his ball back onto the fairway.

"Jesus," he said, throwing his club into the golf cart. "So what's going to happen to your clients, Frank?" he asked.

"They don't know it yet," Coyle said, chipping onto the green, "but I'm going to convince them to take a plea agreement, and when I'm through spinning their heads, they'll think it was their idea. Sanchez will get, let's say, three years, and Blu will get three to five. That'll keep Bryant happy."

"Sounds about right," the Judge said, hitting his ball out of the rough with a five iron. "My wife and I are going to spend Christmas in Hawaii, so I want to clear my calendar of this nonsense."

When all the men reached the green on the eighteenth hole, it was time for them to tie up all the loose ends before they went into the clubhouse. As Frank Coyle lined up his putt, Judge Tores, Governor Maxwell, and Senator Bryant stood on the skirt of the green.

"If my inside information is correct, Bill," Judge Tores said, "there will be a vacancy on the Supreme Court in about four years. The timing couldn't be more perfect. With you in the White House, you could exert your influence toward my nomination and confirmation."

Coyle sank his putt. "You're up, Bill," the governor said.

"I can assure you, Judge," Bryant said, walking toward his ball. "You'll be our guy."

Senator Bryant took a couple of practice swings and then sunk his putt. "You're up, Judge," Bryant said.

"Since you're in such a generous mood," the governor said to Bryant, "my wife and I always wanted to take an extended stay in Italy. An ambassadorship would be nice."

"Ouch," Bryant said.

"Wow, he's not bashful," Coyle said.

Judge Tores sank his putt. The governor took his favorite putter out of the golf cart, and as he walked up to his ball, he turned to Coyle. "Hey, Frank, you ever heard of the saying that all good things come to those who wait? Bullshit." He tapped in his putt. "You have to strike while the iron is hot. Now let's get into the clubhouse. I'm dying for some cold ones, and I have a big appetite today."

"In more ways than one," Coyle said, and all the men laughed.

As they drove the golf carts to the clubhouse, Bryant rode with Coyle. "When this Silver Verde thing is over, I'll make sure that your firm has more legal work than you can handle."

"Thank you, Senator. My son just got accepted to Harvard, and you know what that costs. I never checked the score card. Who won the game?

"I guess we all did," Bryant said, giving Coyle a high five.

When the men entered the clubhouse, a private bar and appetizers had been set up for them. Oysters on a half shell served with horseradish, hot sauce, and lemon wedges; jumbo cocktail shrimp; and mushrooms stuffed with panko bread crumbs and crab meat had been prepared for them.

When their table was ready, they were escorted to another private room overlooking members playing tennis. They enjoyed a surf-and-turf lunch of stuffed lobster, baked stuffed shrimp, and sizzling filet mignons. As they feasted on their lunch, complements of Senator Bryant's expense account, they laughed and savored the ironically appropriate moment and drank a toast to their future prosperity with chilled bottles of red and white wine from Blu Vineyards.

→▬ ▬←

The newswire services picked up the story and played it up for all the newspapers and advertising it would sell. It went viral on the Internet. Articles about the implications of what happened in Silver Verde ranging from prominent politicians to ordinary citizens filled the editorial pages. Radio talk shows and intellectual magazines analyzed, overanalyzed, and debated all aspects of what was referred to as "the incident at Silver Verde."

Senator Bryant was not happy that the incident at Silver Verde became a public issue. He did not want anyone examining his connection to California Power and Light. He called the Prince of Darkness, who told him not to worry. The media attention surrounding Silver Verde was not what he had envisioned when he had set the events in motion. Many of the public were skeptical of the storyline. They viewed Billy Ray's plight as another example of the erosion of individual rights and freedoms. However, the Prince of Darkness had fed misinformation to the press about Billy Ray's military record, which was sure to curb public sentiment and put out the fire he inadvertently started. He assured the senator the story would play out in a normal news cycle and then disappear.

→━◎ ◎━←

In Columbus, Ohio, Kenneth "Wiz" Castle's family owned Wizard Electronics. He had served in the Special Forces unit with Billy Ray in Afghanistan. He spent hours surfing the Internet reading stories and comments about the Silver Verde incident. He also read the spin the Prince of Darkness had disseminated to the press about Billy Ray's military career. When he came upon Blu Vineyard's website, a devious idea formed in his mind. He went into the backroom where the electronic wizardry took place that earned him his nickname. He was careful in writing the text to dispel the propaganda. He knew that only the CIA, military intelligence, and a handful of men knew the true details of Billy Ray's discharge, and it could be traced back to him and the other men in his unit.

Using over a dozen servers and a program he had written that had an oscillating IP that could not be traced back to the originator, he flooded the Internet with millions of bits of information and e-mails with simple text, highlighted with the heading "Free Billy Ray and Ocho," with a large cobalt-blue bird as a symbol of the movement. He dubbed the pirate website "The Black Parade" after one of the songs he used to listen to while he was working in his shop.

In the weeks that followed, graffiti artists from all over the country who did not even know Billy Ray or why he was incarcerated, began tagging billboards, trains, highway embankments and bridges, and any empty walls that could be used as a canvas with "Free Billy Ray and Ocho." Contrary to what the Prince of Darkness told Senator Bryant, the story did not die.

→━◎ ◎━←

On a demolition site in New Jersey, Robert "BB" Brazoli was sipping a coffee from the catering truck as he awaited the all-clear horn to begin the countdown to demolish the building. On his white hard hat were his initials, BB, with the company name, Phoenix Demolition. BB had learned and perfected his use of explosives from his years in the military. The building that would be raised was a dilapidated twenty-five-story masonry-and-steel building. He had supervised the weakening of the structure's support beams and wired shape charges, prima-cord, and hundreds of pounds of plastic explosives.

As he waited for the countdown, he saw an old military ID of Billy Ray in the *New Jersey Advocate* and the article detailing the current charges and incorrect military information. The newspaper article ended with the caveat: "Efforts to confirm the allegations concerning his military record were denied under Title 4 of the US Secrecy Act."

The all-clear siren began. As BB put down the newspaper, he looked at the two missing fingers on his right hand. He quickly shook off the phantom pain, along with the bad memories associated with his loss, and waited for the countdown. Over his Nextel, he was given the signal and the countdown began. When it reached zero, he flipped a serious of switches, and within a few seconds, a series of synchronized explosions went off in rapid succession and the building came crashing down. As the huge cloud of billowing smoke rolled over the area, he picked up his newspaper and threw it into a trash barrel.

--==○==--

In Detroit, Michigan, John Rollins, a black auto-assembly worker, was eating lunch in the cafeteria. He had just finished reading an article about Billy Ray in the *Detroit Free Press*. He had a difficult time digesting what he had just read, along with his half-eaten lunch. John was a big man with bold, chiseled facial features and a muscular frame, like a linebacker. He kept to himself most of the time, and when he did speak, it was with a quiet, reserved voice.

The shift supervisor came marching into the cafeteria with a tray full of food and sat down next to John. As he began eating, he was talking about the front-page story to other men at the table. The supervisor was constantly telling and retelling war stories about his days in Vietnam, or about how his only son had been killed by an IED while serving in Iraq.

"I hope they throw the book at that clown," the supervisor said with his mouth full of shepherd's pie. "Hey, Big John, what do you think of that asshole? Didn't you serve in Afghanistan?"

John looked at the supervisor but did not respond.

"Oh, I forgot. You never talk about your days in the military. What's your opinion of that coward who got his men killed?"

John got up from the table, opened the shoot of the trash bin, and dumped the remainder of his lunch and the newspaper into the receptacle.

"Oh shit," one of the men at the table said. "I think you upset the big guy."

John turned toward the supervisor as he made his way to the door. "Don't believe everything you read in the newspaper."

"And I suppose you know better?"

As John opened the door, he spoke to the supervisor without turning around. "The two men they were talking about in the newspaper who were killed in Afghanistan were in my unit. They were killed ten feet away from me.

The men at the table said whoa in unison. "I guess he told you," one of them added.

"Big John, I wasn't trying to upset you. I'm entitled to my opinion."

"I guess you are, and you know what they say about opinions," John said, closing the door to the cafeteria behind him.

Tywater Federal Penitentiary

It was the best of times, it was the worst of times,
It was the age of wisdom, it was the age of foolishness,
It was the epoch of belief, it was the age of incredulity,
It was the season of Light, it was the season of Darkness,
It was the spring of hope, it was the season of despair,
We had everything before us, we had nothing before us...

—Charles Dickens, *A Tale of Two Cities*

TYWATER FEDERAL PENITENTIARY was located in an isolated rural area, ninety miles north of Silver Verde. The high-security facility had been converted into a prison from the former Dwight D. Eisenhower Air Force Base. Surrounding the gray granite prison walls were two twenty-foot-high fences covered with razor-sharp stainless-steel ribbon wire. In between the two fences was a security corridor with armed guards and highly trained German Shepherd attack dogs. The air traffic control tower now served as a watchtower, manned with armed marksmen. In the fifteen years since the facility had been added to the federal prison system, there had never been a successful escape.

For his first three weeks at Tywater, Billy Ray was placed in solitary confinement in the intake center awaiting permanent assignment. He received all of his meals in his ten-by-six-foot cell and was only allowed out one hour every day to shower and exercise in the prison "yard" by himself, under guard. It took him a while to become accustomed to the inescapable odors that permeated the prison. It was a combination of institutional food coming from the cafeteria, musty damp cement, and the cloying medicinal smell of pine-oil disinfectant liberally applied each morning at six by the overly enthusiastic inmate custodial staff.

At 7:00 a.m. on the last day of the third week, Billy Ray was transferred to the supermax wing and placed in administrative detention. Administrative detainees, like Billy Ray, wore an orange jumpsuit designating that they were high-risk prisoners and under a full restraint order—never allowed out of their cell without arm and leg shackles.

The supermax block commander was Lieutenant Brian O'Rourke. He pushed Billy Ray toward his cell with his black baton. O'Rourke was a large, middle-aged, burley man about six foot two and 250 pounds. His face always seemed to be flushed red on his large head, almost as big as a basketball. His hair was cropped short in a marine-style crew cut. The graying hair on the sides of his head was cut so short that it was barely visible. When they arrived at Billy Ray's cell, O'Rourke pushed the door open with his baton.

"You don't get the privilege to hear the news in solitary, hero! The word is that the SEALS just killed bin Laden. If you and your fuckups in Afghanistan were doing their jobs, it might have not taken ten years. So you're Billy Ray, the one everyone's been making all the fuss about. You don't look so tough to me! Here's the Tywater handbook," he said, throwing it on the floor of the cell. "On my block, I enforce my own set of rules," he said with a grin. "From this day on, you *are* only two-five-one-six. You lost the right to have a name the minute you entered the gates of this prison. You're just another piece of shit under my boot, along with the other thirty shitheads on my block. Got that, hero? Anyone who fucks up on my block, I crack 'em in the fuckin' head," he said, slapping his baton against his hand. "And FYI, hero, I've been jumped, shanked, and scumbags like you have thrown shit and pissed at me, and I'm still standing! I just can't wait to have you make a move on me so I can crack you in the fuckin' head."

O'Rourke spoke slowly with a rough, guttural accent and a methodical sarcastic demeanor. "I read your civil and military jacket. I served *honorably* in ninety-one, Iraq, second battalion, marines," he said. "You hurt a lot of good soldiers in that hick town you're from and got your men killed in Afghanistan. On this block, you're the worst piece of shit here!"

Billy Ray raised his eyes slightly to observe the lieutenant. When evaluating a potential opponent for a chess match, conflict or combat, he would always look for a weakness to gain an advantage. He noticed that O'Rourke was pigeon-toed and carried his weight on his heels, unbalanced. In his mind's eye, he envisioned rendering him unconscious with two quick strikes or killing him instantly with one lethal blow. Billy Ray grinned and looked directly into O'Rourke's eyes.

"Don't eyeball me, hero! And wipe that grin off your face. Do it again, and you know what will happen?"

"Yeah, yeah, yeah. You'll crack me in the fuckin' head," he said, mimicking him.

"Don't back sass me," O'Rourke said, raising his baton as if he was about to strike him. As O'Rourke tried to show off, he spun his baton, and it fell to the floor. Billy Ray picked it up. Before he handed it back to O'Rourke, he spun it so quickly it became a blur. O'Rourke became startled and fumbled as he tried to reach for his can of mace.

"I think you dropped this, Lieutenant."

As he quickly grabbed the baton away from Billy Ray, another guard came over.

"I've come to escort the prisoner, sir."

"Where am I going?"

"You don't ask the questions, here! It's visiting day, and you got some, so get your ass movin'."

When Billy Ray was escorted into the visiting room, Junior and Jenny were seated on the opposite side of a one-inch-thick Plexiglas booth outfitted with phones. As he glanced at Jenny, he smiled. It was as if he was alone in a desert and found a momentary oasis. As their eyes met, he turned away, which did not escape her notice. Then he sat down and picked up the phone.

"How you holding up?" Junior asked.

"OK. We have about five minutes and a lot of ground to cover. Our conversation is being recorded, so keep that in mind. Did you get my messages from Coyle and the instructions?"

"Yes. I met him in his office. He looks a little shady. Do you thrust him?"

"At this point, my life is in his hands."

"We already started moving all the vines starting with your stock from France to the new farms. We hired a nursery with a wire-basket balling machine to move all of Jenny's avocado trees. Oh yeah, her mother and father asked me to thank you. How did you manage all this?"

"I was planning to expand our farm but not under these circumstances. When the price of gold was a little under three hundred dollars an ounce, I bought options and futures with my military pay. When Fredrick's Farms was about to go into foreclosure, I bought it from them at a fair price before the bank took it. I put both farms in our mother's maiden name," he said, looking up at Junior and Jenny, nodding his head. Junior nodded his head, acknowledging that he got the implied message. In actuality, Billy had purchased several pieces of property, but he didn't want anyone to know who may be listening in on his conversation.

"Junior, this is very important. Have Coyle transfer all of the properties, including Blu Vineyards, into your and Jenny's names. He said if I went to trial, I'd probably lose and get seven to ten years. I'm going to accept the plea agreement and get around four. There's an ambiguous clause in the agreement that he didn't explain to my satisfaction about restitution. That's why I don't want anything in my name."

"I'll get it done as soon as we leave. They're fast-tracking this buyout. We have about four months to get out. Surveyors and heavy machinery have already arrived. They already started building the road to the new dam, and that new condo development near the interstate is almost completed."

"In the basement of the Fredricks' house is a safe. The combination is the month, day, and year we were born. Got that? There's more than enough to give us a cash flow," he said, looking up to make sure he got the message.

"I understand. Have you seen Ocho in here?"

"I'm in solitary, twenty-three hours every day. Coyle is preparing a plea deal for him. He'll get maybe two and a half to three years. His wife won't be able to make their rent payments. Have our guys move their family into one of the farmworkers' houses on the property."

"We received an e-mail from Renard. He wanted assurances that, with all that has happened to you, his future shipments can be filled. Processing all of the Blu Select wine is going slow. Renard did have one great piece of information."

"Take Ocho's brother-in-law out of the field. He can operate all of the machinery. E-mail Renard and tell him that his next four years' allotments will be on schedule."

Junior opened a large manila envelope, took out a certificate, and placed it against the Plexiglas for Billy Ray to read. The guard behind Billy Ray watched him as he read the document. For the first time since he came into the visiting room, a smile appeared on his face.

"I know it's not much of a consolation, but it's something to look forward to when you get out. Blu Select was chosen best of show worldwide from over two hundred entries, including three from Domaine Romanee Conti. I wish Dad was here to see this."

A buzzer rang, indicating that visiting time was over.

"Finish up, two-five-one-six," the guard behind Billy Ray said.

Junior handed the phone to Jenny. Her voice was soothing but melancholy. "How you doing, Billy?"

"I'm holding up. Can't sleep, though."

"We wanted to tell you," she said, reaching out for Junior's hand, "with all this going on, we didn't see a need to wait. We're getting married in about a week in a private ceremony."

"I'm glad for the both of you. Don't worry about me. I'll be fine. Be happy and start a family."

"OK," the guard behind him said. "Time's up."

As Billy Ray left, Jenny kept looking at him until the door closed behind him. As he was escorted back to his cell, he tried to hold on to her image, but it quickly faded. As the reality of where he was imprisoned his thoughts, it was as if seeing her was only a temporary reprieve, a fleeting mirage.

On his way back to Silver Verde, Junior called Coyle and relayed his brother's instructions to him. He scribbled down several notes on a legal pad and called Senator Bryant. He talked to him for several minutes, hung up the phone, and smiled. Then he took the yellow paper and fed into his shredder.

→▭ ▭←

Four months had passed since Billy Ray entered Tywater. He had accepted the plea agreement and received three years, two months. He could feel his spirit and strength of will sinking under the weight of knowing that his sentence took away what should have been the most productive years of his life.

Today he was scheduled to have a psychological examination. He welcomed any change in routine to relieve the boredom of his monotonous existence. As he waited for the guard to escort him to his appointment, a trustee came to his cell. Every few weeks an inmate came by pushing a cart of books and magazines from the prison's outdated library. This time he picked out an old, tattered copy of Charles Dickens's *A Tale of Two Cities* and several *Popular Science* and horticultural magazines.

Billy Ray was escorted to the administration building, past Warden Vincent Van Leeston's office and into the office of the prison psychiatrist, Dr. Catalina Vibes. Dr. Vibes was seated at her desk. She instructed him to sit down, without looking up. The guard took up a position several feet behind him.

Under her white lab coat was a conservative gray-and-black tweed business suit. Her dark hair was cropped short and a pair of bifocal glasses hung from a black necklace around her neck. She was matronly in appearance but attractive and well kept, with a shapely figure for a woman in her early to middle fifties. Billy Ray noticed an indentation and discoloration where a wedding band had recently adorned her long, slender ring finger.

As she read his file, he observed the many framed professional degrees and personal photographs that hung on the wall behind her or were neatly displayed on her desk. Although he knew it was Dr. Vibes's profession to evaluate him, he already formulated a composite of her from the information her professional and private artifacts disclosed, but more important, from what it failed to reveal or what he believed she tried to keep private.

Dr. Vibes had a soft, demure voice. "Perhaps you would care to tell me what I hope to accomplish today?"

"We are here so that you can evaluate my psychological frame of mind to determine if I'm a potential threat to myself or others."

For the first time since Billy Ray entered the room, she looked up to see what type of man had just given her that textbook answer. "Very lucid, but not unexpected for a man with an IQ as high as yours."

Billy Ray knew that a psychological profile could be used to keep a prisoner locked up beyond his original sentence. "Haven't you overlooked something, Catherina?" he asked.

"It's Dr. Vibes to you, two-five-one-six. What is it that you believe I forgot?"

"Since I've already accepted a plea agreement, the court never ordered a psychological examination. We cannot proceed without my consent."

"And you know a little about the law?" she asked sarcastically.

"Enough to know that's the release form on the top of my file."

"And I suppose that you won't sign it," she said, placing the form and a pen in front of him.

"There's no reason not to. I'm as sane as the next guy, as long as it's not the guy in the next cell," he said, signing the form and sliding it back to her.

"Fine. I'd like to begin with your military career. Do you believe you are suffering from posttraumatic stress disorder?"

"No."

"You were a marine, in a Special Forces unit stationed in Afghanistan?"

"Yes."

"And while engaged in the line of duty, you killed the enemy?"

"Yes."

"And how did that make you feel?"

"Overjoyed it was them and not me."

"Can you estimate how many men you killed?"

"Real soldiers never keep count."

"Humor me. Was it five, ten, twenty...more?"

"Quite a few."

"I see here that you received two Purple Hearts and a Silver Star for distinguished service. Then, something happened that was removed from your file resulting in your dishonorable discharge. What happened?"

"It was at the end of my tour. Contrary to whatever is written there, it was a mutually agreed upon voluntary discharge. And I have the signed documents at home to prove it."

"I'm sure you do," she said patronizing him. "You have a history of violence. You were involved in a double homicide when you were in your...early twenties," she said, looking down at Sheriff Roy's report.

"It was justified homicide, and I don't care to discuss the matter any further."

Dr. Vibes read excerpts of the report, looked up at him with a curious expression, and decided not to press the issue. "Perhaps you would care to detail the events in Silver Verde that resulted in us having the pleasure of your company at Tywater?"

Billy Ray shrugged his shoulders, nodding, as if to say "Why not?"

"The indictment stated that you attacked Senator Bryant and members of his staff and injured about a dozen ISS soldiers, some of them severely. Is that what happened?"

"One man attacked twelve, resulting in injuries to the twelve. Does that sound plausible?"

Dr. Vibes did not answer him. She jotted down a few notes and continued. "Do you believe you are a man prone to violence?"

"Actually, I'm a pacifist."

"And a comedian," she said, mocking him. "How do you explain this violent confrontation?"

"I used the force I deem necessary to protect my family, friends, neighbors, and myself."

"Then I suppose you felt no remorse over the injuries and suffering you caused those soldiers. According to the indictment you were...'Out of control, in a violent rage,'" she said. "Didn't you realize you could have killed some of those men?"

"No, not some of them, all of them. Had I been out of control, and if it was my inclination, I could have easily killed every one of them."

The guard behind him shook his head and smirked.

"So I may better understand your thought process, if you feel a real or perceived threat, you feel there is nothing illegal or immoral about taking the law into your own hands. Isn't that the way a vigilante thinks? Suppose everyone in the country thought the same way you do?"

A piece of information quickly surfaced in his mind from a novel he had read in college that he remembered telling General Nault at his military inquest. He altered it slightly to answer her question. "If everyone in the country thought the same way I do, wouldn't I be insane to think any differently?"

Dr. Vibes opened her mouth and raised her hand to correct him but hesitated as she thought about the implication of his response. His response had caught her by surprise. The guard, who was now leaning against the wall several feet behind Billy Ray, smiled at his answer, which seemed to annoy her.

"How very glib, Mr. Blu," she said sarcastically.

He smiled. It was the first time since he arrived at Tywater that anyone had addressed him by his name instead of his number. He could feel and sense a personal sexual tension, and oddly enough, an attraction between them.

"Court documents indicate that you believe that the lives of yourself, your brother, and others were in peril, and that there is some type of conspiracy against all of the residents of Silver Verde. For a man of your intelligence, doesn't that seem delusional and a little paranoid?"

"A little paranoia is not necessarily a bad thing. It can keep you sharp, save your life."

"And how did you arrive at the conclusion of this impending doom, and this conspiracy theory?"

"I know everyone in Silver Verde. There were strangers there who didn't belong, outside agitators. And there was one person in particular who gave credence to my belief that something wasn't kosher."

"And that person was?"

"A person known to me to be with the CIA."

"The CIA! Really! The Central Intelligence Agency! Your story gets better and better all the time," she said, shaking her head in amazement, mocking him.

"You of all people should know that things aren't always the way they appear to be. Sometimes things are perceived the way they are *made* to appear to be."

Once again she reflected on what he had just said. "You based your actions upon your keen powers of observation, this unique gift to be able to analyze a situation in a split second, to access a potential threat, to look into a person's character and intent, and then act upon your precognitions?"

"Maybe not as easily, or with the keen powers of observation as a professional, like yourself," he said, mocking her.

"Well educate me, please. I'm more than curious to see how your unique talent works. Show me on maybe…this guard behind you."

"Too easy," Billy Ray said, looking over his shoulder at the guard.

"Well then, demonstrate your powers of observation on, let's say, me."

"Are you sure?"

"I can hardly wait."

As he spoke, he seemed to be looking through her, not at her. The tranquility in his voice mesmerized her, which caused her facial expressions to turn blank as she went into a trance.

"You were the only child of loving parents…who were well off. Nice home in the suburbs. Private schools. An overachiever. Graduated from an Ivy League college. Earned your Harvard medical degree with distinction. You believed in love once. Married for many years. After the recent divorce, you no longer trust or believe in lasting relationships. You never had children for the sake of your career. You work out at an all-women empowerment spar. Jog before work. Maybe yoga classes twice a week. Eat health foods. Your nights are spent alone with your one or two cats, sipping tea in your flannel pajamas, channel surfing between the Science Channel and the Food Network. All the while reading professional texts and *Psychology Today.*"

Dr. Vibes snapped out of her trance. Her face was flushed with embarrassment. Then she let out an uncharacteristic laugh. "This is a joke, right! Who put you up to this? Who gave you that information?" she asked, looking up at the guard.

The guard shrugged his shoulders.

"Shall I continue?"

"Yes—I mean no!" she said, trying to regain her composure, and then quickly changed the subject.

"Do you have any hobbies?"

"I used to play chess, therapy for my mind and soul."

"And you no longer play?"

"There aren't any chess boards or players in solitary confinement. But that's a matter of perspective. I'd like to think I'm playing chess all the time, metaphorically speaking."

"How so?"

"Chess helped me form strategies for problems and adversaries. It taught me caution. To think before I act," he said, looking directly at Dr. Vibes. "You develop foresight and deferred gratification, sacrificing in the short term to gain in the long term. It taught me the consequences of my actions, and maybe more important," he said, hesitating as he remembered the last words his mother had

69

told him before she died, "the consequences of inaction. And it taught me how to put into perspective every event, no matter how trivial or insignificant and see its relationship to the whole picture."

A smile appeared on Dr. Vibes's face as she came to realize what he had been doing during the whole evaluation. "And have *we* been playing chess this morning?"

"How lucid," he said, mimicking her once again. "But I fear you have me at a distinct disadvantage."

"Is it part of your strategy…to have me think that? All right, I'll play. It's your move. How so?"

"You're the one holding the pen," he said, smiling.

"Did you have a girlfriend? Your file does not say if you were married."

"I had a girlfriend," he said, recalling Jenny's smile, "but it didn't work out."

"And why's that?"

"You know how it goes, Dr. Vibes."

"One final category. When your time is served, how will you be making a meaningful contribution to society?"

"I will resume my duties running our family business."

"And that is?"

"Blu Vineyards. We make wine."

"Is this commercial enterprise successful?"

"We do our best. When our chess match is over, check out our website," he said, making his final move. He knew that the information would enlighten and confuse her.

"I will, Mr. Blu. Good day."

After Billy Ray left, Dr. Vibes looked at her notes and began a preliminary evaluation. She knew what type of evaluation would put her in the good graces of the administration and Warden Van Leeston. Psychological abnormalities like "prone to fits of uncontrollable rage, delusional, suffering from a persecution complex, paranoia, and a danger to himself and others" could easily be assigned to him. Out of curiosity, before she continued, she Googled Blu Vineyards. She read the document that Jenny had posted on the front page of the website announcing that William Raymond Blu, co-owner of Blu Vineyards, was the recipient of the prestigious Best of Show for his Blu Select wine from all of the entries worldwide at the Wine Expo held in Burgundy, France.

She was now more confused as to her prognosis. Over the years, she had written thousands of evaluations of incorrigible inmates. She could not determine, with any degree of certainly, how much of what he was telling her was the truth or the elaborate ruse of a pathological conman.

⇥⊟ ⊟⇤

A week after Billy Ray received his psychological examination, he placed his lunch tray on the sliding receptacle on his cell door. He barely touched his meal. He felt uneasy all morning. He had a premonition, a free-floating anxiety that something wasn't right. Then his suspicion was confirmed when he heard several guards talking near his cell door. Two guards and the assistant warden, Carl Curtis, were talking to Lieutenant O'Rourke in whispering voices. As he listened, he only heard bits and pieces of their conversation.

"What's up, Captain?" he heard O'Rourke ask. "It's not visiting day."

"The mayor of Silver Verde asked Van Leeston for a favor." Then Captain Curtis said something, and O'Rourke laughed. "You are not to tell him anything. He'll find out soon enough. And be civil. Do you hear me, O'Rourke? Civil."

Billy Ray was placed in shackles and escorted to a small annex room outside of the visiting room. He heard a buzzer opening a door, and Mayor White and Father Pat were escorted by another guard into the room.

Father Pat's eyes were red, and he appeared to be wiping tears from his eyes.

"What's wrong?" Billy Ray asked as he could feel his heart racing. "What happened?"

Mayor White could see that Father Pat couldn't speak. "It's your brother," the mayor said, lowering his head. "He's...dead. He died this morning."

Billy Ray could feel adrenaline pumping through his body as his emotions and senses heightened. "How?"

"He received the settlement check for your property," the mayor said. "As soon as the check cleared, the government seized the funds. Judge Tores issued the court order. Something to do with your restitution."

"Coyle was supposed to take care of that. But what happen to my brother?"

"I wasn't there until after…"

Father Pat cleared his throat and interrupted the mayor. His eyes glazed over as if he were recalling the event as it was happening. "The demolition crew showed up. Your brother climbed aboard a bulldozer armed with your father's rifle and blocked the entryway.

"They called the sheriff and the state police. The state police called in the ISS. The ISS called General Bishop. Then all hell broke loose. When I got there, about twenty ISS soldiers had already arrived, some of them the same ones you tangled with in town. They were wearing bulletproof vests and carrying automatic weapons. Sheriff Roy and Jenny convinced Junior to get off the bulldozer. As he was climbing down, he slipped, dropping his rifle. The shots rang out," he said, flinching as if still hearing the shots. "It never seemed to end. Jenny was clutching my hand as she looked at Junior. We were both covered in his…blood."

The mayor nudged Father Pat, who momentarily stopped. "Jenny dropped to the ground, still holding my hand so tight…so tight. She opened her mouth to scream, but nothing came out. Then she went into shock, eyes open, but not responsive. Your brother was pronounced dead at the scene, and Jenny was taken to the county hospital. Doc Horton attended to her. She's still in shock, but stable."

To the best of anyone's knowledge, no one had ever seen Billy Ray show any outward signs of emotion. He was always austere, stoic in nature. He tried to remain faithful to the warrior's code from *The Art of Violence*, which postulated, "In order not to cloud or interfere with his judgment or actions, a warrior must always remain unaffected by grief or pain. He must accept all occurrences as the unavoidable result of divine will." Although he tried to suppress his emotions, they surfaced. His eyes welled up, and tears fell down his face.

"I asked Warden Van Leeston if you would be allowed to attend the wake and funeral under guard," the mayor said. "He said it was out of the question. You are a flight risk, and he already was doing me a big favor by just letting us come in to see you."

"Will you do me a favor, Mayor?" Billy Ray asked in a voice slightly above a whisper.

"Sure, anything Billy."

"Take care of all the arrangements for my brother, and take care of Jenny… anything she needs."

As Billy got up to leave, he wiped the tears off on the sleeve of his jumpsuit.

"We'll take care of everything," Father Pat said. "Your brother, Jenny, and you will be in my prayers."

"Pray for them, Father, but not for me. And say a prayer for all those responsible for everything that's been happening. One day, they'll need all the help they can get!"

As the door was buzzed open, the mayor and Father Pat stood up. Father Pat wanted to leave Billy Ray with some last words to console him. "Your brother is now in heaven with your mother and father."

"Maybe, Father," he said, without turning around, "but that's not where I'm going."

"…we were all going direct to Heaven,
we were all going direct the other way,
in short, the period was so far like the present
period, that the noisiest authorities, insisted
its being received, for good or for evil, in the
superlative degree of comparison only."

—Charles Dickens, *A Tale of Two Cities*

As news of the events of Silver Verde was broadcast throughout the country, once again it did not escape the notice of the men who had served with Billy Ray in Afghanistan. Nor did it escape the attention and interest of people ranging from ordinary citizens to radical militant groups who had come to believe that if ominous events by government soldiers could take place on "Main Street," it could be soon happening everywhere.

Dr. Vibes's shift was ending. As she cleaned some papers off her desk, she wondered why Warden Van Leeston was pressuring her to complete Billy Ray's profile. She was just about to leave when the assistant warden's secretary came into her room quickly and told her to turn on the television.

A CNN reporter was detailing the events at Silver Verde with the backdrop of a large-claw bulldozer tearing down the remnants of Billy Ray and Junior's home.

"Once again, violence has broken out in the normally peaceful town of Silver Verde, California," the reporter said. "Raymond 'Junior' Blu armed with a rifle, was shot and killed by ISS soldiers while resisting arrest. As you may remember, Raymond Blu is the is the brother of William 'Billy Ray' Blu, who is serving a four-year term at Tywater Penitentiary for assault upon Senator Bryant and ISS soldiers. We will keep you updated as more information comes in. This is Ron Clark reporting to you live from Silver Verde."

As Dr. Vibes turned off the television, part of her interview with Billy Ray came to mind: "You believe that the lives of yourself, your brother, and others were in peril..." As she closed the door to her office behind her, she remembered what Billy Ray had said and wondered how much of what just happened was what it was "made" to appear to be.

⟶⟝ ⟞⟵

O'Rourke removed Billy Ray's shackles with a wide grin on his face. When he entered his cell, Billy Ray turned and faced him. "No one is gonna lose any sleep over one less scumbag in the world," O'Rourke said, taunting him. "Except maybe for you. Just thought I'd give you something to think about when you're all alone at night in your cell."

"So you believe in the saying 'every dog has its day'?"

"You bet your ass I do. Your brother got what was coming to him, just like you got what was coming to you."

As the expression on Billy Ray's face changed, it alarmed O'Rourke. He had seen that look before, guarding men on death row at another prison. It was a look of despair, hopelessness—from men who had nothing to lose.

"O'Rourke, I know you're not as dumb as you look. Did you ever take the time to figure out how a dozen or so ISS were put down, armed with batons just like the one you have there, and I didn't even get a scratch…until a sniper's rubber bullet took me out?"

The smile disappeared from O'Rourke's face as he thought about what Billy Ray had said. He stepped backward quickly and closed the cell door with his baton.

"Just thought I'd give *you* something to think about when you're all alone at night walking the cell block."

From that day forward, O'Rourke never went to Billy Ray's cell without being accompanied by another guard or two.

That night, as Billy Ray lay awake thinking, reflecting about his past, present, and his alltoo-uncertain future, it was indeed the best of times for him. He had achieved one of his lifelong goals, which exceeded his dreams, when his wine was selected as the best in the world. But it was also the worst of times. His brother was dead. He would be in Tywater for almost three more years, and the other person he dreamed about was now a widower and would be crying herself to sleep every night. He felt that everything that had happened was interconnected, but he couldn't put the pieces together—yet.

Big Brother

*"There was of course no way of knowing whether you were being watched
at any given moment. How often, or what system, the Thought Police
plugged in on any individual wire was guess work. It was even conceivable
that they watched everybody all the time but at any given rate they could
plug in your wire whenever they wanted to. You had to live—did live, from
habit that became instinct—in the assumption that every sound you made
was overheard and except in darkness every movement scrutinized."*

—George Orwell, *1984*

THE PRINCE OF Darkness arose every morning at five without the aid of an alarm
clock or a wake-up call. On whatever continent or time zone he was located,
his internal clock awakened him each day just before sunrise. He had just spent
the last three weeks in Afghanistan and was adjusting to the time difference. He
was dressing in his dark-blue pinstriped suit, which had been neatly laid out the
night before on his bedpost. As the first shreds of light filtered into his room,
he looked out his bedroom window over a small body of water in the rear of the
expensive townhouse condominium he had purchased in Alexandria, Virginia.

He was content in his new permanent residence, surrounded by a quaint community made up of mostly professionals working in or around Washington, DC.
He was within walking distance of gourmet restaurants featuring a broad range of
world-class cuisine, expensive men's haberdasheries, and upscale women's boutiques.

As he looped his dark-blue tie slowly and methodically into a perfect config-
uration, he turned his head from side to side, looking at himself in his bathroom

mirror, observing the slow progression of gray hair on his neatly trimmed side-burns and around his earlobes. As he looked at his reflection, he became self-absorbed and enamored by his good looks and masculine physique and marveled at how well preserved he was for a man approaching fifty.

He had a slight but noticeable obsessive-compulsive behavioral disorder that mirrored and coincided with the way in which he viewed his place and purpose in the world. He believed it was his calling to remake, reshape everyone and everything to fit into his perception of perfect order: a place for everything and everything in its place. The expensive clothing in his closet was always neatly arranged. The toiletry articles in his medicine cabinet as well as all the cans in his pantry and food in his refrigerator were always positioned with the labels facing out and never more than a quarter of an inch apart.

Before he opened his laptop, he adjusted the two books on his night table that he considered the bibles of his personal philosophy of life. The books were Machiavelli's *The Prince* and Tsiang Kiuen's *The Art of Violence*. He opened his lap-top and typed in his code. An EMC—emergency message communiqué—was flashing on his screen. He read all the newspaper accounts and opened the links to all the television reports detailing Raymond Blu's death. As he read Sheriff Roy's account of the incident, he wondered what effect this development would have on the long-term plans he had for Billy Ray. Would he still be able to turn him into a valued asset, under his control, or would this make him a loose cannon, a liability bent on revenge that he would have to address personally one day? He had not planned on seeing General Bishop until later in the month, but this incident warranted an unscheduled visit. He e-mailed Bishop and advised him that he would be arriving around nine.

Every morning, whether heading into DC or taking the expressway to the Pentagon or the NSA, he would take a shorter route through the rear entrance of Arlington National Cemetery, which was a five-minute drive from his con-dominium in Alexandria. Sometimes, he would stop and observe a military ceremony in progress or relatives of the departed placing flags and flowers on the gravesites of their loved ones killed in the line of duty. He drove his black Crown Victoria to Fort Meade, Maryland, to the NSA Building. The new of-fices of the Internal Security and Surveillance program were located on several floors of the building. After passing through several checkpoints, he took the elevator to General Bishop's office. He carried a small black valise and a hatbox under his arm.

"Good day," General Bishop said, extending his hand.

"Is it?" he replied, not extending his hand. He rearranged a few papers and a pen on the general's desk. "People usually aren't overjoyed to see me!"

The Prince of Darkness opened his valise and handed several documents to the general. Then he handed him a hatbox and a small manila envelope. "The board approved your promotion and your position as director of the ISS. Here is the order, your designation, a general's cap, and new clusters."

"The board?"

"Yes, the board. The men behind the men behind all the men. A group of individuals who have made all of the significant decisions in this country, with the utmost discretion, since, let's say, November 1963. With their endorsement and blessing, you are now among the elite who have complete autonomy. They are the only authoritative body who holds us accountable. Let's hope you never have to meet them. It is *never* a good day when they call you in. I've got a feeling that they'll be requesting the pleasure of my company after the recent ISS fuckup. Come on; let's go for a walk."

"Where are we going?"

"It's about time I took you to see what you are *really* in charge of."

They took an elevator down deep into the hardened underbelly of the building and entered a long, dimly lit corridor past the first guarded checkpoint.

"I suppose your reference to the fuckup was what happened to Raymond Blu. I sent you an EAC, but the Pentagon said you were out of the country at an undisclosed location."

"I was in Afghanistan with my counterpart in intelligence, but his classification would be an overstatement, taking care of company business…briefing some of our foreign allies to…neutralize some radicals who have been trying to destabilize their government and undermine our agenda."

"Neutralize?"

"You're one of us now. You know how it goes. So little time, so many people to assassinate. Only kidding…or was I?" he asked rhetorically. "And yes, I was talking about Billy Ray's brother. Did you read the sheriff's report?"

"Yes, but I have been assured that our men were justified in their actions and will be exonerated."

"They are your men, not mine, and that's not the point. According to the sheriff's report, he was giving himself up."

"I agree that they may have overacted, but after the Silver Verde altercation with Blu, they were not taking any chances."

"Overacted is an understatement. They shot him what? Forty, fifty times? Where the fuck did you recruit those men at, Soldiers R Us? In Silver Verde, your old nemesis Blu took them apart. He could have killed them all. The whole event is recorded. I'll send you the link, and you can see for yourself how inept your so-called elite forces were."

"We're getting better. I recruited the only member still in the military from Blu's unit to train them, Major Macky. In no time they'll be a force to reckon with."

"I hope so, but I'm concerned how Billy Ray reacted to his brother's death."

"I wouldn't worry about him."

The Prince of Darkness stopped walking. "You should be. You of all people know what he's capable of. You ever heard the expression 'Let sleeping dogs lie'? Psychologically, he was almost where I wanted him. His will was all but broken; a drowning man in a dark whirlpool of hopelessness and despair looking for someone to throw him a lifeline. That's where I would have come in. I hope his brother's death didn't give him a quest, a vendetta."

"He's not going anywhere for quite some time."

"And what about when he gets out? The board and I have plans for him."

"What plans?"

"That information is above your pay grade."

They arrived at the final checkpoint. They stood before a gray vault door with the letters ISS engraved into the door outlined in gold leaf. To the left of the entrance was a keypad. After the Prince of Darkness typed in his name, an automated female voice gave him instructions to proceed.

"Code in," she requested.

He entered a code and placed his thumbprint on the screen of the keyboard.

"Processing. Facial recognition and retinal scan complete," the voice said.

"Now that you're officially the director," the Prince of Darkness said, "have the duty officer code you in. You're going to be spending quite some time down here."

As the red lights surrounding the vault door turned to green, a beeping alarm rang, and the door began to open slowly. They entered the amphitheater, which had descending platforms with dozens of operators at computer terminals processing incoming data. At the bottom of the room was a theater-size screen displaying live satellite feeds of surveillance in progress. General Bishop stood awestruck by the scope, magnitude, and sophistication of the high-tech surveillance equipment. As the Prince of Darkness and Bishop observed the operation, a few of the operators looked up, recognized them, and quickly resumed working.

"How many people know this program exists?" Bishop asked.

"Big Brother operates three shifts, twenty-four seven. Except for a few congressmen who appropriated the money for this covert program and those who operate and oversee it, no one."

"How did this all come about?"

"Some time ago, the board decided that this program was not only necessary but essential for our country to remain a strong nation. They came to the conclusion that like all great empires of the past, our nation could only fall from within."

"But what is the purpose of gathering all this information?"

"Not only is it my duty, but it will be my pleasure to enlighten you. It all begins with the fiber-optic lines that come in on the West Coast in San Obispo, California, and on the East Coast in Atlanta, Georgia. We spliced into the fiber optics, and all incoming information is routed here. The Big Brother supercomputer compiles and categorizes millions of pieces of information daily and highlights certain keys that we have selected the program to isolate. Once a pattern is found, it triggers a full-scale investigation. Additional information is collected from IRS filings, Department of Motor Vehicles records, credit cards, banking, mortgages, everything that is bought and sold anywhere, even on Amazon and eBay. All e-mails and phone conversations. Research conducted on the Internet, books taken out from libraries, YouTube, Myspace, Facebook, Twitter, et cetera, and of course, the new form of electronic transfer of money, Bitcoin. Once that information reaches a predetermined threshold, the file is forwarded to the board for review to determine if the intel is innocuous or a more comprehensive level of investigation or interdiction is warranted. Big Brother is the most comprehensive mega-data-mining program in existence. I recorded all of the correspondence between the president, his cabinet, advisors, and campaign personnel focusing in on his reelection. I extracted all pertinent intel and gave it to Bryant, who shared it with Morton. Of course, they don't know who or how it was acquired," he said with a cunning grin.

"Is this all legal? What will the courts and the government say if they found out?"

"You still don't get it. We're the government! It this all legal? Well, that's a matter of perspective. After nine eleven, and the recent terrorist attack, we've been given carte blanche, unrestricted power to act at our own discretion and unconditional authority to carry out our mandates. As far as the courts, we have enough influence to persuade them in accepting our belief that the constitution in not a stagnant but ever-evolving document. In order to preserve and ensure our way of life, certain liberties and freedoms that the American public has taken for granted will have to be modified or surrendered."

"Is this an extension of Operation Pin Thread?"

"Pin Thread? To compare Pin Thread to Big Brother is like a comparison of an abacus and a supercomputer.

"And the citizens of this country will just accept the covert surveillance and loss of privacy?"

"Maybe not at first. Sure they'll be some resistance. That's why your ISS forces have to be up to the task to persuade them to accept our way of thinking, if you know what I mean," he said with deadpan seriousness. "And those citizens who are suffering from constitutional constipation will be forced to accept an enema of reality and joyfully wipe their asses with the Bill of Rights."

"And this is the goal of the Big Brother program?"

"In part. Big Brother is one of the tools we will use to implement our agenda. You know," the Prince of Darkness said, as if he were looking up at an apparition, "it is both a blessing and a curse to be a visionary. And one day, historians will thank us for this foresight, and we will be spoken of with the same reverence as our founding fathers." The Prince of Darkness opened his black valise and took out a folder. "The persons on this list are to be submitted to the full spectrum of surveillance," he said, handing the file to the general.

Bishop opened the folder and read down the list. "You have a governor, lawyers, senators, a judge, a mayor, a sheriff," he said, moving his finger down the list, "and even a Catholic priest?"

"No one's above suspicion," he said, taking a pen from the inside pocket of his suit jacket. "I think we can cross out Raymond Blu. No need to put him under surveillance, is there, General?"

"No, sir. Not anymore."

"Big Brother hasn't overlooked any aspect of our society that may unbalance the equation. The program is in the process of compiling a list of books and movies that soon will be deemed un-American and subversive. In the near future, they will be blacklisted and removed from circulation. The masses must be kept under surveillance to monitor their progress, or more important, lack thereof, in attaining enlightenment. We must be ever vigilant to keep them in the dark, leading unexamined lives. We are going to give them an obscure, convoluted view of their little pathetic lives as if they were looking at the world through wax paper, and reading Braille will be the only means of perception.

"I agree, sir. An ignorant society is a blissful one."

"So you're on board with everything we have to do?"

"Absolutely. Your will be done."

See No Evil, Hear No Evil, Speak No Evil

AFTER HIS BROTHER'S death, Billy Ray became lethargic and lost in a malaise of hopelessness and depression. After a period of grief and introspection, he turned his anger inward. Late at night, undetected in his cell, he kept in shape with the exercise methods of calisthenics and isometrics. He spent countless hours honing the precision and lethality of all his martial-arts disciplines. He was now in the best physical shape of his life, but he didn't know, as of yet, at whom to vent the anger that had been building inside him. He remained sharp and focused and ready for anyone or anything that he would possibly confront.

Weeks turned into months, and months into years. He had been at Tywater for three years with only a little over six months left to serve, or at least that's what he thought. He'd had several appointments with Dr. Vibes over the past three years since his first visit. He looked forward to his meetings with her and felt that she enjoyed their conversations. She gave him several favorable evaluations, which would not interfere with his scheduled release date, but the findings did not meet with the approval of Warden Van Leeston.

In sharp contrast to other regions of the country, the economy of Silver Verde was thriving. The dam would be completed just about the same time that Billy Ray would be released from Tywater. The influx of thousands of construction workers, and the businesses servicing those men, had made Silver Verde more vibrant and economically stable than the small but quickly growing town had ever been.

Mayor White and Father Pat visited Billy Ray regularly, sometimes alone and at other times together. Jenny had only been up to visit him a few times since Junior's death, but she wrote to him every month. Today was visiting day, and from Jenny's last letter, Billy Ray knew that she would be up to see him. Today he thought he would tell her, but he had mixed emotions as to how she would react. Billy Ray was escorted into the visiting room and waited for Jenny. As she walked into the room, all eyes gravitated toward her. She was radiant, and the other visitors kept looking at her until she sat down and picked up the phone.

"I've been counting down the days, Billy. Your release date is marked on my calendar. We're planning a welcome-home party. Everyone can't wait to see you. And I..." she said, lowering her head.

"How's everything going at the farm?" he asked, trying to change the subject.

"Fine. Everything is almost up to full production. Ocho's wife said he's getting out in about a month. You wouldn't recognize the town. It's grown so much in the last three years—with all the people working on the dam. We now have a Taco Bell and a McDonald's in town. A Dunkin' Donuts and a Starbucks are located across the street from each other. Sparkey's has been renovated and can hold nearly two hundred people, and they're breaking ground for a CVS Pharmacy Superstore next month. The oddest thing happened last month at the library, where I still read to the children at story hour. We received a letter with a list of books that are to be removed from circulation and sent to a depository in Maryland. Do you believe it?"

"Nothing surprises me these days. How are you and the mayor getting along?"

An odd expression appeared on her face. She didn't know how to respond, or what he was implying. "Great," she said cautiously. "He's always there when I need him."

"Good, I'm glad."

"What do you mean by that, Billy?"

"He's a handsome man with a good, stable career."

Jenny was speechless. She opened her mouth to respond, but nothing came out. Then she thought for a moment, cleared her throat, and spoke softly. "I see what you're doing. Don't you care for me, even a little?"

"Don't take this the wrong way, Jenny, but it would be for the best if you didn't come here to see me or write any more letters."

"Why, Billy? Why?"

"You have to trust me. I'm only thinking of your welfare. You don't think everything that has happened came about by chance, do you? No one has anything I care about in this world to hold over me. The people who are responsible for all this may hurt you or use you as leverage to get to me. I can't have that. I can't have anyone else I care about hurt because of me. So please don't write or come to see me anymore."

Jenny bowed her head and started to cry. As she wiped the tears from her eyes, he turned away. "You're breaking my heart...and it's not the first time. Seeing you, thinking of you, is all I have to look forward to. You're all I have left. There's no future for me without you in it."

"Jenny, this is the way it has to be. Ask the mayor; he'll tell you I'm right."

She wiped the tears from her eyes and composed herself. "I loved Junior, and I know he loved me more that I could ever hope for. But as I lay awake at night, alone, I wonder if I loved him because he reminded me so much of you. I never really understood you, Billy. No one does. Why won't you let somebody love you? I can't help it, but I do."

The buzzer rang. Visiting time was over.

"The months will go by quickly and maybe..." he said, hanging up the phone without finishing his thoughts.

When Billy Ray was escorted back to his cell, Lieutenant O'Rourke was waiting for him. "Movin' day, asshole."

"What do you mean?"

"Some fuckin' imbecile decided that you've been a model prisoner, so you're going to spend the remainder of your sentence in the general population. They even rescinded the full restraint order."

Billy Ray wondered why Van Leeston would place him in the general population, where his life could be at risk or an altercation might occur.

"Will you miss me, asshole?" O'Rourke asked, taunting him. "But you'll be back here soon, or better still, maybe you'll end up in the morgue."

"Why's that?"

"You'll see soon enough," he said, smiling a devious smile. "It's only a matter of time before you'll fuck up or tangle with a maniac like yourself out there," he said, pointing his baton in the direction of the yard.

"Can't be any worse than being in here with you."

"What the fuck's that supposed to mean?"

"Sometimes prisons hire men with the same criminal sadistic tendencies as the men they are guarding—sort of as a deterrent to their own kind."

"Maybe, but the difference is that I'm the one wearing the uniform with the power and the stick," he said, slapping his baton against the palm of his hand.

"And that, O'Rourke, may be the only difference."

⇥⊙ ⊙⇤

On Billy Ray's first day in the general population, his block was escorted to the cafeteria and then into the yard. He walked around the perimeter, along the twenty-foot-high inner fence with the stainless-steel ribbon wire coiled on top. Occasionally, men would deliberately walk in his path or bump into him, or at least that's what he thought. Each time, he would just sidestep the men and keep on walking. He observed men playing basketball on several full-length basketball courts. Shirtless members of a Latino gang displayed gang-related tattoos as they lifted weights. Several men were jogging around a quarter-mile black cinder track that encompassed the entire yard. After a while, he came across two black men playing chess, one old and one young. As they played, several other men were huddled around the game, watching their moves.

"Checkmate," the old man said. "Next pigeon."

The young man got up and a middle-aged man wearing thick black-framed glasses took his place.

"Next time, old man," the young man said.

"In your dreams," the old man said, without looking up.

Billy Ray observed the old man's hands as he reset the pieces on the board. His knuckles were enlarged, and there were elongated scars on the backs of his hands. It appeared to him that these were the hands of a man who had worked hard all his life. The old man won every match he played, but he was no match for him, Billy Ray thought. After there were no other men to play, the old man glanced up at him with hollow, world-weary eyes. Then he lowered his eyes and arranged the pieces on the board for another game.

"You play, young man?" he asked, without looking up.

"Not for quite some time," Billy Ray said, smiling.

"Well, sit down, boy, but before you do, would you mind turning around?"

Billy Ray turned around with a puzzled look on his face. "What was that all about?" he asked as he sat down.

"I was looking for a bull's-eye."

"A what?"

"That's my way of telling you something without telling you something. In the yard I mind my own business, and I'm left alone."

Billy Ray extended his hand. "I'm William Blu. People call me Billy Ray."

"I'm Roscoe Clements. People call me Roscoe Clements," he said, smiling. "I know who you are, and so does everyone else in the yard. So you're the one, ha. The one who has all the wackos comin' in their pants. I thought you'd be bigger, mean-looking, tough. You're just a young man. Not really much to meet the eye."

Roscoe made a move, and Billy Ray quickly countered.

"What did you mean by the bull's-eye?"

"I'm surprised they let you out of solitary. They must have gotten the word. The word, like a man's rep, travels fast in here," he said, moving another piece.

"I don't understand," Billy Ray said, moving and then taking one of the old man's pieces.

"In your three years here, boy, you haven't learned nothin' about Tywater. Rumors, like a man's rep, can get blown all out of proportion. First thing you know, a guy like you is ten feet tall. These sick fucks in here have a twisted code they live by, same as any other prison. The more dangerous and greater a rep a man has, the more status is gained by someone making his bones on you. You know what that means?"

"I get the picture."

Roscoe made his signature move in an attempt to capture Billy Ray's queen. He had seen the ploy several moves before and quickly blocked his attempt.

"My, my, my. I've got to pay attention here. I may have underestimated you, boy. I think you're much better than you led me to believe."

"So the word is that I've been targeted. Targeted for what?"

Roscoe laughed quietly. "Right now you got the biggest target on your back that anyone has had in Tywater in the six years I've been here. You're the brass ring, the Super Bowl, and the World Series all rolled into one trophy for some psycho to place on his mantelpiece."

"I'm not looking for any trouble. I just want to do my time and go home."

"I've got the feeling that trouble has a way of finding men like you."

Lieutenant O'Rourke was walking in the yard. He appeared to be looking for someone as he stopped by several groups of men, asking questions. He stopped and talked to two Latino men who were playing dominos.

"Shiiit," Roscoe said, glancing up at O'Rourke. "What the fuck's he doing in the yard?"

Billy Ray looked up. "I was in his block for three years."

"When I first got here, I smacked a guy for disrespecting me. Gotta stand your ground in here. Got two months in solitary. How many times did he threaten to crack you in the fuckin' head'?" Roscoe said, mimicking O'Rourke.

Billy Ray smiled and made another move.

"He's a sadistic cocksucker," Roscoe said, shaking his head from side to side. "A lot of inmates on his block have gone to the infirmary with busted heads, ribs, and teeth from his big black billy club."

One of the men playing dominoes pointed in Billy Ray's direction, which Billy Ray noticed but said nothing. After he made another move, he noticed six skinheads standing in the alleyway that led to the gymnasium. All of their heads were cleanly shaven. They had tattoos that covered their arms and ran up to their necks. Most of the tattoos were void of color except for their gang colors, which were blue-black indigo ink outlined in red. They were all tall men, well built, with overly muscular frames. The more they tried to look inconspicuous and blend in, the more they stood out. He could sense that they were evaluating him, planning strategy. Two of the men looked in his direction and then walked down the alleyway.

"You, two-five-one-six," one of the guards said. "Get up and get your ass movin'. You're wanted in the gym."

"I'll be right back," Billy Ray said to Roscoe. "And no cheating."

Billy Ray's senses heightened as he walked down the alleyway. He looked up at the security cameras and noticed that there was a blind spot, and by walking against the brick wall, his movements could not be recorded. As he was almost at the end of the alleyway, Roscoe glanced up and noticed that the other four skinheads had followed him.

"Seemed like a nice young man," Roscoe said to himself. "Looks like we're not going to finish our game."

About a minute later, Billy Ray walked out of the alleyway and sat back down, which startled Roscoe. As Roscoe was studying the board, a shrieking siren rang out.

"What does that siren mean?" Billy Ray asked.

"The only one who really knows is you. It means everyone in the yard has thirty seconds to get down on the ground, face first, and place their hands behind their heads or get shot by the guards on the tower."

As they hit the ground, Roscoe smiled. "That's twice I underestimated you. I'm getting the feeling that there's a lot more to you than meets the eye, Billy Ray Blu. Yes, siree!"

As Billy Ray was returning to his cell, he saw Lieutenant O'Rourke talking with two other guards. He knew O'Rourke wasn't smart enough and didn't have the connections to have arranged the hit, and wondered how far up the conspiracy went. As he passed by, O'Rourke spotted him and stared with his mouth open, aghast, almost paralyzed.

An hour after Billy Ray had returned to his block, three guards opened the door to his cell and escorted him to T-1, the administrative section of the prison. As he waited outside the assistant warden's office, Dr. Vibes walked by.

"Are you all right?" she asked, touching his arm.

"Never better."

"There's a lockdown in the prison. Someone said you were attacked in the yard?"

Billy Ray was about to give her an evasive answer when the door to the assistant warden's office opened.

"Bring him in and wait outside," he said.

When Billy Ray entered his office, the assistant warden was standing up with his back toward him, staring out the window that overlooked the yard.

"Sit," he said with an angry voice. "Mr. Blu, I'm the assistant warden, Captain Carl Curtis," he said, turning around, "and right about now I'm fucking pissed. Do you know who runs this prison? Well, do you?" he asked, raising his voice.

"No, sir."

"I do. Warden Van Leeston was appointed to his position. These days, he's a politician, not an administrator. I've been here since day one, worked my way up. I earned my position. The warden was conveniently away at a celebrity fund-raising golf tournament for vice-presidential candidate Senator Bryant. I don't like anyone fucking around in my prison, especially on my watch!" he shouted at Billy Ray. "What the fuck happened in the yard?"

"I was playing chess when the alarm went off."

Captain Carl sat down at his desk and flipped through Billy Ray's file. "Nothing here adds up. Except for the obvious. College grad with an IQ off the charts. You won some kind of award for making wine. Recipient of the Silver Star. Vibes gave you a decent evaluation. But still, I think you're seven miles of bad road. Why are we sending periodic updates on your status to a CIA agent, a Mr. Standz, in Alexandria, Virginia? Why would someone in the Pentagon be so concerned about your welfare? Do you know who I'm talking about? His name is Colonel Alexander Clay."

"Yes, sir. He commanded my unit in Afghanistan."

"Nothing adds up except, and I'll say it again, the obvious. I have six skin-heads in the infirmary, some of them in serious condition with broken arms and legs, fractured skulls, cracked ribs, and busted faces and teeth, and you know nothing about it. Stand up, turn around slowly, and show me the backs and fronts of your hands and arms."

Billy Ray stood up and did exactly what the assistant warden instructed.

"Not one defensive wound and not one trace of blood. We confiscated and cata-loged all the weapons those skinheads had. Then I get to thinking, what kind of man has such deadly skills? Where does a man lean how to exact this type of controlled violence with such pinpoint precision and restraint to have disabled those men but still not have killed them? Not in any combat training in the military I served in. The snitches in the yard said those skinheads were here to whack you."

"Maybe they're mistaken."

"Oh, I don't think so! Those skinheads arrived here a week ago. Common sense tells me that they were transferred here for one purpose. As soon as they are well enough to travel, they're out of here. And you know nothing about it?"

"No, sir."

"That leads me to my next questions. What is it that you know, or what have you done, that both the CIA and the Pentagon are interested in you? Why were these men sent in here to whack you? If I asked you a personal question, would you answer it honestly?"

"I worked on our farm all my life, sir. I respect a man with a good work ethic who earned his position, as yourself. If you are the one who really operates this prison, it must be a great burden that carries great responsibility. If I can answer your question honestly, I will."

Captain Carl looked up at Billy Ray. He immediately took a liking to him. Maybe it was because he believed that a person like Billy Ray didn't belong in Tywater, or maybe it was because what had been obvious to him was now sublime. He knew that someone with powerful connections had tried to make Billy Ray a victim of circumstances above and beyond his control. "Are you now or were you ever a spook?"

Billy Ray smiled. "No, sir. I was in the Special Forces, marines, but I was never assigned to the CIA to carry out Black Ops."

The assistant warden's secretary came into the room quickly. "You have an urgent call, sir. It's the warden."

Captain Carl picked up the phone. "I have to take this call. It's probably about you. Bad news travels fast with all these rat bastards in here!"

An inmate with the custodial staff entered the next office. As he began cleaning, he turned on his portable CD player and turned down the volume. As Captain Carl continued talking on the phone; Billy Ray listened to the barely audible music. The song playing was "Another One Bites the Dust" by the group Queen. As he listened, he recounted the confrontation he'd had earlier, replaying the event to the lyrics, beat, and tempo of the music.

As he went down the alleyway, he walked cautiously against the brick wall, out of view of the security cameras. He knew the skinheads would be waiting around the corner to ambush him. As with any chess match, Billy Ray anticipated their moves and planned his in advance. Just before he turned the corner, he took a deep breath and remembered a section from *The Art of Violence*: "All battles are won or lost before they begin."

As he turned the corner, the skinheads were carrying makeshift prison weapons: shanks made from sharpened kitchen utensils, toothbrushes that had been whittled down to resemble ice picks, and wooden clubs that had been made in the woodworking shop. He smiled at the men, which elicited an odd expression on a few of their faces. The other skinheads came up from behind and trapped him.

"It's your move, boys."

Two of the men tried to rush him. The first man came at him with a shank, raising it above his head in an attempt to stab Billy Ray in his chest. He ducked and bent the man's wrist backward, breaking it as his shank fell to the ground.

Another one bites the dust...

At the same instant, he swept the second man's legs out from underneath him and placed a hard downward thrust to the side of his kneecap. A loud cracking sound rang out as his knee and part of his shin were snapped in half.

Another one bites the dust...

The third and fourth men swung at Billy Ray with makeshift ice picks and clubs. He spun and hit one of the men with a roundhouse forearm smash under his clavicle, breaking his jaw and collarbone.

Another one bites the dust...

He hit the fourth man with an open palm to the bridge of his nose, splintering the cartilage into pieces as torrents of blood came spurting out.

And another one's gone...

Billy Ray lunged forward, jumping high off the ground, and kicked the fifth man in his solar plexus, knocking the wind out of him. As he stumbled backward, he grabbed the man by his arm and snapped it back with such force that bone connecting his elbow to his forearm was broken and protruding through his skin.

And another one's gone...

The last man backed up and attempted to run away as he saw the other men either lying unconscious or writhing in pain, covered in blood, on the ground. Billy Ray grabbed the man by the back if his neck and spun him face first into the brick wall. Teeth, blood, and torn flesh flew in all directions as the last man fell to the ground and passed out.

Another one bites the dust...

⋯⊨◉ ◉⊨⋯

Billy Ray was brought back to the reality of the moment as the assistant warden hung up the phone and began speaking to him.

"That was Van Leeston. He was calling from the clubhouse at the golf tournament. His spies gave him all the details. Ass-kissers waiting in the wings to take my job. But that's my problem. Now, let's get back to your problem. There's nothing you can tell me to shed some light on what's really going on here?"

"You must have surmised by now that those men had inside help. I'm just curious as to who signed the transfer orders for those men?"

"What are you alluding to?"

"Maybe that's my way of telling you something without telling you something," Billy Ray said, remembering what Roscoe had said to him earlier.

Captain Carl knew that Van Leeston had signed the transfer orders, but he avoided answering his question by redirecting the focus of the question.

"Let me answer that question by asking, were you ever in a catch-22 situation that could make or break your career? In this case it would be the latter. The more I try to figure out what really happened, I'll probably find that I won't really want to know what happened. You see those brass monkeys on my desk?"

Billy Ray looked at three highly polished small brass monkeys his desk. The first monkey had its hands over its eyes, the second had its hands over it ears, and the third had its hands over its mouth.

"That's the mind-set here at Tywater. See no evil. Hear no evil. Speak no evil. Get the picture?"

"Clearly."

"I'm the daily operations officer, but this is Van Leeston's prison. He said there's going to be an official inquiry when he returns. You have to remember you have little to no rights in here. The inquiry won't be conducted as if you were in a court of law. If I can help you, I'll try. If the board votes that you are culpable for those men's injuries, it would be solely up to Van Leeston's discretion to add more time to your sentence. In the meantime, what am I going to do with you?" For your own safety, I'd be inclined to remand you back to solitary. Do you want to go back to solitary?"

"No, sir. I can take care of myself."

Captain Carl smiled. "That's obvious," he said, looking directly at Billy Ray, raising his eyebrows. "Maybe that's *my* way or telling *you* something without telling you something," he said, tongue in cheek. "You're dismissed, and please, Mr. Blu, behave out there."

As he got up to leave, he brushed his hand over the three brass monkeys. "You know what they say about evil, Captain Carl?"

"No, not really."

Billy Ray opened the door to leave, and without turning around, he said, "All it takes for evil to thrive is for good men to remain silent and do nothing to stop it."

Paradise Lost

"In dim eclipse, disastrous twilight sheds
On half the nations, and with fear of change,
Perplexes monarchs."

—John Milton, "Paradise Lost"

It was a dark and bleak time in America. In order to keep the people "safe from themselves," as the board described the crisis, certain safeguards were implemented. The ISS forces were increased to over ten thousand soldiers to quell any disturbances that may arise if the conditions deteriorated. All of the little fires were converging into one wildfire of discontent, just as the Prince of Darkness had predicted. The doomsday scenarios that the board had foreseen and tried to prevent were now forming a "perfect storm" of events, stacking up like dominos. All it would take was one or two catastrophic events and the fragile fabric of society would unravel. The board realized that if the government did not learn from the mistakes of the great civilizations of the past, this young nation, less than 250 years old, could end up in the trash bin of history. They began questioning whether the remedies they had prescribed to cure a critically ill nation had contributed to its condition and actually accelerated its decline.

The seeds of anarchy were just beginning to sprout and break through the surface of society. As the president implemented measures through executive order, they had the opposite effect of what they had planned. The citizens could feel the stranglehold of government intrusion and the erosion of their personal freedoms and inalienable rights. These thoughts supplied a fertile medium that nourished the roots of rebellion to take hold and grow strong. Violent outbursts were an everyday occurrence at food markets as scarcity, hording, gouging, and the price of everyday staples went much higher than people were willing to pay or could afford. All entitlements, along with municipal, state, and social-security pensions came late, greatly reduced, or not at all. The US dollar was on the verge of collapse. The more pressure the board applied to tighten their grip, the more it seemed to slip from their grasp.

The political team of Senator Randolph "Randy" Morton from Texas and Senator William Bryant were far ahead in the polls. They ran on a platform using all the politically charged buzz words, like *reform, change, our pledge,* and *our promise,* all the while chanting the words that had become the mantra of their campaign—"Jobs, jobs, jobs" and "We will protect our country and our friends abroad from the radical Islamists." They told the people everything they wanted to hear to alleviate the fears of their base and give them hope, empty promises to get elected that they knew they couldn't possibly deliver.

If America's reign was nearing its end, if this was the twilight of its last gleaming moment in history, its fall from grace would be so pronounced that the angels would look down from the heavens, bow their heads, and weep at another paradise lost.

It was late winter, almost spring. The temperature was warmer than usual for this time of the year in Silver Verde. At the new Four Strong Winds avocado farm and Blu Vineyards, the buds on the avocado trees and grape vines had already opened.

Jenny was at the front desk of the library until the children got out of school for story hour. Her arms, long legs, and face were lightly tanned, which gave her a soft glow and contrasted against her pale yellow and pink floral sleeveless dress. Her long brown hair was neatly tied back and held in place with a bow matching her dress.

Jenny didn't see the stranger when he came in. She was busy checking out some books for an elderly couple. He seemed to have appeared from out of thin air. She didn't recognize him, although he looked strangely familiar. She glanced up at him. He looked dignified wearing black slacks, highly polished black leather Cordovan shoes, an open-collar, short-sleeved tan shirt, and a pair of almost transparent, lightly tinted sunglasses.

Maybe it was because she was daydreaming about Billy Ray at the time that she thought the stranger resembled him. When she finished checking out the books, she looked up to get a better look at him, but he had vanished as quickly as he had appeared.

From the second-floor balcony, in between tiers of books, the stranger observed her from a vantage point unseen. He had read the transcripts of their conversations and envied Billy Ray.

A woman of such beauty had professed her love for him and desired to be with him when he got out of prison. And just as Billy Ray had feared, he would use her love for him as a bargaining chip if it became necessary.

Jenny thoughts were preoccupied in the quiet of the library. She remembered when she was twenty years old, sitting on a blanket with Billy Ray on the grassy banks of Silver Verde Lake, as the late-afternoon sun reflected off the shimmering bluish-green water. They had just finished eating an early dinner that she had packed in a small wooden slat-weaved picnic basket. He had opened a bottle of wine from his vineyard. They sipped the wine and teased each other while he ran his fingers through her long brown hair. She had a small portable CD player, and her favorite song, "Four Strong Winds," by Neil Young, was playing. It was a perfect day.

It was a moment frozen in time, a place she visited often for refuge, a temporary respite. That was the day when Billy Ray said that he would love her forever and sealed his promise with a soft, lasting kiss. Her memory faded as she looked down at her ring finger, where a wedding band once sealed her promise to his brother. She was so absorbed in her recollection that she didn't notice the stranger was standing in front of her.

"If you gaze long into the abyss, the abyss will gaze back at you," the stranger said, which brought her back to the reality of the moment.

"Pardon me?" she said, startled, shuffling some papers on the desk.

"I'm sorry. It looks like you were lost in thought," he said, smiling. "I said if you gaze long into the abyss, the abyss will gaze back at you."

"Yes, I see," she said, returning the smile. "Milton's *Paradise Lost.*"

"A rare find. Not only are you a beautiful woman, but you're also a scholar."

Jenny blushed, embarrassed, not knowing how to respond, and changed the subject. "I haven't seen you around here before," she said, looking into his eyes. He does resemble Billy Ray, she thought. "So many new faces with the building of the dam, new roads, and bridges. Your accent is from back east."

"How perceptive. Originally, I was from Baltimore. Now I'm living just outside of Washington, DC. I'm just passing through on my way to visit an old acquaintance."

"May I help you find something? As you can see, we're in the process of rearranging many books after we were given the list."

"The list?"

"Yes. A list of books that are to be removed from circulation and sent to a depository in Maryland," she said, smiling as she got a better look at the man and wondered if Billy Ray would look like him when he was about his age.

"As a person who's obviously very literate, I'm interested in your opinion as to why you believe these books are being removed," he asked, knowing the answer but interested in gauging her response.

"Probably the censorship of ideas."

"Not only are you beautiful and a scholar but you also possess a keen insight. You're going to make some man very happy one day. But I'm sure the removal of those books is only a temporary measure that won't last."

Jenny blushed once again. She thought his comments were a little forward, but she took them as compliments anyway. "I hope so. Many of the banned books are classics."

"Perhaps you can direct me to the section that contains works by Milton. I want to brush up on my *Paradise Lost.*"

"I'll take you to the section."

As the stranger followed her, he drank in the hypnotic fragrance of her jasmine perfume that permeated the air in her wake. As she walked with her floral dress moving from side to side, he observed the sinewy muscles in her long legs and shapely body. Jenny took one of Milton's books from the shelf and handed it to the stranger.

"Thank you," he said, smiling. "You've been most helpful."

The stranger sat down in a booth and opened the book. He watched her graceful stride as she made her way back to the front desk. A short while later, Jenny looked in the direction where the stranger had been, but he was gone.

→≔● ●≕←

It was another routine, mundane day at Tywater, or at least that's what the administration thought. Dr. Vibes was on her laptop when she heard the commotion. Secretaries and administrators were scurrying in the corridor outside her office, talking in loud, nervous voices. She opened the door and saw the warden's secretary walking briskly, almost running, down the corridor, carrying several files in her folded arms.

"What's going on, Cindy?" Dr. Vibes asked.

"We're getting a visitor in about a half hour. He's CIA and requested a meeting with Van Leeston and then with prisoner William Blu."

"The CIA? The Central Intelligence Agency wants to see the warden and then William Blu!"

"That's what I was told. The warden wants to review Blu's files before the meeting."

As Dr. Vibes closed the door to her office, she remembered bits and pieces from his evaluations and wondered if the story that she thought Billy Ray had fabricated could possibly all be true.

→≔● ●≕←

When Billy Ray was escorted past the visiting area to the interview room, the Prince of Darkness was standing near the doorway. Billy Ray was not surprised to see him. Word had traveled at lightning speed throughout the prison population that someone from the CIA was there to see him.

"Guard, before we enter, I want you to turn off all the surveillance equipment in the room," the Prince of Darkness said matter-of-factly.

The guard looked at Billy Ray and then back toward the Prince of Darkness. "I can't do that without the warden's approval."

"Is this a federal prison?"

"Yes."

"Yes what?"

"I don't understand," the guard said, bewildered.

"Well, let me enlighten you. The correct response would be 'yes, *sir*,'" the Prince of Darkness said in a calm but stern voice.

"Yes, sir," the guard said, straightening up at rigid attention.

"If I have to run it by the warden out of professional courtesy, I will, but I assure you, no one here has any authority over me. So don't embarrass yourself, and do exactly as you were told. And if it's possible, have someone from the cafeteria bring up a pot of hot coffee with some sugar and cream on the side."

"Yes, sir."

The Prince of Darkness had made his first move in the psychological chess match before the game even began. By grandstanding, he wanted to demonstrate to Billy Ray who was in charge and that the surveillance equipment had been turned off so they could talk in confidence with complete candor. Billy Ray knew that he would have to use all his cunning and guile, along with all the best strategies he had mastered to even hope for a draw. Knowing that the Prince of Darkness had already made an opening move, Billy Ray was devising his counter.

The Prince of Darkness took a seat. "Sit, William," he said, gesturing for him to sit across the table from him.

"Mr. Richard Standz," Billy Ray said, as if he were addressing an old friend, and extended his hand. "I knew it would only be a matter of time…and circumstance…before you came up to see me. How are you?"

The Prince of Darkness was taken aback by his unexpected friendly demeanor and by the fact that he had not heard anyone call him by his birth name for quite some time. Except for members of the board, very few people knew his real name. Billy Ray thought it was a nice opening move.

"Fine, William," he said, regaining his footing as he shook his hand. "And you?"

"I've been better."

"Sit. Relax. We have many issues to discuss today. We've actually never met…face to face."

"No, but you've been lurking in the background, conspicuously present at certain times in my life."

"Actually, four times, counting today."

"Four. I thought it was three. Once at my hearing in Afghanistan. Once in Silver Verde, and today."

"There was a fourth time, but there's no way you could have known. You were unconscious on the operating table after that mission went sideways. That was a bad time for everyone."

"A worse time for some than others," Billy Ray said.

"I guess it was," he said, nodding in agreement. "I was there outside the operating room. I saw your vital-signs monitor flatline. I saw you die. Then they hit you a couple of times with the paddles, and your strength of will brought you back. I'll never forget that."

"Well, that's what they say happened."

"I'm going to speak frankly. What we discuss here is confidential. There are a few things that I feel imperative to clarify. I am sorry for what happened to your brother some years ago. I know you were close. It was an unfortunate, unnecessary action taken by young, inexperienced ISS soldiers. Secondly, I know you are smart enough to have figured out that the agency had no involvement in the attempt on your life. That was amateur time. If the board had wanted you dead, you'd be history. It would have been made to look like an accident or a suicide."

"I guess I can sleep a little better knowing that," Billy Ray said, insincerely. "And I suppose you had nothing to do with what went down in Silver Verde?"

"I was there, and I know that you know I was there. I wouldn't have missed it for the world. The way you took out those men—magnificent piece of work—but then again, I expect nothing less from a man of your talents. Silver Verde was an assignment to watch over the board's investment in the next vice president, Senator Bryant. And yes, there were covert agents there."

"And that's your entire involvement?"

"Not entirely. When it got out of control, we had to step in."

"And I suppose you were in Afghanistan at my hearing for...?"

"Actually, I was there to clean up Bishop's mess. In you, I saw an opportunity I couldn't pass up. Everyone at the agency was disappointed when you refused our offer."

Billy Ray could not determine if everything the Prince of Darkness was telling him was the truth. Sometimes, men like him would intersperse truth, half-truths, and misinformation so seamlessly that the truth and lies would become indistinguishable. Everything the Prince of Darkness told him was plausible, but Billy Ray remained skeptical.

The guard knocked on the door, and an inmate wheeled in a cart carrying a stainless-steel carafe of hot coffee and smaller dishes containing sugar and cream. Both Billy Ray and the Prince of Darkness made a cup. He took a sip and waited for the door to close before he spoke.

"I've come here to give you the keys to the front gate, William. If you accept the terms of my offer, you'll be out of here in one week, sentence reduced to time served."

"You have nothing to hold over me. Nothing to offer me that I need...or want."

The Prince of Darkness took another sip of coffee. "You're playing in a game that you can't possibly win, but you don't know that yet, not without my help. All the charges against you in Silver Verde will disappear, along with your prison record."

"And you have this power?"

"I assure you, I do."

"Even if you do, the question is, why?"

"The board and I have discussed our plans for you. I'm retiring from the field in several years. I can easily see you as my protégé. You'd be a perfect candidate to succeed me. One day, you'll be in charge of the whole network."

"And until that day comes, I'd be...a government asset, an assassin?"

"That may be part of your duties, along with protecting our country from threats from without and within. I can see by the look on your face that you're not buying this. Keep an open mind until you hear the entire proposal. William, do you like music?"

In midspiel, the Prince of Darkness had changed the direction and focus of his questions. Billy Ray didn't know if this disjointed strategy was an attempt at misdirection, a red herring. Maybe the nonlinear line of questioning was meant to throw him off his game and make him lose his concentration, he thought.

"Music?"

"I enjoy music. Music has the power to inspire, incite, give one hope, or take it away. It can become intertwined in one's memories and preserve and unlock good and bad memories. Many times the lyrics and melody can form an inseparable bond with events in one's life—nothing deeply philosophical like Nietzsche or Plato—and become inseparable from our memories. The song conjures up the memory and vice versa. I'm partial to the group the Eagles. I saw them in concert several times when I was younger. Do you know their music?"

"They're a little before my time, but I like their music."

"Good, because there are some lyrics from one of their songs that may apply to both our lives."

"What are they?" Billy Ray asked, not really caring but trying to figure out where the Prince of Darkness was going with this.

The Prince of Darkness took another sip of coffee. "'Hotel California.' Everyone build walls around themselves. I have mine. You have yours. We are all prisoners of the private hells we make for ourselves. The line from the song is, 'We are all just prisoners here of our own device.' For you it may be a literal and figurative prison. For me, it's the one I imposed upon myself. We have a lot more in common than you think. In many ways, you're just like me."

"I'm nothing like you!"

"Don't be so sure!"

The Prince of Darkness opened his black leather valise and took out a few documents. He placed one document on the table in plain view of Billy Ray, knowing that he could see the cover page. He took another sip of coffee and flipped through the pages of the other document.

"I was refreshing my memory of the official transcript of what happened in the yard. You stated that when the sirens went off, you were playing chess with another inmate."

"If that what it says."

"You may not know that I fancy myself as quite a chess player. I play online with masters from all over the world. I used to enjoy matches with a player whose online name was Big Blue, without the *e*. Oddly enough, he stopped playing just about the same time that you were incarcerated. The best I could ever do against him was a draw. Today, I think my luck is going to change."

Billy Ray had always suspected that his online opponent Black Knight was the Prince of Darkness. Maybe, he thought, the Prince of Darkness was trying to tell him something without telling him something. Once again, the Prince of Darkness used his strategy of changing the direction of his questions.

"I guess a belated congratulations is in order."

"For what?" he asked, puzzled.

"Your wine that is distributed by the Consortium has been selected several times in the past few years as one of the finest in the world."

"You are a wine connoisseur?"

"Heavens, no. I couldn't tell the difference between a five-dollar bottle of wine and a bottle of Dom Perignon or your wine. I just returned from some unfinished company business in Afghanistan. On my way back, I went to Riyadh for a dinner with some of the sheik's relatives. Would you believe they served me your wine? Blu Select is a big hit in Saudi Arabia, even at over five hundred dollars a bottle. It's quite an accomplishment; then again, nothing you do surprises me. All that said, I think you're missing the big picture. There are higher callings."

"Not for me. When my six months are done, I just want to return home and tend to my vineyards."

"Really. That's the only ambition a man of your superior intellect and talents wants out of life?"

"Not everyone wants to rule the world. I'd be content just being the master of my own simple little safe world."

"What I'm offering you is a way out, a life preserver for a drowning man in an ocean of politics who cannot possibly fathom that he's in way over his head. I can give you your life back. Your freedom. Your vineyard. The woman," he said, looking directly at Billy Ray. He was making one of his final moves before the end game and wanted to gage Billy Ray's emotional response.

"The woman?"

"Jenifer. I went to the library in Silver Verde today to see her. What was it that she said to you on your last visit? Oh yes, 'There's no future for me without you in it.'"

"I knew our conversations were recorded."

"Would you expect anything less...from me? All the transcripts are right in front of you. I know if I were so fortunate to have a woman of her beauty and intelligence, and so full of life, love me, I'd be grabbing for that life preserver. After all she's been through, don't you think she deserves a little happiness? What was it that she said—'Don't you care even a little for me?' Well, do you? I think you have all along. Am I wrong? Are you heartless? You know, everyone thinks I'm heartless, but I'm not."

"Then I suppose your alias, the 'Prince of Darkness,' is a misnomer?"

The Prince of Darkness became introspective as he stared into the abyss, a place in which he often took comfort and refuge. As he spoke, in a voice slightly above a whisper, he was in a trance, with a sad expression on his face that appeared genuine, as he recalled his past. "We were young. In love. She was beautiful, not as beautiful as Jenifer, but she was mine. My princess, as I used to call her. Finished my tour of duty with the Navy SEALS. Married. Got a nice high-level civil service job with a defense contractor. We were planning a family. And then, like that," he said, snapping his fingers together, "she was gone. She wasn't feeling well. Nothing out of the ordinary for a woman who's four months pregnant. She went downhill fast. Miscarriage. Three months later... it was over. Ovarian cancer. If my wife had lived and carried our baby to term, he would have been just about your age. I never told anyone that story. I never had a reason or saw a need to open up and confide in anyone. I can give you the chance of happiness that he took away from me," he said, looking up toward the heavens. "And if you refuse, the greatest prison you would have made for yourself is going through this life all alone, like me."

"Pleased to meet you
Hope you guessed my name,
But what's puzzling you,
Is the nature of my game?"

—Mick Jagger/Keith Richards, "Sympathy for the Devil"

Billy Ray reflected about what the Prince of Darkness had said. The entire strategy became clear to him. What a crafty, well-played move. It was the kind of game he would play. He comes to you when you're weak, vulnerable. He confides in you. Attributes human frailties and emotions to himself in which you could sympathize and identify, as maybe a kindred spirit. Tempts you with dreams of happiness and gives you a glimpse of paradise, just a fleeting glimpse. Then, when he believes he has you, he offers you a bite of the apple. That's when you realize the dilemma of your choice. To receive the paradise he offers you, the asking price is your soul, and you're damned forever. That's the game he plays. In order to win, you have to lose.

"You seem lost in thought. Are you considering my offer? It's your choice. Only you can make a hell of your heaven, or a heaven of your hell."

Billy Ray smiled a becoming smile, knowing how appropriate it was that the phase the Prince of Darkness had chosen was from Milton's "Paradise Lost."

"Damned if I do, and damned if I don't. Is that my choice? To reign in hell or serve in heaven? It's a tempting offer, but I only have six months left to serve, and then I'm going home."

Billy Ray could sense something was wrong. For the first time since he had learned the rudiments of the game, he couldn't see the next move. He knew the game was near its end, but it wasn't over. He could see that the Prince of Darkness was overly anxious, overly confident, which was usually a tell that an opponent had yet to play his coup de grace. Billy Ray thought that he would bait him to expose his play.

"Since we're almost at the end game, how do you think the match is going?"

"Up until now, it's been a draw, but I have at least one more move left that you could never foresee. One that has no countermove. One that you could never recover from.

Billy Ray smiled. "Well, let's see it."

The Prince of Darkness appeared to be gloating, savoring the moment. His cell phone rang. Standz used the first cords of the Eagles song "Hotel California" as his ringtone. He looked at the caller's number and let it go to voice mail.

"The board at Tywater convened yesterday. They voted three to two against you. The only two who voted in your favor were the assistant warden and the prison psychiatrist. The warden said minimum-sentencing guidelines for violent assaults state six months for each count. Looks like you'll have thirty-six months added to your sentence to consider my offer. Checkmate!"

Billy Ray looked off in the distance and thought for a moment. There was no countermove. Although he knew he had lost, he thought he'd give the Prince of Darkness something to think about.

"I've always known what you're capable of…just about anything. But I don't think you really know what I'm capable of…not really. There will be no need for you to be visiting anyone in Silver Verde again," he said, looking directly at him as he got up to leave. "Jenny is not a bargaining chip, a pawn. She is *not* to be used to get to me! You said you held the keys to the front gate, well maybe so do I. What makes you think if I ever wanted to get out of here that these walls could hold me?"

"Before you go, I never told you the other line from 'Hotel California' that applied to you. In light of what you just said, it may be more appropriate than ever."

Billy Ray stopped without turning around. The Prince of Darkness was still playing the game, he thought. Maybe there was still time to make a final move.

"The line is 'You can check out anytime you like, but you can never leave.'"

He opened the door to leave. The guard was waiting outside. He turned briefly and looked into the Prince of Darkness's eyes. "Did you learn anything meaningful from our little game?"

"Nothing I didn't know before I came."

"Are you sure, because I learned something. I now know that you may have been right all along."

"How so?"

"Deep inside, I may be one step away of becoming a man just like you."

"I'm curious. In what respect?" the Prince of Darkness said, leaning forward with growing interest.

"If you really wanted to gain some insight into my character, to see my dark side, who I am, and what I'm capable of becoming, all you had to do is…look into a mirror!"

As Billy Ray closed the door behind him, he left the Prince of Darkness thinking, pondering, and analyzing his last move.

The Id, Ego, and Superego

THE LOCKDOWN AT Tywater had been suspended. When the inmates in the yard would see him coming, they would whisper to each other, clear a path, and give him a wide berth. As he made his way toward Roscoe, he passed by the members of the Latino gang who were lifting weights. Ramon "La Muerte" Santiago was the leader of the Latino gang. His word was law in Tywater. He looked up at Billy Ray and gave him a slight nod. Billy Ray gave him a similar nod in acknowledgment and respect to the prison code. When he approached the men playing chess, he turned around puzzled and wondered why the inmate who had been playing stood up quickly and let him take his place without finishing his game.

"Sit down, boy. Nice to see you're still alive and kickin'."

"What was that all about?"

"It's the code. Respect. You made your bones in the yard, in a big way. No one's gonna fuck with you now. They're all scared shitless of you. No one liked those skinheads. They hate everyone, 'cept for their own kind. Smiles and whispers was the word 'round here when you smacked down those motherfuckers."

As Roscoe and Billy Ray began playing chess, the men watching them did so at a distance.

"May I ask you a question, Roscoe?" he asked as he moved a chess piece.

"Sure, but if I don't get the right answer, you ain't going to get pissed off. Wouldn't want to make you angry," he said jokingly.

Billy Ray smiled. "It's not that type of question. I just wanted to know what you did to end up here."

"You haven't learned anything in the joint, boy. We're all innocent here, aren't we, boys?"

The men surrounding the game laughed.

"Sure 'nough," one of the inmates said. "Mistaken identity."

"I was framed," added another.

"How about you?" Roscoe asked.

"I did almost exactly what they said I did," Billy Ray said with his head down, studying the table. "I just couldn't prove that my actions were justified."

"Well," Roscoe said, moving a piece, "I am innocent!"

"Then, what happened?"

"In almost seven years, I still can't figure it out. The Clements family had been farming in the valley for four generations. I bet you didn't know I knew your father, and my father knew your grandfather. We had a modest forty-five acre farm next to the interstate ramp."

"The land that had a large billboard on it saying something to the effect that it was the future development site of the Village at Silver Verde?"

"Future, my ass. You've been out of touch, boy. Where my farm once was is now fancy townhouse condominiums, apartments, and a shopping plaza. The whole shebang is almost fully occupied with all those people working on the dam, new roads, and bridges. When you get out, you take a ride by and take a looksee for yourself."

Billy Ray looked up at Roscoe. "You'll be getting out of here many years before me. Van Leeston added three years to my sentence because of what happened with those skinheads."

"And I thought I got fucked. They gave you three big ones with no proof."

"They said I don't have any rights here."

"Ain't that the truth," he said, nodding his head in agreement.

"You still didn't tell me what happened."

"About seven years ago, this three-piece-suit lawyer comes to see me. He said he represented a group of investors who are interested in buying my land. His name was Coyle."

"William Coyle?"

"Sure is. The snake that bit his ass died. He made me a lowball offer. Thinks that because I'm a black man and a dumb farmer that I'd jump at a million dollars. Oh, my Lordy Lord, not one million whole dollars, Mr. Lawyer Man. I refused his offer, and that's when the trouble started. I had no mortgage. Had borrowed fifty grand for farm equipment—that's all. Mysteriously, the loan was called in. I go to pay off the loan, from an account at the bank I've been doing business with for forty years, and they tell me all my accounts are frozen. Some smartass broad at the head office tells me that she don't even have to tell my why because of the Patriot Act. Next thing I know, a sheriff shows up and serves me with a foreclosure notice at lightning speed. So I make an appointment to see my senator, after all, he the chairman of the banking commission in DC."

"Senator William Bryant?"

"Yeah, another two-faced fucking snake. I put on my Sunday best, drive almost two hours, and wait four hours in his office before he finds the time to see me. I give him all the papers, tell him my story, and he assures me that there's been a mistake. He tells me that he'll take care of everything. I still remember the bullshit he told me. He says, 'Mr. Clements, that land has been in your family for over one hundred and fifty years. It's hardworking farmers like your family who are the breadbasket of this great nation. Put your trust in me, and I'll have this travesty cleared up on one week.' One week to the day, four sheriffs show up and throw me off my property. My boys and I get into a scuffle, and we end up in county jail. When I get out, I bust into Bryant's office and get charged with trespassing and assault on a public official. No money for a good lawyer. The public defender is green out of law school and don't know his ass from his elbow around a courtroom. I get convicted of trespassing, assault on a public official, and fraud in a so-called check-knitting scheme, trying to pay off the debt with my own frozen money. Some paid-off weasel of a bureaucrat from the county records office testifies against me."

"What was his name? " Billy Ray asked rhetorically, pausing as he tried to remember his name. "Was it Cook?"

"None other. Then the federal judge, Tores, throws the book at me. I get almost eight years."

"Judge Arthur Tores?"

Roscoe looked up with an odd expression on his face. "You seem to know all the motherfuckers who framed me."

"Among other charges, I was also charged with assault on Senator Bryant. Judge Tores administered my plea agreement, and Coyle was my lawyer."

"Jesus, what a coincidence!"

Without Roscoe realizing the ramifications of what he had told Billy Ray, he had just given him some of the missing pieces to the puzzle he had been trying to put together since he arrived at Tywater. "There are no coincidences as big as these, Roscoe."

"My boys moved away from California. They come to see me now and then. I asked for help from the very man who put me in here. Take a guess who's one of the owners of that investment company who wanted to buy my land. Senator Bryant himself. My great-great-grandpappy was allowed to homestead that land for serving in the Civil War. Now it's all gone. I was just a nigger in their way. They took everything the Clements had and everything we were ever going to have. What am I going to do when I get out? Live with one of my boys? I have nothing left, 'cept for my old guitar that I used to play for my boys on our front porch at night."

Both men played the remainder of the game in silence. Although they were both distracted and lost their concentration, the game still ended in a draw.

⇢▄▄◑ ◐▄▄⇠

On the East Coast, it was just before dawn in Washington, DC. It was cold and a light dusting of snow had fallen during the night. Sand trucks were preparing the roads for the morning commute. The Prince of Darkness drove from Alexandria, Virginia, through the rear entrance of Arlington National Cemetery. The dim sunlight was just breaking through the gray clouds over the distant horizon. It was too early for visitors at the cemetery. Two men, one operating a backhoe and the other with a spaded shovel, were digging a grave.

The crisp morning air was filled with white smoke from the backhoe and the smell of burned diesel fuel.

The Prince of Darkness had obtained the itinerary of Senator Bryant. He knew he would be in his office earlier than usual before he flew out to join former Senator Morton on the campaign trail. He wore a black pinstriped suit, a black, three-quarter-length Chesterfield coat, and a pair of black transition teardrop sunglasses.

When he entered the building in the capitol that housed the offices of many congressmen, he showed the security guard his credentials and took the elevator to Bryant's office. Then he turned off the lights, sat down in a plush leather chair, and waited. At six o'clock in the morning, Senator Bryant entered his office, turned on the lights, and was startled to see the Prince of Darkness sitting in his office with his legs crossed.

"Jesus Christ! You scared the hell out of me!" he said, holding one of his hands over his chest.

"Obviously not! Are you out of your fucking mind!" he said, standing up quickly.

"How dare you come into my office and talk to me in that tone with such vulgarity!"

"You know why God gave men like you two eyes, two ears, and only one mouth?"

"No. Humor me."

"So you could see and hear more than you speak. Now, sit down and shut the fuck up. I asked you if you were out of your fucking mind!"

"I don't know what you're talking about," Bryant said, feigning bewilderment.

"Don't ever play poker, at least not for money. You can't keep a straight face. Sometimes, Senator, a lie is more revealing than the truth. Don't play cute with me. It was you. What kind of agent would I be if I couldn't find out who tried to have Blu killed. You left a trail a child could follow. I don't give a rats ass what you, Coyle, Tores, the governor, and now Van Leeston are up to, but it's going to stop or else!"

"Or else what? Is that a threat?"

"You bet your vice-presidential nomination it is! You still have aspirations of higher office, don't you?"

"Have you seen the polls? Nothing short of divine intervention could stop me from becoming the next vice president."

"What, do you have a mind like a sieve? You retained nothing from my last visit. The voting public is very fickle. One scandal and you'll go from the front runner to the butt of jokes on the late shows."

"Let me worry about that. Everything is under control."

The Prince of Darkness washed his hands over his face and rubbed his eyes.

"How did a man like you, so arrogant, so stupid, and so inept, ever amass your fortune or even get elected? Oh, yes, I forgot. You made your money the old-fashioned way; you inherited it."

"My constituents love and respect me. I've been elected to congress six times, and the seventh election will be the charm. Soon, I'll be the second-most-powerful man in the free world, and one day the most powerful."

"Not if you keep making such monumental fuckups like you did with Blu."

"He's a nobody...a dumb hick from a nowhere town."

The Prince of Darkness washed his hands over his face once again. Then he opened his black leather valise, took out a document labeled "National Security," and threw it at Senator Bryant, hitting him in the face. Bryant opened the file and began reading the notations.

"You have no idea who you been fucking with! Read this file in its entire graphic splendor. Blu is a patriot, in every sense of the word. He's a warrior in a class all by himself. Superior intellect with a unique set of skills. I've trained many assets under my control—real assassins, not like the dipshits you sent in to whack Blu. Blu makes most of them look like Boy Scouts. I have an idea why you're trying to silence him. For your sake, you better hope he never finds out."

As Bryant viewed some of the pictures in the dossier, he grimaced as if he had hit a nerve. There were many gruesome pictures of Al-Qaeda soldiers, some of them with their heads or other body parts lopped off. The ground under the corpses was covered with pools of dried blood. As he continued to look at the pictures, he wondered if it was too late to call off his backup plan.

"He's just one man," Bryant said, trying to ease his own conscience. "You speak of him with reverence, almost as if you admire this criminal."

"You made him a criminal, and I now regret having taken any part in it. And I do admire him. He's a man of conscience, loyalty, and integrity, not like some men I know," he said, looking directly at the senator.

"After all the rumors I've heard about the governments you help topple and all the men you arranged to have assassinated, you're lecturing me about conscience?"

"That's who I am. That's what I'm authorized and paid to do. I keep the delicate balance around the world between good and evil, without moral turpitude. Deceit is part of my craft in pursuing amoral goals, but it shouldn't be the tools of a senator! I am the final court, impartially judging between the lesser of greater evils to determine which are to be eliminated, which are benign, and which are allowed to continue because it may be in this country's best interest. Normal constructs and restraints of morality are outside the realm of my purpose and function."

"Wow, how Machiavellian! Have you ever found a home?" he said, still flipping through the pages of Blu's file.

"I'll take that as a compliment. You look at those pictures carefully. That's the work of the man you called a nobody from nowhere."

"How come so much of the file has been blacked out? You gave me a censored file!"

"National security issues."

"After your last visit, I did a little research. Called in some favors. There's a rumor that in Afghanistan, Blu was either dead or dying and you saved his life. Any truth to that story?"

"I don't know where you got that bad intel. Even if it were true, what makes you think I'd discuss it with you?"

"If Blu's as dangerous as you claim he is, all the more reason to have him eliminated."

"You'd like that, wouldn't you? Me doing your dirty work. Cleaning up your mess. Eliminating the one man who could bury you literally and politically. If and when that decision is ever made, it won't be made by the likes of you or your cronies, even if and when you become the vice president."

"Are you suggesting that a Secret Service detail won't be able to protect me?"

"No. If you listened more carefully that last time I was here, you would have paid more attention to all those little fires that were glowing brightly all over this country. Haven't you read the papers or seen the turmoil and rioting in the streets? All those little fires have merged into one firestorm of sedition, mistrust, and rebellion. You ever heard of the saying to never give a firebug a can of gasoline to play with? Well Blu could easily become the Rembrandt of all arsonists, not only for you, but for this whole country."

"What the hell are you talking about?"

"Nice choice of the word *hell*, which will soon become apparent," he said, reaching into his pocket and removing a Blu Bird key chain. He dangled it in front of the senator. "Do you know what this is?"

"An empty key chain," he said, shrugging his shoulders.

"Oh, there are keys on it, but you're too blind to see them. This Blu Bird key chain may hold the keys to open the gates of hell for you, me, and maybe arrange for Blu's early release. There's a pirate website that's dedicated to Billy Ray Blu. He doesn't even know it exists. He's portrayed as sort of a folk hero, a champion of the common man, fighting the good fight against insurmountable odds, against evil government men and conspiracies. Against men like you. The site gets millions of hits every day. This Blu Bird is not only a symbol of him, but also one that the downtrodden have taken to heart and identified his plight as their own. They're rallying behind him and the movement is growing. They even have a name and an anthem for the movement: The Black Parade. With the taking of his land, the killing of his brother, and now an attempt on his life, you gave the movement more credence than ever to a conspiracy theory. The Big Brother program can usually track, locate, and identify the people responsible for this site. This hacker has such an advanced and sophisticated oscillating IP that is routed and rerouted every few seconds to locations all over the world. I've been told it is impossible to pinpoint."

"I'm not going to worry about a couple of hackers with computers in their basement spewing out propaganda."

"You should," the Prince of Darkness said, shaking his head. "The Blu Bird key chain was originally given out by the Wine Consortium from France as a way of promoting Blu Select. This corporation imports, exports, and controls most of the premium wines in the free world. The consortium also owns a substantial interest in the multitrillion-dollar Barclays Bank. Their power, wealth, and connections would make you and your cronies look like a bunch of paupers. After Van Leeston added three years to Blu's sentence, who was conveniently playing golf with you on the day of the botched hit, the consortium got a little worried that the flow of their prized commodity may be in jeopardy. If you fuck with them, they may be inclined to put together a team of foreign and domestic lawyers that would make OJ's dream team look like public defenders. You wouldn't want their investigators looking up your ass with a microscope, would you, Mr. Former Vice-President Nominee? Now, if you're done with that file, I'll have it back. Can't have that type of information falling into the wrong hands."

The Prince of Darkness stood up and placed the file back into his valise. "I know you have a full agenda today, so I'll show myself out. As he was leaving the room, he began humming the melody to the song "Hail to the Chief," mocking Senator Bryant.

"A ballbuster right to the end," Bryant said, without looking up. "Always a pleasure."

"Heed my warning, or there'll be hell to pay. Who knows, maybe the next time I see you, you'll be the second-most-powerful man in the free world. Then you can do to this country the same thing you're still doing to your secretary, Cynthia."

⇥⊙ ⊙⇤

The late-morning sun in the cloudy sky was casting long shadows in the yard at Tywater. Billy Ray and Roscoe had about an hour left to finish their chess matches before yard time was over.

"Did you ever think that the people trying to have you wacked had a backup plan, or if you might still be a target from one of Tywater's psychos?" Roscoe asked.

"Never gave it much thought."

"After you made your bones in the yard, none of the ordinary maniacs are going to fuck with you. But there's always the really sick wackos whose wiring in their heads is short-circuited. The kind of guys who'll slice and dice someone in the morning, have a nice lunch in the afternoon, and sleep like a baby at night. Men who don't give a fuck about the consequences of their actions. Men with no conscience. That's the kind of guy I'd worry about."

"Why, have you heard something?"

"The word is that they let this guy out of solitary who's been there for a long time. He's one scary motherfucker. They say he doesn't talk to anyone, and no one has the balls to talk to him. His yard privileges start today. You don't think that's only by chance, do you? I caught a glimpse of him coming out of the cafeteria yesterday. He's a fucking monster out of a fifties horror movie. Towers over everyone. Arms and legs like tree trunks. Looks like three hundred pounds of all muscle. I know you can handle yourself, but if he makes a move on you, I don't know if you can stop him without killing him. Then you're really fucked. That's how dangerous he looks, at least from a distance."

Billy Ray didn't seem overly concerned. "I'll keep an eye out for Mr. Frankenstein," he said, and they both laughed.

As their match was nearing its end game, a strange silence washed over the yard as quickly as the fast-moving clouds blocked out the sun over the landscape. The guards in the yard and in the towers became apprehensive and alert as they tried to figure out what was going down. Roscoe sensed that something was wrong. He looked up quickly and noticed that the man he had seen in the cafeteria was making his way toward them. As he walked, a path cleared, like Moses parting the waters.

"Don't panic, boy, but that scary guy I was telling you about is coming...in a hurry. I think he's going to try to make a move on you right in the yard."

All the inmates were now watching the man as he quickened his pace. Billy Ray looked at him from the corner of his eye and smiled.

"What do you want me to do?" Roscoe asked, picking up the stool he was sitting on to help Billy Ray defend himself.

"Nothing. I can handle this."

As the man was several feet away, Billy Ray stood up and faced him. The man reached around him with his massive arms, hugged him briefly, and then put both of his massive hands on top of Billy Ray's hands as a form of a handshake. It was Ocho.

"Roscoe, it's all right. He's a friend of mine."

"Thank God," Roscoe said, breathing a sigh of relief as he put down his stool. "I was about to give him a whoppin'," he said, deadpan.

"We're going for a walk in the yard. Then I'll be back to finish our game."

As Billy Ray and Ocho walked around the cinder track, the yard returned to its normal level of activity.

"I thank you, Mr. William, for what you did for family," Ocho said with a low, echoing voice.

"No, thank you, Ocho, for what you did in Silver Verde. I never meant for you to get into trouble for me."

"Soldiers had no right. I know difference between right and wrong. I see," he said, placing one of his massive fingers up to his eyes. "I do it again. Same men, they kill Mr. Junior." He tried to hold back the tears from his eyes.

"When are you getting out?" Billy Ray asked, changing the subject.

"One month," he said.

"When you get out, I want you to help Jenny with her farm and your brother-in-law at the vineyard."

"How long you stay here? I hear bad things. Some men try kill you. But they don't know about you. You showed them," he said, smiling. "Men say now you be here for long time."

"You don't have to worry about that. When you get out, you'll be in charge. I want you to do me a favor, but you can't tell anyone."

"Anything, Mr. William."

"I want you to watch over Jenny. If you ever see any strangers near her farm, be very careful. I think she may be in danger."

"No one hurt Miss Jenny. I break them in half," he said, mimicking breaking something in half with his massive hands.

A short while later, Billy Ray resumed playing chess while Ocho looked on. No one, not even the men who normally watched the game, approached within twenty feet.

"You got your own personal bodyguard," Roscoe said, looking up at Ocho. "Blu, I'm not a chess master, but I've played long enough to know when someone is toying with me, stringing me along. I want your best game. The kind of game you gave those skinheads."

Billy Ray laughed as he made another move.

Dr. Catalina Vibes knocked on the door of the assistant warden's office and entered. She wore a beige jumpsuit with a sash tied around her midsection, which accented her shapely body. She pushed up the glasses that slipped down to the bridge of her nose before she took several files out of her carrying case.

"I have the recent psychological examinations you wanted to review with me, sir."

Captain Carl barely acknowledged her presence. He was staring out his window that overlooked the yard. It was late afternoon. The yard should have been empty. Two men, one wearing a military uniform and the other in a prison uniform walked along the perimeter of the yard on the cinder track.

"Sir, I have the files you requested," she said once again.

"I wonder what they're talking about?" he asked rhetorically, without turning around.

"Who, sir?"

"William Blu and Colonel Alexander Clay from the Pentagon."

"A colonel with the Pentagon is in the yard talking with William Blu?" she said, moving closer to the window to get a better look. "First the CIA comes to see him and now a colonel with the Pentagon. What's going on, sir?"

"I'd be damned if I know. Something ominous, I would guess. I've been in the prison system long enough to know the difference between a couple of psychos who got a beef with an inmate and whacked him and what appears to have been an orchestrated assassination attempt." Captain Carl turned around and sat down at his desk. "I want to review all the new inmates' psychological examinations, Doctor. But still," he said, looking back in the direction of the window, "I'd love to know what they're talking about."

→═◑ ◑═←

Colonel Alexander Clay wore a dark-green uniform with a matching beret tipped slightly to one side. His uniform was covered with the medals he had earned for his many years of combat military service. Clay was a respected and seasoned veteran, a warrior having served in both Iraq wars and two tours in Afghanistan. He was slender and tall, and his reddish-brown hair was cropped short and interspersed with various shades of gray. He was part Cherokee, on his mother's side, with high cheekbones and steel-blue eyes, which contrasted sharply against his dark skin and muddy complexion. On the right lower side of his face was a long, barely noticeable scar from an injury he received from a roadside IED that killed his driver and injured him.

"Why are you limping, sir?" Billy Ray asked.

"The Wiz performed a minor surgery on my ass. Anyone above a certain pay grade in the Pentagon has a global GPS tracking device implanted in their ass cheek supposedly in the event that we're kidnapped or go rogue so they can locate us. I think those paranoid bastards just want to keep track of our movements. The Wiz took it out and attached a devise to it so I can turn it off when I don't want anyone to know where I am, like today."

"Richard Standz came by to see me a week ago."

"Speak of the devil," Clay said, looking at Billy Ray as the afternoon sun shined brightly on his face. "I haven't seen you in what, six years? You know something odd? Now that I got a good look at you, I never realized how much you resemble Standz."

"I am aware that we have similar characteristics, but I'm nothing like him... where it counts," he said, holding a closed fist up to his heart.

"I figured he'd be around to see you after someone tried to whack you. Did he make the same offer he did in Afghanistan?"

"I turned him down. Tempting offer, especially when he told me Warden Van Leeston added three years to my sentence."

"I know. That's why I'm here. They're going to kill you, you know! It's only a matter of time...three more years to get it done, and maybe next time you won't be so lucky."

"Standz said the agency had nothing to do with what happened, and I believe him."

"You're probably right. That's not their style. If the board gave the green light, they wouldn't have sent in amateurs. No, it's someone else, but who? You know that they must have someone on the inside?"

"Yes, I know."

"I already went to see all the men in our old unit. They're all on board with my plan to get you out of here."

"I could never ask them to do that. They have their own lives and families now. Why would you throw away your career?"

Colonel Clay stopped walking. "Why? The same reason why they would. We're not going to sit by and let them kill you. None of us would be alive if it wasn't for you. And what did it cost you? You were the sacrificial lamb who got thrown to the wolves so that the brass like that asshole Bishop wouldn't go down in flames for their fuckup. Did you hear he's a general now with the ISS?"

"I heard about it."

The colonel looked up at the guards in the towers watching them. "And this is what it comes down to. The greatest hero to come out of the Afghan War, who no one outside of us even knows about, makes his home in a federal prison, waiting for someone to kill him. What a military disgrace. This is no longer the America so many of us fought to defend and died to protect. There are a great many top military people like myself who don't like the direction this country is heading. However, there's also a growing number of those in the military who view everyone not wearing a uniform as the enemy. Unfortunately, the principles and ideology of fascism and socialism have filtered into the policies of our military and government. This ISS is pure fascism masquerading as the only hope our country has to preserve its security. In a few years, we'll be a police state. Why do you think the ISS has already over ten thousand troops? Remember Macky?"

"Sure, how is he?"

"He's still in the military, promoted to major. After you did a number on those ISS soldiers in Silver Verde, they called in Macky to train their forces. Bishop and the ISS have been busy little bees. You know what they're planning now?"

"In the brave new world they're creating?"

"After the first of the year, ordinary citizens will need travel permits to travel from state to state. Come next year they're going to start conducting McCarthy-like hearings. They're calling it the Committee to Investigate Un-American Activities. They'll parade high-profile people before the televised inquisition to provide names of subversives. The president has sent out a trial balloon to try to banish the private ownership of all guns. I tell you, when that happens this country will be heading down a very slippery slope."

"How are the rest of the men doing?"

"BB is as happy as a kid in a candy store. He's blowing up buildings for his cousin's demolition company. He's got a drinking problem though. Trying to drown out his bad memories at the bottom of a bottle, but he'll be OK. Rollins will go to hell and back for you. The Wiz is the key to the whole operation. He has to keep us under the radar of all the surveillance programs. The only problem we may have is with Midnight."

"Captain Midnight," Billy Ray said, smiling as he shook his head. "What a piece of work. How's he doing?"

"As usual. He's off his fucking rocker, very unstable. But you never know when we'll need a world-class sniper, and only you, BB, Midnight, and I can pilot a Black Hawk or Apache. I went to see him a week ago. He's self-committed in a VA looney bin, jacked up on meds, watching reruns of *Family Feud*, just repeating over and over to himself, 'Who's your daddy?' When I told him about my plan, he wanted to check out that very minute. I told him to sit tight and that I'd be in touch."

They both laughed. "Well what do you think about our offer?"

"I can't see the end game. You know all hell's going to break loose when I'm out."

"I'm hoping on it. It'll be a wake-up call. It will no longer be your hell but their hell. Once you're out and safe, I may have a way to clean up part of this mess, but we're going to have to figure out why someone is trying to kill you and if it has to do with what happened in Silver Verde."

"How are you going to clean up part of this mess?"

"I have your file."

"Which one?"

"The only one that counts. It was redacted and parts mysteriously deleted, but not before I made an uncensored copy. Many careers are going down the drain when this is made public. When the time is right, I'll give it to the Wiz to send out over the Internet on his pirate website."

"Pirate website?"

Colonel Clay reached into his pocket and pulled out the Blu Bird key chain. "Over a million people click onto the Black Parade website each week. It's dedicated to one person's fight to clear his name...you. I've thought this out carefully. I don't see any other way out for you. I'll give the Wiz the codes for a military depot to requisition everything you could possibly need. But the end game is up to you. Got any ideas?"

"Last Friday night they showed an old war movie in the prison annex called *Force Ten from Navarone* that gave me a few ideas. If I do this, they'll be no turning back. Every bridge I've ever built in my life will be burned behind me," he said, reflecting for a moment and thinking that this decision also meant that he would be cutting all ties and severing any possibility of a future with Jenny. He let out a deep breath and lowered his head. "All right, set it up. My life is in your hands."

"As ours were in yours that night, and we're all grateful. We all died a little that night, and you...well, you actually did die...for us. We're going to make the most of our lives...the lives that you gave back to us. Can you trust anyone in here?"

"Outside of a few inmates, there's only two. The assistant warden is a good man, but he turned a blind eye to what's going on. He wants to be the next warden. I guess the only one I trust is the prison psychiatrist, Dr. Catalina Vibes."

"I have a voice-activated tape recorder in my pocket. You tell me what you want the men to do. Leave the escape to me, and William, stay alive until we can get you out."

⋙ ⋘

Captain Carl and Dr. Vibes were finished reviewing the evaluations. He stood up and looked out his window to see if the men were still in the yard. "I talked with Colonel Clay before he went out to see Blu. He was civil but did not hide his feelings that he believed whoever tried to have Blu killed could not have done so without inside help."

"I agree, sir," Dr. Vibes said, placing her files back into her carrying case.

"You spent some time with him, Doctor. What can you tell me about him? He seems to be a man of honor."

"I like him too. Not our typical inmate. He's smart. He has charisma. Handsome," she said, lowering her head as she tried to conceal her true feelings. "When I first evaluated him, I thought he was a conman, a pathological liar. Now I don't know what to believe."

"The colonel said he had never commanded a soldier with Blu's loyalty, lethal skills, and dedication. What I'm worried about is what happens when a man of his ability is backed into a no-win situation?"

"I think he has something inside him that he must battle constantly, buried deep, and suppressed. If he's backed into a corner, it all depends how his mind will cope when he's pushed to the brink. In Freudian terms, it's called the id, ego, and superego. The id in him would be unbridled emotions like violence, rage, and sexual impulses unrestrained without consequence. The superego in him would suppress these urges and rationalize them, acting like a conscience, defining for him the consequences of his actions. The ego is like a referee in a sporting event, mediating and overseeing a balance between the two opposing forces. If he's pushed too far, there could be a breakdown in his mental process. The dark side of his personality could dominate the good I see in him. With his near-genius intellect, military training, knowledge of weaponry, and lethal skills, he could morph, transform into a person unrecognizable even to himself, a person capable of unimaginable acts on an epic scale that one could barely fathom. Then again, he's very complex. He may be in control, knowing the consequences of his actions, and still carry out certain acts, suspending morality in the same way he must have when he killed the enemy in battle."

"Then let's hope it never comes down to that. Maybe this colonel has a way out for him. If not only for Blu's sake, maybe for the rest of us."

Captain Midnight

THE WIZ AND BB had arrived several weeks before the other men to prepare the site that would become the command bunker and make it undetectable to even the most sophisticated government surveillance. Although both men were combat buddies and had a mutual respect for each other's talents, they were an odd couple with almost opposite personalities. The Wiz was quiet, introspective, and reserved. BB was loud, obnoxious, and outgoing. There was always tension and a playful animosity between the men that manifested itself in constantly taunting each other.

Kenneth "Wiz" Castle's family owned Wizard TV and Electronics in Columbus, Ohio. He was thin and had nervous, squirrel-like mannerisms. He talked quickly and always appeared wired, or at least that what BB had always said. His short dirty-blond hair was cut short, reminiscent of the way Ivy Leaguers wore their hair in the fifties. His clothing was always about a decade out of style. He did not keep up or care for his personal appearance. All he cared about was computers and electronics.

BB's real name was Robert Brazoli. Everyone called him BB, in part for his initials, but mostly because he was a "ballbuster," always needling the men around him with sarcasm or playing practical jokes on them. Since he had left the military, he gained forty pounds and was overweight for his six-foot frame. He had dark-brown wavy hair, large dark-brown eyes, a pencil-thin mustache, and a wide, childlike, devious smile. His mannerisms were typical for the neighborhood he grew up in and his language was crude and punctuated with profanity and slang Italian insults. He usually chewed an unlit cigar in his mouth all day.

Their first order of business was to commandeer two army transport vehicles and disconnect the GPS tracking devices on board. Colonel Clay had supplied ISS uniforms, each with the rank of sergeant. They drove the vehicles to a highly secure military depot in the Nevada desert near the secret government testing facility known only as Area 51. Using the proper military protocol, codes provided by the colonel, and forged requisitions documents, the equipment and weapons they had requested were loaded into the two vehicles. No one questioned the authenticity of the orders, especially when the colonel threw in a twist by having the Wiz laser-sign General Bishop's name to the requisition order. The documents stated that all the equipment and weaponry was to be used for training and fortification by the ISS at a classified, undisclosed location.

Billy Ray had purchased property that became the new location of Blu Vineyards and Four Strong Winds avocado farm. He had also acquired two additional properties. When the Wiz and BB entered Silver Verde, they unloaded the equipment and weapons at the Kramer homestead, located ten miles southwest of the center of town. The Kramers were Mormons, members of the Latter-Day Saints, who kept to themselves, never traveled, and seldom went into town. They were survivalists, "doomsday preppers," always fearing and believing that Armageddon was quickly approaching. Their property consisted of a modest white ranch-style house, two small outbuildings, and two football-field-long prefabricated metal buildings that were used to store their farm equipment and machinery. One of the buildings housed several ten-thousand-gallon stainless-steel tanks they used to distill the excess of their corn crop into ethanol for the petroleum industry. The Kramer's farm mirrored their lifestyle and their philosophy of life: self-sufficiency and self-reliance. They were completely off the grid, without phone or cable lines entering their home, believing this would prevent the government from monitoring their activities. On the top of the south-facing roof of both of the metal buildings were photovoltaic cells that converted sunlight into electricity and a satellite dish that the Wiz said would come in handy. Inside the building were battery-storage systems and a diesel generator for backup power.

What had made their farm the crown jewel and an ideal location for the men to carry out their mission was the large, hardened fallout shelter under one of the metal buildings, undetectable to even the most thorough search. The Kramers were prepared for what they thought was inevitable, whether it was from a biological catastrophe, disintegration of society, or an economic melt-down. Even though they considered their property safe, they sensed a crisis was coming and became exceedingly paranoid. They sold their farm and moved to a relative's compound, a four-hundred-acre farm in the middle of Montana.

Billy Ray had left a suitcase of cash for the men to purchase whatever they couldn't requisition or pilfer. They purchased two vans and attached magnetic signs, as if they were subcontractors for the regional cable company. Under the guise of installing fiber-optic lines, they installed video cameras at strategic locations at key intersections in Silver Verde and along the new road leading to the hydroelectric facility. The last cameras they set up around the Kramer farm were equipped with infrared motion detectors and a facial-recognition program to monitor and alert them to anyone near their command bunker.

Both men had been in Silver Verde for about a month. They notified Colonel Clay that they were ready for the other men to join them. John Rollins came in on schedule, but Captain Midnight was overdue, which gave the men cause for concern. Rollins was sitting at a table drinking coffee and listening to the Wiz outline all the tasks they had to complete before they could spring Billy Ray. Behind him was a wide array of electronic hardware, computers, monitors, and servers that he had FedEx deliver to their cover apartments in the Village at Silver Verde.

To say that John Rollins was a very dark-skinned man would be an ethnic understatement. His almost coal-black skin reflected his Liberian ancestry. Big John, as the men in his unit referred to him, was an ominous-looking man with broad shoulders, defined muscles in his biceps and forearms, and huge hands, which, when closed, resembled a baseball catcher's mitt. For such a big man, he had a calm personality and spoke with a soft, small voice. He seldom initiated a conversation and was quiet and introspective. Even though he was considered a gentle giant, everyone knew he was not the type of man you would want to make your enemy. If he liked you, he would show it. If he didn't like you, he would ignore you, and you would avoid him because of what his silence implied.

The Wiz was sitting at his array of electronic equipment, surfing the Internet. BB, who was eating a large Italian grinder that he had made earlier, looked at Rollins and winked. Rollins knew BB was up to something and quickly suppressed his smile.

"Ma-dorn, Wiz!" BB said with mock alarm. "I think some of your equipment is burning."

The Wiz shot up and quickly began checking the wiring and connections on his servers that were blinking and buzzing as they were processing information.

"I don't smell anything," the Wiz said, still checking his equipment.

"It's coming from right here," BB said, pointing to an area near the monitors.

The Wiz leaned over and took in a deep breath. "Jesus Christ!" he said, turning away in disgust as Rollins and BB started laughing. "What the fuck have you been eating?"

BB took another large bite of his Italian grinder and passed some more gas with a resounding blast. With his mouth full of food, he began singing the first line from the song Lou Canova sang in the movie *Broadway Danny Rose*: "*Agita, my goomba, in the bonzo…*"

"In English," the Wiz said, moving away from him quickly.

"What you smell is the four cloves of garlic I fried up with the broccoli rabe that I put on my veal parmesan *grinda*."

"Have some manners, you degenerate!"

"Yeah, we're up to our armpits in culture here," he said, smiling.

"You guys started up right where you left off in Afghanistan," Rollins said as he got a whiff of what the Wiz smelled. "That's nasty, BB. Thank God this place has a good ventilation system."

"See what I have to put up with, Rollins? Look at that pig eat. He's nothing but a degenerate!"

"Now you've really hurt my feelings," BB said in jest. "I resent being called a degenerate. An educated derelict maybe, but I'm not a degenerate."

The lights in the room began blinking, and an alarm rang, alerting the men that the perimeter had been breached. Rollins and BB got up quickly and both men grabbed M-16s. The Wiz sat in front of the monitors, looking at the figure with the infrared cameras.

"How many are there?" Rollins asked. "Do you want us to go outside?"

"Quiet!" the Wiz said, rotating the cameras as he tried to get a better look.

A lone figure with a knapsack slung over his shoulder walked near the ranch house in a zigzag pattern. He stopped at brief intervals to touch the foliage of the shrubs and leaned over to smell the fragrance of the wildflowers that were in bloom.

"It's Midnight," the Wiz said, smiling. "Rollins, go outside and show him the way into the bunker before he blows a gasket."

When Aloysius Smith, a.k.a. Captain Midnight, was born, his mother was a patient in the Dix Building at the Institute of Mental Health in Cranston, Rhode Island. It was presumed that she was impregnated by either another mental patient or one of the staff. She died shortly after giving birth, and her son was remanded to the custody of the state, where he was transferred to the Saint Aloysius Orphanage. The nuns at the facility wanted to give him an unblemished start in life, so they petitioned the courts to change his name to Aloysius in honor of the patron saint of the orphanage, and the surname of Smith. Before leaving the orphanage at the age of eighteen to join the military, he was given his file detailing the circumstances of his arrival.

Aloysius Smith was an unimpressive, ordinary-looking man in his early forties who had spent more than half his life in the service of his country. His hair was dark and short. Anyone looking into his dark, hollow, foreboding eyes could sense that there was something not quite right about him, that he wasn't all there.

Captain Midnight was a warrant officer in charge of training and planning operations for the Nightmovers, an elite unit of snipers. The men in his unit gave him his nickname because all his missions were conducted from midnight till dawn. He felt safe and at ease in the darkness of his nocturnal world, where he would track, target, and kill his prey as if he and his men were merely on a hunting expedition.

The Nightmovers had successfully carried out so many classified and unclassified missions that their exploits has become legendary and elevated and distorted to almost mythic proportions as they were retold countless times.

Midnight was not a dedicated soldier for the glory, medals, or rewards. He was simply a stone-cold, amoral killer and did his duty to earn the respect of his men and for the sheer exhilaration and joy that only ultraviolence could provide. He always fought as if there were no tomorrow because he really didn't care if it came at all. Even though he was fearless, but never reckless, in battle, he never placed any of his men in harm's way. The men under his command felt safe with him. He led a charmed life in the battle zone, and to his credit, none of the men in his unit had ever been killed or even seriously wounded. Midnight was nearly twice the age of the men in his unit and became like an overly protective father figure for them.

Because of his success rate, his odd, sometimes psychotic behavior was not only tolerated but actually encouraged and rewarded by giving him as much latitude and leeway as the military could overlook. He requested a transfer for himself and a few select Nightmovers to serve in Major Clay's command out of boredom and because Clay's region had an abundance of targets.

Rollins escorted Captain Midnight into the command bunker. As he entered the room, BB approached him with open arms. There was camaraderie among the men, an inseparable bond that had been forged by the deaths of the other men in their unit and from their anointment by the baptism of their own blood.

"Buono sera, Capitano Mezzanotte," BB said, hugging him.

Midnight was not a man to openly express his emotions, but he was happy to be in the company of the men in his former unit. *"Buono sera, Signore Roberto,"* he replied, smiling slightly.

Midnight sat down, poured a cup of coffee, put in seven teaspoons of sugar, and stirred it slowly. Then he took out a package of Victory brand, English Oval cigarettes and a small roll of Scotch tape from his knapsack. He taped two cigarettes together and lit them up simultaneously. He took in a deep drag and blew out the smoke slowly from his mouth and nostrils. BB looked to the other men and then back at Midnight. He took a long sip of bottled water, still keeping a curious eye on him.

Midnight took in another deep drag, stared at the other men, and smiled. "OK, boys, when does the killing start?"

BB, who had not yet swallowed, choked, sending water in all directions.

"Hold on, Captain," the Wiz said in a serious tone. "In case you didn't get the memo, Billy Ray said no killing unless your life is in jeopardy, and absolutely no collateral damage to the townsfolk!"

"Lighten up, Wiz. I was only kidding. I'm in control; that is as long as I'm on my meds," he said, smiling a Cheshire grin, which quickly disappeared. "BB, did you get the message I gave to the colonel?"

"Yup."

"Well, did you get the package for me?"

"Yup. The supply sergeant in charge of the depot used to be a sniper. He grilled me. Wanted to know what the ISS wanted with that model of rifle, special ammunition, and the AIVC. I didn't know what the fuck to tell him. I had to play stupid."

"Shouldn't have been too hard for you, and what a believable performance it was," the Wiz said, sitting down at his keyboard as the other men laughed.

"Keep it up, douchebag," BB said, walking behind him and giving him a slight tap on the back of his head. "Hey, Midnight, what the fuck is an AIVC, anyway?"

"An AIVC is an ambient invisibility cloak. It's a self-contained blind that a sniper climbs into, and once activated, it adjusts the inside air to the ambient temperature outside, reducing the infrared signature of the sniper to the point that he becomes almost invisible to anyone trying to locate or target him."

"All right," the Wiz said, standing up. "Unless you want to spend a decade in a federal penitentiary, pay close attention. On this desk are four Navy SEAL megaphones running through a computer program and a router switching device. Each man's name is above a phone with a clock adjusted to the time zone where he lives. If we are probed, and we most certainly will be when Billy Ray gets out, when the phone rings at your home, it will be transferred here. That will tell whoever is probing us that you're at home and not here. Rollins, that will not apply to you because you're leaving the day before we spring Billy Ray."

"If it's all the same, I'd like to see him before I go."

"You'll be cutting it close. After he's out, they'll run the full spectrum of surveillance trying to figure out who got him out. We'll be the primary suspects. All right, I guess one or two days won't make that much of a difference. Midnight, sit down in this chair. I have to take your picture for your new IDs."

Midnight sat down. The Wiz took his picture and laminated his new California driver's license and a US Geological ID and attached them to a black lanyard.

"Our US Geological uniforms are on those hangers," the Wiz said, pointing to a clothes rack. "On Monday we'll start the last assignments, and then it's…

show time. Rollins, here's your IDs, and give BB his," he said, with a devious smile.

Rollins looked at his new license. "Looks like I'm going to be William Washington," he said. Then, looking at BB's IDs, "And you're going to be Mr. Stewart Cazzo."

"Give me those fucking things," BB said, snatching the IDs from Rollins hands. "Stewart Cazzo. That's my new name! You son of a bitch." He looked at the Wiz, shaking his head. "Stewart Cazzo, Stu Gotz!"

Rollins didn't know what the name meant, but Midnight did, and he laughed.

"What's BB pissed about?" Rollins asked.

"In Italian, it means this prick, or this cock," Midnight said.

"I gave him a name that suits him," the Wiz said as the men laughed.

"Go ahead; encourage him," BB said. I don't give a fuck." He turned toward the Wiz, placing the back side of his palm under his chin and flipping it in his direction. "Stu Gotz," he said, grabbing his crotch.

TCB—Taking Care of Business

IT WAS ALMOST 1:00 a.m., one week before the men would put Colonel Clay's plan into motion to break Billy Ray out of Tywater Penitentiary. Midnight and Rollins had applied a stencil to the vans and were just finishing spray-painting the US Geological lettering and logo on the door panels. The Wiz was attaching the black government license plates on the vans. When Rollins and Midnight were finished, they went back to the bunker to play hi-lo-jack. The Wiz went to the other metal building to see if BB needed any help. BB was chewing on an unlit cigar as he loaded super sacks of ammonium nitrate fertilizer with a forklift into one of the huge tanks the Kramers had used to make ethanol. He was distilling nitro methane and fertilizer into a highly explosive liquid form of plastic, similar to C-4.

"Is it safe in here?" the Wiz asked. "I hope you know what you're doing."

"Don't worry about me. I got the mixture right."

"That's not what you said yesterday."

"I'm not making pasta-fa-zool, pinhead. I got it right."

"Yeah, and even a broken clock is right twice a day."

"Now you're talking through a paper asshole! What the fuck is that? Bumper-sticker wisdom?"

"Ah, *paison*, I call it like I see it."

BB turned around and gave the Wiz "the look" as he removed the unlit cigar from his mouth. "If it's not right," he said with a crooked smile, tipping his head to one side, "they'll be finding body parts of us in Nevada."

"I know the colonel explained Billy Ray's instructions to you, but I'm still not clear how it works."

"See those tanks of hydrogen, sacks of powered aluminum, and the oxidizer we pilfered a couple of weeks ago? That's the trigger, the blast wave to set off the forty tons of this home-brewed C-4. I've taken down skyscrapers with seven hundred fifty pounds of plastic, primer cord, and shape charges.

"You think it will work?"

"Well I really don't know. I'll tell you one thing; the second blast force and shock wave will be of such magnitude that it will show up on the Richter scale as a seismic event."

After he finished each batch of distilled AMFO, BB would take several hundred pounds and mix it in a wheel barrow, adding a plasticizer and varying amounts of galvanized roofing nails left behind in a large drum by the Kramers. Then he would shape the mixture to resemble the boulders alongside the road leading to the dam. In the middle of each boulder, he took Ball jars that the Kramers used to preserve fruits and vegetables and put a mixture of powered aluminum, oxidizer, and an accelerant. The following morning, he would paint the hardened rocks using an airbrush to resemble the color and texture of the boulders on the road leading up to the dam. Every day, when the men would go out, he would take what he made the night before and place them along the roadside.

The Wiz was curious as to what BB was doing. "What is all that stuff for?"

"Technically, these are some of the largest claymore mines ever made. Each rock will explode twice. The second explosion," he said, shaking the contents of one of the Ball jars, "are mini thermobarics. They'll burst organs twenty yards away. I've embedded each one with the synchronized chips you gave me. I'm going to place them along the road leading to the dam to form a gauntlet, a killing zone. If Billy Ray has to use them, he'll press the trigger, and they'll detonate about five seconds apart, shredding everyone coming up behind him."

The next morning, the men started out from their cover apartments at the Village at Silver Verde. They drove to the sheriff's department, where a deputy sheriff accompanied them for a traffic detail. As soon as they arrived and began setting up their equipment, a security unit drove up to them in a Jeep and asked them their business. They showed them their work order that stated they were directed by California Power and Light to install seismic equipment to comply with the permitting process. The paperwork, along with the sheriff's detail, gave them an unquestionable air of authority and access. The security staff read the paperwork, talked briefly with the deputy sheriff, and told all the men to have a good day as they left.

BB had brought a small CD player and a CD containing a compilation of the eclectic music the Wiz had downloaded for him. He enjoyed music ranging from Billy Joel, Elton John, ELO, and Meatloaf to Frank Sinatra, Nat King Cole, and Roy Orbison. Every morning as the men began working, they would listen to the first song on the CD, "Taking Care of Business," by Bachman Turner Overdrive.

The deputy sheriff directed the constant flow of traffic safely around the work area as BB and Rollins were setting forms for concrete pads. The Wiz was holding a GPS unit and a marker as Midnight looked through the sights of a surveyor's transit, directing him to the exact location of the pads. Midnight had painted two small *x*'s in the middle of the road, designating the only safe places to be standing when the devices they were installing were activated.

The men took a late lunch. Midnight sat on a grassy slope admiring the panoramic view of the valley and Sliver Verde Lake. That was the area that used to be known as Blu's bluff, where Billy Ray had spent most of his leisure time. He finished eating and took out his V Brand Oval cigarettes. He taped two together and lit them up. The other men, who had finished eating, walked over and sat with him.

"Hey, Midnight," BB said, "Cortez told Macky bits and pieces about of one of your missions outside of Kandahar. I want to know what really happened."

Midnight took in a deep drag and blew the smoke out slowly. "Cortez told Macky? Cortez was a good man," he said, lowering his head. "There was no need for a warrior like him to go out the way he did. If he told Macky, why do you need my account?"

"Cause it sounded like bullshit to me," BB said, smiling as he gave him a nudge.

Rollins, who had been lying back against a large gray boulder, leaned forward. He finished the rest of his water to quench his thirst in the hot California midday sun. "Hey, Wiz, got an extra bottle of water?"

"I only have two bottles left for the rest of the afternoon."

"Here we go, Big John," BB said, tossing him an ice-cold bottle of water. "You asked the wrong guy. Wiz is a fuckin' tightwad. Wouldn't give you the sweat off his balls." The other men laughed.

"I heard the same story from Macky," Rollins said. "All right, Midnight, what's the skinny?"

"You boys know that I don't talk about that shit, like some FNG talking out of his ass."

"Now I'm curious," the Wiz said. "If Midnight won't come clean to what really happened, what did Macky tell you?"

Rollins took a long drink of water. "He said the Nightmovers had just spent a rough night and eliminated about a dozen high-priority targets. The sun was just rising, and they were waiting for their evac to pick them up. The chopper took a hit and returned to base, leaving Midnight and his boys stranded until another evac could arrive. The Taliban knew they were stranded, and they sent the word out. They all came out of the desert, like fucking vultures smelling certain death. Al-Qaeda knew all about Midnight and his Nightmovers. Bin Laden put out a $1,000 reward for the head of any Nightmover and a $10,000 bounty on Midnight's head, and they all wanted to collect. They surrounded his unit and had them trapped in crossfire.

Now here's the part that seems hard to believe. Cortes told Macky that the enemy was advancing, closing in their trap. Midnight stood up, grabbed a belt of grenades and an M-16, and walked into the middle of the firefight. Then he slowly and methodically walked to every location where the enemy was hiding, tossed in a few grenades and mowed them down. He casually advanced, as if he was taking a pleasant stroll in a park. The force of the bullets striking his body armor pushed him back. When the evac team arrived, they found him sitting next to a couple of dismembered bodies, eating an MRE. All he kept repeating was, 'Who's your daddy?' Back at base, when he took off his body armor, they say it had over a dozen slugs in it. Now, for the record, is that what really happened?"

The men looked at Midnight for an answer, not realizing that he was having an episode. His medication must have worn off. Violent images danced in his head, and a full gamut of expressions flashed across his face intermittently every few seconds. The electrical impulses skipjacked across the synapses of his brain much like a steel ball at the mercy of gravity in a pinball machine. His blood pressure and heart rate elevated quickly. He was savoring the memory of the ultraviolence, madness, and mayhem as he relived Rollins's account of the event.

"I think his medication wore off," Rollins said in a voice slightly above a whisper.

"What's wrong with him?"

"Wiring's all fucked up in his head. Some shrink told him the psychotic episodes were a result of temporal lobe epilepsy and that he'd be OK as long as he stayed on his meds."

"Well, he's out of it now," Rollins said.

BB called out to him several times, trying to snap him out of his state of mind. "Midnight, is that what happened?"

Midnight glanced at BB. The men could tell he was not fully aware of his surroundings. They had seen him go off before but not to this severity or for this long a duration. He was rocking back and forth and just kept repeating, "Who's your daddy." Then he reached into his top pocket, took out two vials of pills, and popped several into his mouth. A short while later, he acted as if nothing had happened. As he returned to reality, his brain registered the question that BB had asked. "I guess so," he said as his face returned to normal. "If that's what Cortez told Macky."

"Why did you do it?" BB asked. "Outside of the obvious."

"Which is?" Midnight said, leaning back to relax.

"That you're insane," BB said in jest. "If that's what really happened, it sounds like the death wish of a man with more balls than brains. We're all a little crazy, and we *know* you're crazy, but are you really that insane? Cortez said you have the biggest set of balls he's ever seen."

Midnight turned and let out an odd laugh. "Then I guess it's a wonder of science that I can even walk," he said, dismissing what BB had said.

"Were you scared or afraid of dying?" Rollins asked.

"In order to have a fear of dying, you have to have something to lose. Someone you care for or who cares for you who'll miss you when you're gone. I have no one—except maybe for you guys—who cares if I live or die."

"And you have no fear?" Rollins asked. "Nothing scares you."

"Not really. I never feared anyone or anything except…"

"Except what?" the Wiz asked.

"That night in Afghanistan," Midnight said, lowering his head.

"In Afghanistan!" BB said. "That motherfucker had just cut off my fingers." He held up his hand. "He just gutted Ranaldi and cut Cortez up into pieces. You were next. If my memory serves me right, you were laughing at Labuti, taunting him to get on with it."

"I wasn't scared of dying. I was worried about Rollins."

"Me!" Rollins said. "You were worried about me?"

"I never had a…family," he said slowly. "You have a family. I remember you telling us that when your tour of duty was over, you were looking forward to teaching your two little boys how to play baseball. I was worried that your boys were going to have to go through life without a father."

The men returned to work and were silent and introspective the rest of the afternoon. When BB thought the men were not watching him, he took a pint bottle of Southern Comfort out of his cooler, poured a generous amount into a paper cup, and drank it in one gulp. Although he tried to hide his renewed drinking problem from the men, it did not escape their notice. BB looked at his wristwatch. It was almost three thirty. The downward-looking satellites would be out of range for another two hours. He returned back to the bunker, picked up a full tanker truck of the liquid explosives, and drove it to the abandoned silver mine using the access road on the other side of the valley. After he pumped the entire contents of the truck deep into the airshaft of the mine, he returned to the bunker.

The next day the men removed the forms they had installed for the concrete pads and installed two weapons cleverly disguised as seismic monitoring devices equipped with photovoltaic panels attached to the top for power. The words *US Geological* and logos had been stenciled on the front and back of the devices. The Wiz was busy wiring the equipment and remote control devices to detonate the first explosion of the series in the mine. BB and Midnight were grading the soil around the cement pads. After the Wiz finished wiring the device, Rollins came over to him. He turned around to make sure that the deputy sheriff could not hear their conversation.

"What is all this for?" Rollins asked.

"These two weapons are called Metalstorms."

Midnight knew, in theory, what a Metalstorm weapon was, and he smiled.

The Wiz tested the remote controls for the Metalstorms several times to make sure the mechanisms were operating properly. "Each one is driven by a computer system that fires fifty thousand bullets electronically in less than a minute. The only place to be standing when these are activated is where Midnight painted the x's on the pavement."

Rollins shook his head in amazement. "I thought Billy Ray said the rules of engagement were that we don't kill anyone unless our lives were in jeopardy."

"You know how Billy plans, John. He's thinking that this might be the biggest end game he's ever played, contemplating every move for the best- and worst-case scenarios. Odds are he's never going to have to deploy them. Maybe he's figuring better to have too much firepower than not enough, better to be safe than sorry."

Midnight, who was listening to their conversation, spoke without looking up from raking the soil. "Fuck 'em! If they took my land, put me in the can for four years, and killed my brother, I'd kill all of them!"

"Let's hope it doesn't come to that, for Billy Ray's sake. The colonel said that if we can find a few more pieces of the puzzle, he may have a way of exonerating him, so he can have a normal life, and a future, and maybe all this will be unnecessary."

That evening the men dropped the vans off at the Village at Silver Verde, and drove unmarked vehicles back to the bunker. On the way back to the bunker, BB spotted Handsome Butch's Firework Emporium.

"Hey, Wiz, that place is probably wired. You think you can bypass the alarm?"

"And why would I do that?"

"I'd like to pick up some shells, you know, put my personal touch on the event—a finale for the finale. I'll pay for them from that suitcase of cash Billy Ray left in the bunker."

"Is this really necessary? And besides, I don't think Billy Ray would approve."

"Of course he would. What the fuck! Let me have some fun."

All the way back to the bunker, BB taunted the Wiz, trying to convince him to break into the fireworks factory. Later that night, the Wiz reluctantly bypassed the alarm system, and BB took boxes of three-, six-, and nine-inch Japanese chrysanthemum shells and boxes of floral mines. When Handsome Butch went to his office the next morning, there was an envelope containing $3,000 in cash and a Blu bird key chain. He had a vague idea what it meant; he stuffed the cash into his pocket and smiled.

The next morning BB and the Wiz arose at dawn and took the US Geological van up the access road on the south side of the valley. The Wiz wired the remote detonator to the thermobaric device while BB set up the fireworks finale.

In the afternoon, Colonel Clay arrived wearing civilian clothing so he would not draw any unnecessary attention to himself. The Wiz drove BB and Midnight to Beale Air Force Base in Northern California to acquire two military helicopters. Colonel Clay remained in the bunker, sitting by the Navy SEAL megaphones, waiting for a relay to give the final authorization and codes to complete and verify the requisition. The relay was patched to the bunker, but it appeared to be located in Maryland.

Although they were following the proper protocols and their forged paperwork appeared in order, they were worried that they had overlooked some minute detail that would result in them getting arrested. The relay was patched to the bunker appearing to come from General Bishop's office at the ISS headquarters in Maryland. After the base commander talked with Colonel Clay, who was posing as General Bishop, the helicopters were released. The Wiz disarmed the GPS tracking devices aboard the transport helicopter and the Black Hawk, and they flew off without anyone suspecting what had just transpired. When they arrived in Silver Verde, the men hid the helicopters in one of the storage buildings using a rail system to roll them out of sight.

Later that evening, the men stood around the Wiz as he attempted to hack into the Federal Bureau of Prisons site. He had been trying to break into the system since he arrived in Silver Verde. Each time he tried to gain access, the computer screen would flash the words *Access Denied.*

"Come on, Wiz kid," BB said. "You hacked into the government satellite systems, the CIA, and the NSA, and you can't hack into this site?"

"Even using the hydra I got from the granddaddy of all hackers, I can't get in."

"Why don't you ask him to help you?" Rollins asked.

"Because," the Wiz said, looking up at the men behind him. "He's in a federal prison."

"Mr. Castle," Colonel Clay said in a calm but stern voice, "the primary objective of this mission is to get William out without detection and without loss of life. This mission is for naught without those codes to shut off the surveillance cameras at Tywater and doctor the phony transfer orders."

"I'm trying, sir. They must have a real sharp IT guy. The multiple firewalls are impenetrable, and the codes appear to change every week."

"You keep trying, but if you can't get in soon, I may have a way to get the codes. I'll take a gamble on human nature. If it doesn't work, I'll be a fugitive from justice, wanted for, among other charges, treason. Then we'll have to come up with another way to get him out before they kill him. You'll also have to break *me* out of prison. Do you understand?

"Yes, sir," the Wiz replied.

"If it all goes sideways, you set the timers for, let's say, twenty-four hours, notify someone in the local government so that we don't have any collateral damage, and get the hell out of here! If I do get the codes, I'm off to DC. I'll be back after William is out. Remember: TCB. Does everyone understand?"

"Yes, sir," they all replied in unison.

Sometimes Things Aren't What They Are Made To Appear To Be

THE PORCELAIN KETTLE was whistling in the kitchen of Dr. Vibes's townhouse condominium located twenty miles north of Tywater Federal Penitentiary. She made a cup of raspberry-pomegranate tea, holding it up to her nose to savor the aroma before taking a quick sip. Then she returned to her living room, moving her laptop slightly, before sitting down on her tan leather sofa. On the ottoman in front of her were folders containing the files she had been reviewing before finalizing the psychological evaluations of several inmates. She picked up the remote control for her widescreen television and switched to the Food Channel Network to watch a segment of *Iron Chef America* that was already in progress. One of her multicolored Siamese cats jumped up on the sofa with one leap, rubbing its fur against her pink flannel pajamas before curling up into a ball as it settled in and closed it eyes.

"Freud," she said, caressing the cat as it purred, "where's your brother, Sigmund? Getting into trouble again?"

The other cat heard its name called and climbed out from underneath a cabinet and came to rest on a Persian carpet in front of the warm, smoldering embers of her fireplace. A sweet but subtle lilac fragrance filled the air from a brass incense holder resembling a cat on the mantle of her fireplace.

When the doorbell rang, she became startled and wondered who would be calling at this late hour. She put on a deep burgundy robe and tied it quickly with a matching sash. Then she looked at the video monitor on the wall and saw a military man in uniform wearing a dark-green beret tipped slightly to one side.

"May I help you?" she asked, pushing the intercom button.

"I know it's late, Dr. Vibes, and I hope I haven't come at an inconvenient hour. I'm Colonel Alexander Clay."

Dr. Vibes buzzed him in. He climbed up the stairs and she opened the door.

"Thank you for seeing me, Dr. Vibes," the colonel said in an apologetic tone. "I just need a few minutes of your time."

"Sit, Colonel. I just made some tea. Would you like a cup?"

Colonel Clay took off his beret as he sat down, and placed a large manila envelope on the table next to him. "Yes, thank you. Just a little sugar, please."

As Dr. Vibes made his cup of tea, Colonel Clay observed the cozy décor. On the walls of the living room were prints by Chagall, van Gogh, and Salvador Dali. "How appropriate," he thought as he looked at one of Dali's works, "that a psychiatrist would have prints by a surrealist like Dali, depicting the workings of the dreamlike subconscious mind." He saw a pair of lightweight blue plastic dumbbells lying next to an exercise bicycle. On a small desk on the side of the sofa was a Tiffany-style stained-glass lamp and a neatly stacked pile of various trade magazines. Everything was exactly as Billy Ray told him it would be.

Dr. Vibes handed Colonel Clay his cup of tea and then sat down across from him on the sofa.

Colonel Clay took out his wallet and handed her his military ID. "As I said earlier, I'm Colonel Alexander Clay, currently assigned to the Pentagon."

"I know who you are, Colonel. You came to Tywater to see William Blu a little over a month ago. I don't understand the nature of your visit."

One of her cats jumped onto the colonel's lap. "Sigmund is always getting into something," she said, shushing him away. "Do you like cats, Colonel?"

Colonel Clay could sense that she was apprehensive at his presence. He thought he'd break the ice with a little levity. "Of course I like cats. They taste like chicken," he said in a matter-of-fact, serious tone, waiting for her reaction. Then he looked directly at the doctor and cracked a smile, which in turn brought a smile to her face.

"You want to know why I'm here," he said, taking a sip of tea. "I would like your honest assessment of William."

The question caught her off guard. She took a sip of her tea, looking up at the colonel as she thought for a moment. He could see that she was becoming skeptical and tentative. She couldn't figure out, with all that had happened to Billy Ray, if the colonel was there to help him or if he was part of the conspiracy that she had become convinced, now more than ever, existed against him.

"He's a very intelligent, complex man who has been through many personal hardships in the past few years. But he's a hard one to figure out as far as what's going on inside. He keeps that hidden."

"Well, let me tell you what I know about William. I've been in the military for thirty years. William is a patriot and the most dedicated and loyal soldier I've ever had the privilege of commanding. And I agree with you that he keeps his feelings, opinions, and emotions to himself. Maybe that's his way of keeping his composure and sanity and the dark side of himself in check. You really have no idea of the hell he's been through. I tell you this with one caveat. There is also another side of William that I'm sure you and others at the prison suspected. When threatened, he's a lethal killing machine, but he can also exercise restraint, as he did with those skinheads at Tywater. He has a conscience and an unwavering sense of right and wrong. The kind of person people should admire and certainly want on their side. Is there anything else you could tell me about him, Doctor?"

"I'll be quite frank with you, Colonel. I'm a little reluctant to discuss private, privileged information about William with anyone. With all of the secretive, covert, and mysterious things that have been going on, I don't know if you have ulterior motives. I can't judge what side you're really on."

Colonel Clay smiled and nodded his head in agreement. "That's why he trusts you, and I now know why he likes you."

"Who?" she asked, with a look of skepticism on her face. She felt she was being played.

"William. You know how tight-lipped he is. For him to have said that, you must have really of made a connection and an impression upon him. But it was wise for you to be cautious. That's why he told me to tell you something that would ease your mind and assure you that I have his best interests in mind. He said to tell you that sometimes things aren't always what they are made to appear to be."

Dr. Vibes thought for a short while and smiled. She remembered Billy Ray telling her that statement on his first visit. "I believe you, Colonel, but I still don't see how I can help."

"Well, if everything goes as planned, he'll be getting out soon. When he does get out, you'll always have to keep in mind what I just told you, because nothing will be what we will make it appear to be."

"He's getting out soon? I haven't heard anything. He has about three more years to serve."

"We're going to arrange an early release for him," the colonel said, with a devious smile on his face.

"Really," she said doubtfully. "And how will you manage that? Is he going to receive a pardon?"

"In a manner of speaking. The problem is, Dr. Vibes, we believe the very people who could grant him a pardon have a vested interest in seeing that he never leaves Tywater...alive. They're going to have him killed, you know! And we're not going to sit by idly and let that happen."

"Who's going to have William killed?"

"We don't know all the players involved—yet—but make no mistake about his fate at Tywater. It'll go something like this. One morning you'll come to work and hear that he's dead. He'll be poisoned in his cell with an undetectable chemical agent. Make it look like a brain aneurysm, or he'll be shot supposedly during a staged escape attempt, or maybe they'll send in some professional assets to kill him, not like the clowns they sent in last time."

"Is this a theory of yours? Do you have any hard evidence or proof of this conspiracy?"

"Some, but we don't have all of the pieces of the puzzle. William believes he has put together some of the pieces, and when he gets out, he's going to find the rest. Once he's out and safe, and all of the information is released, the powers that be will have no other choice than to exonerate him. But he can't stay at Tywater much longer. What's the point if he's exonerated posthumously? You must have suspected that whoever tried to have him killed did so with help from someone on the inside."

"The assistant warden and I agree, but I still don't understand how he's going to be granted an early release."

"I'm not going to sell you a false bill of goods, Dr. Vibes. You deserve to know the truth. You are aware that William is a chess player."

"Yes, he mentioned that to me, but I'm still not seeing the whole picture."

"William is too modest to mention the fact that he's not just a good chess player but a world-class chess player. When he gets out, he's going to play the end game of all end games. It will be catastrophic! He's going to take back everything that was taken from him. And the people responsible for his brother's death, and framing him, will pay a high price...with interest."

Dr. Vibes thought for a moment as she finished her tea. She could sense that he was holding back something. "What is it that you're not telling me, Colonel? I still don't see where I fit into all this."

"When I said we were planning an early release for William, what I failed to mention is that it won't be an authorized one. We're going to forge phony transfer orders from the Federal Bureau of Prisons. We have everything in place except for...the prison codes."

There was an awkward silence in the room. "Oh, I see," she said softly.

"We've worked out all the details. No one will discover what transpired until he's already out. Believe me—there's no other way to get him out safely without the loss of lives."

Colonel Clay reached into his inside top pocket and handed her a disposable, prepaid phone. "If you agree to send us the codes, this phone has been modified to be untraceable. You just text the codes and then throw the phone in your fireplace. If you decide not to give us the codes, I'll understand."

"You're asking a lot from me, Colonel. For argument sake, let's say I won't or can't get you the codes. What happens next?"

Colonel Clay looked up at the ceiling, thinking, groping, as if the answer would materialize from out of thin air. He collected his thoughts and answered her question bowing his head. "If we don't get him out," he said, beginning slowly, "or if an accident should befall him, there are highly skilled ex-military men who would not take the news kindly. One of those men, in particular, is beholden to William, like the brother he never had. He's very unstable and, without his medication, certifiably insane. He's an amoral killing machine, but unlike William, this psychotic killer doesn't have a conscience. God only knows what a warped mind like his is capable of doing. Tywater could easily become a war zone with massive casualties!"

"You paint a pretty graphic picture."

Colonel Clay reached over to where he had placed the large manila envelope and took out a document labeled "National Security." He handed it to the doctor. "Before you make your decision, this file may shed some light on part of the mystery of what's been going on. It's a copy of an uncensored file before the CIA doctored it to save the careers of the brass who, pardon my French, fucked up. When William is released, the contents of this file will be made public at the appropriate time, along with anything else we can uncover. You won't want to be on the wrong side of this when it comes out. Many careers will be drastically altered or ruined."

"I'll read the file, but I can't keep thinking about what both you and William said about how appearances are deceiving and that sometimes perceptions can be manipulated. How do I know, and more importantly, how do you know, that everything in this document is the truth and not just misinformation?"

"Because, Dr. Vibes," the colonel said, getting up to leave, "I was there, and I was one of the men he saved. After you read the file, it would make excellent kindling for your fireplace, if you catch my drift. We'll understand if you don't want to get involved. There's nothing more I can say to persuade you, except that William's life is in your hands. Good night, Doctor."

You Can Fool Some of the
People Some of the Time...

LIEUTENANT O'ROURKE WALKED over to Billy Ray's cell, accompanied by two guards. He had a wide grin on his face as he took the baton from his holster and rattled it between the bars of his cell. One of the guards unlocked the cell door slowly.

"Stand up, hero," O'Rourke said. "It's movin' day. When I heard the good news about your transfer, I just had to come down personally to celebrate your send-off," he said sarcastically.

"Should I cuff him?" one of the guards asked O'Rourke.

"Absolutely! Can't take any chances with this asshole."

Billy Ray placed both of his hands together and one of the guards snapped the manacles in place. O'Rourke pushed him down the dimly lit corridor with his baton. "I hope you like water sports, hero. Rumor is that you're off to Gitmo with all the other scumbags. Seems that some information has come to the warden's attention that you're no longer safe at Tywater. Don't know where he gets that idea from," O'Rourke said, winking at one of the other guards. "A military transport will be landing in the yard in a few minutes. After a little 'rendition' at Gitmo, you'll be *dying* to be back here."

Billy Ray didn't say a word. He just turned toward O'Rourke and smiled a becoming smile that was more like a sneer. O'Rourke's elation was suddenly tempered with disappointment. He was puzzled and disconcerted as he wondered why a man going from purgatory to hell would be smiling.

When Billy Ray was escorted into the yard, two military helicopters had already landed, the blades of the aircrafts still rotating. Two ISS soldiers wearing flight helmets were standing in front of the open doors of both helicopters and toting M-16 assault rifles. One of the guards took off Billy Ray's manacles, and as he was escorted into one of the helicopters, he heard Lieutenant O'Rourke laughing and shouting loud enough so that he could hear him over the rotating blades. "Remember you said to me that every dog has its day? Well, today is yours, asshole!"

Then all the ISS soldiers appeared to split up into the two helicopters, and they took off slowly. The first indication that something had gone drastically wrong was when the guard in the watchtower saw a bright flash in the distant dark horizon, followed a few seconds later by a loud, resounding concussion. It appeared that the two transports had flown too low and crashed into the high limestone cliffs in the distance.

June 29, 5:45 a.m. eastern standard time
When the Prince of Darkness arose the next morning, it was still dark. An EAC (emergency action communiqué) was flashing on the screen of his computer. When he read the e-mail and viewed the attachments, his first reaction was bewilderment and anger. But as he thought about the message, he nodded as his anger turned to skepticism. Then he smiled with a sense of wonderment and marveled at how his protégé had pulled this off.

He dressed with a sense of urgency and then headed quickly to the ISS headquarters in Maryland. As he drove, he kept replaying the conversation he had with Billy Ray at Tywater. The words kept echoing in his mind. "You said that you held the keys to the front gate. Well, maybe so do I. What makes you think that if I ever wanted to get out of here, these walls could hold me?"

When the Prince of Darkness entered the Big Brother amphitheater, he immediately began gathering intel, using all the highly sophisticated programs at his disposal. At 10:00 a.m., General Bishop entered the room.

"I got your e-mail. Tragic," the general said smiling, with a touch of irony in his voice, "about what happened to Blu. Looks like whatever he knew...about that night...died with him."

The Prince of Darkness was busy reading some information at the computer terminal. He shook his head at the general's remark. "How the hell did you ever make the rank of general? Oh yes, I forgot," he said, looking up. "Someone pulled some strings. I hope you're not buying this contrivance. Doesn't it seem a little too convenient? You can fool some of the people some of the time, but this just doesn't fly, and no one, absolutely no one, makes a fool out of me!"

"I don't understand. The trouble with you is that you think everything is either a cover-up or a conspiracy."

"That's what keeps me and countless others whom I'm responsible for alive. You really think Blu is dead? Accordingly to my information, the Federal Bureau of Prisons never issued a transfer order. I ran a probe to find out the origin of those military helicopters that supposedly crashed with all on board. They came from Beale Air Force Base in California. Do you know who signed the requisition orders for the choppers?"

"No. Enlighten me."

"According to the perfect match of the signature, you did."

"I did no such thing."

"I know that. Someone is amusing themselves at your expense. Do you think they went through all of this planning to end up crashing into a cliff? It was a clever distraction, but not clever enough. I had Big Brother get me a list of all the men in Blu's former unit."

Major Breelin entered the Big Brother room and walked down the descending stairway to General Bishop. He saluted him, and they exchanged pleasantries. The major had been recently appointed as the operations officer in charge of overseeing the program.

The Prince of Darkness looked up and read the rank and name of the major. "Major Breelin," the Prince of Darkness asked, without looking up from the screen, "who's the brightest and best analyst you have in the program, one who is proficient in electronic tradecraft?"

"I didn't quite catch your name," the major said. "General, is this man an aide of yours? Does he have the proper clearance to be here?"

The Prince of Darkness looked up briefly, mildly annoyed. General Bishop pulled the major aside and whispered a few words to him.

"Yes, sir," the major said, coming to full attention. "That would be Lieutenant Patrice Suni."

"Would you have her come down to this terminal? I have a few assignments for her."

When Lieutenant Suni came over, the Prince of Darkness stood up. She sat down and coded in. She was a short, dark-haired Asian with dark-brown almond-shaped eyes. The Prince of Darkness noticed that when she saluted the general and greeted him, her mannerisms were animated, almost rigid, strictly business, and void of emotion. Her facial movements were like a mannequin. She was exactly the kind of analyst he wanted to perform the tasks.

"General, if my assumptions are correct, this could not have gone down so smoothly without someone on the inside with a complete knowledge of military protocol and procedure; in other words, one of us. What was the name of the commander of Blu's unit?"

"That would be Major Alexander Clay. I think he's a colonel now, assigned to the Pentagon."

"Really! Luck favors the prepared mind. He fits the bill. Lieutenant Suni, run a program on Colonel Alexander Clay. Locate him from his implanted GPS. Tell me where he is now and run a history of where he's been for, let's say, the past month."

She typed in the information and the colonel's current location and history came up on the screen. "Right now he's in his office in the pentagon. For the past month he's been in and around Washington, DC, in Maryland for two days, and three days in New Jersey, where according to the file, he owns a small cottage on a lake."

"That seems like a dead end," General Bishop said.

"I was sure it was him," the Prince of Darkness said. "Lieutenant, run a detailed program for all the colonel's cell phone and hardline correspondence and give the printout to the general, but not quite yet." The Prince of Darkness looked at the printout of all of the men in Blu's unit. One name stood out as a probable collaborator, a Sergeant Kenneth Castle, communications and electronic warfare specialist. "First, send a probe and a spike to Kenneth Castle. Make sure you activate the voice-recognition program."

She entered the program, and the phone rang at the Wiz's home phone. The call was immediately relayed to the SEAL megaphone in Silver Verde. All the men were sleeping late from the celebration the night before. When the phone rang, they jumped up quickly, and the Wiz turned on his computer. "I'm away at the moment," the taped message said. "If you need assistance or if this is an emergency, call me at the office at Wizard Electronics, at 1-800-999-WIZZ."

"I knew it," the Wiz said to the other men. "It's a very sophisticated probe coming from Maryland, either the NSA or the ISS."

About twenty seconds later, the megaphone rang again, displaying the number of Wizard Electronics. The Wiz turned to BB. "BB, pick up that cordless drill, and when I'm talking on the phone occasionally press the trigger for some background noise, and don't overdue it."

When the Wiz answered the phone, Lieutenant Suni handed the phone to the Prince of Darkness.

"Wizard Electronics," he said.

"Is this Mr. Kenneth Castle?"

"Sure is. What may I do for you?"

"I'm trying to locate and eliminate a problem. You see, there was a crash, and I can't figure out what really happened."

"A crash?"

"Yes…with…my computer."

The Wiz thought for a moment. He could sense that the person on the other end of the line was being coy. "No problem. Would you like me to come out and pick it up?"

"That won't be necessary. I'll be in your area in a few days, and I'll drop it off."

As the Wiz was just about to hang up, BB pressed the trigger on the cordless drill a few more times. "Just ask for the Wiz. See you then."

→—● ●—←

"All right. Lieutenant, where did the probe locate him, and did the voice recognition verify it was Castle?"

"He's in Cleveland, Ohio, and yes, the voice is a perfect match."

"Another dead end," General Bishop said.

"Not really, sir," Lieutenant Suni said. "Big Brother has had Kenneth Castle, a.k.a. 'The Wiz,' under surveillance for about three months. He's a high-priority target as the possible source of a subversive and antigovernment pirate website. So far, there isn't any hard evidence linking him to the site."

"Good work, Lieutenant," the Prince of Darkness said. "Step up the surveillance on him."

In the meantime, the Wiz was running his own program on the outside chance that his voice-recognition program could tell him who was on the other end of the line. After scanning the database and voice comparisons, the screen flashed a 98 percent match. "I got that son of a bitch."

"Who was it?" Billy Ray asked.

"It's Richard Standz, the Prince of Darkness himself. Thinks he could trap me with that lame tradecraft."

"It figures," Billy Ray said. "We're still one step ahead of him. If he's probing all of the men in our unit, our ruse didn't fool him. I didn't think it would. That means he's still not sure who helped me and whether I'm still alive. BB, did you forget about the errand you have to run for me this morning?"

"An errand?"

"You know…the delivery."

"Shit, I forgot all about it. I'll get on it right now," he said, putting on his Los Angeles Angels baseball cap.

→▶◎ ◎◀←

June 29, 11:30 a.m. Pacific time

Jenny had just finished breakfast. Her mother was in their small kitchen preparing her husband pancakes and corn beef hash with eggs. As was customary each morning, her father would read the local newspaper and watch the national news on TV and then switch to the Weather Channel to see the local forecast.

That morning, Jenny had planned on helping the farmhands prune the avocado trees. In the afternoon she planned on going to the library, where it was her day to read to the children at story hour. Just as she was about to leave, the breaking news flashed across the television screen about the helicopters that had crashed, killing all aboard including a Silver Verde resident who was being transferred from Tywater Federal Penitentiary to an undisclosed location, William Raymond Blu.

The CNN reporter, who was standing outside the front gates of Tywater, read from a prepared text and stated that, "a spokesman for the Federal Bureau of Prisons was not aware of any transfer orders, and government officials were still trying to determine the details and at this time had no comment." The reporter went on to say that "a spokesman for the Federal Aviation Administration said several investigators were dispatched to the site of the crash to determine the cause."

Jenny watched the report in silence, paralyzed at what the reporter said. Her mother came running into the living room as she overheard the news. Jenny turned slowly and returned to her room, closing the door behind her. She lay down on her bed fully clothed, staring up at the ceiling, and started to cry. She was still in her room when the doorbell rang. Her father got up slowly, still keeping his attention focused on the news program.

A slightly overweight man wearing a Los Angeles Angels baseball cap was standing on the front porch. "I have a special delivery for Jenifer Blu," the man said, handing him the small package. "Good day, sir," he said, returning to the white delivery van.

Jenny's father took the package, shook it, and wondered what was inside.

"Who was that?" Jenney's mother asked.

"A delivery man with a package for Jenny."

Jenny's mother knocked on her door gently. "Honey, you have a delivery." Jenny did not respond, so she repeated it again.

From behind the closed door, Jenny said in a barely audible, hushed voice, "Open it if you like, and put in on the table."

Jenny's father opened the package. Inside was a small metal bluebird attached to a key ring, and a note. He held up the key chain to show his wife, giving it a flick with his finger. He opened the letter and read it to himself, puzzled by what was written.

"Well," Jenny's mother said, "who is it from, and what does it say?"

"It's not signed. All it says is, 'There's no future for me without you in it.'"

Suddenly, Jenny came from her room. "Let me see that note," she said, taking the piece of paper from her father's hand. As she read the note to herself, she thought for a moment, and then a smile appeared on her face. She wiped the tears from her eyes with the back of her hand.

"What does it mean, honey?" her mother asked.

"It's what I told Billy Ray the last time I visited him in prison. I think it's his way of telling me that he's alive."

Jenny's mother and father looked at one another in amazement and joy. Jenny picked up the key chain and her cell phone and headed to the door.

"Where are you going?" her father asked.

"I have a busy day ahead," she said, heading out the door. "And it looks like it's going to be a beautiful day."

"Jenny, wait," her mother said, stepping out onto the porch. "If Billy Ray wants everyone to think he's dead, it must be for a reason. Keep that in mind."

⇒━● ●━←

8:30 a.m. Pacific time, Tywater Federal Penitentiary

A media circus had gathered outside the gates of Tywater Federal Penitentiary and at the location of the crash site several miles away. All the regional and national networks had dispatched camera crews and reporters to cover the story. Investigators from the Federal Aviation Administration assisted by several local fire departments were searching the area and dragging the deep, dark rushing waters under the high cliffs of the former limestone quarry. Occasionally they came up with debris of what they believed was the remnants of the military helicopters. Cadaver dogs with escorts were searching the banks of the river. Although they had been scouring the area of the crash since daybreak, they still hadn't recovered any bodies and presumed that they had been washed downstream from the swift-moving current that flowed through the ravine.

When the inmates were let out into the yard, an eerie quiet had fallen over the men as the word spread about what had happened to Billy Ray. For the first time in any of the inmates' recollections, Roscoe Clements had not set up his chess board. He just sat alone on the upper tier of the metal bleachers overlooking the track. He was staring out in the direction of the cliffs in the distance, wondering what had really happened to his friend.

Dr. Catalina Vibes looked out her office window toward the front gate, observing the reporters. She wondered if in an attempt to save Billy Ray's life, she had actually contributed to his death, or was this all part of the misdirection of the colonel's plan to "make things appear the way he wanted them to be."

⇢▬◉ ◉▬⇠

11:30 a.m. eastern standard time

On the East Coast, the Prince of Darkness was still giving instructions to Lieutenant Suni. "Continue running the full spectrum of surveillance on all the men under Colonel Clay's unit, and add his name to the list. Key into their military IDs for facial recognition and tie into all the security cameras at all airports and bus and train stations in California and in the vicinity of where the men live."

"Is there anything you want me to do on my end?" General Bishop asked.

"Retask all the satellite surveillance to focus on Silver Verde."

"If Blu is still alive, and I have my doubts, that's the last place I would go if I were him."

"But you're not him, General. I have a feeling that he thinks we're still playing the same 'game' when I visited him in prison. He still thinks he can win! If he is in Silver Verde, I have to figure out, in advance, what his end game is. I gave him a way out, but he wouldn't take it. I can tell you this: the board is not going to be pleased by this latest development. At some point in time, very soon, they'll want to see me…and you. If this isn't resolved soon, you know what they instruct us to do. We still have some time to figure out what really happened and who helped him escape and then—there will be hell to pay!"

"If Blu is alive, I wouldn't worry about him. I have an idea to smoke him out and then take him out, once and for all!"

"Don't underestimate him or whoever is helping him. I tell you this for the sake of your career. I have to figure out who and how they got him out."

⇢▬◉ ◉▬⇠

The night before, after the prison guards took off Billy Ray's shackles, the ISS soldiers who took custody of him appeared to split up and enter the two military helicopters. The men had rehearsed this part of the plan countless times, and it was executed with perfect precision. In reality, all the men had actually entered the Black Hawk helicopter. The Wiz had set up a remote control for the other helicopter made from spare parts of video games and a joystick from an old Atari game.

Midnight was piloting the remote controls from the Black Hawk, until he drove the first helicopter that BB had wired to explode upon impact into the high cliff at full throttle.

When the men arrived at the command bunker, they hugged Billy Ray and began the celebration they prepared for his homecoming. BB popped the cork of a magnum of champagne, and they all drank a toast to Billy Ray, Colonel Clay's plan, and the success of the mission. The more the men drank, the more silent and introspective they became.

Later that evening, Rollins was preparing to leave. Everyone knew that the window of opportunity was growing short for him to return home without being detected. They knew that the next day the government would be using the full scope of surveillance and investigative skills to determine who helped Billy Ray escape, and they would be on the top of a very short list.

Rollins put his duffel bag into the Black Hawk. He entered one of the metal storage buildings with Billy Ray. Midnight and the Wiz prepared the helicopter for takeoff.

Although Billy Ray and Rollins both talked softly, their hollow-sounding voices echoed off the massive expanse of the building and the metal walls.

"Are you going to make it back safely, John?"

"Wiz has it all figured out. He and Midnight are going to fly me to my brother's house. He lives outside the city, in the sticks. He'll drive me the rest of the way. I'll be back to work tomorrow. They think my family and I have been on vacation for the past few weeks."

"Good."

Rollins looked down as he heard the engines of the helicopter starting up. Billy Ray could see that Rollins was thinking, trying to compose his thoughts before he spoke. "You got a real raw deal, Billy, over there and then over here."

Billy Ray nodded his head in agreement. "You know the deal, Big John. You play the cards you're dealt."

Rollins took out his billfold and handed Billy Ray two pictures. "These are my two boys. The older one is twelve and the younger, ten. I never really had a chance to thank you for...you know..." he said, turning his head so that Billy Ray would not see his eyes getting teary.

"You know that's not necessary, Big John."

"I can never thank you enough. I know what it's like to grow up without a father. My father abandoned our family when I was just an infant. If you didn't come get us, my boys would not have had a father. My wife's expecting," he said, which brought a smile to his face. "It's going to be a boy. Know what name we picked for him?"

Billy Ray handed the pictures back to Rollins and shook his head.

"William Raymond Rollins," he said, holding up his head high with pride.

"Billy Ray Rollins," Billy Ray said, nodding. "Has a nice ring to it." They both laughed.

The Wiz and Captain Midnight entered the building. "Big John, we're leaving in five," Midnight said.

"Sure enough," Rollins said as he stood.

Before the Wiz left the building, he turned to Billy Ray. "Do me a favor and keep an eye on BB. He's having nightmares again, and he fell off the wagon. He does stupid things when he's out of booze."

"I think he's out for the night, but I'll babysit him for you," he said as Rollins laughed.

The Wiz shook his head and left the hanger.

"It's time I got going, Billy," Rollins said. "I'd really like to stick around and see it all go down. It's going to be something else," he said, looking up as if visualizing the event.

Billy Ray reached into his pocket and pulled out a manila envelope. "I want you to have this," he said, handing the envelope to him. "It's a little something for you and the kids."

Rollins opened it up. The envelope was filled with crisp one-hundred-dollar bills. Once he saw what was inside, he tried to hand it back to him. "I can't take this."

"Of course you can," Billy Ray said, holding up his hands and refusing to accept the envelope. "I have an envelope for all the men. Trust me; I have more than enough to last me for the rest of my life. You take this and do some good for you and your family. It's all we really have in life. It's the only thing that really matters."

"When all this mess is cleared up, like the colonel says it will be, you will come by and see me and the family."

"Sure, Big John…someday."

Billy Ray walked with Rollins to the awaiting Black Hawk. As Big John entered the helicopter, he turned to Billy Ray and gave him a big thumbs-up before he closed the door behind him.

A Piece of the Puzzle

June 30, 1:00 p.m. Pacific time, four days to the reckoning

THE DAY WAS overcast with a cool mist and drizzle. BB wore a lightweight, full-length army duster, and Billy Ray wore a dark-blue nylon parker. Before they left, the Wiz handed BB Billy Ray's new IDs. BB looked at it, puzzled. "Who's John Galt?"

"It's an inside joke," the Wiz said as Midnight and Billy Ray understood its significance and smiled. They left the command bunker and headed to the Village at Silver Verde to exchange their vehicle for the white US Geological van.

"What do you hope to find at the county records office?" BB asked.

"I've had an itch I couldn't scratch for four years. Today we're going there to get a large piece of the puzzle."

When they arrived at the Village at Silver Verde, Billy Ray was just about to get out of the van when BB grabbed his arm. "Hold up, Billy. Look at that black SUV that just pulled up...the one with the government plates."

A late-model black SUV with darkly tinted windows had pulled into the front entrance under a large porte cochere. Six men got out and immediately started unloading luggage and what appeared to be long black leather gun cases. They looked like military men, tall and well built, with marine-style short haircuts.

"BB, did the Wiz place any surveillance cameras near here?"

"Or course, right across the street."

Billy Ray took out a disposable phone that the Wiz had modified to alter and scramble his voice to make it unrecognizable and undetectable to any voice-recognition program. He dialed the number, and it rang in the command bunker.

"What's up, Billy?" the Wiz asked.

"We're at the Village at Silver Verde. Looks like company men...spooks. They're unloading at the front entrance. See if you can identify who they are, and keep an eye on their movements. See what they're up to."

After Billy Ray hung up, the Wiz zoomed in and recorded the men entering the building. After they had all entered the building, BB and Billy Ray quickly got into the US Geological van and left. The Wiz slowed down the tape and fed the images into the facial-recognition program he had hacked from Langley. As he replayed the tape, Midnight saw something and asked him to freeze-frame the tape.

"Well, well, well! Who's your daddy?" Midnight said slowly as he moved closer to the screen. "I know two of those sons of bitches. The other four I don't recognize. They were in black ops. We were on a mission together on the border of Pakistan killing Taliban operatives. They're real good. Both elite fucking snobs. They think they shit vanilla ice cream. Last I heard they were doing wet work for the CIA. See those gun cases they were carrying? State-of-the-art sniper rifles, just like the one you got me from the military depot. With the velocity and explosive power of the ammunition, even if you're off the kill zone on your target, you'll still blow them apart. Very messy, but deadly. Someone wants somebody dead in a bad way!"

"We're fucked now," the Wiz said.

A devious, almost insane smile broke out on Midnight's face. "No, we're not!"

"How do you figure that?"

"'Cause they don't know *I'm* here."

--→━◑ ◐━←--

As they drove on the interstate, Billy Ray noticed that BB's hands were shaking as he gripped the steering wheel, almost as if he was going through withdrawals or the DTs. He reached into his top pocket and dumped a bottle of aspirin into the cup holder next to him. Every once in a while, he would grab a few and pop them into his mouth as if he were eating M&Ms. Billy Ray could sense that his mind was elsewhere as he occasionally looked at the two missing digits on his hand.

"Are you all right, BB? Do you want me to drive?"

"I'm fine."

"What's bothering you? You know you can confide in me."

BB remained silent for a while, but then he opened up as he began to talk slowly, still looking at the road. "You'd think after all these years I could put it all behind me. I can't get it out of my head. Every night. Every fuckin' night, the same nightmares. I hear Rinaldi and Cortez screaming. I see their faces as that motherfucker was gutting them, blood gushing out everywhere. Their insides falling out right in front of them. They didn't gag them or us. They wanted the rest of us to hear them screaming. Savoring the horror. To let us know what was in store for us. And I was next. Labuti put his cigarette out in my face. Then he wiped the blood off his bayonet on my arm before he cut off my fingers. I see it every night. But you got them all, Billy. And Labuti, well, he got his."

"I guess so," Billy Ray said, not knowing what to say to comfort his friend. "Take the next exit. We're almost there."

⇀═◉ ◉═↼

In the meantime, the Wiz was monitoring the black SUV. He had run the facial-recognition program on all the new arrivals and confirmed that they were all ex-military men assigned to the CIA, Department 6, which the Wiz knew to be the black ops division for counter insurgency and covert assassinations. As the men entered the SUV and headed toward town, the Wiz followed their movements.

Midnight had gone outside and was sitting under a large tree, drinking iced coffee and smoking his customary two cigarettes taped together. As he was relaxing, observing the various trees that were foreign to him, a brightly colored hummingbird, in unnatural hues of florescent blues and reds, flew within inches of his face. Its wings were moving so fast, they were not visible to the human eye. At first he marveled at this tiny wonder of nature. It didn't seem real to him, like an animation from a Disney cartoon. Then the hummingbird tilted. It appeared to be looking directly into his eyes. He smiled and reached out to touch it, to verify in his mind that the bird was real and not just an illusion. It flew off in quick, erratic flight and disappeared as fast as it had appeared. Then he began wondering. He couldn't determine, with any degree of certainty, if what he just saw was real or if he was having an episode. He reached into his top pocket and popped a few pills just in case.

When the SUV reached the center of town, the Wiz called for Midnight to come inside over the intercom system.

"What's up?"

"I don't know. All six just arrived in town. They split up in groups of two and they're just walking around town."

Midnight looked at the monitor at the men walked about town. They were all wearing sunglasses and dressed in conservative civilian clothing. As they walked, they appeared to be looking up at the rooftops of the buildings.

"What are they up to?" the Wiz asked.

"Exactly what I'd be doing if I were given this assignment. They're looking for vantage points, the best positions to carry out their mission...to take out their targets without being detected."

"Image the collateral damage to the civilian population. They're going to turn this town into a war zone."

"No they won't. They're looking to take out their target with the precision of a surgeon. And their target is Billy Ray. Their arrogance and overconfidence will be their undoing. They think they're shooting ducks in a penny arcade. If that's the way they want to play it, so be it. The more spooks they send, the more body bags they're going to need. I can't wait," he said, smiling.

→►◉ ◉◄←

As BB and Billy Ray got off the exit, there was a traffic jam outside a gas station. Some customers had created a disturbance at the gas station and were fighting with the attendants over gouging the already high price of gasoline. When they passed by a supermarket, protesters were outside carrying signs and asking people to boycott the big store chain over their outrages prices. The economic conditions had deteriorated to the point where a strange foreboding descended over the country like a plague of locusts. The fear and tension were palpable. People could feel and sense that the fall and collapse were imminent. As chaos and civil disorder erupted in every state, it was a harbinger of events to take place that had been smoldering for quite some time. The dominoes of misfortune, impending doom, and dissent were all stacked up, only waiting for that one event, that one little push, and the whole tattered fabric of society would unravel and come crashing down.

When they arrived at the county records office, they waited almost until closing before they entered. A light mist was still falling, and occasionally the sun tried to break through the gray sky. Landscapers were cutting the lawn and trimming branches off the trees outside the building. As they were about to enter the building, BB saw a pair of tree loppers near the entrance. He picked them up and hid them under his army duster.

"What is that for?" Billy Ray asked.

"Trust me," BB said, with a devious look on his face. "Just follow my lead."

"This guy has to know something," Billy Ray said, opening the door. "How do you want to play this—good cop, bad cop?"

"No, no, no," BB said, shaking his head. "How about good cop and a really sick, demented bad cop," he said, smiling. "Believe me, when I'm through with him, he's going to tell you everything you wanted to know…and then some!"

Just before they entered the office, BB mussed his hair, giving him the disheveled look of a madman. When they entered the office, Billy Ray recognized the senior records clerk, Daniel Cook. He seemed annoyed at their presence and looked up at the clock above him before continuing with his paperwork. He wore a light-green tweed suit, white shirt, and a dark-green bowtie. There was a small television on the desk with the volume turned down. As he looked up at the screen, his horned-rimmed glasses slipped down to the bridge of his nose. He pushed them back in place looking at the CNN update about the crash at Tywater. Billy Ray listened as the commentator said something to the effect that the incident was now determined to have been a botched prison escape, killing all of the unknown perpetrators aboard the helicopters, including prisoner 2516, William Raymond Blu.

"It's nearly closing time, gents," Cook said. "I hope this doesn't take long. I have a long way to travel before I get home."

"You can't get there from here," Billy Ray said, looking directly into Cook's eyes.

Cook put down his pen and looked at Billy Ray, puzzled. Then he stood up. "That's the most asinine statement I've ever heard."

Billy Ray turned toward BB. "Lock the door."

As BB locked the door, Mr. Cook became alarmed. The cocky, arrogant expression drained from his face as he began twitching.

"I agree, Mr. Cook. It was an asinine statement when you said that to me four years ago. You see, Mr. Cook, your home may be far away, but you are here, and you may not be able to make it there from here," he said, mocking what he had told him years earlier. "You don't remember me, do you Mr. Cook? Let me refresh your memory."

"N-n-no, I don't," he said. "Why...should I?"

"I see you were watching CNN when we came in. If I told you I am William Raymond Blu, does that ring a bell?"

Cook shook his head. "Can't be. He's dead."

"Not quite yet! And if you think back four years ago, I came in looking for the seismic charts for my land in Silver Verde."

Billy Ray could see by the expression on his face that he now remembered, but he shook his head as if to say he didn't know what he was referring to.

"Don't play cute with me. You know exactly what I'm talking about...the piece of land on which California Power and Light built the hydroelectric dam."

"I have no idea what you're talking about."

BB walked up to Cook slowly. His eyes were rolled back into his head. He took a pencil off his desk, smelled it, licked it, and then put in into his mouth.

"W-what's w-wrong with th-this man?" he asked as his stammer grew more pronounced.

"They don't let him out much, except in a straightjacket."

"You got kids?" BB asked, tilting his head.

"Y-yes."

"You don't force them to play the piano, do you?"

"N-no."

"Are you sure?"

"Y-yes."

"My father, God rest in pieces," BB said, with a demented laugh, "used to make me play the piano. Day in, day out. One day I played the wrong notes, and he slammed the piano case down on my fuckin' fingers. He pushed his hand with the two missing digits into Cook's face. BB leaned over and whispered into Cook's ear. "You know what I did? Do you know what I did?" he said, increasing the volume of his voice. "You know what I did!" he shouted. BB dropped his head and feigned crying. Then his somber mood changed to one of insane laughter.

"It was tragic, Mr. Cook," Billy Ray said in mock sincerity. "Perhaps you read about it in the newspaper. First he cut off all his father's fingers. Then he cut him up into small bite-size pieces—and fed him to the two family dogs."

BB turned to Billy Ray and winked. Then he reached under his army duster and slowly removed the pair of tree loppers. "Can I cut off a few of this douchebag's fingers now, Billy?" he asked, clicking the loppers in front of Cook's face.

Cook was now twitching uncontrollably. He had involuntary movement, and urine puddled on the floor under his feet.

"That depends. I've got a feeling that you've been here long enough to know where all the bodies are buried. A weasel like you would keep files on certain things, for leverage...to protect himself, you know, if the shit ever hit the fan. So I figure, you're going to give me what I want—now!"

Mr. Cook entered the back vault room. He walked down a long row of dark-green metal filing cabinets and fumbled with his keys as he opened one of the lockers, all the while keeping a watchful eye on BB. After he open the cabinet, BB pushed him aside using the tree loppers.

In alphabetical order," BB said, "Adamo, Blu, Clements."

"Did you say Clements?" Billy Ray asked, reaching out to take a look at the file.

He flipped through the file, looking at canceled checks and bank drafts and a letter from Coyle with instructions for Cook. "What the fuck is this all about?" Billy Ray shouted, grabbing him by the jacket collar.

"It wasn't me. It was Senator Bryant's office and his lawyer, Coyle. That dumb nigger wouldn't sell them his land, so..."

"So they railroaded him. That black man happens to be a friend of mine. He's rotting in prison for what you assholes did! Let me see my file, BB?" Billy Ray flipped through the pages of his file, occasionally turning the file sideways to look at charts and graphs or to read. "I knew it," he said, looking at the original designation for the fault line that ran under the old silver mine. "The questions are who and why."

"It's all in there," he said, nodding toward the file. "It was Bryant and the board he controls at California Power and Light. It was the only location in California that had the requirements and was economically feasible enough to build the facility. It was perfect except—"

"Except," Billy Ray said, interrupting him, "it was too close to a fault line, so they had you move it just far enough away to meet the permitting requirements. Is that about right, Cook?"

"Yes, it is."

"And what did you get in return for helping them with this fraud?"

Cook seemed reluctant to answer Billy Ray until BB gave him a nudge. "M-my son got a job with the state, and my daughter is a congressional aide in DC."

"Suppose there was an earthquake strong enough to cause the dam to fail. Thousands of people downstream would have been killed. And that would be all your doing. Injustices like this cannot happen without bureaucrats like you selling out!"

"I'm just a p-public servant. I do w-what I'm told."

BB grabbed hold of Cook's hand as if he were about to begin cutting off his fingers. "Shut the fuck up, you sniveling bastard," BB said. "Come on, Billy; let me cut off just a few fingers."

"Please, make him stop," Cook pleaded. "W-what's he g-going to do? I have a family."

"So did I," Billy Ray said, trying to control his rage. "You want to know what he's going to do? It all depends on you. You can be smart and not tell anyone about our visit, or stupid, and my friend will have to come by to pay you a visit...alone. Come on BB, let's get out of here. This servant of the public makes me sick, and leave the loppers here as a reminder for what may be in store for him if he opens his mouth."

BB threw the tree loppers on the desk, which make Mr. Cook jump and wince. Just before BB closed the door, he stuck his head back inside. "Remember what I said about piano lessons," he said, shaking his head.

Semper Fi

ON THE WAY back to Silver Verde, the Wiz sent Billy Ray a text message and told him that Colonel Clay had returned and would be waiting for them at the Village at Silver Verde. When they arrived, they quickly switched vans. The colonel was wearing civilian clothing and a wide-brimmed leather Stetson hat. The Wiz had told the colonel about the "visitors," and he got into the van quickly, keeping a watchful eye to avoid being detected.

"Nice to see you in better surroundings," the colonel said, patting Billy Ray on his back.

"And what am I, chopped liver?" BB asked jokingly.

"Nice to see you too, BB. How'd you like my plan, William?"

"It was flawless, but I don't think Bishop or Standz bought it. Why else would they have sent those spooks here?"

"By the time anyone, including Standz, sifts through the rubble and figures out what really happened, you will be in the final moves of your end game. If everything else goes as planned, you'll be cleared, exonerated...at least from the former charges," he said, smiling. "You were right about Catalina. She's some woman. If not for her, you'd still be in Tywater."

"She is a good person," Billy Ray said, recalling her sad smile. "Lonely though. I guess life doesn't always turn out the way people plan."

"Why, William Blu," the colonel said, eyes squinting as he tried to figure out his admiration for the doctor. "If I didn't know any better, I'd think you have a hard-on for her."

"It's not like that."

"Good, because she's more my type...and age. I'm retiring next year. If I'm still alive or not rotting somewhere in a brig, maybe I'll look her up."

"Maybe if I'm still alive and not rotting in a prison," Billy Ray said, ribbing the colonel, "maybe we'll double date."

"Could be," the Colonel said, nodding. "Why not? Did you find what you were looking for at the county records office?"

"Ah, Mar-dorn, I'll say," BB interjected. "I used my charming personality to persuade that weasel to give it up!"

"Knowing you, BB, I don't think that's what happened," the colonel said, laughing.

"BB terrorized the clerk. He literally pissed his pants," Billy Ray said as he handed the colonel the files.

The colonel flipped through the files. "What's this Clements file all about?"

"He was one of my friends at Tywater. He used to own the land where they built the Village at Silver Verde. My lawyer, Coyle, Senator Bryant, and his partners stole it right out from underneath him. It's all in there."

"Wow, what a bonus! What do you want to do with this?"

"I don't know yet. You have to figure that Bryant has the governor and most of the government officials in California in his pocket."

"I agree. I served in Iraq with the man who was appointed the US attorney general in California. He's a straight shooter...former head of the state police. I'll get it to him, and maybe justice will be served, but you never know. You never know if the power of those pulling the strings can turn a man. What's in your file?"

"Everything I've always suspected. Bryant was behind the whole thing. Since the fault line that ran thorough my property was never well defined, he had them move it just far enough from the proposed site of the dam to get through the permitting process."

"That intel should be released soon, but not yet."

"I agree."

"Now for the bad news," the colonel said, raising his eyebrows. "I overheard in the Pentagon that Bishop is going to declassify some of the information from your doctored file, so it can be released. Now that everyone thinks you're dead, he doesn't want the public turning you into a martyr. He's trying to dispel the mystique that the Wiz built up about you on his pirate website to bury you, destroy your reputation, and discredit the website, all in one shot. You're going to be portrayed as an insubordinate disgraced soldier who disobeyed orders, resulting in some of your comrade's deaths. But remember, I have the uncensored file and transcript. We'll wait until Bishop releases the phony file, and then we'll shove the real one right up his keister. In that way, you'll be cleared, at least in the public's eye, and we'll catch that son of a bitch in a lie, a cover-up."

When they arrived back at the command bunker, the colonel said he was exhausted from the long trip and went to sleep. Billy Ray was also tired. As he lay in his bunk, he read through the report and transcript of his military-court proceedings. It brought back memories that he had pushed deep into the recesses of his mind in an attempt to forget them. His eyes were growing heavy. He put down the file and drifted off to sleep.

⇥▬◉ ◉▬⇤

All the witnesses at his precourt hearing were transferred to the US command headquarters in Kandahar, Afghanistan. The décor of the small courtroom was stark and drab. The walls in the room were pale yellow and peeling. Metal folding chairs were set up to accommodate about twenty people.

In front of the courtroom was a long oak table. A small US flag was positioned in the corner of the room, sprouting from the mouth of a cast-bronze eagle floor stand. On the oak table were papers, portable filing cabinets, a pitcher of ice water, several glasses, and a Bible. Sitting next to the table was a male military stenographer, waiting to record the testimony. A creaking Casablanca fan was spinning slowly and did little to cool the stifling hot and stuffy room. As the officers entered the room, everyone rose to attention.

US Marine Major General William Nault had been appointed as the judge advocate and would preside over the hearing. Flanking the general were Lieutenant Colonel Richardson and Colonel Plasse. As Major General Nault sat down, he immediately began sorting through the papers in front of him. He was in full dress uniform, displaying the many medals he was awarded over his forty years of service. He was frail looking, tall and thin, with deep-blue eyes set deeply in an angular, gaunt face. His hair was cropped short. The hair that was visible was almost pure white.

The stenographer stood to address the courtroom. "In compliance with the Uniform Code of Military Justice, this finding of facts, case number A4211, comes to order. Major General William S. Nault, presiding. All seated."

"Proceed," Nault said to the prosecutor.

The military prosecutor reviewed his paperwork and called Colonel Bishop to the witness stand. After he was sworn in, the colonel looked at Billy Ray and then up at the ceiling, avoiding making eye contact with him.

"Colonel Bishop, describe for the court the details on the night of April twenty-second, at approximately eighteen hundred hours."

"Sergeant Blu had just returned from stateside, where he was attending his father's funeral. Base told him that his unit had not returned from their mission. All attempts to communicate with them were unsuccessful. The last location of their GPS was several klicks—I mean miles—into Pakistan. Sergeant Blu wanted to take a unit and go after them. I told him that command had been notified and were formulating an extraction plan."

"And what happened next, Colonel?"

"He became enraged, belligerent, and disrespectful and said it was a 'cluster fuck, and by the time command made a decision, they'd all be dead.' I immediately remanded him to base and restricted him to his barracks."

"And then, Colonel?"

"About an hour later, I was informed that he had commandeered a Black Hawk and flew into Pakistan. Several hours later he returned with five men. Lieutenant Cortez and Sergeant Ranaldi had been killed and were not returned to base until the extraction team arrived the next day. While on the mission, Sergeant Blu was shot. A bullet grazed his heart—the left ventricle, I believe the doctors later said. He underwent emergency surgery, and when his condition stabilized, he was flown to base hospital in Kandahar."

"So it is your testimony that you remanded Sergeant Blu to base and placed him on barracks restriction and he disobeyed those orders?"

"Yes."

"That will be all, Colonel."

Billy Ray was directed to take the stand and sworn in. As the prosecutor was reviewing his notes, Major General Nault addressed Billy Ray. "Sergeant Blu, you have the condolences of the court on the death of your father. We acknowledge that it's been a trying couple of months for you. Are you fully recovered from your injuries, Sergeant?"

"Yes, sir."

"It was touch-and-go there for a while."

"Yes, sir."

"You may proceed," Nault said to the prosecutor.

"Sergeant Blu, a yes-or-no answer to the questions will suffice." He turned his back to Billy Ray and paced the floor as he spoke. "After learning that the men in your unit did not return from their mission, did Colonel Bishop remand you to base?"

"Yes."

"And did Colonel Bishop, in fact, restrict you to your barracks?"

"Yes."

"And did you, in fact, commandeer a Black Hawk helicopter, contravening a direct order to remain on base?"

"Yes. I took the Black Hawk to rescue the men in my unit."

"A yes-or-no answer will suffice, Sergeant," the prosecutor said, approaching him.

"I swore two oaths," Billy Ray said, looking directly at Colonel Bishop. "To tell the truth, the *whole* truth, not half-truths to cover up someone's mistake."

"Your Honor," the prosecutor said to Nault. "Direct the defendant to answer the questions asked in the manner requested."

Major General Nault waved his hand at the prosecutor as if to say *enough*. "Lieutenant, Sergeant Blu is not a defendant yet. In light of the fact that he waved his right to counsel at these proceedings, we'll grant him some leeway, a little leeway," he said, looking at Billy Ray, "to express and define his answers. I am curious though, as to what was the other oath you swore to, Sergeant Blu?"

"The same one all marines follow, sir. The same code you swore to when you first joined the marines: to leave no man behind. I believe I have fulfilled both of my oaths, sir."

Nault bowed his head and smiled.

As the prosecutor reviewed his notes, Lieutenant Colonel Richardson handed Nault a file containing photographs of the enemy base where the men had been rescued. As he viewed the pictures, he tilted several on their side to get a better view of the graphic carnage inflicted on the enemy that had been attributed to Billy Ray. The last photograph he viewed was of an eighteen-inch, blood-soaked sai sword deeply imbedded in the neck of a Taliban soldier.

"Lieutenant, I have one question for Sergeant Blu before you proceed," Nault said, with a half smile on his face. "Is a sais sword standard issue for the marines these days, Sergeant?"

"No, sir," he said, quickly repressing a smile.

"Proceed, Lieutenant."

"So is it your testimony that you disobeyed several orders issued by Colonel Bishop on the night of April twenty-second?"

"Yes."

"The prosecution rests, sir."

"Sergeant Blu, you may step down," Lieutenant Colonel Richardson said.

The stenographer stood up and told everyone that there would be a twenty-minute recess and then the court would render its judgment. After the board returned into the courtroom, Billy Ray was asked to stand.

"Sergeant Blu," Nault said, "the judicial board and I have taken into account many factors in arriving at our decision. We have reviewed your military record. It has been exemplary up until now. Your two Purple Hearts and your Silver Star for," he said, looking down at his notes, "conspicuous gallantry and intrepidly in action against the enemy is well noted." He held out his right hand with an open palm. "However, on one hand, your action took great bravery and is to be emulated and commended, but on the other hand," he said as he raised his left palm, "your insubordination is to be condemned. It is these conflicting circumstances that not only presented us with a dilemma but conversely helped us to reach a unanimous decision. We gave great weight to the testimony of the survivors in your unit who all testified that at the time of their rescue, they were being systematically tortured and summarily executed. However this is not germane to the issue of your insubordination. At the time you disobeyed several direct orders, you could not have ascertained with any degree of certainty that these atrocities were in fact taking place. In retrospect, your intuition and insight were correct. Do you agree with our assessment up until now, Sergeant?"

"Yes, sir."

"Furthermore, it is a fact that these men were rescued from sovereign Pakistan soil. Even though your action saved the lives of most of the men in your unit, your insubordination could have caused an international incident with our already strained relationship with the Pakistani government. Sometimes, Sergeant Blu, there are issues that are vital to the national interests of our government that are more important and outweigh the life or lives of an individual or individuals in the military. If orders are disobeyed for matters of conscience, there would be a breakdown of discipline, and chaos would reign. I ask you, Sergeant Blu, suppose every marine thought the same way you do?"

"In all due respect, sir, I believe they all do, well most of them," he said, looking over his shoulder in the direction of Colonel Bishop. "If every marine thought the same way as I do, yourself included, then I would not be *semper fidelis* to the code of the marine corps to have acted any differently."

Major General Nault raised his eyebrows as he thought about what Billy Ray said. He smiled, along with the other members of the board. "Looks like I stepped on a land mine with that question, Sergeant Blu." General Nault looked to the far corner of the room, where the Prince of Darkness sat. "It has come to our attention that you have received an offer to serve this country in, let us say, a far different capacity, where the powers that be felt that your unique set of skills and lethal talent would have been, hopefully, put to better use. And are we correct in assuming that you refused this offer?"

"Yes, sir."

"Then Sergeant Blu, in accordance with the finding of facts, it is the decision of this Military Judicial Board that your behavior did not exceed the threshold, nor is there sufficient grounds to proceed with a military court-martial. However, we find that sufficient evidence exists that you have violated the Uniform Code of Military Conduct befitting a US marine. Since you only have two months left on your tour of duty, you will be dismissed from service at the conclusion of this hearing. It will not be an honorable or a dishonorable discharge, merely an early termination of your military service. This proceeding contains testimony and details that fall under the US Secrecy Act. As such, the accounting of this hearing will be sealed. You are so informed that revealing any of the details of this hearing is a serious crime punishable under the US Secrecy Act as treason. Do you acknowledge and accept the findings and mandates of this court?"

"I do, sir."

Major General Nault banged down his gavel. "This finding of facts is concluded."

As the members of the board gathered up their papers and files, Nault called out to Billy Ray. Although he was addressing him, he was staring at Colonel Bishop with a look of disdain. Bishop became uneasy and quickly turned away. "Sergeant Blu, good luck. Off the record, I wish I had a dozen men like you when they gave me my first command in Nam. Semper fi," he said, saluting Billy Ray.

"Hoo-rah," Billy Ray responded, saluting the general.

Pinheads and Patriots

June 30, 6:00 p.m. Pacific time

MIDNIGHT WANTED TO survey the topography outside the town to locate vantage points in the event that he would have an encounter with the snipers. BB joined him, and they parked their van in the woods on the outskirts of town.

"While you're up there," BB said, nodding his head toward the hills surrounding the town, "I'm going for a little stroll in town."

"You think that's wise?" Midnight asked, raising his eyebrows.

"*Va fungool!* Don't let your head explode, Midnight. I'm just gonna go to a package store. I'll be right back."

"All right," Midnight said reluctantly as he began walking up the steep incline. "And BB, behave."

It was almost sunset. The large orange orb setting over the distant horizon casted long shadows over the area and illuminated the waves of clouds in a backdrop sea of blue with a soft pink and orange glow.

Midnight surveyed the town through a pair of military infrared binoculars equipped with a range finder to pinpoint certain locations. He identified several locations where he believed snipers would set up. Then he picked out the best vantage point for himself to pick them off. As he looked through the binoculars, he scanned the area near the van and became alarmed because BB was nowhere in sight. A half hour earlier he saw him trying to enter a liquor store, but it was closed. He assumed that BB had returned to the van. He returned to the van and waited twenty minutes before he called the Wiz and told him that BB had disappeared. The Wiz rewound the surveillance tape of Main Street and located him entering Sparkey's Tavern.

"Did you locate him?" Midnight asked.

"That lush went into a bar. This is a recipe for disaster!"

"Where's Billy?"

"He's still sleeping."

"Wake him, now!" Midnight said, with concern in his voice. "You know how ornery BB gets when he's drunk. He's liable to start a riot."

"All right, return to the bunker. I'll let the colonel sleep and wake Billy. He knows the town better than we do, and the best way to get BB out undetected."

The Wiz woke Billy Ray and told him what had happened. As soon as Midnight entered the bunker, he went into the anteroom where the weapons and equipment were kept.

"Midnight and I will go into town and get BB," the Wiz said to Billy Ray. "You're too hot. They'll just be waiting for you to make a mistake like this."

"He's my responsibility. I'll be in and out before anyone knows I'm there."

Midnight came back into the main room wearing battle fatigues. His face was painted with black-and-dark-green camouflage makeup. Slung over one of his shoulders was the duffel bag containing the AIVC and over his other shoulder was a long black case containing his sniper rifle. Strapped on his belt were cartridges with high-ballistic rounds and a long black steel night bayonet.

Billy Ray first looked at Midnight and then at the Wiz and laughed. "What, are we going on one of your 'Midnight Madness' search-and-destroy missions?"

"Better to err on the side of caution, that's my motto," he said, with deadpan seriousness. "Just drop me off on the outskirts of town. I'll cover your ass."

Billy Ray took the Stetson hat that the colonel was wearing when he arrived in Silver Verde to hide his face. "All right Midnight, let's go, but don't turn this into something that it's not."

"Wait," the Wiz said, opening up a small metal box next to his electronic equipment. He took out two small mics and earphones similar to the ones the secret service field operatives wore. "Put these on so we can communicate with each other."

Jack and Loretta Sparks owned and operated Sparky's Tavern. With the influx of construction workers to build the hydroelectric dam and the service sector, the population grew in Silver Verde. They expanded and renovated the old pool hall into a tavern with a full kitchen, serving finger foods and deli sandwiches. Strategically placed, high up on the walls of the tavern, were six widescreen, high-definition TVs on closed-caption except for sporting events. To the rear of the tavern was a game room with six pool tables and various electronic, coin-operated games. Because many off-duty ISS soldiers frequented the tavern, Jack had placed a sign at the entrance stating that weapons of any type were not allowed in his establishment.

BB sat at a table in the far corner of the tavern. He sat alone with a half-empty bottle of Jack Daniels. He was intoxicated but still lucid. On the top of the table, set up in front of two empty chairs, were two full shot glasses of whiskey, one for each of his dead comrades, Rinaldi and Cortez. A cover band was setting up their equipment on a small stage next to a long red oak-and-mahogany wood bar with shiny brass step rails and trim. Scantily clad waitresses were scurrying throughout the crowded tavern carrying trays of beer, mixed drinks, and food. Sitting at the table next to BB were off-duty ISS soldiers in their midtwenties; some of them in their early thirties. They were loud, horsing around, and mildly intoxicated.

Fox News Network's *Factor* program had just begun. As the host, Bill O'Reilly began with the "Talking Points" segment of the show, and a military photograph of Billy Ray was posted to the right of the screen. Next to the picture was the Special Forces insignia worn by the men in his unit. One of the McFarlane brothers, who was playing pool, saw the picture and yelled out for Jack to turn up the volume.

As O'Reilly spoke, the patrons became silent. "I don't like to make light of a tragedy," he went on to say, "but according to a file recently declassified by General Bishop, director of the ISS, William 'Billy Ray' Blu, a resident of Silver Verde, California, who died along with unknown accomplices in a botched prison escape from Tywater Federal Penitentiary, disobeyed a direct order, resulting in the deaths of two soldiers in his unit. According to the file, former Special Forces Marine Sergeant Blu was dishonorably discharged for his insubordination.

Federal authorities are still trying to piece together who his accomplices were that apparently died along with him when they crashed their helicopters into the side of the high cliffs outside Tywater.

They are also investigating how they were able to commandeer two fully armed helicopters, and where the breakdown in military security was. If the contents of these files are correct, Mr. Blu and his inept gang are pinheads, and they may have gotten their 'just deserts,' ironically, at their own hands. We'll keep you informed."

As O'Reilly went on to the next topic, the tavern returned to its noisy activity. In the command bunker, the Wiz and Colonel Clay had been watching the Fox program.

"I knew that asshole Bishop would feed the media that doctored file," the colonel said. "Wiz, scan in the real file and send it out to all the news outlets. Make sure Fox gets the first copy. Bishop wants to play hardball. Well, let the games begin."

After seeing what O'Reilly had said, BB raised his glass for a toast. "B-bullshit," he said, slurring his words. "Here's to you, Billy Ray."

The ISS soldiers at the next table heard his toast and gave each other an odd look. One of the younger soldiers nudged one of his comrades next to him. "I wish I could have come up against that pinhead, Billy Ray," he said, loud enough so that BB could overhear him. "I would have fucked him up, just like we took out his brother."

"You hear what that dipshit said, Rinaldi?" BB said, talking to the empty chair next to him. "That FNG thinks he could take out Billy Ray."

"You talking to me, country boy?" the young soldier said, standing up.

BB laughed. "Careful what you wish for, FNG."

"What did you call me?"

"I think he called you an FNG," one of the soldiers said, ribbing him. "A fucking new guy."

"Fucking new guy! Fuck you, country boy, and that pinhead Billy Ray," he said, standing up.

The lieutenant at the table grabbed him by his arm. "Sit down. Don't start any shit with the locals. He's drunk. Leave him alone."

In the far corner of the room, sitting with his back against the wall, Ocho sat with several other farmworkers watching the confrontation. He kept an eye on them as he wrapped his massive hand around a mug of beer and took a sip.

Carla stood outside the tavern, looking through the window at the crowd. Because of her nocturnal activities, Jack Sparks banned her from entering his establishment. She wore a low-cut rose-colored dress, exposing the top portion of her large, protruding breasts. Her makeup was overdone as she tried to hide the ravages of her age and appear younger. Inside the tavern the cover band started to play. As the female singer took the stage, the noise in the room subsided. She began with an old Mary Hopkins ballad, "Those Were the Days."

As Carla heard the song, she remembered it all too well. Each time she heard that song, at various periods of her life, it had a more profound meaning and would always make her introspective and sad. It brought back memories of better days, all the wrong decisions she had made, and unfulfilled dreams.

> Once upon a time there was a tavern
> Where we used to raise a glass or two,
> Remember how we laughed away the hours
> Think of all the great things we would do.
> Those were the days my friend…

As she listened to the song, she reminisced about better times in her life. She was young, and the future looked bright and full of promise. She remembered dancing with Billy Ray at the Harvest Festival. Whenever the reality of her life would bring her down, she fantasized of being with Billy Ray, if only for one night. She knew he loved Jenny. Everyone in town knew that, and it was a forgone conclusion that one day they would get married. But as it is with human nature, sometimes the more you know you can't have something, the more you desire it. She remembered the last time she had seen Billy Ray and he said that he would take a rain check on someday. As the years of hardship and disappointment had weighed her down, she came to realize that for people like her, someday usually meant never. And now, Billy Ray was gone, and with that, any hope that her dream would ever be realized. She looked at her reflection in the window and a tear ran down her cheek. She was approaching forty and realized that the better part of her life was now behind her.

> Just tonight I stood before the tavern
> Nothing seemed the way it used to be,
> In the glass I saw a strange reflection
> Was that lonely women really me?
> Through the door there came familiar laughter
> I saw your face and heard you call my name
> Oh my friend we're older but no wiser
> For in our hearts the dreams are still the same.
> Those were the days...

Carla was so absorbed in the memories that the song invoked that she did not realize that someone was standing behind her. Suddenly, there was another reflection in the window next to hers. At first, she thought the image of Billy Ray was merely a projection of her thoughts. Then she heard a familiar voice, a reassuring voice, call out her name. When she turned around, she was so startled that she took a step backward, nearly falling down. When she realized that it was really him, she threw her arms around him, hugging him tightly. She kissed him several times as tears of joy filled her eyes.

"How? I mean...they said you were dead."

"Are you glad to see me?" he asked as they both laughed.

Carla wiped the tears from her eyes, smearing her makeup. "I still can't believe it," she said, kissing him again. Does Jenny know you're alive?"

"I think so, but I'm not sure."

"Should I go to her ranch and tell her?"

"For your sake, hers, and mine, you can't tell anyone you saw me. I know it's abrupt, but you really have to be going. It may get very dangerous around here very soon."

"I have so many questions."

"We'll see each other again, but I can't make any promises," he said, patronizing her, trying to get her to leave the area.

"Someday," she said, smiling.

"Sure, someday."

Carla hugged him again and began walking down the dimly lit street. He watched her until she disappeared around the corner. Then he looked into the window of the tavern and spotted BB sitting in the far corner of the room. Inside the tavern, the soldier who had confronted BB nudged the soldier next to him. He noticed that BB had a tattoo on each of his forearms.

"Watch me goof on this hick. Hey, country boy," he said, leaning over toward BB, "what does that tat stand for?"

BB drank down a shot with one gulp. "W-which one?" he slurred.

"How 'bout that one?" he asked, pointing to an old faded tattoo on his left forearm.

BB winked in the direction of one of the empty chairs. "This o-one," he said, trying to point to the tattoo on his left arm. The tattoo was of a black, round bomb with a lit fuse, the kind usually seen in cartoons. Surrounding the bomb was a faded red heart with the words *Moms and Bombs* underneath. "That's w-what I do for a livin'. I b-blow things up. No, l-let me corr-ect that. I blow th-things down."

"Really!" he said, laughing as he turned toward the other soldier. "You want to see a real man's tattoo?" he said, rolling up the sleeve of his uniform, exposing his bicep with the ISS tattoo.

BB looked over and laughed. "*Wow!*" he said, mocking the soldier. "An ISS tattoo? Not *the* ISS?"

"Sure is," he said, moving his bicep from side to side for BB to get a better look.

"The ISS is a…a fucking joke," BB said, laughing in the soldier's face.

"Are you rat-fucking my unit, country boy?" the soldier asked, growing irate. "You'll never have anything like it!"

"You got it backward, FNG," BB said, moving his other forearm to display his other tattoo. The tattoo was an inverted ace of spades with a marine corps emblem in the middle and a yellow lightning bolt running through it. Underneath the tattoo were the words in Latin, Potius mori Quam Foedare, *Death before Dishonor.*

A lieutenant at the table saw the tattoo. "Hey, Garcia," he said to the young soldier, "that's the insignia that was just displayed on the screen a couple of minutes ago. It's the one that the men in Blu's Special Forces unit wore. You there," he called out to BB, "were you in the Special Forces, in Blu's unit?"

BB laughed at the lieutenant's question. "Hey, GI Joe, ask him," he said, nodding in the direction of one of the empty chairs.

"Hey, country boy," Garcia said, shoving BB. "My lieutenant asked you a question!"

"*Fuck* you!" BB said, laughing in his face. "And in case you didn't hear me the f-first time, *fuck* you again!"

Billy Ray was just about to enter the tavern when Midnight began talking to the Wiz and him. "The area is hot. Repeat, the area is hot. Do you copy?"

"Copy that," they both answered.

"Located five, but can't find the sixth. Can see your position. Get the package and get the hell out."

As Billy Ray entered the tavern, the band began playing their rendition of an old Marshal Tucker Band song, "Heard It in a Love Song." He made his way through the crowd and saw Ocho slouched over, several tables down from where BB was sitting. As their eyes met, Ocho straightened up, and a wide smile appeared on his face. He was about to get up, but Billy Ray motioned for him to stay put. Another man, sitting in the far corner of the room with his back against the wall, was keeping an eye on him. He took a small picture out of his top pocket and then looked once again at Billy Ray. It was the sixth CIA agent who came into the tavern to pick up some cross talk and intel from the locals. He couldn't be sure it was him; the cowboy hat obscured his facial features. Although weapons were not allowed in the tavern, he reached under his jacket and cocked his 9-mm Glock handgun.

Private Garcia was now so infuriated with BB's laughter and insults that he grabbed him by the back of his shirt collar. "You got a big mouth, country boy. Maybe I'll have to close it for you!"

Billy Ray took the soldier's hand off BB. "Time to leave, Robert. Your wife is worried sick about you."

"Another cowboy," the soldier said, sizing up Billy Ray. "You know this asshole?"

"Don't mind him. He means you no disrespect. He's just drunk. I apologize for anything he might have said. Come on, Robert. Dinner's getting cold."

BB looked up at him and smiled. "OK, Billy Ray, I'm coming."

Billy Ray winced. He quickly helped him up and began walking toward the exit.

"Did that asshole just call you Billy Ray?" the soldier asked.

Billy Ray did not turn around. He just kept on walking with BB in tow. The group had just finished their song. As they were taking their bows, he noticed that two of the McFarlane brothers were between him and the exit. Although he put his head down and tried to avoid them, the older brother spotted him.

"Blu," he said, aghast, mouth open, nudging his brother. "It's Billy Ray!"

Billy Ray rolled his eyes. He tried to plan a course of action, but with the unexpected chain of events, it left him with very few options without inflicting collateral damage and injuries to the locals. The CIA agent began talking into his mic, giving a description of Billy Ray to the snipers waiting in the darkness. He got up quickly, reached under his jacket, and pulled his gun.

Private Garcia yelled out across the room to the other ISS soldiers. "It's Blu! Billy Ray Blu!" He tried to put a choke hold on him. Billy Ray grabbed his wrist, twisting it backward. Then he spun and hit him with a roundhouse forearm just under his Adam's apple, knocking the wind out of him. Garcia reeled backward against the bar and slithered down to the floor, holding his neck.

BB laughed as tables, chairs, and beer bottles flew across the room. He leaned over where the soldier was on the floor gasping for air, trying to regain his breath. "Wow! You r-really fucked up Billy Ray," he said, mocking him. "Told you, FNG, to be c-careful what you wished for."

The CIA agent pushed his way through the crowd with his gun held high, trying to get closer to Billy Ray. Ocho saw him and quickly picked up a table. Using it like a battering ram, he smashed the agent into the bar. His neck snapped backward, breaking his collar bone, and his gun discharged. Billy Ray turned as he heard the shot and saw the unconscious agent on the floor and Ocho standing over him. He pointed to Ocho, who in return pointed back to him. As Billy Ray grabbed BB by the back of his collar, he saw that the McFarlane brothers had cleared a path for him to the exit.

"Get going, Billy," the older brother said. "We've got your back."

As they left the tavern, Midnight told Billy Ray that a convoy of ISS was heading into town from the north, cutting them off from the van, and to head south and then double back. As they headed south, someone came up from behind them.

"Halt! Hands up where I can see them, or I'll blow you apart."

Billy Ray put his hands up and glanced over his shoulder. It was one of the CIA snipers, and he had his rifle trained on Billy Ray. He saw someone coming quickly from behind the sniper. The sniper's rifle went off, nearly striking Billy Ray, as Carla hit him from behind with her pocketbook. As his rifle fell to the ground, he fell backward but quickly gained his footing and reached for his handgun. A shot rang out in the distance, and at almost the same instant, the agent's chest exploded, sending fragments of bone, pieces of flesh, and torrents of blood covering Carla, Billy Ray, and BB. The agent was lying on the ground in a contorted position with a gaping hole through the middle of his chest.

Carla stood dazed, wiping the blood off her face and then looking at her hands. She didn't know if the blood was her own.

"Carla, you're all right. It's not your blood. Get down."

A few more shots rang out as the other snipers tried to take him out. One hit a car in front of them and the other shattered the windows of Sparky's Tavern. They crouched over as they made their way to Carla's car. They heard several more shots in the distance. Every time a shot rang out, he heard Midnight's insane laughter in his earphone followed by him saying, "Who's your Daddy?"

Carla helped Billy Ray put BB into the backseat of her old green Toyota Camry. As they drove, BB leaned over and looked at Carla with his eyes barely open. "Hey, Billy Ray, is this J-Jenny?"

"I wish," Carla said.

"Mar-done, Billy. What a rack on her!"

"Behave, BB," Billy Ray said, turning around.

"OK," he said, slouching back just before he passed out.

"Don't mind him, Carla. He's drunk."

She looked back at BB, who was out cold, snoring. "I think he's cute. Is he a friend of yours?"

"Like a brother."

Carla didn't answer him at first. She thought about how close Billy and his brother were. "I'm sorry about Junior. Everyone liked him."

He just nodded his head in agreement. They drove down a dark dirt road until he told her to stop. Billy Ray helped BB out of the back of the car. He was still groggy but able to walk.

"Where are you going, Billy? We're in the middle of nowhere."

"It's better if you don't know."

"Who was that man that was killed in front of Sparkey's?"

Billy Ray held up BB and began walking toward the brush. "Men that were sent here to kill me...and more will come."

"You take care of yourself, Billy Ray. A part of me died when they said you were dead. I don't think I could take that again."

"Go right home, Carla. Main Street is not going to be a safe place tonight."

"Will I see you again?" she asked as he disappeared into the darkness.

"Someday, Carla. Someday."

"Sure...someday," she said to herself, shaking her head. "Someday."

Billy Ray returned to the bunker and put BB to bed. Colonel Clay and the Wiz were monitoring the activity around the town. Dozens of ISS soldiers were scouring the streets, armed with M-16 automatic rifles, looking for Billy Ray and interrogating anyone they would come upon.

"Did Midnight return?" he asked.

"No," the colonel said. "We've been trying to contact him, but he's maintaining radio silence."

"He's smart," the Wiz said. "He knows they may be trying to triangulate his position if he talks. What happened out there?"

"Everything that could go wrong did, except for Midnight. I think he killed all the snipers, except the one in the bar."

Colonel Clay smiled. "That's my boy!"

Suddenly, the outer perimeter motion detectors rang inside the bunker. Midnight drove the van into one of the metal buildings and then leisurely walked into the bunker. He had a distorted grin on his face. His hands, arms, and camouflaged clothing were covered with dried blood.

"What happened, Captain?" the colonel asked.

"It's not my blood. I hope everyone had as much fun tonight as I did. I never feel more alive than when I'm killing someone."

The Wiz looked at Billy Ray and the colonel, shaking his head. "What did you do, Midnight?"

"After I took out all those spooks, I rounded them up—we're going to have to hose out the van…messy business—and I gift wrapped all of them, except for the ones inside and outside the bar room, and dumped the bodies in the village green's gazebo."

"Jesus, I wonder how this is going to play with the media?" the colonel asked. "But more important, thanks to BB's stupidity, they now know, for certain, that you're alive. Most of the blame for this will be pinned on you."

"No, it won't, Colonel," Midnight said as he took out his customary two cigarettes taped together and lit them up. "Not if the Wiz still has the military photographs of the spooks I killed. Well, do you, Wiz?"

"Yes, I do."

"You send out their military IDs to all the stations you sent the other information. How're Bishop and the other brass going to explain what CIA assassins were doing operating illegally on domestic soil in Silver Verde? Am I right, Colonel?"

"You are, Captain. It just might work. Depends how the media spins it. Wiz, send it out ASAP. Let's see how it plays."

→►◙ ◙◄←

The next morning Main Street became inundated with agents from the FBI, AFT, CIA, Homeland Security, and members of various other state and local agencies. Several ISS Black Hawk helicopters were continually crawling across the sky above Silver Verde. The area surrounding the gazebo had been cordoned off with red caution tape, and a line of state police were blocking access to the road. Curious residents were made to stay hundreds of feet away. The state coroner examined the bodies, and after dozens of pictures and forensic evidence were taken, their bodies were transported to an undisclosed location.

Once again, Silver Verde became the center of the news media's attention as every national and local newspaper and station had dispatched cameramen and reporters to cover the breaking story. They were interviewing any of the residents of Silver Verde who had any information about what took place in Sparky's Tavern. They were also trying to gather details and verify whether Billy Ray was in fact alive, and if he was responsible for the carnage.

As the Wiz looked at the activity in the location of the road leading to the dam, he became curious and alarmed. There were dozens of men working with heavy equipment, digging foundations and unloading huge crates with fork lifts from a flatbed trailer. He couldn't figure out what they were doing. Men from California Power and Light were in a bucket truck tying into electrical lines and inserting thick black wires into gray PVC conduit leading to the area where the men were working. Other men were erecting tall fencing with barbed wire all the way up the incline to the hydroelectric facility.

As he continued watching the men, he received an e-mail on his oscillating untraceable site from the Fox News Network legal department. They were interested in running the story but needed to verify the accuracy and authenticity of the information he had sent. He immediately sent additional documentation to satisfy their inquiry.

-->===◎ ◎===<--

8:00 p.m. Pacific time

The next night the men in the bunker were playing hi-lo-jack, waiting for *The O'Reilly Factor* on Fox News Network to begin. As the program began, O'Reilly began with his talking points segment. Then he held a stack of papers in his hand that he collated by tapping them on the desk several times.

"Tonight we have a bizarre and interesting story. It almost reads like a Hollywood script that has so many implausible plot twists and turns that you'd have to suspend all disbelief just to follow the storyline. We ran a story the other night that seemed pretty straightforward about William Blu, a Special Forces marine sergeant who died in a failed prison escape from Tywater Federal Penitentiary along with his accomplices. The information we received from General Bishop, director of the ISS, was that Sergeant Blu was dishonorably discharged for disobeying a direct order, which resulted in the deaths of two men in his unit. We at Fox now know that the information in this first story was false, and the failed prison escape and subsequent deaths of Blu and his accomplices was an elaborate ruse, carried out with military precision.

"Before Fox ran this story, we asked General Bishop for a comment. A spokesman for the general denied all allegations stating for the record that the claims were elaborate fabrications. Legal staff representing the government went before Federal Judge William Anthony requesting an injunction preventing Fox from reporting the story. In court they cited the precedent-setting Reynolds case, claiming privilege and that the information was in the interest of national security and should not be divulged. After taking testimony and reading the briefs, Judge Anthony did not grant the government an injunction, citing that General Bishop had already declassified most of the information and that millions of citizens had already seen the entire file, which was leaked on a pirate website. Judge Anthony granted the government one stipulation that Fox could not reveal the exact geographical location of where the incident took place.

So with all this nonsense behind us, here's what we now believe to be true. Sergeant Blu did in fact contravene a direct order. It did not lead to the deaths of two men in his unit. According to testimony of the survivors, they had already been tortured and some of their comrades killed before he arrived. Sergeant Blu rescued the remaining six men and killed approximately a dozen Taliban who held them captive. He sustained life-threatening injuries in the rescue when a bullet grazed his left ventricle.

Now to the matter of what really happened last night, where five men were killed and one seriously injured in Silver Verde. Verified by the military photographs we received, all of the men killed in Silver Verde last night were members of an elite CIA assassination squad. The CIA would neither confirm nor deny that those men were CIA agents. Since it has been alleged that the men were acting on orders from General Bishop, we'd like to know if he has an answer to why CIA agents were carrying out illegal covert operations on domestic soil.

But we at Fox cannot forget that in fact Mr. Blu *is* a fugitive from justice, as he escaped from Tywater Federal Penitentiary. However, we received information that six men attempted to kill him in the recreation yard. And in the court transcript of the arraignment and plea agreement that lead to his incarceration, Mayor White of Silver Verde stated that he believed that the situation that led to the charges was a setup. Hey, who knows? Maybe Blu felt that Tywater was no longer a good place for some much needed R and R," he said, tongue in cheek. "I wonder what Mr. Blu knows that would make so many ominous men try to kill him on two separate occasions.

"Sergeant Blu is the recipient of a Silver Star and two Purple Hearts. He should have received another Purple Heart and possibly a Congressional Medal of Honor for his actions in Afghanistan. Instead, he was drummed out of the military and thrown under the proverbial bus to cover up the malfeasance of military officers. We consider Mr. Blu a hero, a patriot.

"And we consider General Bishop a pinhead for his attempt to besmirch the reputation of Mr. Blu and for trying to deceive the American public with misinformation.

"We will keep you informed about this story, for this *is* the no-spin zone... because," he said, pointing toward the viewers, "we're looking out for you. The word for tonight is canard, c-a-n-a-r-d. Look it up, General Bishop," he said, shuffling his papers with a cunning smile.

The Board

ON THE EAST Coast, the Prince of Darkness received an EAC detailing the sketchy events that had taken place in Silver Verde. He, along with General Bishop, had been summoned for a meeting with the board.

The Prince of Darkness met General Bishop in his office. Then they took the elevator as far down as it would go and were met by two security guards. They entered the elevator and turned two separate keys simultaneously for the elevator to proceed to the bottom floor of a small amphitheater fifteen stories underground.

"Before we meet with the board, is there anything you would like to tell me?" the Prince of Darkness asked.

"About?" the general asked, being coy.

The Prince of Darkness shook his head. "About the monumental fuckup last night in Silver Verde."

"In the event that you were correct that Blu was still alive, and in Silver Verde, I put a plan in place to take him out."

"And they missed! I told you not to underestimate him or his accomplices. The board is not going to be pleased by this latest development."

They entered the dimly lit room and walked down the descending carpeted stairs to where the board had already convened. They were sitting around an elliptical mahogany table on an elevated platform. The board was comprised of two former congressmen, two retired judges, a retired navy general, a former owner and CEO of a military defense contractor manufacturing high-tech weaponry, and two former CIA agents. Several appeared to be in their late sixties and a few of them in their middle seventies or early eighties. An appointment to the board was for life. The only ways a member was replaced was upon death or for an illness that prevented them from performing their duties. They were in charge of all of the personnel and programs certified top secret and above top secret. Under their auspice were many covert operatives to implement their policies and execute their mandates.

The chairman, a former senator, was an elderly, well-dressed, distinguished-looking man. He poured a glass of water, took a sip, and cleared his throat. He spoke in a slow, deliberate manner, never changing the inflection of his voice. "General Bishop, I hope you now understand the gravity of the situation you have placed us in. You opened up a can of worms when you declassified the Blu file in an attempt to further destroy a dead man's reputation; a dead man who is apparently alive and creating havoc in Silver Verde. The people we have planted at various media outlets informed us that Fox News had received sensitive information, including the entire transcript of Blu's finding of facts inquest. Our legal staff went to federal court to get an injunction preventing Fox and other news outlets from making those files public under the US Secrecy Act and failed. MSNBC, as well as NBC and CBS, did not cover the story, but Fox and CNN have already run it. Your office was contacted by Fox for a statement. We issued a release on your behalf denying the allegations brought forth and the alleged cover-up as a clever fabrication. But now to the issue at hand. Did you authorize the use of those CIA operatives in Silver Verde?"

"Yes, sir."

"Well, that took initiative, but it failed miserably! That may pose a problem, a black mark on the ISS and possibly...on your career. Wouldn't you agree, General?"

"Yes, sir."

"We're glad you agree. That's why we arranged for you to be on a military transport leaving for the West Coast in two hours. Once there, you will take command of an additional two thousand ISS troops that are being dispatched to Silver Verde as we speak. In addition, we strongly advised California Power and Light to erect a ten-thousand-volt electrified gate on the road leading up to the hydroelectric dam, which they are in the process of installing. The celebration and dedication for the opening of this facility was to take place on the Fourth of July. We have asked California Power to delay the ceremony. This dam was largely constructed on land once owned by the Blu family. We now believe this would have been an excellent opportunity, given the number of dignitaries and government officials who would be in attendance, for him to create a disturbance at this event...or worse. This dam has become a symbol, just like damaging it would be a symbolic gesture. We have a diametrically opposed situation. On one hand, we have an immovable object: the dam. On the other hand, according to you, Mr. Standz—and you claim to know Blu better than anyone—we have an unstoppable force. Can we stop Blu, Mr. Standz?"

"I don't know, sir."

The chairman looked at the other members of the board, shaking his head. "Then we have an imminent threat, a bona fide crisis. Too many people, on the left and right, crossing ethnic and racial lines have become sympathetic to his cause. Given the state of this nation, if he succeeds, this act of civil disobedience could be the catalyst that catapults this country into chaos and anarchy."

The chairman held up his finger as several pictures appeared on the monitors on the computer screens in front of them. An agent had forwarded graphic pictures of the CIA operative's bodies that were killed in Silver Verde. "Mr. Standz, is it your opinion that Blu killed those agents, as some of the news stations are reporting?"

"I don't believe so, sir. That type of killing is not in his repertoire; not his forte. This could only be the work of one man that was in his unit, one of the men he rescued in Afghanistan, Captain Aloysius Smith. Big Brother verified that he checked out of a mental ward at a VA Hospital in Providence, Rhode Island, six weeks ago. The timeline and the profile fit."

"Who are his other accomplices?"

"I suspect Sergeant Kenneth Castle, an electronics and communications expert. Sergeant Robert Brazoli, an explosives and munitions expert. And as of yet, unconfirmed, maybe one of our own, Colonel Alexander Clay, with the Pentagon. Tomorrow, I will know for sure whether or not the colonel is involved.

The chairman looked at his wristwatch. "You are dismissed, General. Wouldn't want to miss your flight. But keep in mind, Blu and his accomplices must be flushed out. Apply a full-court press, and by all means, take the white gloves off. Do you understand this mandate?"

"Yes, sir."

After General Bishop left, the chairman looked over his notes and discussed an issue with the other members.

"Mr. Standz, I have some reservations, observations, and questions," vice chairman of the board and former chief justice of the appellate court Dorothy Weinberg said as she adjusted her bifocal glasses, looking down at the Blu dossier. "There is some obvious bad blood between Bishop and Blu, a vendetta that goes back to their days in Afghanistan. It has clouded the general's judgment. By all accounts, Blu is a remarkable man, near-genius IQ, recipient of the Silver Star and two Purple Hearts, and his vineyard has developed a world-class wine. This is the type of man others should be trying to emulate, not the type of person who should be hunted down and killed like a rabid dog. I was wondering about the extent of your involvement over the past several years in regard to Mr. Blu."

"With his unique talents, I tried unsuccessfully to bring him into the fold, make him one of us, maybe in the capacity as my protégé. My intentions with him have always been honorable."

"Really," she said, looking over her bifocals. "And we know where the road paved with good intentions leads. How did this situation ever get so out of control? Is this the way we treat our heroes?"

"In a perfect world, no, Your Honor."

"This country can't survive four more years of the current liberal administration. My sources tell me that Vice-Presidential Nominee Senator Bryant is somehow knee-deep in all this mess. If Bryant is involved in a scandal, he'll take Senator Morton down with him. See if you can find out what involvement Bryant has in all this mess and make it go away."

"Yes, Your Honor."

"Distance yourself from Bishop and Bryant. The potential fallout from this fiasco will take down everyone associated with them. And make sure all the strings we've pulled to get Bryant the nomination can't be traced back here. Very few know that we exist or how we operate, and we'd like to keep it that way! Do you understand these mandates?"

"Yes, Your Honor."

The Game

July 3, 7:00 a.m. Pacific time

Is there a game
No one wins
If no one loses?
That can end in a draw
If both sides chose
To call a truce, reengage,
And live to fight
Another day.

THE NEXT MORNING, the Wiz arose early and was busy monitoring the activity in and around Silver Verde. Well over two thousand ISS troops had arrived overnight in convoys and were setting up temporary bivouacs, assembling large camouflage tents on the north side of the new bridge. A long procession of military Humvees were arriving and parking in neat rows on a grassy area behind the bridge. A makeshift landing zone had been set up, and dozens of Black Hawk and Apache Helicopters were continually landing and taking off. Armed ISS soldiers had set up road blocks and check points on all roads leading in and out of the area.

The Wiz focused in on the road leading to the dam. Now he could see that the men had been constructing an electrified gate across the road with a guard post on each side. Two-man fortified pillboxes had been set up every hundred feet along the hillside leading up to the dam just above Silver Verde Lake. He ran a test program for the remote triggers that were hidden in the Metalstorm weapons, and his worst fear was confirmed. The high voltage from the electrified gate was interfering and blocking the signal to the detonators.

As he continued to watch the activity, a large military flatbed truck was allowed to pass through the gate. General Bishop, who had set up a command center in the administration building of the facility, walked down and watched the soldiers unload the dark-green crates. The Wiz shook his head as he zoomed in and saw the writing on the crates: Portable Stinger Missile Defense System.

The men, who had been eating breakfast, came over to see what the Wiz was looking at in the monitors. BB was eating a bowl of cereal, dropping it on his shirt and on the floor as he ate. The Wiz showed them the gate and told them about the stinger missiles and the escalating developments.

"You slob," the Wiz said, watching BB eat. "You really fucked up this time."

"How many times do I have to say I'm sorry?" BB said, bowing his head like a little child who had just been scolded.

"Forget about the fact that you almost got Billy and yourself killed. Forget about the fact that they now know for sure that he's alive. The remote trigger that I spent a week putting together is merely a decoration, useless!"

"All right, Mr. Castle," Colonel Clay said, "he gets the picture, and I'm *sure* it's never going to happen again," he said, with a stern voice as he looked at BB. "Now let's move on. How about I fly the Black Hawk over and past the gate. Will we be able to activate the trigger?"

"Maybe, but it'll be a suicide mission. Those stingers will take you out before you get close enough to push the button."

"In that case, maybe we'll send Robert," he said jokingly, patting BB on the back, which made him choke on his cereal.

Billy Ray seemed lost in thought. Many of his well-laid-out plans had changed. Then he remembered the beginning of a chapter from *The Art of Violence*: "If the enemy deploys unanticipated tactics to thwart, capture, or kill the warrior and his forces, he must take appropriate countermeasures to neutralize the threat and once again gain the advantage." By the expression on his face, the men could tell he was not pleased by what he had to do. He would have to alter a vital part of the strategy for his end game.

"Midnight, a little later in the day, you and BB take the USG van, and make sure you have your IDs to get through the checkpoints. The county hospital is twenty klicks south. Go there and pilfer a vital-signs monitor."

"What's that for Billy?"

"A backup plan. I'll tell you about it later. BB, you think you can wire the bridge without getting caught?"

BB thought for a moment. "Maybe. On a remote? Handheld?"

Billy Ray nodded.

"No problem. Midnight and I will take a couple of hard hats and a surveyor's transit. While the ISS thinks we're surveying the area, I'll wire the bridge."

Castle Traps Black Knight

"Mr. Castle, did you find the last pieces of the puzzle?" Colonel Clay asked.

"I got into Bryant's PC, piece of cake. I found some helpful information, but no smoking gun."

"And what about Standz?"

"What's he looking for?" BB asked.

"I remember what Standz told William when he visited him in Tywater. He said he had the keys to the front gate. Maybe what we're looking for is in his PC, but the Wiz can't hack in."

"It's a secure website, and the first password is audio. It could be anything; his voice, a song, a ringtone."

Billy Ray thought about the conversation he had with the Prince of Darkness at Tywater. Then he remembered when Standz's cell phone rang. "Wiz, go to YouTube and download the first chords to the Eagles song 'Hotel California.'"

The Wiz downloaded the beginning of the song as Billy Ray instructed. He replayed the chords, and the first lock opened. A chess board appeared on the screen with the pieces moving themselves on the three-dimensional board. "We passed the first lock, Billy," the Wiz said, "but there's no way of knowing what the second password is. The possibilities are endless."

Billy Ray looked at the pieces on the chess board and noticed that one piece was conspicuously missing. Then he smiled. "Try 'black knight.'"

The Wiz typed in *black knight*, and the chess board disappeared, displaying all his files.

"I don't know what to make of it," Colonel Clay said. "William, you think just like Standz."

After looking through dozens of highly classified files, the Wiz came across a curious file labeled "A Hole in One" with attachments. The men watched with an eerie silence as Senator Bryant, Governor Maxwell, Attorney William Coyle, and Judge Tores were playing rounds of golf, discussing the advantages each man would stand to gain by keeping Blu in prison as long as the law would allow. They watched the video until the men went into the clubhouse.

"Wasn't that your lawyer?" Colonel Clay asked. "And wasn't Tores the federal judge in your case?"

Billy Ray didn't answer him. He just nodded with a look of disgust and contempt on his face.

"You never had a chance," BB said. "Every last one of those motherfuckers was going to gain—at your loss! Well that's it, Billy. All we have to do is give this tape to the authorities, and they'll all take it in the ass. They'll have to pardon you."

"No they won't!" the Wiz said, emphatically. "The video is worthless without the audio. The audio portion of the tape would constitute an illegal wiretap and would be inadmissible in any court. Am I right, Colonel?"

"I'm afraid you are, Mr. Castle. But we're going to give this to a higher court: the court of public opinion. These are some of the most prominent and powerful men in the country. But if we make it public, the outcry would be so loud it would force an investigation. All this is very powerful evidence, Castle, but there's still a big piece missing. See what else is in his documents."

The Wiz opened and closed numerous documents, many of them labeled "top secret" and "above top secret." Many of them were documented assassinations of various individuals in foreign countries. Then he came upon another curious file with a video attachment labeled "American Pie."

As he opened the attachment, it was a video of the village green with the high-school band playing the Don Mclean song "American Pie." As they watched, Midnight told the Wiz to freeze the action.

"What is it?" the colonel asked.

"I recognize that guy in the red-checkered flannel shirt with the LA Dodgers baseball cap. That, gentlemen, is one of the snipers I took out. He's was one of the CIA assassins. I'm sure of it."

"Good work, Mr. Smith," the colonel said.

As the video advanced, they saw the riot begin and the townsfolk scrambling for cover. They saw Senator Bryant and his staff being whisked away to a limousine. They watched in silence and amazement as Billy Ray took out one ISS soldier after another. They had never actually seen him engage in hand-to-hand combat. They only witnessed the aftermath and caught a fleeting glimpse of the lethality he was capable of inflicting on that night in Afghanistan.

As Billy Ray took out the remaining ISS soldiers using the majorette's baton for a weapon, the colonel winked at the other men and smiled. "Look at him go," he said, with pride and exuberance. "They're lucky they're still alive. He could have killed them all!"

All the men heard the conversation between the Prince of Darkness and the CIA agent in the church tower when he told the sniper to take Billy Ray out. After Billy Ray had been brought to his knees and Ocho had thrown one soldier through the windshield of a car and the other through a signpost, the video ended.

"That's about it, William," the colonel said, putting his arm around him. "The last piece of the puzzle. Good work, Castle. What do you want to do with this?"

Billy Ray thought for a moment. "Nothing yet. Give me some time to think about the best time to release it."

"Wiz, put the golf outing and the riot at Silver Verde on a separate disk," the colonel said. "Download everything else in Standz's file on a thumb drive. Never know when we'll need that type of covert intel for leverage. I'll bet Bishop and Standz never saw this move coming."

A battle plan
Under false presence
Attack, retreat
A new defense,

With cunning and guile
A noble cause
To find a weakness
Uncover their flaws.

Black Knight Traps White Knight
7:00 a.m. eastern standard time
The Prince of Darkness drove to an isolated cove on a small lake in New Jersey. There was a thick fog rolling in over the water, and the shoreline could only be seen intermittently. As he approached a small lake house owned by Colonel Clay, he listened to the beeps of a handheld tracking device keyed in to locate his implanted GPS. He rang the doorbell several times and then inserted a locksmith device that had a number of levers and a tip that resembled bobby pins. With one twist of his wrist, the door opened. He called the colonel's name several times, thinking that he may still be sleeping. He had a cover story ready in the event that he was home. He walked around the small, dark cottage, holding and pointing the tracking devise as it blinked and beeped louder as he approached his bedroom. He opened the door slowly. The stark room was nearly empty except for a neatly made bed and only a few pieces of furniture. He moved the device until it made one solid tone. Then he opened up a small top drawer in the night table. He took out a plastic bag and saw the colonel's GPS.

"Gotcha, you son of a bitch," he said, with a devilish grin on his face. "Think you could fool me with that amateur tradecraft. Not in your lifetime!"

1:20 p.m. eastern standard time
Bishop Baits Queen
Jenny had just returned from her volunteer work at the library. She stopped briefly to talk with the ranch hands who were constructing fieldstone and masonry columns at the entryway to the avocado farm. She had taken the iron archway from the old farm that displayed the words "Four Strong Winds Avocado Farm." A few more days of work and the men would reach the height to install the arch above the columns.

She entered her room and began changing, all the while talking to her mother, who asked if she had heard any news about Billy Ray. Four Humvees pulled down the dirt driveway at a high rate of speed. Twenty ISS soldiers got out quickly and surrounded the house. They were all wearing lightweight Kevlar vests and carrying M-16 automatic assault rifles. They were coordinating all of their movements using only hand signals. Two soldiers approached the front porch carrying a steel battering ram and smashed through the front door. Jenny's parents were startled, and they were shoved to the floor at gunpoint. Jenny was half dressed and naked from the waist up. Several soldiers burst into her room and dragged her out by her hair and pushed her to the floor next to her parents. They were ordered not to raise their heads or speak. Some of the soldiers searched the rooms. When they were confident that the house was secure, they radioed to General Bishop to enter. As the general stepped out of one of the Humvees, several Black Hawk helicopters were hovering overhead, securing the perimeter.

"What's going on?" Jenny's father asked, raising his head.

One of the soldiers hit him in his lower back with the butt of this weapon. "Keep quiet, old man, and keep your head down!"

General Bishop walked up the wooden stairs and along the planking of the deck, smiling as he looked at the smashed front door. He walked up to where Jenny and her parents lay prostrate on the floor. He placed the tip of his highly polished shoe under one of Jenny's outstretched arms. "Everyone stand up."

Jenny stood up, folding her arms in front of her to cover her naked breasts. She was trembling, and her face was flushed with embarrassment.

Bishop observed her closely without any outward sign of emotion. Then he motioned for one of the soldiers guarding her, who was smiling. "Take her to her room and let her put something on. Then bring her back, and be quick about it."

→═◑ ◐═←

Ever since Billy Ray had told Ocho to watch over Jenny, he varied his duties each day between the vineyard and the avocado farm. When he saw the military vehicles and the helicopters hovering over her house, he and twenty ranch hands ran up to the front of the house. As the ISS soldiers saw them coming, they pointed their weapons in their direction.

"You there, Jolly Green Giant, get your hands up, way up, above your head!"

Ocho said a few words to the other men in Spanish, and they all placed their hands over their heads. He noticed that one of the soldiers was wearing a neck brace and recognized him as the soldier that Billy Ray had put down in Sparkey's Tavern.

"How's neck?" Ocho asked, taunting him.

"Shut the fuck up. You think because you're a giant that I'm scared of you?"

"No worry for me," Ocho said, smiling. "Now you do this to Miss Jenny and parents, next time Billy Ray see you…he break your neck…for good."

"Is that so? Next time I see him, I'll put a bullet in his fuckin' head…just like I'm going to put one in yours," he said, pointing his weapon toward Ocho's head, "if you don't shut the fuck up!"

Ocho just laughed, which made the soldier more agitated.

⇥ ⇤

When Jenny returned to the kitchen, she went over to her mother and held her hand tightly.

"I don't understand what's going on…General," her father said, looking at the three stars on Bishop's cap.

General Bishop looked at Jenny, who turned away as he stared at her. "Are you Jenifer Blu, formerly Jenifer Haas?"

"Y-yes," she said, choking on her words.

"You're under arrest. Lieutenant, place the prisoner in handcuffs."

"What!" Jenny's mother shouted.

"What are the charges?" her father asked. "Let me see the arrest warrant."

"William Blu is now classified as a terrorist. Under the Internal Security and Surveillance doctrine, we don't need a warrant to arrest your daughter. She's suspected of aiding, abetting, and facilitating the escape of Blu and harboring a fugitive from justice."

"That's nonsense!" her father said. "We haven't seen Billy Ray, and she doesn't know where he is."

"Oh, but I think she does. If Blu surrenders to me personally, I'll think about letting your daughter go. Until that happens, she'll be held at Tywater Federal Penitentiary for interrogation. Lieutenant, take the prisoner to the helicopter."

General Bishop took off with Jenny in the Black Hawk helicopter. Jenny's parents drove into town and met with Sheriff Roy and Mayor White and told them what had happened.

News travels fast in a small town. It wasn't long before most everyone in Silver Verde knew that the ISS had arrested her.

⊷⊨◎ ◎⊨⊷

BB and Midnight went to the county hospital, passing through several checkpoints as the left Silver Verde. When they entered the hospital, they walked down a long corridor and entered an OR scrub room. They both put on three-quarter-length white lab coats. As they left the room, Midnight took a stereoscope, smiled, and placed it around his neck.

As they passed by three teenage employees wearing candy-striped uniforms, BB raised his eyebrows, flirting with them, and said, *"Bella materiale!* And how are we doing today?"

"Fine, Doctor," one of them answered as she smiled a giddy smile.

"A couple rounds of golf, Dr. Mezzanotte, after we perform the lobotomy?" BB said, in a profound serious tone.

"Most certainly, Dr. Brazoli, but only if I can whack a few before we dine at the clubhouse."

After they located a portable vital-signs monitor, BB disconnected it from the stand and hid it under his lab coat. Then they quickly made their way back to Silver Verde, passing through several more checkpoints as they entered. They put on their hard hats and set up a transit on the north side of the bridge. Two ISS soldiers came over and asked them what they were doing. BB produced official-looking papers the Wiz gave them, which satisfied the soldier's inquiry.

Under the newly constructed bridge was the rustling water of a meandering tributary that emptied into Silver Verde Lake. When he was sure he wasn't being watched, BB went under the bridge and placed explosives on strategic structural supports.

–≡◦ ◦≡–

In Tywater Federal Penitentiary, sometimes the word was the gospel truth. At other times, the word was filtered through the prison population by word of mouth and became distorted. At other times the word became so exaggerated it no longer resembled the truth.

2:30 p.m. Pacific time

That afternoon, at Tywater, the prison population had gotten the word that something was going down, but it was vague and lent itself to pure speculation. The inmates in the yard were instructed to clear a large area in the middle of the track for a military helicopter to land. Lieutenant O'Rourke had received the word that Jenifer Blu had been arrested and was being transferred for interrogation to Tywater and would be held on his block in solitary confinement.

As the Black Hawk helicopter landed on the grass in the middle of the yard, Dr. Vibes looked out her window. Both Dr. Vibes and Captain Carl had been busy doing paperwork and didn't get the word about what had transpired. She went to Captain Carl's office to see if he knew what was happening. He said he didn't know, and they both went to the warden's office to ask him.

Warden Van Leeston was busy signing requisition forms for cafeteria staples and looked up at them, seemingly annoyed by the intrusion.

"What's going on?" Captain Carl asked.

"I received a call from the director of the bureau of prisons to grant General Bishop permission to secure a prisoner at our facility.

Dr. Vibes looked out the warden's window into the yard. At first she thought that the ISS had captured Billy Ray.

"The same General Bishop," Captain Carl said, shaking his head, "who was caught in a lie about Blu's military record?"

Van Leeston put down his pen and looked up. "This was the nearest facility to interrogate…her."

"Her!" Dr. Vibes said.

"The woman is Jenifer Blu, William Blu's sister-in-law."

"She doesn't belong here," Captain Carl said. "Since when do we imprison citizens for questioning without due process?"

"William Blu has been classified as a terrorist. They felt that this would be the most secure place for her to be held."

"Really?" Dr. Vibes said. "They're using her to set a trap. He's too smart for this ploy."

"Oh, yes, I forgot, Dr. Vibes; you are quite familiar with Blu's psyche from your *numerous* evaluations. Don't forget, Doctor—Blu is a fugitive from justice. He escaped from my prison! *My* prison! He made me the laughingstock of the entire prison system. If they're using her for bait, that's fine by me. And if it helps capture, or better still, kill him, all the better."

"If there's one thing I learned when my father used to take my brother and me fishing, it's that it never turns out too well for the bait," Captain Carl said.

"For the big fish they're trying to catch either," he said, smiling. "As you can see, I'm quite busy, so that'll be all," he said, looking up, "from the both of you."

In the yard, Lieutenant O'Rourke and several guards waited at a safe distance for General Bishop and the ISS soldiers to take out the prisoner. After Jenifer was escorted out of the helicopter, General Bishop ordered the soldiers to take off her handcuffs.

"Are you sure there's nothing you care to tell me about where Blu is and what he's planning?" Bishop asked, leaning over so she could hear him over the noise of the rotating blades of the Black Hawk.

"I told you," she said, rubbing her sore wrists from the handcuffs, "I honestly don't know where he is."

General Bishop looked at O'Rourke's rank and nametag and motioned for him and his men to come closer. "We're going to let our prisoner have some… quality time in the yard with these killers, rapists, and perverts," he said, talking to O'Rourke but looking at Jenny. "See if it refreshes her memory."

"Yes, sir," O'Rourke said, smiling.

"But we're going to keep an eye on her, and if it gets out of hand, maybe we'll step in…maybe,"the General said.

After the guards left Jenny alone in the yard, the inmates began gathering and circling around her with suspicion and curiosity. Dr. Vibes and Captain Carl returned to his office and were observing the activity in the yard.

"What's going on?" Dr. Vibes asked indignantly.

Captain Carl looked into the yard and saw the inmates surrounding Jenny. "This is not going to happen on my watch. I'm going to put a stop to this. Stay here, Catalina," he said, turning to leave the room. "And if Van Leeston wants my job," he said in a loud enough voice so that the warden could hear him, "he can shove it up his ass!"

→▭ ▭◄

Ramon "La Muerte" Rodriguez was the leader of the Latin gang at Tywater. He was serving three consecutive life sentences, without the possibility of parole, for killing three men in a drug deal gone bad. On the side of his neck was a large colorful tattoo of a scantily clad Spanish woman. On his right arm were numerous tattoos signifying all of the men he killed on the outside. On his left arm were dark-blue jailhouse tats signifying all the men he had killed while in the prison system. In prison he was called by the name he earned from all those men he had killed: La Muerte—Death.

La Muerte walked up to Jenny, sizing her up and nodding. As he walked around her, he caressed her behind, giving it a slight squeeze, which made Jenny wince. *"Agradable,"* he said as all the men laughed.

Suddenly Roscoe Clements came pushing his way through the crowd of men surrounding Jenny. "Excuse me, ma'am, ma'am. You can be no other than the woman my friend Billy used to tell me about. Ma'am, are you Jenny? Jenny Blu?"

"Y-yes," she said.

"La Muerte," Roscoe shouted and pointed toward Jenny. "This woman is Blu, Jenny Blu. The one…the government killed her husband," he said, struggling to find the right words in Spanish.

"Blu," La Muerte said as he backed away from her, speaking in Spanish to all the men surrounding her. He told the men that this was Billy Ray's woman, having misunderstood what Roscoe had said. All the men backed away from her. La Muerte bowed his head. "Jenny Blu, English no good. Your man Billy Ray…one of us. We see," he said, pointing to his eye, "on TV what government do to him. Now...you one of us. You safe here. Go," he said, directing her to Roscoe, "with chess man."

As Captain Carl entered the yard, he saw Jenny walking alongside Roscoe Clements, and he smiled.

"What the hell's going on here? General Bishop shouted.

"I don't know, General," O'Rourke said, bewildered.

"There's a code in here, General," Captain Carl said. "Someone must have told them who she is. She's safer in here than she would be in Silver Verde."

"You just worry about your prison, and let me worry about Silver Verde."

"Oh, but I am, General," he said in a condescending tone. "Now that the word's out, God forbid she should *accidentally* fall and break a fingernail. Why, I could have an all-out riot in here. Couldn't guarantee the safety of you or your men."

"Are you mocking me, Captain?" General Bishop asked with indignation.

"Wouldn't think of it, sir."

"I guess a full body-cavity search is out of the question," O'Rourke said, smiling.

"And what do you think the inmates will do to the guards if she's harmed in any way, O'Rourke?" Captain Carl asked.

The smile disappeared from O'Rourke's face as he realized what the captain meant.

"Lieutenant," Bishop said, motioning to O'Rourke, "get the prisoner and take her to the interrogation room, and be careful," he said sarcastically, looking at Captain Carl. "Wouldn't want her to break a fingernail."

⟶══◉ ◉══⟵

Carla was in the checkout line at the local IGA market when she overheard an elderly customer talking with the cashier about Jenny's arrest and that General Bishop had taken her to Tywater Penitentiary. After she put her groceries in her car, she ran down Main Street, with her two boys in tow, and dropped them off at Margie's Beauty Salon. She drove frantically, backtracking over the same roads, trying to locate the area she had dropped off Billy Ray and BB.

⟶══◉ ◉══⟵

The Wiz had been monitoring the ISS checkpoints and all roads that led to the compound, and he saw the old dark-green Toyota Camry traveling up and down frantically. BB and Midnight had just returned to the compound, and the Wiz asked BB to get Billy Ray, who was resting in his bunk.

"What do you make of this, Billy?" the Wiz asked him.

"It's Carla. I wonder what she wants."

"Who?" BB asked, looking at the monitor.

"The woman who drove us here the other night."

"Oh, that night. It's still a blur to me," BB said, rubbing his face. "I remember now," he said, cupping his hands in front of his chest. "The broad with the big..."

"Smile," Billy Ray said, interrupting him as they all laughed.

"BB, go through the woods and see what Carla wants."

Before BB left the compound, he looked into a small mirror and was primping himself, using his fingers as a comb to fix his hair, and then tucked his shirt into his pants. Colonel Clay saw what he was doing and nudged the Wiz.

"Oh, what's this?" the Wiz asked as the other men saw what BB was doing and laughed.

"Nothing," BB said. "Mind your own business!"

When BB saw Carla racing toward him, he stepped into the road, and she nearly ran him over.

"Whoa, what's the hurry, darling?"

Carla was nervous and disheveled but recognized BB. "Do you remember me?"

"How could I ever forget a beauty like you?" he said, leaning against her car to get a better look.

Carla smiled at the compliment and quickly began rattling off what had happened, barely taking a breath between words. BB thanked her and said he would get the message to Billy Ray. BB double-timed it back to the bunker and told the men what had happened as he tried to catch his breath.

Billy Ray sat down and rubbed his hands over his face. As he sat pondering his next move, his eyes glazed over.

"You know it's a trap, William," Colonel Clay said. "You're going to have to let her go, but it's your call."

"I can't. And it may be a trap, but not for me. I know the layout of Tywater as well as anyone." Then an idea came into his mind, and he turned to the Wiz. "Do you think the codes that Dr. Vibes gave the colonel are still good?"

"Maybe, but there's no way of knowing—until it's too late. If they changed the codes, you'll be walking into a trap. Why, what do you have in mind?"

"They'll never expect me to do something this quick, and they don't know we have another Black Hawk. If the codes are still good, the shift change is at six. Lieutenant O'Rourke will be in charge."

"Bishop's no fool," Colonel Clay said. "Maybe this is just what he's planned. Wiz, do you think they retask the downward-looking satellites?"

"Absolutely, Colonel, but with all the air traffic in the area, it would be hard for them to isolate us."

"There's only a small window of opportunity for this to succeed," Billy Ray said. "This time we'll do things a little differently. We'll leave at five forty-five. BB and Midnight, prepare the Black Hawk for takeoff, and load the sixty MM cannon with the depleted uranium shells. And we're going to need some stun guns."

"Depleted uranium shells," Midnight said, smiling. "Now that's my kind of ammunition. Are we going to get to kill anyone?"

"This time Bishop crossed the line. I don't want to kill anyone, but if it comes to that...I'm going to my bunk to rest, if I can. Midnight, get me at five thirty."

⇥▣ ▣⇤

Carla made her way back to town to pick up her children. As she entered Main Street, she was stopped at an ISS checkpoint. One of the soldiers asked her for her driver's license and took her ID to the guardhouse. A minute later he returned with another guard.

"Are you Carla Beck?" he asked, looking at her and then at the picture on her license.

"Yes, what seems to be the problem? I'm in a hurry. I have to pick up my children."

"Pull your car over to the side of the road. You're going to have to come with us."

"I don't understand. What's this all about?"

"According to Mr. Sparks, you were in the vicinity of Sparkey's Tavern on the night that an act of terrorism took place. Command wants to ask you a few questions."

"I don't know anything about what happened."

"Then it won't take too long, Miss Beck. You still have to come with us."

A few minutes later, a Humvee arrived. Two soldiers got out and placed Carla between them. Then they drove off to the command center at the hydro-electric facility.

Every Dog Has Its Day

King Takes Rook
Blocks Bishop
Saves Queen

BILLY RAY WENT to his bunk. There were cardboard boxes stacked against the walls containing his parents' old clothing, memorabilia, and valuables. He opened one of the boxes and took out a musty album of old photographs. The Wiz was in the main bunker updating information on his pirate website. As Billy Ray flipped through the photographs of his childhood, he heard the barely audible song "The Black Parade" by My Chemical Romance, which was the anthem of the Wiz's underground website.

"When I was a young man
My father took me into the city
To see a marching band
He said, "Someday when you grow up
Would you be the savior of the broken,
The beaten, and the damned?"
He said, "Will you defeat them?
Your demons and all the nonbelievers
The plans that they have made
Because one day I'll leave you
A phantom to lead you in the summer
To join the Black Parade.

Billy Ray stopped flipping through the photographs as he came upon a photo of himself and his brother when they were seven years old, in Saint Mary's receiving their first Holy Communion. They were standing by each other with their hands folded in prayer as a young Father Pat was handing Junior a host. Then he came upon another photo of him and his brother in their Little League baseball uniforms on opening day and another as they were blowing out the candles on two separate cakes on their eighth birthday. When he came across another photograph, he peeled back the protective plastic and removed the photo. As he studied the picture, he rubbed the image of his brother, and his eyes welled up with tears.

<hr/>

It had been a crisp, beautiful day in October. Big events seldom happened in the small town of Silver Verde. Everyone in the community had lined Main Street to attend a parade for the first senatorial bid of William Wadsworth Bryant.

Vendors were walking in the street selling popcorn, cotton candy, and helium-filled balloons. The high-school marching band and majorettes were just coming into view ahead of the procession.

As mothers often do with twins, Billy Ray and Junior were dressed alike for the big day, wearing cowboy outfits complete with cowboy hats, rawhide fringed jackets, and toy silver six-guns in holsters with white plastic handles and caps for ammunition.

Next to his family were the new neighbors from the avocado farm next to their vineyard with their daughter, Jenny, about a year or so younger than the boys.

Mayor Theodore "Teddy" Roy, whose large face was bright red with sunburn, was walking from side to side along the parade route and shaking hands with the townsfolk. Behind him was his younger brother, who had just been appointed as the town's first sheriff.

Bryant's campaign workers were wearing red-white-and-blue straw hats, handing out campaign brochures. Several men with his campaign were dressed as clowns, handing out lollipops to the children.

Just before Bryant's motorcade passed by, Adeline Blu talked with Jenny's parents and placed their daughter between her two boys. She told them to get closer and to place their arms around each other to take a picture. Jenny was wearing a pink ruffled dress with pink bobby socks, black suede shoes, and a pink ribbon in her braided hair, which matched her dress. Adeline moved out several feet into the parade route and asked them to smile as she took the picture using a large, cumbersome Polaroid camera.

As the motorcade passed, townsfolk took pictures, clapped and whistled. Bryant and his wife sat on top of the rear section of a late-model white convertible Cadillac El Dorado. His young children were sitting in the backseat, waving methodically to the crowd. On the sides of the Cadillac were posters displaying pictures of Bryant with a US flag in the background. Above his picture were the words "Honesty and Integrity," and below was his campaign slogan, "Elect William Bryant, a Man of His Word."

Billy Ray tried to hold onto the image, but it became as faded as the photograph he held in his hands. He looked at his brother's image once again and placed the photo into his shirt pocket.

>─● ●─<

Most world-class chess players of Billy Ray's caliber can see many moves in advance. He always had the gift and foresight to see all his options, and every possible outcome. He had applied the discipline and principles he learned from the game and applied them to the decisions he made in his life. He knew that important aspects of his end game had radically changed. He thought it was a bad omen, a premonition that for the first time in his life, he couldn't see beyond tomorrow. He wondered if everything he had—all of his accomplishments, all of his dreams and desires, everyone he ever knew or loved—would soon be gone if the game didn't turn out the way he planned. All that would be left would be old photographs of him, and in time, there would be nothing left to show he ever lived at all.

> But at my back I always hear
> Time's winged chariot hurrying near
> And yonder all before us lie
> Deserts of vast eternity.

—Andrew Marvell, "To His Coy Mistress"

After BB and Midnight had prepared the Black Hawk, they returned to the bunker to continue watching a Blu-ray disc of an old movie that they had watched half way through the night before, *V for Vendetta*. Over the years, BB had seen the movie many times. He liked the plot, but he especially enjoyed the pyrotechnics at the beginning and end of the movie. Midnight had seen the movie a decade before and only remembered bits and pieces of the plot.

When they began watching the movie, it was just before the climax. The character called V, wearing the Guy Fawkes mask to hide his disfigurement, had just set up a vast number of dominoes. He tipped one of them over, which started a chain reaction that tumbled down all the rest of the dominoes in the matter of a few seconds.

"I think I remember how this movie ends," Midnight said.

"Shhh," BB said. "The best part is coming up."

"You know, BB, this story is similar to what happened to Billy and what's going to happen, but doesn't the guy wearing the mask succeed in his goal but die in the end?"

"I see the similarities, but that's not going to be how the story of Billy Ray ends."

"How can you be so sure?"

"Because that's why we're here. As long as there is a breath left in my body, with every ounce of my strength of will, I'll never let that happen."

Visions of ultraviolence danced in his head as Midnight began having a minor episode triggered by what BB had just said. "I'm with you, brother," he said with conviction, his head tilted and twisted with a wry expression on his face, displaying a full gamut of conflicting emotions—amusement, anger, elation, and belligerence—all within a matter of seconds. "I'll fuckin' kill them! I'll kill every last one of them!"

The movie was ending. The Parliament building was demolished, and a massive fireworks display began with Tchaikovsky's "1812 Overture" playing in the background.

At 5:30, Midnight went to Billy Ray's bunk and told him it was show time. All of the men dressed in ISS soldier's uniforms and took off. The Wiz called the prison, and following procedure and protocol, asked to speak with Warden Van Leeston. The call was transferred to Lieutenant O'Rourke at the guard's station in D-Block.

215

The Wiz put Colonel Clay on the phone. Colonel Clay told O'Rourke that he was the duty officer from Beale Air Force Base and said that an ISS Black Hawk Helicopter was in transit from Beale to pick up the prisoner. He also said that General Bishop had requested a transfer order from the Federal Bureau of Prisons and gave him the proper codes to verify the order. In order to expedite the transfer, the colonel told him that they would be landing on the rooftop of D-Block.

After they landed, two ISS soldiers were waiting on the rooftop to escort them down a stairway to the solitary confinement section of the prison. Billy Ray stayed in the helicopter and kept the engine running. As they arrived at Jenny's cell, Lieutenant O'Rourke met them.

Jenny sat on a small bunk, huddled in an upright fetal position with her back against the wall. Billy Ray walked down the damp, musty cement stairwell to D-Block, still wearing his flight helmet. As he walked toward the men, O'Rourke turned toward him briefly and then opened the cell door.

"She was pretty tight-lipped," O'Rourke said to BB. "Maybe you'll get more out of her with your interrogation techniques, if you know what I mean," he said, smiling. "All right, Blu, get up. You're going for a ride."

Billy Ray stood behind O'Rourke. As he took off his flight helmet, he winked at BB and Midnight. When Jenny saw who it was, her eyes opened wide.

"O'Rourke, remember the day when my brother was killed and you said to me that every dog has its day? Well, today's yours!"

With those words, BB and Midnight stunned the ISS soldiers with their Tasers and they fell to the floor, twitching and convulsing from the electrical shock. O'Rourke turned, and when he saw it was Billy Ray, the color drained from his terrified face. He tried to regain his composure and reached for the baton in his holster. Billy Ray grabbed his wrist and twisted it backward, causing the baton to drop to the floor. O'Rourke dropped to his knees as Billy Ray took out an eighteen-inch sais sword and placed it against his neck.

"Jenny, are you all right?"

She nodded.

"Come out of the cell and stay with those men," he said, motioning toward BB and Midnight.

"D-don't kill me," O'Rourke pleaded.

"I should slit your throat for all you put me through," he said, pressing the blade of his weapon so hard against his neck that it drew blood. "All I want to know is who besides you set me up? Who gave the order?"

A puddle of warm urine formed underneath O'Rourke, and by the smell in the cell, it appeared he had a bowel movement too.

"Van Leeston! It was Van Leeston!"

"And what were you both promised for setting me up?"

"Some big-shot senator, I don't know his name, took the warden golfing. He promised him that he'd be appointed as the new director of the Federal Bureau of Prisons. I was to be appointed to the rank of captain. After Van Leeston's promotion, they were going to bypass Captain Carl, and I was going to become the new warden."

"Was that big-shot senator William Bryant?"

"I don't know. Please believe me. I don't know."

"Billy, slit this sniveling douchebag's throat," Midnight said. "Or let me kill him!"

"Don't kill me. I have a family."

Billy Ray turned to BB. "You got all that?"

BB reached into his top pocket and pulled out a small black voice recorder. "Every fuckin' word of it."

Then Billy Ray turned to O'Rourke. "A family! I had a brother before they put me in here, and she had a husband. But I'm not going to kill you. I've done far worse than that! After this, your career and Van Leeston's are finished." Billy Ray nodded to Midnight, and he stunned O'Rourke, who fell twitching to the cell floor. "Gag and tie all of them and lock the door. No one will know what happened here until the shift change at five o'clock in the morning."

Several prisoners in the cells across from Jenny's had been watching silently through small Plexiglas openings in their cell doors.

"Put out the word," Billy Ray said to the men in the cells, "how this tough guy shit and pissed his pants and cried like a baby for his life. He'll never have a hold over any of you again. And you tell them it was Billy Ray."

"We'll get the word out, Billy," one of the men in the cells said. "Don't you worry 'bout that."

After Midnight closed the cell door, Jenny hugged Billy Ray. Tears were in her eyes, and she was still visibly shaken by the ordeal. Then they quickly made their way to the roof and took off.

⊶⊷ ⊶⊷

BB flew the Black Hawk back to Silver Verde just above the tree tops to avoid radar and detection from the unmanned drones. Jenny sat in the rear of the helicopter with Billy Ray, holding on to him tightly. She had stopped trembling, looked up at him, and placed a soft kiss on his cheek.

BB turned around and winked at Billy Ray. Then he began singing, mimicking Dean Martin's version of the song "That's Amore."

"When the moon hits your eye like a big pizza pie, that's amore. Go ahead, Billy, give her a big kiss. We won't look," he said, laughing.

As Jenny laughed along with the men, Billy Ray looked into her eyes. Even though she was disheveled, he couldn't help thinking how beautiful she was. It pleased him to see that the scared, distraught expression on her face had disappeared.

"Who are these men, Billy?"

"We served in the marines. They broke me out of Tywater. "

"I prayed you'd come for me. Then I prayed you wouldn't. I understand now. I was heartbroken when you told me never to visit you again in prison. You knew they would use me to get to you, and by seeing you I was placing myself and you in danger. That awful man, the general, said that if I didn't tell him where you were, he was going to kill you."

"You're safe now, and General Bishop's not going to kill anyone."

"I can still see his face, inches from mine, as he shouted," she said as her face went blank, recalling the ordeal. "He said he was going to put me away for the rest of my life if I didn't tell him what was going to happen tomorrow. Billy, what's tomorrow?"

"It's Independence Day," he said, avoiding the question. "After tomorrow, he's going to come looking for you. Didn't you tell me you had relatives in Canada?"

"My aunt, my mother's sister, lives in Alberta. My uncle works on the oil pipeline."

"I'll get you there with a new identity. You'll be safe there until this all blows over."

"Will you be coming with me?"

Billy Ray thought for a moment. "You'll have to trust me on this; you'll be safer there without me. After tomorrow I'm going away...maybe for a long time."

"Where will you go?"

"It's better if you don't know."

She hugged him and gave him another kiss. "After that general left, I had an interesting visitor."

"Who?"

"The prison psychiatrist, a Dr. Vibes."

"And what did you talk about?"

"You," she said, nudging his side. "She couldn't say much because a soldier was always standing nearby. She asked if I needed anything and said that she missed the sessions she had with you and said if I ever saw you again to tell you that you were right, right all along, and that sometimes things aren't the way they are made to appear to be. She said you'd know what that meant."

Billy Ray smiled. "She's a good woman."

"I bet she is," Jenny said with a coy smile. "I can tell she has the hots for you. Trust me—a woman always knows these things."

"If it wasn't for her, I would never have gotten out of Tywater."

"Well, it's clear to me that she misses you, but not as much as I did. And then as she was leaving, she said something that I couldn't figure out."

"And that was?"

"She nodded as if confirming something to herself and said, 'I can see now; you must be the one.' What did she mean by that?"

Billy Ray smiled. "Trust me," he said, mimicking her. "Shouldn't a woman always know what these things mean?'"

She shook her head, smiling at his answer. Then she hugged and kissed him again.

The Black Hawk began descending on an open piece of land on the perimeter of Jenny's property.

"Are we landing?"

"We're on your property. You'll be safe here until tomorrow morning."

"It's Sunday night. Will it be safe enough for me to go to church with my parents?"

Billy Ray thought for a moment. "Yes, but early tomorrow I'll send someone for you to give your new identity and get you safely to Canada."

"If you're leaving tomorrow, promise me that you'll see me before you leave."

He didn't answer her. The helicopter landed, and BB turned to Billy Ray. "We got to get movin', Billy," he said. "We're sitting ducks out here for the drones."

Jenny held on to him tightly. She was reluctant to let him go, thinking that this could be the last time she would ever see him. "Billy, you didn't promise me. I want to see you before you leave. I have to see you."

"Go, Jenny," he said above the noise of the rotating blades as they kissed. "I promise. I'll see you tonight. And by the way, she was right; you are the one. There has never been anyone else for me except you."

Jenny watched the helicopter until it disappeared over the treetops. As she walked back to her home, tears of joy welled up in her eyes. This was the first time since he had left to join the military that he openly expressed his true feelings for her.

My Word Is...

WHEN THEY RETURNED to the bunker, the Wiz was busy with his electronic equipment. Colonel Clay stood next to him with a broad smile on his face. "I take it everything went well."

"Sure did," Midnight said. "And we didn't even have to kill anyone. What's up, Colonel? Why the big smile?"

"The Wiz located Standz's private residence and his private cell-phone number."

The Wiz looked up and smiled. "After I got his private line, I traced his residence on Google satellite. He lives near Arlington Cemetery in an exclusive waterfront condo development on a small lake in Alexandria, Virginia. He's on his PC as we speak."

"Well, let's dial him up and bust his balls," BB said.

"You really want to dance with the devil?" Billy Ray asked.

"Come on, Billy," BB said, holding his hands together in mock prayer. "Let's rent some space in that asshole's head."

"All right," he said reluctantly. "After the mission we just went through, maybe we need a little levity."

The Wiz dialed up the number, routing the call through Southeast Asia. Then he put the Navy SEAL megaphone on speaker.

The phone rang in the Prince of Darkness's residence. He looked at the CIA display on the caller ID and was baffled by where the call originated. He picked up the phone cautiously.

"Hello, Richard," Billy Ray said.

At first there was dead silence on the other end as he checked the caller ID again. "How did you get this number? Who's this?"

"Just look in the mirror, Richard."

In the background BB snickered. He had to put his hand over his mouth to keep from laughing.

The Prince of Darkness thought for a moment. Then a smile appeared on his face. "Mr. Blu, you're the last person I thought I'd be talking with today. Tell Mr. Castle he's very clever, but tell him not to get too smart for his own good. By the way, General Bishop is looking for you."

"I know exactly where Bishop is, just like I know exactly where you are."

"Really?" he said. "Since thousands of people are looking for you, where are you, William?"

"Maybe I'm right outside your condominium in Alexandria, standing in front of the marina."

Once again there was silence on the phone as the Prince of Darkness stood up quickly and looked out his window. There was no movement in the marina except for an elderly couple tying up their sloop.

"Mr. Castle has been a busy little bee."

"You have no idea."

"It's only a matter of time before Big Brother links him to all his illegal activity and that pirate Black Parade website. Then we'll see how smart he thinks he is in prison. By the way, say hello for me to Colonel Clay, Robert Brazoli, and Aloysius Smith," he said, gloating at what he thought was a brilliant move.

"You just did," Billy Ray said as a countermove. "You're on a speaker phone."

"Good. Then they'll take comfort in knowing that their military records will be taken into account at their sentencing hearing after they're convicted on numerous charges. I have all of you by *the proverbial balls!*" he said, placing an emphasis on his last words in an attempt to intimidate the men.

"There's a alternate view to that, Richard. Do you remember when you visited me at Tywater with your offer of redemption and you said that 'up until now the game has been a draw, but I have one move that you could never foresee, one that has no countermove, one you could never recover from'? Do you remember?"

"Yes, I do."

"Good, because what goes around comes around. You don't have us by the balls. We have you by the *proverbial* balls," he said, mocking him, "and a governor, a senator, a corrupt federal judge, a paid-off lawyer, and a warden!"

"Really? And how do you figure that?"

"I'll get back to that later. Who besides you know about the men who've been helping me?"

"I told the board about my suspicions, but nothing as yet has been confirmed."

"Good, because you're going to keep that information to yourself."

The Prince of Darkness shook his head and let out a sardonic chuckle. "Can't do that, William...unless you give me something substantial in return. You and your band of merry men have a great many people on edge. And what a stroke of genius leaking that intel to the media at exactly the right moment about Bishop. It went a long way toward restoring your reputation, but not in the eyes of the law or the government. They'll stop at nothing to capture or kill you. I told you in Tywater that I could give you your life back, along with the princess and the happy ending. Quid pro quo."

"I already gave you two things of great importance to you."

"Really, and the first is?"

"Your life!"

Once again there was dead silence that spoke volumes. "*My* life!" he finally said.

"See how vividly you can picture this graphic scenario. You leave your townhouse to have a meeting with the board, maybe to arrange a few assassinations of some foreign dignitaries. You get into your late-model Crown Victoria, and when you turn on the ignition, four pounds of C-4 in a shape charge goes off under the driver's seat. Whatever is left of you is interred in your new residence in Arlington. If I thought you had anything to do with what happened today, that morning would have been *this* morning!"

"I still don't understand the reason for the hostility. What happened today?"

"General Bishop and the ISS abducted Jenny and put her in Tywater."

"I had absolutely nothing to do with that. And you have my word on that, and my word is my bible; it's my bond."

"I don't know what anyone's word is worth anymore."

"Let me make some calls. I'll get her released."

"That won't be necessary. I already got her out. And you *will* keep that information to yourself until tomorrow."

"Remarkable," he said, gazing into the abyss. "Bishop's a desperate man. He's trying to salvage what's left of his reputation, especially after you leaked that information to the media and all but destroyed his career."

"He did that all by himself."

"The board told him to take the white gloves off, but I never thought he'd sink to this level. He's a loose cannon. I can't control what he does."

"I wouldn't worry too much about him. He's going to have his hands full tomorrow. Did the board in their collective wisdom ever take into consideration what would happen if I took off the white gloves? Well, did they? They won't be able to fly in enough body bags on C-130s for the dead! And *my* word is carved in the same granite they'll use to make all the ISS soldiers' tombstones."

"Don't do anything rash. The board only thinks you were planning some sort of disturbance at the dedication of the dam. That's why the ceremony was postponed. But I think your end game is on a much grander scale. It's the dam itself, isn't it? If I'm right, you'll be burning a bridge you'll never be able to cross back over...ever. Not even I will be able to help you after that."

"All scores will be settled tomorrow, and anyone or anything in my way won't be there for long. But thanks for the advice, since I know how much you care for my welfare," he said with a touch of sarcasm. "I now know you've been complicit in everything that's happened to me, except for trying to having me killed. And I now know who was behind that. You could have put an end to this any time you wished."

"That's who I am. That's what I'm paid to do. That's what the board instructed me to do. I did a dishonorable thing for an honorable reason."

In the background the Prince of Darkness heard Colonel Clay let out a sarcastic laugh.

"You still think I'm trying to play you, but I'm sincere in everything I just told you. That's why I'm going to tell you that Bishop just classified you as a terrorist. Do you know what that means?"

"Standard shoot-on-sight order," Billy Ray said matter-of-factly.

"My advice is to call it all off. Go underground. Defuse the whole situation. Let it all blow over. If I'm right about your end game and it goes sideways, in order to win, you'll have to lose. And even if you do succeed and live, then what? All the work you did to restore your reputation and exonerate yourself will have been in vain. And you'll be right back where you started, but this time your fate will be of your own making."

"You're not telling me anything that I haven't already considered."

"I'm still your only hope. Turn yourself in to me. I give you my word that I'll clear you."

"You have nothing left to offer me that I don't already have."

"What do you mean by that?"

"If I were you, I'd change the audio and passwords to your PC. The Wiz put everything in your files on a flash drive. The soul that you once thought you held in the palm of your hand is now free from your grasp forever. You no longer have any hold over me."

There was a very long pause on the phone, this time much longer than before as the Prince of Darkness realized that he had been outplayed in his own deceitful game. He knew Billy Ray was right. He had let this soul slip away. There was nothing left in his repertoire of deceit, his bag of tricks, and with all his cunning, that could enable him to regain his hold over Billy Ray. Every game, every move they had ever made against each other led up to this moment. And he knew he was powerless to alter the outcome of the game. Finally, he spoke again, but this time with the low voice of a beaten man. "Well then, I guess this will be the last time we speak."

"Don't get all teary-eyed on me now, and besides, I don't plan on getting captured or killed."

"And then what?"

"Well, since we do think alike, you tell me!"

"I really don't have a clue."

"I'm going deep underground. No one's ever going to find me. And maybe, if I think I'm really free and safe, and everyone that I care about is safe, I'll surface. But then again, maybe it'll be better for everyone's sake if I never surface.

Keep everyone guessing. As long as people like you think I'm still out there, they'll think twice about their transgressions."

Suddenly, a strange metamorphosis, a transformation was taking place right before the men's eyes as Billy Ray talked on the phone. The inner demons that he always tried to keep hidden surfaced. His facial expressions changed, but what was really disconcerting to the men was the unnatural, out-of-character look in his eyes. It made them feel uneasy. His voice became almost a whisper and his language metered, which made the men pay close attention to what he was saying. "If anyone—anyone—uses Jenny again to get to me, if she's harmed in any way, they'll see a side of me that they wished they never brought out... and that goes for you as well! You're going to play a role you're not accustomed to—Jenny's guardian angel. You're also going to forget everything you know about the men with me.

"And what do I get in return?"

"In return we won't disclose where we got the information and, in the process, save your career. You also have my word that we won't come looking for you, so you won't be wondering, looking over your shoulder, worrying every time you turn on the ignition to your car. In that way you can enjoy the life I've given back to you."

"Then it's a draw, a truce. We'll both come out winners."

"That's one way to look at it. Maybe in the grand scheme of things, we're both going to lose."

"You just might be right. Since you've given me my life back, I guess we're even. Someday you'll find out about the life I gave you back."

"I know the story. Maybe everyone would have been better off if you let me die in the OR. Do we have an agreement?"

"You have my word, for whatever you think it's worth. Well, I guess I can't say I'll see you around—"

"Because you won't," he said, interrupting him, "unless you renege on your part of the bargain, and then you still never see me coming."

After Billy Ray hung up the phone, his demeanor slowly returned to his normal personality. He turned to the Wiz. The men could see there was still something bothering him. "Make two copies of the tape BB recorded in Tywater and send a copy to the media and another to the director of the Federal Bureau of Prisons. Scan in all the information we got at the county records office. Send it out along with the tapes of Hole in One and American Pie, but before you do, take Standz's voice out the tape, so he can't be identified."

"Why, Billy?" BB said, biting the side of his hand as a gesture of defiance. "We're got the devil by the balls!"

"Because I gave him my word, and he gave me his."

"His word! His word! He gave you stu-gotts!" he said, motioning his hand in the air by his side as if he was jerking off. "Why do you think everyone calls him the Prince of Darkness? You take the word of the devil?"

"And what are you prepared to do if he doesn't honor his word?"

"Me! Me! I'll shred the bastard. Send him to fuckin' kingdom come," he said as the other men nodded in agreement.

Midnight gave BB a pat on the back, trying to calm him down. "That's the spirit," he said in earnest.

"And Standz knows that," Billy Ray said, trying to put BB at ease. "It may be the only thing that will make him honor his word."

"You're probably right, William," Colonel Clay said, nodding his head in agreement.

"Billy, what was all that bullshit Standz said about giving you your life back?" BB asked.

"You really don't know, Robert?" Colonel Clay asked.

"No, sir."

"The night we took William to the OR, he was bleeding internally, so they could only stabilize him. I was debriefed that night. Rank has its privileges," he said, smiling at the men. "Midmorning the next day, when all of you were being debriefed, I went to the OR. Standz had just returned from the site where we were captured. He was pacing the floor, occasionally looking into the OR at the surgeons operating on William. The doctors had been up all night trying to piece together four soldiers from B-Company who were on S-and-Ds when an IED had blown them apart. William flatlined...twice. One of the surgeons just gave up. He took off his rubber gloves and threw them on the floor in disgust. Standz burst into the room, screaming. He said something to the effect that if they didn't put the paddles on him and try to revive him, he would see to it that they were permanently transferred to a forward position in a hot zone. A nurse energized the paddles, and the surgeon hit William several times until he got a heartbeat. After William was stabilized, Standz left."

Colonel Clay turned to Billy Ray. "I'll never knew why he took such an interest in you. Maybe he saw something in you that was lacking in him. Then again, after he saw what you were capable of, maybe he saw a potential recruit, a man willing to sacrifice himself for his men who overcame insurmountable odds to accomplish the mission. I really don't know if his motives were honorable, but I swear to God that story's true."

"It happened just like you said," Midnight said. "Standz told me the same story when he tried to recruit me."

"I didn't know Standz tried to recruit you, Smith," the colonel said.

"Three months after Billy was discharged, my seventh tour ended. I told command that because they fucked Billy, I was done. I was fed up with the bullshit. Standz comes to see me and asks me to be a spook. He probably told me the story about saving Billy's life so that we'd be simpatico, using it to form a common bond between Billy, me, and him, but I blew him off."

"How'd you do that?" BB asked.

"I lied. Well, it was actually a half-truth. I told him, 'I'm your man. Where do I sign up? I'm ready to kill everyone and everything in my path. Just point me in the right direction.' Then I told him about my medical condition and that sometimes I have episodes and space out, but the doctors said I'd be OK as long as I stayed on my meds. I guess the prospect of having an unstable agent on the loose with a license to kill must have scared the shit out of him because he said he'd get back to me, but he never did. But I tend to agree with BB, Billy. I don't know if we could ever really trust the word of a man like Standz. Lies and deceit are the tools of his trade, just like a sniper rifle is the tool of my trade. When an honest man, a straight shooter, gives you his word, it's like he's aiming at the bull's-eye of truth on a target. He takes his one shot with a rifle. Even if he misses the bull's-eye, you know his aim was true. Men like Standz, when they give their word, they take a shotgun approach to the target. Oh, they'll hit the bull's-eye, along with everything else, mixing and peppering the target with the truth, half-truths, and outright lies. And soon, it will all become interchangeable. He won't even be able to distinguish one from another, much less an honest man. And since he's a crafty marksmen, you can never be sure of anything he says, even when he gives his word. And Billy, he's been aiming at you ever since that night."

"Midnight," Colonel Clay said, putting his arm around him. "Sometimes you amaze me with your intellect. What an appropriate metaphor."

"Well then, Midnight, Billy Ray said, "if Standz is on target about what could happen to me if tomorrow goes sideways, you'll be one of the guys who'll make sure he keeps his word."

Midnight thought about what Billy Ray said and then looked away from him, not wanting to show the other men his emotions. "Then I won't say you can bet your life on that, Billy, because I know you already have."

Billy Ray returned to his bunk. The Wiz began sending out all the information exactly as he had requested. A little later in the evening, Billy Ray returned to the main bunker. He had bathed and put on clean clothing.

"Wiz, give me two secure phones. I'll be back late, or shall I say early, in the morning."

"Where are you going, William?" Colonel Clay asked.

"Church."

"Church? You think that's wise?"

"Colonel, I gave Jenny my word that I'd see her before tomorrow. It's the last place anyone would be looking for me. I'll be hiding in plain sight. Wiz, monitor all roads leading to the church. If there's any activity, call me on one of these phones. If anything happens to me, find a way to activate the trigger, and everyone get the hell out of here."

What can it be!
What is this game?
Where the winners and losers
Think they're one in the same?
What is the answer?
The explanation?

Was the journey more important
Than the destination?
To arrive where you began,
And know this place,
To begin again.

Remembrance of Things Past

"...and so it is with our past, it's a
labor in vain to attempt to recapture it."

—Marcel Proust, *In Search of Lost Time/*
Remembrance of Things Past

WHEN BILLY RAY arrived at Saint Mary's Church, the service had just begun. He opened the large oak doors slowly so he would not disturb the parishioners. Then he stood in the rear of the church, trying to see where Jenny and her parents were seated.

Saint Mary's was a small but majestically adorned church. On each side of the main altar were two smaller altars with alcoves constructed of off-white Italian marble and beige limestone with striations of gold and brown running through the stone. In the middle of the two small altars were life-size carved marble statues of Saint Joseph in one and the Madonna in the other. Under the stained-glass windows that lined both sides of the church were carved reliefs of the Stations of the Cross.

At first, no one realized who had entered the church. As the congregation began to notice that it was Billy Ray, everyone began to turn around to see him. Father Pat looked up over his bifocals to see what was causing the commotion. As he saw Billy Ray standing in the rear of the church, he smiled and continued the service.

Billy Ray spotted Jenny sitting near the front of the church with her parents. As he began walking down the aisle, he became mildly alarmed by people he didn't recognize, thinking that one of them could easily send a text message alerting the ISS to his presence. As he continued down the aisle, all eyes were fixed on him. Some of the longtime residents sitting in the aisle seats reached out to touch him, paying homage to the man they considered their hero.

When he reached the pew, he made a small sign of the cross and knelt down briefly before sitting down next to Jenny. She smiled and reached out to hold his hand.

As the service continued, a duel consciousness occupied his thoughts. He was following the ceremony but also remembering the last time he'd sat in this exact pew with his family.

⋯⋯

His family had attended the seven o'clock Sunday service. It was the brothers' twenty-first birthday. After the service ended, they went to pick up some supplies at Bain's Dry Goods Store and then planned on going to a local restaurant for breakfast. When they entered the store, Mr. Bain was standing behind the cash register, waiting on two customers. Adeline Blu walked down the narrow corridors and began placing various spices and baking supplies into a small wicker basket slung over her arm.

"Good morning, Mr. Bain," Billy Ray said.

The two men at the counter had their back toward Mr. Bain. He looked directly into Billy Ray's eyes and said, "Good morning, Junior."

Billy Ray thought his behavior odd. Mr. Bain had known him since he was born, but he called him by his brother's name. As both men turned toward Mr. Bain, he recognized them. Even though they were older, and one of them was now almost bald, these were the two men who had stolen the silver ore from their mine and accosted him and his father. The man with the long scar on the side of his face had his hand under his jacket. As Mr. Bain gave him another odd look, shifting his eyes in the direction of the men, Billy Ray's heartbeat and adrenaline level increased.

Adeline walked up to the counter and nodded to the two men. "Good morning," she said.

"Mornin', ma'am," the scar-faced man said.

"I haven't seen you men in town before. Are you visiting someone?"

"No, ma'am," he said. "We've been, let's say, on vacation for the past five years—room, board, and meals courtesy of the state of California," he said, nudging the other man.

The other man's face was pockmarked, and he was dim witted and repeated everything his accomplice said. "Yeah, vacation."

"Come on, Mom; we've got to get going," Billy Ray said.

"What's the hurry, Billy? I still have to pick up some flour if I'm going to bake a cake for the birthday party."

"We'll get it later," he said, grabbing his mother's arm, trying to lead her toward the door.

"Hold on, amigo," the scar-faced man said, pulling a gun from under his jacket. "No one's leavin'. You think you're pretty slick, Shopkeep, with those eyes. Now everyone come up here where I can see you."

"I recognize you men," Raymond said. "You're the thugs that stole the silver from our mine."

"My, my, my, old man, what a memory. Just take out your wallets, and you, ma'am, put your purse right here," he said, tapping his gun on the counter.

"Yeah, on the counter," the dim-witted man repeated.

Adeline held her pocketbook with both hands and pulled it close to her chest. "I *will* not!"

"What is it with you people? So little time, so many pigeons to rob. Now, ma'am, give me the fuckin' purse, or *someone*," he said in a sing-song manner, "is not going to make it to *breakfast*."

"No!" she said adamantly.

Billy Ray felt helpless, almost paralyzed with indecision. Everything he had learned from Master Mei and the theories from *The Art of Violence* had not prepared him for this moment. He had acquired the skill, discipline, and knowledge but not how or when to apply it.

"Some people just don't get it," the scar-faced man said, placing his gun sideways in his hand, striking Raymond on the side of his face just above his temple, sending him tumbling back, crashing into a row of can goods.

Billy Ray's instincts took over. He spun around with great force hit the man with an open-hand chop just under his Adam's apple, shattering his windpipe. As he fell to the floor, his gun discharged. The pockmarked man lunged at Billy Ray with a knife. He twisted his wrist backward, took the knife, and thrust it deeply into the man's throat. As he fell to the floor, torrents of blood poured from his nose and the gaping hole in his neck. As he gasped for air, a gurgling sound erupted as blood projected from his mouth. Then there was just silence.

Billy Ray turned toward his mother. She was still clutching on to her purse. Her hands trembled as she dropped it to the floor. Then she placed both hands over her stomach and looked at her blood-covered hands. "Oh, Billy, I think I've been shot," she said, collapsing.

Raymond tried to get up off the floor, but he could not stand up. He looked at the pool of blood next to his wife. "Junior," he shouted, wincing in pain. "Get Doc Horton and the sheriff," he said, before passing out.

As Junior ran out the door, Mr. Bain and Billy Ray knelt down next to Adeline.

"Billy, is your father all right?" she asked, in a voice slightly above a whisper.

"He's all right, ma."

She looked down and saw the pool of blood and felt the warm liquid under her. She knew she was seriously injured. "Billy, have patience with your father. He's a hard man, but he loves both of you boys."

"You're going to be fine, ma," he said, trying to ease her mind. "Doc's on his way."

"Your brother...Junior. Watch over him. You've always been the stronger of the two. Promise me..." She didn't finish her thought. Her eyes closed, and she became limp.

Sheriff Roy came running into the store with his gun drawn, followed by Dr. Horton and Father Pat. Dr. Horton placed two fingers on her neck and shook his head. As Father Pat knelt down, administering her last rights, he could barely speak as tears flowed down his face.

The memory of his mother as she lay dying had always haunted him. When he opened his eyes, he was back in the present. His mother's last words echoed in his thoughts as he remembered the day Mayor White and Father Pat came to the prison to tell him that the ISS had killed his brother. "Billy, watch over your brother."

Everyone stood up in the church and held hands as the congregation recited the Lord's praye. After the prayer, everyone sat down. As easily as he had slipped back to the moment, once again he was back in time...

⊶⊫◉ ◉⊰⊶

After a short investigation, Adeline's death was ruled a homicide and the deaths of the two criminals were deemed self-defense, justified homicide. In the months that followed his wife's death, Raymond became distant from Billy Ray. He felt that Billy Ray's actions had contributed to her death. He stopped talking to him and would not sit down at the same dinner table with his son.

It was late in the day, almost twilight. Billy Ray had just grafted all the scions from the rare stock of grapes he'd purchased from Burgundy, France. When he entered his home, Raymond and Junior were already eating supper. He made his plate and sat across from his father.

"Billy, did you finish?" Junior asked.

"Just finished," he said, looking across the table at his father, who kept his head down as he ate.

Although Raymond had not finished eating, he got up to leave.

"Don't leave on my account. I'll eat in my room."

"Good," his father said, with his back to him. "Because every time I see your face, it reminds me of her lying on the floor dying. You just couldn't let it go, could you?"

"Come on, Pop," Junior said. "That's not true. Those men robbed and killed a convenience store clerk in the next county. If it wasn't for Billy, they might have killed us all."

"You stay out of this, Junior," he said, pointing his finger at him and then turning slightly to look at Billy Ray. "I saw what I saw. All that fancy self-defense nonsense. That's what got your mother killed. All that useless knowledge is just as useless as all those fancy grapes you bought from *France*. You have no idea of the evil that men do, or obviously how to prevent it. If it wasn't for you, she'd still be alive!"

"Nothing I've ever done has been good enough for you. I'll not stay where I'm not wanted. You won't have to be looking at my face much longer."

"Why's that, Billy?" Junior asked, believing what his brother was saying was in anger or in jest. "Where are you going to go?"

"Somewhere where my worthless talents," he said, looking at his father, "might be put to use. I joined the marines."

Raymond began walking out of the room and shook his head in disgust. "Good riddance," he said, without turning around.

⇥▷◁⇤

Everyone in the church stood up and a procession of the faithful filed up to the altar as Father Pat began passing out communion. Billy Ray said an act of contrition for all his past transgressions, and for those he was about to commit, before going up to the altar. As he held out his hand to receive the host, he handed Father Pat a small note as inconspicuously as possible.

Just before the mass ended, Father Pat walked up to the pulpit to address the congregation. "I have been asked by the US Geological Association to inform the residents of Silver Verde of the following," he said, looking down from the elevated pulpit at Billy Ray. "There's is a high probability of a seismic disturbance in the northeast area of the county sometime in the wee hours of the morning, presumably just before sunrise. California Power and Light already owns most of the land in that area. However, those of you who live in low-lying areas are strongly advised to seek temporarily higher ground. For those people, a safe place would be Silver Verde Vista. We pray that their prediction is inaccurate," he said, raising up his hands. "Go in peace."

"Thanks be to God," the congregation replied.

⇥▷◁⇤

After the mass ended, Billy Ray stayed in his pew while Jenny walked with her parents to the rear of the church. After they left, she remained in the rear of the church, talking with Mayor White. Most of the people left the church, respecting Billy Ray's privacy, and just nodded as they walked by. As Dr. Horton walked by, he reached out and touched him on his shoulder. "We're all behind you, Billy. God be with you."

Father Pat motioned for Billy Ray to stay. "Let me change out of these vestments. Before you go, I have something I want to give you."

When Father Pat returned, he held a small box between his hands tightly as if to protect the valuable contents inside. The box was covered with purple velvet and had the presidential seal embossed in gold lettering on the top. He sat down next to Billy Ray, placed the box between them, and crossed his legs.

"William," he said, looking over his bifocals as if he were about to scold a schoolboy for misbehaving, "did you kiss the Blarney Stone, my son? I didn't know that the science of geology had advanced to the point that earthquakes could be predicted in advance."

Billy Ray smiled. "Never could fool you, Father."

"You look troubled, my son. Anything you care to confide with me?"

Billy Ray turned around to look at Jenny, who was still talking with the mayor. "I'm worried about Jenny's future. With all the hardship she's had to endure, she deserves a little happiness. She's relying on me for her future, and I think I'm going to let her down...again."

"My son, that's why you are the selfless man you are. With so many conspiring against you, so many who want to capture or kill you, you're worrying about the welfare of another."

"All my life I could see all my possible choices and plan for them. The consequences of my actions were clear. But for the first time, I can't see beyond tomorrow. The decision I will have to make will affect so many, especially Jenny."

Father Pat looked up as if he were asking from guidance from a higher source to counsel him. "It's the decision a man has to make when faced with adversity that is the true test of his character. I know you're not here asking for forgiveness, and I'm not going to give you absolution for the things you've done or are about to do.

Everyone knows what you've been through, not only in Silver Verde but throughout the whole country, the crosses you've been made to bear and the injustices and hardships thrust upon you, so I believe there's nothing to absolve. If you'll bear with me, I'd like to tell you how a young Irish lad from so far away came to be the parish priest in this small community.

"It was your father who convinced me to come to Silver Verde. I promised him I'd never tell anyone this story, but I can't see what harm it would do to tell you now. It may actually ease your mind and maybe help you with the decisions you'll have to make.

"I was about the age you were when you joined the marines. A punk, a street brawler from the slums of Dublin. The old parish priest sees something in me that I never did. Takes me under his wing. Tells me he's going to put my violent tendencies to good use. Teaches me the fundamentals of boxing. Mostly to keep me off the streets, out of jail, and out of the hands of the IRA. I become a pugilist, as they used to call us back then. Irish Patty O'Keefe, Golden Gloves champeen, the pride of Ireland. Shamrocks on my kelly-green-and-white boxing trunks. Turned pro. Won all my first ten bouts by knockouts. Made big money by the standards of the day. Wore custom-tailored suits. Stayed and ate in all the fancy hotels.

"Everyone wanted to be in the company of the moneymaker, and management took a nice bite of the golden boy's arse. Had my way with the ladies, if you know what I mean," he said, raising his eyebrows. Billy Ray smiled. "Made plans with a beautiful redhead. Oh, what a lass! We were to be engaged after the big bout to unify the light middleweight title. I was to fight a mean Englishman, a dirty fighter with an iron jaw. He'd never been knocked out. The fact that an Irish Catholic was to fight an English Protestant couldn't have been better for the promoters. And they played up that fact for all they could squeeze out of the hatred between the Catholics and the Protestants.

"Tenth round," he said as his eyes went blank, reliving the story as he told it. "I'm cut bad. My eyes look like walnuts. Perspiration burning the cuts over my eyes. I'm almost out on my feet, but so is he. The fight's about even. Just before the bell rings for the final round, my manager says to me, 'Patty boy, we're in England. Don't let it go to the card. Go out there and kill him. Kill him!' With about a minute left, I get lucky and slip in an uppercut. Then I hit him with a right cross. He lets his guard slip and goes against the ropes, trying to recover. I summoned up all I had left and hit him with a flurry of short punches. That's when I look into his eyes. They're lifeless. Big and black like an eight ball in a billiards game. My corner's yelling, 'Finish him! Finish him!' He's going down all on his own, but I still load up. I didn't have to load up. Pop! I hit him on the side of his temple. His legs turn to rubber as he goes down. As soon as I see the way he goes down, I knew something wasn't right. I went to a neutral corner, and the referee counted him out. The longest ten seconds of my life. He raised up my arm, declaring me the winner. All the while I'm looking over my shoulder at the Brit. His manager is lying next to him, screaming for the ringside doctor. He's not getting up. He died right there in the ring, and I never put the gloves on again. It wasn't in me anymore. I kept seeing his eyes. His eyes. After the fight, there were riots in the streets. We barely made it out alive. And that beautiful redhead called off the engagement after I quit boxing. Isn't it funny how sometimes when you need someone the most, they abandon you?

"I left that whole life behind. Traveled to America. Stayed with my mother's relatives. Joined the seminary. After I was ordained, I joined the military. That's where I met your father, in Vietnam. I was assigned to his unit as their chaplain.

"It had been raining for over a week. Hot. Humid. We were drenched to the bone. Our position was overrun. We never saw them coming. I can still hear the forward observers screaming, 'Zips in the wire,' as the mortar shells and flares were exploding overhead. They seemed to come out of the bowels of the earth from tunnels under our base. The casualties were devastating. They shoot the injured and take the survivors to a POW camp in the middle of nowhere, far away from allied lines.

"Our numbers dwindled from starvation, disease, and executions. They worked us sixteen hours a day in the rice patties. Your father and I were skin and bones. The commandant was sadistic. He hated Americans. Disobey even the smallest order and you were put in the hole, and you never came out. After a while the commandant and the guards tolerated me and let me walk about the camp unguarded. They knew I was a man of the cloth, and therefore harmless, or so they thought. And since I was keeping up the men's spirits and morale, it was good for production in the fields. I helped out in the kitchen, preparing the slop for our men and the water buffalo steaks for the Vietcong. Now and then, I'd sneak out some real food for our men. After a while I had a fundamental knowledge of their language, which I knew one day would come in handy.

"I talked with your father every day. He'd pass the time talking about his family's vineyards and about how the small town was going to build a church and a school. That's when I promised him that if we both made it out of that hell alive, I would become their first parish priest.

"One morning when I was preparing breakfast, I get bits and pieces of guards talking. They said something to the effect that the Americans were closing in, and they were going to evacuate the camp. The commandant must have been worried about all the atrocities he and his men had committed because they were going to kill all of us before they left the next morning. That night when I was preparing the guard's dinner, I took a couple of knives and poisoned their food.

"Later that night, when the guards were either unconscious or dead, I began setting the men free, starting with your father's bamboo cell. I told him what was going down and gave him one of the knives. There were still about eight guards who had not come off their shift to eat. When I went to free the rest of the men, your father killed all the remaining guards, some of our men would later say, brutally.

"Two days after we escaped, a reconnaissance team found us, and we were shipped stateside. Seventy-eight men went into the camp," he said, looking down, "and only twenty-five made it out. There was an official inquiry, and your father downplayed his role in the rescue. He wasn't about the medals or the glory. When the time came, he knew what he had to do, and he did it."

Father Pat opened the small purple velvet box. His hands trembled slightly as he handed him a Silver Star. "Your father was awarded this medal for his actions in saving the men. The brass had something much grander in store for me. After I recuperated in a VA Hospital, I was flown to Washington, DC. On the lawn of the White House, with all the media present, President Lyndon Johnson gave me this," he said, taking another medal out of the box and handing it to him.

Billy Ray looked at the medal and then at Father Pat. "The Congressional Medal of Honor," he said in amazement. "No one knows."

"And I know that you'll understand why I'd like to keep it that way. I want you to keep both medals."

"I'll keep my father's medal, but I could never accept yours."

"I want you to have it. It's only been collecting dust for the past fifty years. I've seen the news programs, and so has everyone else. You probably deserve this medal as much, if not more, than I did. After I received this medal, the church would have granted me any parish in the land. Why, there was even talk about a position in the Vatican. Ha! That wasn't the life for a simple man like me."

"Junior and I knew my father was in Vietnam. When we were young, one rainy day we were in the attic playing war with all his military stuff. He came up and was pissed and told Junior to take off his uniform. We asked him about the war, and he just looked away and changed the subject. That night, he burned everything in his footlocker in our fireplace. My mother told us never to ask him about his time in the military, and we never did again. But now, I think I understand."

"I don't think you do, William. Not really."

"How so?"

"I think he saw a lot of himself in you. Maybe he didn't want you to become jaded. Shelter you from the outside world. The horrors of war. He probably didn't want you or Junior to know what men have to become and what they have to do when confronted by evil men. After all you've been through, how ironic. In light of the fact that you did virtually the same thing he did when you rescued your men who were being tortured and killed, I guess he was right in thinking that the apple wouldn't fall far from the tree.

"Talking to you about my past reminds me of that song those two American lads sang 'The Boxer.' Every time I relive the story, the song returns. The song and the memory are forever intertwined." He looked up and recalled the lyrics of the song. "'He carries a reminder of every glove that laid him down or cut him till he cried out in his anger and his pain, I am leaving. I am leaving, but the fighter still remains.' Inside me is the remnant of a prize fighter, but that young, cocky Irish lad, full of promise and foolish pride, is long gone, and in his place is the old priest you see before you.

"Every decision I've made—many good, some bad—has led me to this point in my life, and what a strange, unforeseen trip it has been. I'm not complaining. I've had a good life. I'd like to think a full life, a meaningful, productive life. I never regretted the promise I made to your father or lost any sleep thinking about all those Vietcong I killed. But I've relived that final round a thousand times in vain, wondering what my life would have been like if I had held back on that last punch. It was my pride. My pride. One day I have to atone, answer to him," he said, looking up, "for what that foolish young man did.

"I know all too well the worldly pursuits I gave up to become a man of the cloth. I've been fortunate to have tasted that life. Maybe when He judges me, He'll take that into account. I would like to have had a wife and a family. And if I would have had a son, I would have been blessed and proud to have called a man like you my son.

"William, you never know what destiny, and since I am a man of the cloth, what God has in store for all of us. And now, both of us know that lesson all too well. Sometimes," he said, looking back at Jenny and then at Billy Ray, "life pulls away the things you want the most, no matter how hard you try to hold on to them. And in an attempt to avoid your destiny, sometimes you run right into it."

Mayor White called out to Father Pat that he was leaving.

"Father," Billy Ray said, "before the mayor leaves, there's something I want to ask him, without Jenny there."

Father Pat called out to the mayor to wait, and asked Jenny to come to him.

"Here I am, your confessor, and I end up telling you my confession," he said, smiling and nodding his head.

When Billy Ray came up to the mayor, they shook hands. "I was talking with Jenny. I asked her about her ordeal with the ISS and how she got out of Tywater so soon. She said I should ask you."

"Let's just say she got out on good behavior," he said, with a cunning smile, raising his eyebrows.

"I see," the mayor said, smiling. "Say no more."

"I have a favor to ask you," Billy Ray said. He looked at Jenny, who was talking with Father Pat.

"Anything, Billy. What is it?"

Billy Ray told the mayor what he wanted him to do. He was puzzled by his request but told him he would honor it, if possible. Then he made a small sign of the cross and left. As Billy Ray was making his way to the front of the church, both the cell phones in his pocket began vibrating.

"What's up, Wiz?"

"Someone must have ratted you out in church. There's three ISS Humvees speeding toward you, and two more about a mile behind them. Get out of there...now!"

"All right, keep me posted."

Billy Ray quickened his pace until he reached Jenny and Father Pat. "Father, the ISS are on their way here now. We have to be going."

"Not by the front door," he said, taking hold of Jenny's hand. "Follow me."

Father Pat led them behind the altar to the vestry, where the ceremonial garments were kept. He pushed aside the vestments, removed a shelf, and pulled a latch. He opened a small door and turned on a light to a narrow stairway. "Those stairs lead to a room under the church.

I take refuge there when I want to be alone with my thoughts. All the privacy and creature comforts of home," he said, winking at Billy Ray.

"Are you coming?"

"No, no. Don't worry about me. I think I can take care of the ISS," he said as they descended down the stairs. "I'll say a prayer for you, William." Maybe two, he thought.

When the ISS burst into the church, Father Pat had a long instrument in his hands, extinguishing the lit candles. The soldiers were wearing full body armor and carrying M-16 assault rifles. Two soldiers secured the entrance while a dozen entered and fanned out, taking defensive positions behind pews and marble columns. Several other soldiers began searching the church.

"Good evening, gentlemen. You're a little late for service."

The lieutenant talked to the other men, speaking into a mic fastened to the lapel on his uniform. "It appears to be secure," he said, to the other men. "He's not here. We're looking for a terrorist, Father. We received intel that he attended service here tonight. Is he in the area?"

"As you can see, I'm the only one in the church."

"You'll have to come with us, Father. It's merely a formality. General Bishop may have some questions to ask you."

"Let me finish extinguishing these candles, and we'll go to see the famous, or shall I say, the infamous, General Bishop."

The Devil Is in the Details

DR. VIBES HAD just settled in for the evening. She made a cup of orange pekoe tea, relaxed on her sofa, and began channel surfing. Her two cats, Sigmund and Freud, were cuddling next to her as they warmed themselves against her checkered flannel bathrobe. She'd had a long, exhausting day at Tywater, and her eyes were heavy, almost closing. She was just about to turn off the TV and retire early when she switched the channel to CNN and saw the caption "Breaking News" flashing across the screen. Wolf Blitzer appeared on the screen with a picture of Billy Ray in the background. Dr. Vibes sat up and turned up the volume.

"Because of the magnitude and political implications of the story CNN is about to reveal, we've extended the 'Situation Room' tonight and have special reports from Anderson Cooper and Jake Tapper," who appeared on a split screen behind him. "Anderson, you have viewed the tapes and documents. What can you tell us about what the viewers will see?"

"Wolf, the tapes and documents seem to implicate Senator Bryant, Governor Maxwell, Federal Judge Arthur Tores, Attorney William Coyle, and others in an ongoing conspiracy, obstruction of justice, as well as a host of other civil and criminal offenses perpetrated against William Blu. We've edited the tapes for time constraints without taking the damaging allegations out of context. And Wolf, although the hour is late, due to the graphic violence in the second tape, entitled," he said, looking down at his notes, "American Pie, viewer discretion is advised."

After the tapes were played, Anderson Cooper made a comment to Wolf Blitzer. "The American Pie tape seems to confirm the allegation made by Mayor White of Silver Verde several years ago that the disturbance that led to Blu's incarceration was initiated by outside agitators. One of the agitators identified by a facial-recognition document supplied to CNN was a former agent of the CIA who was recently killed in Silver Verde. Back to you, Wolf."

"Alarming details, Anderson," Wolf Blitzer said, shaking his head. "We also have a document from the California County Records Office that seems to indicate that Senator Bryant, who is on the board of California Power and Light, may have used his influence to alter the fault line in order for the hydroelectric facility to meet permitting regulations. Evidence suggests that the dam was constructed very close to a fault line.

"We also have evidence in the form of a tape of a yet-to-be-identified corrections officer at Tywater that implicates Warden Van Leeston in an attempt on William Blu's life while he was incarcerated at the federal prison. The tape also implicates an unknown powerful senator in the plot. Could this unnamed senator be in fact Senator William Bryant?"

"And if that isn't enough," Anderson Cooper said, "in a somewhat related matter, in documents provided to CNN, it would appear that Senator Bryant and his partners committed fraud to obtain a large tract of land on a project in Silver Verde from a man identified as Roscoe Clements. He is currently serving a seven-year sentence in Tywater. On that property is now a twenty-million-dollar mixed-use project called the Village at Silver Verde. It would appear that the property was confiscated by illegal means and that the cover-up led to the imprisonment of Mr. Clements."

"After the break," Wolf Blitzer said, "Jake Tapper is in Studio B with two former federal judges to discuss the legal ramifications of the tapes and documents and whether the US attorney general will move to vacate all the judgments against William Blu. Jake Tapper will discuss whether these developments will end the political career and the vice-presidential nomination of Senator Bryant, who seems to have been the architect of these conspiracies and the cover-up."

Dr. Vibes watched the CNN report until it ended. She finished her cup of tea, turned off the TV, and smiled. As she got into bed, a sense of sadness and foreboding enveloped her like the blanket she had just pulled over herself. All her training and sessions with Billy Ray gave her a unique insight into his personality, but more important, what he tried to hide. In light of the CNN report, she wondered if this was the goal of his end game or a prelude to his vendetta. She knew of his inner demons and that it had something to do with death, the death of others, and although she prayed she was wrong, ultimately his own demise.

⊶≡◉ ◉≡⊷

The Prince of Darkness was playing chess with an opponent from China over the Internet when an EAC flashed across his screen. He was unaware of the CNN report until the board requested his immediate presence at an emergency meeting. He quickly read the attachments in his communiqué with highlights of the news report. He dressed, and as he entered his Crown Victoria, he thought twice and hesitated before he turned on the ignition, remembering what Billy Ray had told him earlier in the day. On his drive to Maryland, he placed his laptop on the passenger's seat and reviewed the CNN report.

When he entered the amphitheater, some of the board members were dressed in leisure clothing, having been summoned at such a late hour. The chairman was reviewing parts of the CNN report on a computer screen.

Vice-chairperson and former US appellate judge Dorothy Weinberg called the meeting to order. Then she looked over her glasses at the Prince of Darkness. "Mr. Standz, may we assume that you have had time to digest and evaluate the ramifications of the CNN report?"

"I have, Your Honor."

"In light of what Mr. Blu has accomplished in gathering and revealing this information, I believe I speak for the entire board when I say we have a new-found respect for his talents. Speaking for myself, I now understand why you have tried to recruit him as your protégé all these years—unsuccessfully, I might add. It would seem that the devil, as well as the truth, is in the details of this CNN report, and this presents a dilemma for us."

"A dichotomy to be sure, Your Honor."

"This will present a public-relations nightmare for anyone who opposes him. From this point on, he'll be viewed as a cult figure, a folk hero, and hence, untouchable. Is this a fair assessment?"

"Yes, Your Honor."

The chairman finished replaying segments of the CNN report. He covered his microphone and asked the vice-chairperson a few questions. "Mr. Standz, if what you say is true, how are we to proceed with the Silver Verde matter?"

"Further involvement or intercession would be unwise and not in the best interest of the board."

"And how did you arrive at this conclusion?"

"I have the details and confirmation that the Silver Verde matter will be resolved in the near future."

"At what timetable?"

"Tomorrow, Mr. Chairman, and the solution will be catastrophic."

"And the board is powerless to control the outcome and the storyline?"

"Yes."

"We don't like being put in a situation in which we're damned if we do and damned if we don't," the vice-chairperson interjected. "Are you advising us that our further intervention can only result in a lose-lose situation for the board?"

"You are correct, Your Honor," the Prince of Darkness said, lowering his head. "My recommendation to the board is to order General Bishop to rescind his classification of William Blu as a terrorist, which carries a shoot-on-sight mandate. Blu knows that in all likelihood he will be exonerated of all of the charges against him. There may be a chance, a slim one at best, that he will stand down from his end game."

"I am curious, Mr. Standz," Weinberg said. "When was the last time you talked with Mr. Blu?"

"Earlier today."

"Really?" she said. "And are we correct in assuming that he revealed the details of his end game?"

"Not in so many words, but I have a pretty good idea of what it is."

"We first thought that he was going to create some type of disturbance at the dedication of the hydroelectric facility to bring attention to his plight, and you now believe his end game is something on a much grander scale?"

"Unfortunately, you are correct. It is the dam itself," he said as the board members looked at each other in bewilderment.

"Refresh my memory, Mr. Standz," Weinburg said. "What will this act symbolize?"

"Everyone here is familiar with the Black Parade website. Posted on the first page is a quote from the Declaration of Independence, which states, 'When a long train of abuses and usurpations pursuing invariably the same object evinces a design to reduce them under absolute despotism, it is their right, it is their duty, to throw off such government and to provide new guards for their future security.'"

"And how does that apply to this situation?"

"In laymen's terms, it means that when the public perceives that the government has become oppressive, those who can act should act. William Blu is not a crusader. He's a man of principals and conviction. It just so happens that some of his goals run parallel to the citizens'. The people have taken up his plight as their own. His end game of taking down everyone who conspired against him is almost complete. When he takes back everything that has been taken from him, including the land on which the dam was built, the people believe his act of defiance will be their act of defiance, and he will become their surrogate, acting on behalf of the people who are unwilling or unable to take back what they believe was taken from them."

"General Bishop and over two thousand ISS troops can't stop him?"

"Try as they may, if they stand in his way, he'll take out Bishop and the ISS, and if it means he'll have to make the ultimate sacrifice to accomplish his goal, he will. After tomorrow, we'll have to brace ourselves for the aftermath and the chaos and anarchy that will ensue."

"How severe and for how long a duration?" she asked.

"It's hard to predict."

"If what you believe is inevitable, then I guess we'll just have to expect the worst, hope for the best, and ride out the storm along with everyone else."

"Yes, Your Honor."

"Now, Mr. Standz," the chairman said, "on to the matter of Senator Bryant. This will be the most important election in our lifetime. His political career is finished. He must be persuaded to stand down, take sole responsibility for his actions, and go away quietly. We don't believe that arrogant S-O-B will. The people will be so outraged by his actions that he'll take down his whole party, including Senator Morton's chances of becoming the next president. The current president is driving our nation off a cliff, and his foreign policy has the entire world at the precipice. Our enemies no longer fear us, and our allies no longer believe we have their backs. Domestically, there are so many people on the government tit of entitlements, they'll be reluctant to vote against Santa Claus. This president's ideology of altruism and his experiment in socialism—the redistribution of wealth, reliance in the government instead of self-reliance—will ultimately lead this country to become a dystopian society. And now we're dealing with ISIS, the Islamic takeover of the Middle East, and a serious threat to our country. We're about to come under attack from without and within. It may truly be the twilight's last gleaming. We have scheduled a military transport to leave for the West Coast in two hours. You'll be the only passenger. Arrange a meeting with Bryant and persuade him to see the light. If he resists, do you have a satisfactory solution to his problems?"

"I have several in mind."

"Excellent. Be advised that our future good graces and the latitude that we have granted you to operate in the field with total impunity are dependent upon a successful resolution to this problem. You are hereby granted the board's executive authority to carry out this mandate with all of the discretion that it warrants. Do you fully understand the parameters of this order?" he asked, staring down at him.

"Yes, Mr. Chairman."

"Well then, that will be all, Mr. Standz. Have a good trip, and Godspeed."

⊷═● ●═⊶

Father Pat had been taken to the temporary headquarters of the ISS at the hydroelectric facility. As the soldiers waited for General Bishop to arrive, he entertained the troops with various stories and anecdotes. When the general arrived, the soldiers stopped talking and stood at attention as they saluted him. Bishop was tired and gave the soldiers a look of disgust. He sat down and noticed an EAC flashing across his screen. He opened the e-mail and read the directive from the board, ordering him to rescind William Blu's classification as a terrorist and the shoot-on-sight order. He took off his general's cap, flung it across the room at one of the soldiers, and deleted the message.

"Two thousand troops in this rathole of a town, and you'd think we'd have him by now," he said to no one in particular.

"He wasn't in the church, sir," the lieutenant said.

"And what does this priest know?"

"We didn't question him yet. We were waiting for you, sir."

"And how about the female witness?"

"Nothing, sir. She said she didn't see anything on the night in question."

"I'll make her talk," he said as he stood up and walked over to Father Pat. "I'm General Bishop, *Padre.*"

"I know who you are," Father Pat said matter-of-factly. "You're the general who got caught in a lie when you tried to tarnish the reputation of our local hero."

Several of the soldiers grinned and quickly hid their amusement, which did not escape the general's notice. Bishop stared down the men. "We received a text message that the terrorist William Blu attended service in your church. Was he there, Padre?"

"All sinners as well as the faithful are equally welcomed in the house of the Lord. Perhaps, when you have some time, you'll attend one of our services."

"Save your sermons for the sheep in your flock who give a fuck! If you talked to him, I want to know every last detail."

"Do you believe in God, general?" Father Pat asked in earnest.

"I ask the questions here, Padre! Cut the bullshit!"

"It was a simple question. I just wanted to know if you believed in a deity, a higher power."

General Bishop looked up in the air, not caring to respond to the question. "You want to know what I believe in? I believe in these United States of America, our military, myself, and very little else. And that's my gospel, Padre!"

"That's really a shame, because I have a feeling—no, actually it's more of a premonition—that you may be seeing your maker sooner than you think."

General Bishop's patience was wearing thin. He put his face within inches of Father Pat's face, trying to intimidate him. "So you did talk to him!" he shouted.

"He didn't tell me anything of use to you, but even if he did, as William's confessor, there's nothing you could do or say to make me violate the sanctity of what he may have confessed to me."

General Bishop looked at his men with a devious smile. Then he hit Father Pat with a backhanded slap to the side of his face. The ring on his finger cut his lip. Father Pat put his hand up to his mouth slowly and wiped off the blood. The soldiers were embarrassed by the general's action and looked at the floor. "I don't want any surprises that I can't see coming," Bishop shouted. "Are you going to tell me what I want to know?"

"Not a chance in hell!"

As General Bishop raised his hand to strike him again, Father Pat looked up. "Forgive me, Father," he said. This time when Bishop went to strike him, Father Pat could feel his instincts take over and his hand close into a tight fist. Then he blocked Bishop's hand and hit him with a left hook and then a sharp uppercut, sending him reeling back over a chair and then crashing into a filing cabinet. He looked over to where the general lay on the floor and then at his closed fist. "I still have it," he said, smiling. "Didn't see that surprise coming, did you, General?"

General Bishop became enraged as the soldiers in the room could not suppress their laughter. "Wipe those fucking grins off your faces and grab that son of a bitch!" he shouted, standing up as he adjusted his uniform, trying to regain his dignity and composure. Two soldiers took hold of Father Pat. Bishop slowly walked over to him and grabbed him by his collar. "Priest or no priest, you're going to tell me everything I need to know, because I have a feeling—no, actually it's more of a premonition," he said mockingly, "that you'll be seeing your God long before I do, Padre!"

Desire and Epiphany

BILLY RAY TOOK off his three-quarter-length jacket and laid it next to a large antique Victorian bed with a canopy of fretwork and ornamental lace. He wore a tight-fitting purple T-shirt that BB had given him, which accentuated his lean, muscular upper body and had the motto of New Hampshire printed in front with bold white lettering: "Live Free or Die."

Next to the bed were a large, barricaded bulkhead and a storage area with church artifacts. There were Christmas and other religious holiday decorations and ornaments and a large crèche with life-size statues of the Nativity.

Jenny was walking around the room looking at all the religious material. She picked up a box of long wooden matches and lit a few decorated church candles that were affixed on top of highly polished brass candleholders. The candles cast a soft flickering glow in the otherwise dimly lit room. Then she sat down next to Billy Ray on the ornate bed, leaned over, and gave him a soft, passionate kiss.

"What were you and the mayor talking about?" she asked, putting her arm around him.

"You," he said, smiling in a joking manner, which immediately put an expression of doubt on her face about the validity of his answer. "And what were you talking about with the mayor?"

"You," she said, playfully returning his quip as she squeezed her arm tighter around him.

"I could tell by the way he was looking at you that he has the hots for you," he said in jest, mocking what she had said earlier about Dr. Vibes's interest in him.

Her first instinct was to rebuff what he had said, but then she thought she would tease him. "Maybe. Why not. He's a handsome man, and he could do worse," she said, putting her head in his shoulder.

Her hair smelled like jasmine, and he drank in the fragrance as it brought back the memory of that perfect day on the banks of Silver Verde Lake.

Billy Ray reached into his pocket and gave her a cell phone. "Just before dawn, some of those men you met earlier will call you. Go with them to Silver Verde Vista. They'll have a new identity for you and will take you to your relatives in Canada."

"Will you be coming with us?"

"Maybe a little while later, when I'm sure we'll both be safe there."

Jenny put her hands under his T-shirt, caressing his body. Then she began pulling it off.

"Do you think this is the time and the place?"

She was a little put off by his question. She knew he was always shy and bashful around women, but if he wouldn't take the initiative, she would. "I can't think of a better place," she said in a voice a little above a whisper. "And time, who knows the next time we'll be together," she said, pulling his shirt over his head.

On his right shoulder she saw the same Special Forces tattoo that all the men wore in his unit. On his back and chest were the elongated scars from the operation that saved his life in Afghanistan. As she moved her hands over the scars, she looked into his eyes and kissed him.

He watched her undressing as the dim, flickering light from the candles gave her body a soft glow and displayed her naked body in silhouette. As she pulled the thin sheet half over them, she kissed him passionately. "You have no idea how many times I desired and dreamed of this moment."

For the first time in many years, Billy Ray's thoughts were not on the events of his past or his future plans but only on the moment. He caressed her sinewy body and soft skin of her legs, thighs, and backside. Jenny could feel her nipples hardening against his chest in her heightened sense of arousal as they moved slowly in unison. The pace of their rhythm increased, along with their beating hearts, as they reached the ecstasy of their rapture. She was breathing heavy and let out a pleasurable sigh as she kissed him on his neck. They made love several times, staying intertwined as one. As they lay facing each other, the expression on Jenny's face was one of bliss and contentment. Her eyes were growing heavy. Just before she closed her eyes, he gave her a soft kiss of reassuring love as she drifted off to sleep.

⋯≡◉ ◉≡⋯

As Billy Ray watched Jenny sleeping, the reality of the coming day began to occupy his thoughts, and his temporary respite became short lived. As the flickering candles obscured the setting, he recalled the events that had shaped and changed the course of his life.

⋯≡◉ ◉≡⋯

His unit was far from base in the mountainous regions, laser-targeting a Taliban stronghold buried deep in the caves. Overhead were B-I Stealth bombers waiting for them to pinpoint the coordinates to enable them to drop thermobarics and deeply penetrate bunker-buster ordinance on the enemy.

When he arrived back at base, a telegram had arrived from Junior telling him that his father didn't have long to live. He had accumulated time for R and R and took the first transport to the States. When he arrived in Silver Verde, his father had already passed away and been buried in the family plot next to his mother. Billy Ray, wearing his full military uniform, stood with his hands folded in prayer in front of the freshly dug gravesite. The grave was adorned with flowers in vases and many funeral arrangements.

As he recalled the memory, he thought it odd that both the Prince of Darkness and Father Pat, one amoral and one pious, had both shared with him the same observation that sometimes a memory or event in one's life becomes intertwined with a piece of music, one recalling the other. For him, each time he thought of his father, the Cat Stevens song "Father and Son" would come to mind and vice versa. In light of everything he had been through, the words were never more poignant than they were now.

It's not time to make a change
Just relax, take it easy
You're still young
That's your fault,
There's so much you have to know.
Find a girl, settle down,
If you want, you can marry,
Look at me, I am old
But I'm happy.

As Billy Ray was lost in thought, trying to focus on the better times he'd had with his father, a Jeep pulled up behind him. Jenny walked over to the gravesite. He turned and smiled. She looked radiant with the early-morning sun behind her.

"Junior said you just got back. I knew you'd be up here."

"I came back as soon as I could, but it was too late. You look well, more beautiful than ever."

She didn't acknowledge his compliment. "Junior and I were with your father when he passed away. In case you wanted to know," she said sarcastically, "he had bone cancer. In his last moments, when he knew he didn't have long, he just kept looking at the empty doorway and asking Junior when you were coming. Junior lied for you. He told your father that he talked to you and that you were on your way. He was in great pain, and when he felt himself slipping away, he grabbed Junior's hand tightly and said, 'Tell him. Tell Billy I was wrong. I'm sorry.' Then he closed his eyes and kept whispering, 'I'm sorry, I'm sorry,'" she said, wiping the tears from her eyes.

Billy Ray turned away from Jenny. He didn't want her to see the tears in his eyes.

"It's OK to cry. At least it'll show there's still something in there," she said, pushing her finger sharply into his chest.

"My tour is over in several months," he said, trying to change the subject. "Then I'm coming home. I'll help Junior with the vineyard and bottle the wine from the grapes from France that he fermented.

"I'm with Junior now," she said, looking away.

"I'm glad for the both of you."

"That's all you have to say? At least I know he loves me! What happened to you, Billy? Are you that heartless? You never said good-bye or even wrote one letter! I thought you cared for me!"

"I didn't know when or if I'd ever be coming back, and I wanted you to move on with your life. All I meant was…I'm glad you did."

Jenny turned around to leave. "Well, I guess you did your job well!"

Billy Ray called out for her to stop, but she just kept on walking, waving her hand in the air. She got into her Jeep and sped away.

I was once like you are now
And I know it's not easy,
To be calm, when you found
Something's going on.
But take your time,
Think a lot, why, think
Of everything you've got,
For you will still be here tomorrow,
But your dreams may not.

When Billy Ray returned to base, he looked in all the usual places where the men in his unit hung out, but they were not there. As he walked to the LZ, he noticed that some of the men were going out of their way to avoid him, while others, when they saw him coming, looked away and hurried on with their duties. When he reached the landing area, Sergeant Brendon was standing on a metal staging, repairing the rotor on a Black Hawk outside a metal Quonset hut. He was wearing baggy grease-stained coveralls and chewing on an unlit cigar.

"Hey, Brendon, where's the boys?" he asked.

Brendon came down from the staging, wiped the grease off his hands, and looked behind him to make sure no one could overhear their conversation. Then he lit his cigar and took a few puffs. "They never came back. Mission started at two o'clock in the morning. There's been no contact with them in fourteen hours."

"What was their last GPS?"

"North, on the Pakistan-Afghanistan border. It's a bad sign, Billy. The GPS system was disabled. The colonel sent them out with Labuti, who was to lead them to a Taliban staging area and weapons cache. Major Clay told Bishop that the men would feel safer if they waited for you to return, but Bishop would have none of it."

"Bishop should have known better," Billy Ray said, looking out in the distance. "I never trusted Labuti. He led them into a trap."

Just then Colonel Bishop came marching up briskly with two privates by his side.

"Colonel," Billy Ray said anxiously, "let me put together a team and go after our guys."

"Command is formulating an extraction plan. Sometime tomorrow I'll get the green light to proceed."

"Tomorrow! Tomorrow! This is a cluster fuck! They'll all be dead tomorrow, if they're not dead already!"

"I said no, Blu! You are to stand down, and that's an order. You are restricted to base, and as a matter of fact, I'm restricting you to your barracks! You men," he said to the two soldiers flanking him, "escort Sergeant Blu back to his barracks."

A short while later, Billy Ray returned to the landing area wearing two harnesses tied to his legs, containing sais swords, a century-old Hattori Hanzo samurai sword that Master Lei had given him as a graduation gift strapped to his back, and an M-16 slung over his shoulder.

"Brendon, fuel me a Black Hawk with a whisper jet, fully armed."

"Can't do it, Billy. You heard the colonel. I ain't going to the brig over this."

Brendon looked into Billy Ray's eyes and saw his rage growing as his inner demons surfaced. He looked at the weapons he was carrying. He knew the stories about his lethal talent and became concerned for his own safety, thinking that maybe Billy had finally "lost it," as he would later testify at the finding of facts court hearing.

"I said fuel the fucking Black Hawk, now! You let me worry about Bishop. I'll take all the flack!"

It was twilight. The setting sun cast long shadows over the hot, dry, wind-blown landscape. Billy Ray sat on a large, rust-colored slab of stone, out of sight, behind the LZ. As Brendon fueled the Black Hawk, he saw Billy Ray looking over the horizon. He was planning his strategy and wondering if the men in his unit were still alive. When the helicopter was ready, he took off, flying low in the direction of their last known GPS position.

When he was close to the coordinates, he put the Black Hawk into the whisper jet mode to avoid detection. Then he switched on the TIS—thermal image system—and flew in a grid pattern until he located thermal signatures near a small ravine. Several hundred yards from the camp, he saw the thermal image of the running engine from a small vehicle that he presumed was a lookout.

After he landed, he put on a pair of night-vision goggles. As he moved toward the area where he believed the men were being held, he killed every soldier in his path, severing arms and legs and decapitating a few in silent, deadly precision.

All the men in the first tent were strung up on a metal pole wedged into the top. Their hands and feet were bound. Rinaldi and Cortez had been gutted; their entrails were either dangling from their bodies or spilled out on the ground beneath them in a pool of blood. BB had been badly beaten about the face and was barely conscious. One of his eyes was blackened and swollen almost closed. Dried blood covered the right side of his face.

Sihar Labuti wore a light-gray turban. He lit a Turkish unfiltered cigarette that he held in between his first three fingers as if it was a pointer. In his other hand was a bayonet covered with dried blood. He looked over at Midnight and squeezed his two cheeks together with the hand that held the cigarette. Midnight moved his head to push him away.

"We thank Allah for delivering you. The bounties for these two dogs," he said, waving his bayonet up toward Rinaldi and Cortez, "only bring one thousand American dollars each, but you, Mr. Midnight Smith, bin Laden put ten-thousand-dollar prize on your head. How many brothers you kill? One hundred, one hundred fifty? You make us rich men."

"Well then, you sick fuck," Midnight said defiantly, "you think I'm afraid of dying! Do it! Do it now!" he said, raising his head, offering his neck to Labuti.

"No, no, no. You I not to kill so easy. First, I think make suffer. Then," he said smiling, as he tilted his head, "I cut off head."

Labuti slapped BB across the face twice to wake him from his semiconscious state. "What's the matter, funny man? Tell joke. Break balls. Make Sihar laugh."

"Fuck you!" he said, spitting in his face.

Labuti wiped the spit off his face and cleaned his hand on BB's blood-stained uniform. "No. Fuck you!" he said, putting out his cigarette on BB's face. "Fuck America! You Americans think you come my country to do what? Impose will and *democracy* on us! This our land for thousands of years. You think we thank for being here? He took out a pair of shears and placed them around two of BB's fingers. "Go ahead, funny man, scream. No shame. No one hear you. No one save you," he said, squeezing the shears and cutting off two of his fingers.

As Billy Ray heard BB scream, at least he knew, or hoped, that he and the other men were still alive. A guard stood outside the two tents, carrying an AK-47 assault rifle. He crept up behind him, put his left hand over his mouth, and slit his throat. The second tent was dimly lit with small propane torchlight. He could see the silhouette of a guard inside. With one quick straight thrust, he pierced the tent and the guard inside, twisting the Samurai sword and killing him instantly. Major Clay, Lieutenant Macky, and Rollins were strung up and bound in the same way that the men were in the other tent. He could see the expressions of joy on their faces but motioned for them to remain silent. His face, hands, and uniform were covered with the blood of the men he had killed. The men saw his demonic eyes, which contrasted sharply with the red blood on his face. He cut them down and gave Macky the M-16. Then he gave the men hand signals, telling them to secure the area while he went into the other tent.

When Billy Ray burst into the other tent, Labuti was so startled he fell back into the corpse of Rinaldi. He tried to stand up and stab him with his bayonet. Billy Ray bent his wrist backward and the weapon fell to the ground. Then he thrust his sais sword deeply in between his shoulder blades.

BB mustered all the strength he had left to speak. "Billy, thank God, Billy. Don't kill him. Cut me down."

He cut down BB and Midnight, all the while keeping an eye on Labuti. BB took one of the sais swords from Billy Ray's harness and stood over Labuti. His face was frozen with terror. "Who's laughing now, you motherfucker!" he said, slicing through his neck so deeply he almost cut off his head. Then, in an insane rage, he stabbed him repeatedly until Midnight stopped him.

"You can stop now, BB. I think he's dead," Midnight said. "Let's get the fuck out of here."

When the men were all assembled, Rollins and Macky were about to retrieve the bodies of Rinaldi and Cortez when one of the Taliban soldiers who had been hiding came out from a small rise of stone and opened fire.

"Watch out, Macky! Billy Ray yelled out as he stepped in front of him and pushed him out of the line of fire. Then he pulled a sais sword and hurled it deeply into the insurgent's neck, just below his Adam's apple. In the distance, the lights of the vehicle came on and began firing in their direction. As the men followed Billy Ray to the Black Hawk, machine-gun fire whizzed over their heads.

After Billy Ray took off, he switched on the TIS, tilted the helicopter slightly, and targeted the vehicle with thirty seconds of minigun fire until it exploded.

A few miles outside their base, the men noticed that Billy Ray was flying erratically. He turned around to look at Midnight, who was in a trance.

He called out several times to get his attention. "Midnight, are you fit to fly us back?"

"What's the matter, William?" Major Clay asked. That's when he looked down on the floor and saw a pool of blood under where Billy Ray was sitting. "Midnight, get up here on the double. William's been hit!"

Midnight took over the controls as the other men helped Billy Ray into the rear of the Black Hawk. Then he slumped over and passed out.

When they arrived back at base, nearly fifty men were watching as the helicopter touched down. BB was the first man out. He had a rag over his bloody hand. He yelled out for the men to get a stretcher. Colonel Bishop was standing defiantly, arms folded, with two MPs at his side. As the men helped Billy Ray out of the Black Hawk, the colonel instructed the two MPs to place him under arrest. BB pulled one of the M-16s from the MPs hands.

"What are you going to do with that?" Colonel Bishop asked.

"Whatever I have to, asshole! You were just going to leave us there to be butchered. They cut Rinaldi and Cortez to fuckin' pieces! Pieces! Billy's going to the MASH, and I'm going to see to it that he does. Any objections, Colonel?" he asked, pointing the gun in his direction.

Several men came running over with a stretcher. All the men in his unit carefully placed him on it and double-timed it to the mobile hospital unit.

⊷▅◉ ◉▅⊶

July 4, 3:30 a.m. Pacific time

As Jenny lay sleeping, Billy Ray dressed slowly and looked at Jenny's partially nude body. He took a piece of stationary from Father Pat's desk, wrote her a brief letter, and placed it in her coat pocket. As he covered her body with the thin sheet, he gave her a soft kiss and wondered if he would ever see her again. He would like nothing more than to grow old with her, have a few children, and lead a simple life, tending his vineyard. As he turned to look at her, he had an epiphany. He wondered if the illuminating flash, the vision, was genuine and had been brought about by his spiritual surroundings. He saw Jenny on a beautiful summer day at a large celebration surrounded by hundreds of people, some wearing military uniforms, others people well known to him. She was radiant, smiling, and laughing as she handed out food and beverages to a crowd. Two small children came running up to her. She patted the boy on his head and gave him a piece of cake. Then she picked up the little girl, whose hair was braided with banana curls, and gave her a kiss. He looked at their eyes. They were the brightest blue, like the California sky on a perfect day—his eyes. As the epiphany was fading, he looked for himself in the vision, but he was not there.

Gethsemane

THERE WAS AN eerie silence in the bunker when Billy Ray returned, a palpable somber mood. He took off his jacket and placed the purple velvet box that Father Pat had given him on the table. They had all been preparing for this day. Now that it had arrived, they had mixed emotions of exhilaration and trepidation. It was the same mind-set and emotions they experienced before embarking on a dangerous mission. Even though they had prepared the "theater" for any contingent that could be anticipated, they knew the outcome of Billy Ray's end game was still uncertain.

The Wiz was sitting at his electronic equipment, monitoring a transmission from the sheriff's department about a call for a rescue squad that had been dispatched to the hydroelectric facility.

Colonel Clay sat down next to Billy Ray. "What's in the box, William?" Billy Ray slid the box over to the colonel. He opened it and took out the two medals. "My, my, my. What have we here?"

"The Silver Star belonged to my father, and the Congressional Medal of Honor was awarded to the priest in my parish for his distinguished service in Vietnam."

Colonel Clay looked at Billy Ray as he examined the Congressional Medal of Honor. "They should have given you both of these along with another Purple Heart for what you did in Afghanistan."

"Well, I guess that's just water over the dam," Billy Ray said as they both smiled at the pun.

"Not quite yet, William. Not quite yet. You know, you'll probably be exonerated and all judgments vacated against you. I talked with the other men, and we'll all understand if you don't want to go through with your end game. You're in control of the game. It's not controlling you."

262

"I know what I'd like to do. I know what's in Jenny's heart, what she would want me to do. But sometimes there are things one just has to do. I've thought about walking away, but do you really think the ISS and Bishop are just going to forget about me, let me lead a normal, peaceful life? They'll never stop, even if I'm cleared of all the charges."

"Well, whatever you decide, we're behind you. It's your call."

The Wiz turned up the volume of the communication between the sheriff and his deputies. "Billy, what was the name of that woman who came here to tell us about Bishop taking Jenny?"

BB overheard the Wiz and raised his eyebrows. "You mean my honey? The one with the big...smile?" he said, looking at Billy Ray.

"Carla, Carla Beck," he said with concern. "Why?"

"A rescue squad just brought her to the county hospital."

Billy Ray stood up and walked over to the Wiz. "What happened?"

"I caught some crosstalk. It's vague, but it seems that she was being interrogated by the ISS and..."

"And?"

"She was admitted to the hospital with a broken jaw."

"Those fuckin' motherfuckers!" BB said.

The Wiz looked away from Billy Ray. He could tell there was something else he wasn't telling him. "What is it, Wiz? What else happened?"

"That priest who gave you those medals, what was his name?"

"Father Patrick O'Keefe."

The Wiz looked away again. "He's dead, Billy," he said, bowing his head.

"Can't be. There has to be a mistake. I was just with him a few hours ago."

"The sheriff was pissed, screaming as he put in a call to the AG at his home. They took the priest's body to county in the same rescue squad as Beck, DOA. The ISS told the medics that he had a heart attack while he was being interrogated. The EMTs told the sheriff that the priest had bruises and contusions on his face and body."

Billy washed his hands over his face in disgust and sorrow. The men could see him trying to suppress his inner demons and rage. "You see what I mean, Colonel? They're out of control. They got to them...because of me. They'll never stop. Sometimes things beyond your control force your hand. I'm no longer in control of the game. It's controlling me. I'm going to burn them all! Burn it all down! Wiz, come with me. It's time to hook me up."

The Wiz picked up a box of electronic devices and a small bag of hardware and toiletry items and followed Billy Ray into his bunk. "All right, Billy, take off your shirt." He took out a small disposable razor and shaved two spots on his chest and one on his arm, just above his elbow. Then he applied electrical conductivity gel and affixed diodes, holding them in place with silver duct tape. After Billy Ray put on his shirt, the Wiz plugged the diodes into a vital-signs monitor and then into the master trigger. "That's it, Billy."

Billy Ray removed his military footlocker from under his bed and began putting on his military uniform in a slow, methodical manner. Then he strapped a harness on each leg, containing three sais swords each. When he was through dressing, he put on the army duster that BB had given him.

"Billy, you never told me what this device was for. The other men don't know what it is, but I do. It's a death sentence; a suicide mission. Give me some time to figure out something else. Please Billy, there has to be another way."

"It's too late for that. I don't plan on it being used, but I can't take that chance...and fail. And besides, I don't plan on getting killed. Too many things I have yet to do with my life. Too many things to live for...especially Jenny. So, don't worry about me," he said, forcing a smile. "I'll be all right. Just get me an RPG case and maybe a small-caliber weapon and several clips."

Billy Ray returned to the main bunker. A few minutes later, the Wiz walked in carrying a long dark-green transport box containing a rocket-propelled grenade launcher, several rounds of ordinance, a small-caliber weapon in a leather holster, and several clips. Colonel Clay was opening a bottle of Blu Select wine with a silver corkscrew. He poured a glass for each of the men. When he went to put the corkscrew into the sink, he noticed that there were empty vials and pills scattered about. "What the hell's this?" he asked, picking up an empty vial.

BB picked up one of the vials in the sink and read the name on it. "Jesus, these are Midnight's psycho meds. What the fuck's this mean?"

"Where did you say Midnight went?" Colonel Clay asked.

"He said out for a smoke."

264

"Well, it looks like he's AWOL," the colonel said, shaking his head.

The Wiz looked over at an empty shelf above his electronic equipment. The color seemed to drain from his face. "Colonel, the remotes for the Metalstorm are missing!"

"Midnight, Midnight, Midnight. What the hell are you up to?" he asked rhetorically. "BB, see what else is missing."

BB double-timed it to the back room where they kept the weapons. A short while later, he returned out of breath. "Colonel, his sniper rifle is missing, some body armor, and a minigun."

"A minigun! Jesus, of all times for him to lose it," he said, looking up at the clock. It was 4:45 a.m.

"I want to spend some time alone, outside," Billy Ray said.

"Not quite yet," the colonel said, handing each of the men a glass of wine. "To William. It took great loyalty, courage, and testicular fortitude when you saved us." The other men smiled. "And we'll never forget that." After he finished his wine, he took the two medals out of the purple velvet box and pinned them on Billy Ray's army duster. "These are the two medals they should have given you for saving us. Good luck, William."

"BB, it's going down just before dawn," Billy Ray said. "Pick up Jenny and—"

"Don't worry about anything, Billy; we know everything we have to do."

"I have another favor to ask you. After you take Jenny to Canada, take a stack of money and see Carla in the hospital. Tell her it's from me...for someday. She'll know what that means. Take the rest of the money to Jenny's parents. And don't tell Jenny about Father Pat."

"Sure thing, Billy."

"One last thing for all of you. There's an envelope for each one of you. Take it."

"No, no, no," the colonel said.

"I insist. I have more than enough to last me...for a lifetime."

The men hugged him, and he left. Once outside, he sat on the edge of a large outcrop of gray stone, looking at the diminished light of the waning moon at the very end of its cycle. It was just a sliver, a fingernail of light against the clear blue-black sky, surrounded by dim, twinkling stars. He took the picture from his top pocket of himself, Junior, and Jenny when they were children at the parade. He rubbed their faces with his thumb as if to animate them.

A man awaits his end
Dreading and hoping all.
Many times he died,
Many times rose again.

—William Butler Yeats "Death"

In the bunker, the men observed him on the infrared surveillance camera.

"What's he doing out there, Colonel?" BB asked.

Colonel Clay looked at the monitor. Billy Ray was staring up toward the heavens. "Even *he* had to go through the garden of Gethsemane but once."

"He who?"

"Him," he said, looking and pointing up. "Sergeant Brenden said William did the same thing that night just before he came to rescue us. Imaging the anguish and uncertainty he must have been feeling wondering if we were still alive and if he was heading toward certain death. And now he's going through it for a second time. Sometimes when a man like William sees the die has been cast, that things have become so out of whack, he'll do whatever it takes to set things right, even if it means the end of him," he said, looking at the monitor, but he was gone. "Well, I guess it's time, but before you go, help me push the Black Hawk out on the rails."

"What are you planning, Colonel?" BB asked.

"When the die *is* cast, I'm going to make sure the dice are loaded in our favor."

"You know they have stingers set up at the hydroelectric facility," the Wiz said.

"I know. The Black Hawk is still loaded with the depleted uranium shells. They'll never see me coming—until it's too late. Once the trigger is set, I'm going to fly Billy Ray out. This isn't going to be a one-way trip for either of us. All right, men, it's show time."

The Ultimate Sacrifice

*When the Warrior is called upon to make the Ultimate Sacrifice,
it is the culmination, sum, and consequences of all his actions that
will define his legacy.
The nobility of his choice is dependent upon it being made without
regret or remorse.
Fore, the avocation the Warrior has chosen and his destiny is
inseparable from his karma, and the path that has been chosen for him.*

—Tsiang Kieun, *The Art of Violence*

AFTER THE WIZ and BB picked up Jenny at Saint Mary's Church, they drove to Silver Verde Vista, the highest point in town, with a panoramic view of the region. As they walked up the steep incline toward the summit, the only sounds that could be heard were the chirping of crickets, far off voices of residents that had already arrived, and the crushing of pine needles underfoot, which gave off a distinctive aroma. None of the residents knew what was about to happen. Some of them came out of curiosity or to heed the warning that Father Pat had given them during the mass.

Some of the residents had set up portable propane lanterns and small campfires. Others were toasting marshmallows for their children. In the distance, dim lights could be seen coming from the town and street lights leading up to the hydroelectric facility. The dam was illuminated with bright spotlights, which highlighted the magnitude of the project and contrasted sharply against the pitch-black sky.

A steady flow of residents were making their way to the summit. As the Wiz was setting up his laptop and other monitoring equipment, Jenny went over to talk to some of the townsfolk who had heard about her arrest by the ISS and had been concerned for her safety and wanted to know the details.

"All right, BB," the Wiz said. "I'm all hooked up. I just hope everything you rigged up is going to take out the dam in one shot."

"That's not how it works, Einstein," he said, slapping the Wiz playfully with an open hand to the back of his head. "Nothing short of a nuclear device could take out the dam in one shot. The base of the dam is over one hundred feet of reinforced concrete."

"Then tell me how your handiwork is going to take it out."

"The dam was constructed with a sloping arch, a curvature that gives it enormous strength and stability by diverting the pressure outward to where it is pinned to the mountainside. The thermobaric will trigger the forty tons of explosives at the bottom of the mineshaft. The blast wave of the second explosion will take out the whole side of the mountain, unbalancing the engineering equation."

"And then it will come down?"

"Nooooo. Then, in theory, we'll wait for the weight and force of the trillions of gallons of water behind the dam to take it out."

"In theory?"

"Trust me. I've taken down skyscrapers with only a fraction of the explosive power that's in the shaft. What I'm worrying about is the blast wave. It will vaporize, disintegrate anyone within a mile of the blast. Say a prayer and cross your fingers that Billy can get far enough away after he sets the trigger so he doesn't become a casualty of his own device.

⇥≡◯ ◯≡⇤

No one knew the area and terrain around Blu Bluff better than Billy Ray. He took a path well known to him using the low brush and topography for cover as he made his way from Silver Verde Lake up the steep slope. He knew the ISS had set up two-man fortified pillboxes to guard the road. He drew two sais swords and came up from behind the soldiers at their post.

Much to his surprise, the two soldiers were already dead; one with a large gaping hole in his chest, and the other killed from a head shot. He smiled and looked into the darkness with the knowledge that Midnight had cleared a path for him.

As he came up upon the road leading to the hydroelectric facility, he walked close to the embankment, using it for cover. He was unaware that as he made his way up the road, he tripped a hidden motion-detector. Alarms began alerting the troops below the bridge and in the hydroelectric facility. Mercury vapor spotlights kicked on and illuminated the roadway and the area around the dam. Billy Ray knew that within minutes the road would become inundated with hundreds of ISS troops. He reached under his army duster, pushed two buttons, and the structural supports began exploding in rapid synchronized succession, sending the bridge into the dark, rushing waters of the ravine below.

In the distance, the Wiz and BB looked at each other as the road became illuminated and they heard the low resounding thumps of the explosions.

"Here we go," BB said as he lit up a long cigar he had been saving for this day. "That's the bridge," he said, holding his head up high as he let out a long puff of smoke.

A multitude of residents scurried to the edge of the summit to see what was creating the disturbance. Jenny came running over and stood next to the Wiz, out of breath.

"What was that?" she asked.

"Billy Ray is fine," he said, looking down at his monitor. "Don't worry. Everything's going as planned."

The ISS commander stationed south of the bridge radioed General Bishop and told him they were under attack from a possible mortar barrage. He told him to take up defensive positions, and to send as many troops as possible up the road to the dam. The Apache and Black Hawk helicopters pilots scrambled to the landing zone in an attempt to get them airborne before another attack.

Colonel Clay was observing the activity at the landing zone from a hidden vantage point using the thermal-image system in the Black Hawk. He located his targets and moved in quickly. Then he began firing hellfire missiles and depleted uranium shells, which gave off an unnatural green hue as they shredded the helicopters and drones as if they were made of paper. As the shells hit the fuel tanks, the dark sky became illuminated as huge orange fireballs arose high into the air.

"What just went down, Wiz?" BB asked.

The Wiz looked at the infrared monitor positioned on a telephone pole near the bridge and saw all of the helicopters burning. "It must be the colonel. I think he just took out all of their air support south of the bridge."

The remaining ISS soldiers north of the bridge began making their way up the road. Billy Ray was trapped between the advancing soldiers and the ISS soldiers who were coming toward his position from the hydroelectric facility. He waited until the soldiers below were half up the road to inflict the most carnage and casualties. Then he opened his army duster and pressed in a series of numbers. The faux-rock claymore mines that BB had made began exploding in rapid succession. The ISS soldiers that were trapped in the gauntlet were either killed by the shrapnel or from the secondary blast wave of the minithermobaric devices.

In the command bunker, General Bishop had summoned Major Macky to the observation tower. They both watched in horror as the troops below the electrified gate were decimated.

"What the hell's going on down there, Major?"

Major Macky was talking to the commander at the bridge. "He took out all our helicopters and most of the advancing troops, sir."

"Who?" Bishop asked.

"It's him. Billy Ray."

General Bishop's jaw dropped, and he quickly tried to hide his displeasure and nervousness. "Then tell me, Major, if he took out all our helicopters and most of our troops from the north, how can he be in two places at once?"

"I don't know, sir. He must have assistance. He's systematically taking out our strategic offensive and defensive capabilities. We still have two Apache helicopters up here."

"Well, get them airborne—now!"

Major Macky ordered the helicopters to take off and take up defensive positions. Billy Ray was still pinned down and taking sporadic fire from the ISS beyond the gate. Suddenly, a Black Hawk helicopter flying barely above the road came crawling through the smoke. Billy Ray began loading a projectile into the RPG.

"We've got him now, Major. It looks like at least one of ours made it out."

Before he could fire the weapon, the Black Hawk began firing at the transformer that supplied power to the gate. As the transformer exploded, an orange-white waterfall of sparks cascaded to the ground. All the lights on the road went black. The red spinning lights on top of the electrified gate blinked and then went out. The backup generator at the hydroelectric plant kicked on and restored power to the facility. Then the helicopter fired a hellfire missile at the gate and blew it apart. As the Black Hawk tilted and turned on its cabin lights, Billy Ray smiled. Colonel Clay gave him a thumbs-up.

"What the hell's going on?" Bishop shouted.

"It's not one of ours," Macky said.

"Tell our pilots to shoot it down!"

Colonel Clay attempted to land to pick up Billy Ray, but the two Apache helicopters closed in on him. He ascended quickly and fired on the lead helicopter. He ripped through it, and it exploded in midair. Before he could target the second helicopter, the Apache got tone, locked in on him, and hit the tale section of his helicopter with a hellfire missile. The Black Hawk spun wildly out of control, and it tumbled down the steep slope and crashed into the lake. Billy Ray looked out over the water to see if the colonel had survived, but it was too dark for him to see.

On the summit, the Wiz, who had been monitoring the activity, lowered his head.

"What?" BB asked. "What happened?"

"This isn't good. I can't pick up the colonel's signal. I think it was his Black Hawk that went down."

The Apache began firing at Billy Ray's position with multiple miniguns. As the helicopter swung around to zero in on him, Billy Ray stood up and fired the RPG, striking the helicopter, which exploded into a fireball before crashing against the embankment.

General Bishop stood aghast in silence with his mouth open, his lower lip trembling. "Major, this has to end! You served with him. You know how he thinks."

David J. Aiello

"Yes, I served with him, and that's what scares me. The Black Parade website said he was coming today to burn it all down. If that's what he's up to, I can't see how we can stop him!"

"Take everything and everyone that's left. Take the fight to him."

"I'll try, sir, but you're right; I do know him, just about as well as anyone, so I can tell you this: after he's done with us, he's coming after you."

"Since your ass is on the line, Major, you better stop him!"

It was almost dawn. Thin shreds of light were starting to break through the dark horizon. Billy Ray checked the monitor on his belt, indicating to him that the trigger could be activated, but he was still pinned down by gunfire.

Major Macky made his way toward Billy Ray with a dozen soldiers by his side. As he came upon his position, he called out for all of the soldiers to cease fire. Then he put down his weapon and walked down the middle of the road with his hands held high above his head. "Billy Ray," he shouted. "Billy, it's me, Macky. Come out. Let's talk. No one's going to fire."

Billy Ray hesitated at first. Then he put down his RPG and walked through the mangled and twisted remnants of the gate. They both met and stood on the x that Midnight had painted in the middle of the road.

As they engaged in small talk, several soldiers flanked the major, including Private Garcia, who was still wearing a neck brace from the altercation he had with Billy Ray at Sparkey's Tavern.

"I dreaded this day, Billy. Everyone said it was coming, but I hoped—no, I prayed—that we'd never meet face to face. Everyone's scared shitless, including Bishop, although he'd never admit it. Rumor is you're going to burn it all down. And I wouldn't blame you. I know what you've been through. And your brother, well," he said, shaking his head. "Tell me, Billy. I know you wouldn't lie to me. What's going down?"

"You trust me, Macky?"

"With my life. I know what I owe you. You took a bullet meant for me. If you didn't come for us, I wouldn't be here today, but I also have my duty."

"I'm going to save your life for the second time, Macky," he said, opening up his army duster slowly.

Macky looked at the blinking lights on the device attached to his belt. "It is true," Macky said in astonishment.

"When the dam goes, and believe me, nothing can stop that now, everyone within a mile of ground zero will die. No one else needs to die. Take your troops and leave."

Private Garcia came up and stood beside the major. "That's him," he said. "It's Billy Ray, the asshole I almost took out in the bar the other night. Why is he still alive? The general ordered us to shoot him on sight," he said, pointing his M-16 at Billy Ray.

"You! You almost took out Billy Ray," Macky said with sarcasm. "The only reason you're still alive," he said, pushing his finger into Garcia's chest, "is because he spared your life. So lower your weapon, stand down, and shut the fuck up!"

A camouflaged Humvee came screaming down the roadway and screeched to a halt. Six ISS elite forces jumped out of the vehicle, carrying M-16 assault rifles. General Bishop was the last one to exit the vehicle flanked by his bodyguards. About a hundred ISS troops came down the road to see what was going on.

General Bishop did not look at Billy Ray as he began talking to Major Macky. "I see you captured him. The question is, why is this terrorist still alive?"

"I didn't capture him, sir. I asked him to come out to talk."

"Talk!" Bishop asked as he scoffed at his answer. "I asked you—why is he still alive?"

"He's wired, sir," he said, not knowing how else to answer the general.

"Wired," he said, taking a step backward. "Wired for what?"

"He wouldn't lie to me, sir. He said the whole area is rigged to blow, and he's the trigger."

General Bishop walked up to Billy Ray, within an inch of his face. "You think you're going to make a fool of me again?"

"You did that all by yourself."

"You son of a bitch! That will never happen again because today it all ends!"

"I know it does, maybe for all of us. How it ends...I'll leave that up to you."

General Bishop looked at the medals pinned to Billy Ray's army duster. He shook his head and let out a sarcastic laugh. "These are real medals," he said, pounding his chest. "Where did you get those from, a gumball machine?" The elite soldiers surrounding the general laughed.

"The Silver Star belonged to my father," he said, bowing his head, "and President Johnson awarded the Congressional Medal of Honor to the priest you killed!"

General Bishop opened his mouth but could not think of a response. Finally he said, "That was his fault. He just wouldn't cooperate."

"It means more to me that he gave me his medal than if the president pinned one on my chest himself. All these years in the military and you still haven't got it! It's not the medals they pin on your chest but the ones that you live by that count. You're going to pay a high price for killing him…here—and in the hereafter!"

"Enough of this bullshit, Major! Shoot him and put an end to this."

"No, sir. I'll take him into custody, but I won't kill him. I owe him that much, and none of my men are going to shoot him either. From what I've been led to believe, the shoot-on-sight order against him has been rescinded, and he'll probably be exonerated of all charges against him."

"Not by me!" General Bishop shouted. "And certainly not after what he's done here today!"

"I'll shoot him, sir," Private Garcia said, moving forward as he pointed his weapon at Billy Ray.

"Stand down, Garcia," Macky shouted, "and that's an order!"

"It looks like all the men in your former unit have a habit of disobeying orders," Bishop said, looking at Billy Ray.

Billy Ray looked at Private Garcia. "How old are you soldier, twenty-four, maybe?"

"That's none of your business. I'm not afraid of what everyone's been saying about you. You're just a man. One man. I was there when Bishop gave us the green light to shoot your brother. Give me the order, General. I'll kill him."

Billy Ray's eyes glazed over as his rage grew. "Keep taking orders from men without honor," he said, nodding in Bishop's direction, "and you'll never make it to twenty-five."

General Bishop nodded his head to the private. Before he could get off a shot, Billy Ray flipped two sais swords in his direction with lightning speed. The first sword went through his hand with such force that it pinned his hand against his ribcage. As the second sword went through his other hand, he dropped his weapon and shrieked with pain.

"Jesus Christ!" the general said, ducking. The elite ISS who were guarding Bishop all pointed their weapons at Billy Ray. He held his hands outward, showing that they were empty.

"Are you going to shoot him now, Major?"

"No, sir!"

"Are you disobeying a direct order?"

"Yes, sir," Macky said, drawing his revolver and pointing it in Bishop's direction.

Everyone's attention was so focused on General Bishop, Billy Ray, and the major that no noticed that a ghostly figure had emerged from out of the darkness. He was standing on top of a large gray piece of ledge across the road on the embankment. He was wearing full body armor, and his face was painted with black camouflage makeup to resemble the mask of a Halloween skeleton. Only the whites of his horrifying eyes could be seen through the darkness as he focused his attention on Billy Ray. He held a minigun in his hands, with a long belt of ammunition slung over his arm.

General Bishop unsnapped his holster. "Looks like I'm going to have to do it myself," he said, removing his pistol. He fired two shots, one striking Macky in his forehead, killing him instantly, and the other hitting Billy Ray in his chest. Billy Ray fell to his knees. As his heartbeat quickened, and his blood pressure dropped, the vital-signs monitor relayed the message and activated the trigger. "Now I'm going to finish this once and for all," he said, pointing the pistol at Billy Ray's head.

Before the general could get off a shot, a scream pierced their ears from out of the darkness. "You motherfuckers!" Midnight screamed as he pressed the trigger of the minigun, first mowing down the elite guards and then moving the minigun from side to side as ISS soldiers dropped to the ground.

General Bishop hit the ground for cover. Billy Ray knew the trigger had been activated. He pulled off the monitor and flung it to the ground. On the summit, the Wiz saw the vital-signs monitor flatline. As the billows of smoke came from the minigun and the metal clips clanked on the ledge below, Midnight began taking fire. Each time a round hit his body armor, he was propelled back, unfazed as he kept firing. Finally, a bullet went between his body armor and struck him in the neck. As he fell to the ground, the minigun stopped spinning. When the remaining ISS soldiers saw that he went down, they came out from their cover and advanced on his position.

"Jesus Christ," General Bishop shouted as he looked at the carnage. Suddenly he, along with the remaining ISS, ducked as the first barrage of fireworks, which sounded like mortar shells, exploded in the sky.

At the summit, the crowd was delighted and awestruck as the array of chrysanthemum shells and floral mines filled the sky with color and sound.

"Here we go," BB said as his pyrotechnic display began.

The Wiz was frantically typing commands into his laptop, trying to figure out why Billy Ray's vital-signs monitor flatlined, only looking up occasionally at the fireworks. "This isn't good," he said to BB. "Something's really wrong. I think...he's...dead."

Neither man realized that Jenny was standing behind them and overheard what the Wiz said. BB turned around abruptly.

"What do you mean he's dead?" she asked as tears filled her eyes. "Who's dead?"

BB gave the Wiz a little shove. "He wasn't talking about Billy," BB said, trying to ease her mind. "Don't worry about Billy. He's invincible."

Midnight looked up at the fireworks and smiled. He knew that the trigger had been activated. As he lay still, he winced with pain as he watched the ISS soldiers advancing on his position. He reached under his body armor and activated the two Metalstorm weapons. "Who's your daddy? Who's your daddy now?" he said as his eyes went blank and closed.

The two Metalstorm weapons ascended slowly from the USG containers. When they were locked in place, a strange, unfamiliar pulsing sound filled the air as the one hundred thousand rounds of small-caliber ammunition began firing electronically, covering every square foot of the road except where the *x*'s had been designated. When the smoke cleared, the only sound that could be heard was the fireworks. The only two men still alive in the road were General Bishop and Billy Ray.

General Bishop stood up slowly. He was covered with debris, blood, and pieces of flesh and bone from the men who had been guarding him. He looked around, his face expressing horror, and examined himself to see if he had been hit. Billy Ray was slouched over on his knees. There was a pool of blood under him on the pavement.

The progression of fireworks was accelerating as the finale was almost beginning. General Bishop looked in both directions on the road and realized that he and Billy Ray were the only ones left alive. "Imagine that," Bishop said, shrugging his shoulders, "I guess it all comes down to me and you. You've been a thorn in my side ever since that night!" he said, picking up his revolver from the ground. Then he reached over, snatched the medals off Billy Ray's army duster, and threw them on the pavement.

"You ever play chess?" Billy Ray asked, looking up.

Bishop gave him a look of indifference. "Never had time for that foolish game."

"Didn't think so. You could never make the ultimate sacrifice...to win. Oh, you'd sacrifice your men, and leave them for dead, but never yourself."

"All pawns, peons," he said, looking at the dead soldiers scattered in the road. "But you're wrong; I've never been afraid of dying. And if today was to be my last day, which I don't see happening, at least I'll have the satisfaction of seeing you go first. I'd be the hero. They'll probably build monuments to me," he said, looking off in the distance as he envisioned what he had just said. "But I do know when the game of chess is over. Checkmate, Mr. Congressional Medal of Honor," he said, raising his pistol.

Suddenly, there was a strange gurgling sound coming from the general's throat, and blood spurted from his mouth. His face was frozen with horror, panic, and pain. The hand holding his revolver lowered and was trembling uncontrollably until the gun dropped to the pavement.

Billy Ray looked up and saw a large black bayonet protruding through Bishop's chest.

"Who's your daddy now?" Midnight said as he twisted the bayonet, thrusting it deeper. "It's me, Aloysius Smith!" he said, whispering into his ear as he pulled out his knife and shoved the general to the pavement.

The finale of the fireworks was beginning. Midnight took off his body armor and helped Billy Ray to his feet.

"Midnight, save yourself," Billy Ray said. "It's going to blow any minute."

Midnight's neck was covered with blood, and it was flowing down his arm. "You're the closest thing I've ever had to a brother. After all we've been through, I'd never leave you here."

"She's never going to understand why," Billy Ray said, looking over his shoulder at the fireworks.

"Who?"

"Jenny."

"Then I'll race you to the bottom, so we won't disappoint her. We either both make it out, or we both go down together."

Arm in arm they hobbled down the road as fast as their injuries would allow.

A thin shred of sunlight was just breaking through the horizon. The fireworks finale had almost ended. So many fireworks were exploding in such a rapid succession that a common pyrotechnics phenomena was taking place. The mind's eye could not assimilate or process all of the visual information. The faster the shells exploded, the slower the motion seemed to take place. When the finale ended, there was a five-second lull, followed by one very large shell as a customary signature to BB's pyrotechnic artistry.

After the fireworks ended, there was a series of small explosions on the south side of the mountain, which could be heard from the summit.

"What was that?" the Wiz asked BB.

"That's the first part of the thermobaric filling the mineshaft with the aerosol mixture, and when it reaches the bottom..."

BB didn't finish his thought. The entire area behind the mountain lit up as bright as midday, followed several seconds later by a thundering blast.

"Any second now," BB said. "Wait. Wait. Wait for it..."

When the thermobaric ignited the tons of explosives in the bottom of the mineshaft, the entire area began glowing, and the ground began to tremble as an orange-white fireball arose in the air and lingered above the dam. One by one, the bright lights on the dam went out. When the blast wave and the deafening echoing concussion reached the summit, some of the residents fell or had to hold on to each other to keep from falling as the ground shook violently, as if a high-level earthquake had just hit the area.

The Wiz held on to his computer equipment as the blast wave hit the summit. "Well, did it work?" he asked BB.

"We'll know soon enough," he said, looking at the calm water on the lake below.

Everyone at the summit became covered by a light mist until it fell like a driving rain as the winds suddenly picked up in intensity. Then there was a loud rumbling that sounded like a freight train as a fifty-foot wall of water, like a tsunami, traveling at a high rate of speed, kicked up a cloud of vaporized water in advance of its arrival. As the wall of water sped by the summit, it came three quarters up to the peak, taking along with it trees, debris, and anything else in its path.

The early-morning sun was shining through the still-lingering orange haze from the explosion. BB smiled as he saw the water flowing over the remnants of what was left of the dam and the half-mile-long hole on the side of the mountain. When the residents saw what had happened, they stood in silence and awe at the spectacle they had just witnessed.

"I guess that answers your question, Wiz," BB said, smiling as he relit his cigar. "Now let's get the fuck out of here and see what happened to the Colonel, Midnight, and...Billy Ray. Then I'll take Jenny to Canada."

"If they're still alive," the Wiz said, picking up his computer and electronic equipment. "If they're still alive."

The Wiz, BB, and Jenny drove to the Village at Silver Verde. BB dropped off the Wiz and pick up the other USG vehicle. As Jenny got into the front seat with BB, he rolled down the window. "Pack up your stuff, check on the other men, and get the hell out of here. In a few hours, this place will be swarming with FBI, CIA, and ISS. After I drop off Jenny in Canada, I'll check on my sweetheart at the county hospital. Then I'll come by your home to see you before I go home. See you later, brother."

"Godspeed," he said, heading toward the van.

As BB drove onto the ramp to the interstate highway, he could see Jenny trying to hold back the tears. There was a look of sadness and concern on her face.

David J. Aiello

"Jenny, don't worry about Billy. He wrote the book on escape and evasion. No one's going to find him until he wants to surface."

She nodded, but his words did not console her. As the tears streamed down her face, she reached into her coat pocket to get some tissue. Along with the tissue, she pulled out the neatly folded letter Billy Ray had placed there. As BB picked up speed, she opened the letter slowly.

Jenny,

I don't know if I'm coming to Canada. For your safety, I may have to disappear for a long time. You'll know when I'm coming; a bluebird will tell you. You know what that means.

She stopped reading the letter and remembered when BB had delivered the bluebird keychain when she thought that he had been killed in the helicopter crash. Then she read on.

If you don't hear from me in a couple of months, it means something went wrong, and I won't be coming back. You must move on with your life, as you once did before. Sometimes things just don't turn out the way we plan, and for that, I'm sorry. You deserve happiness and a good life, and I'm sure it will happen for you...someday. I've always loved you. You have been, and will always be, the only one for me.

Love,

Billy

She read the letter again, folded it neatly, and placed it back in her coat pocket.

When the Music Stops

AT ABOUT THE same time that the dam came down, the Prince of Darkness arrived at Senator Bryant's California office. He had talked with him on his flight to the West Coast and waited in the darkness for him to arrive. He searched through his desk and found exactly what he was looking for in his top right side drawer.

When Bryant arrived, he turned on the lights and was startled to see the Prince of Darkness sitting with a black valise on his lap. The senator was wearing a dark-blue designer jogging suit and sat down quickly, fumbling with and sorting the papers on his desk.

"I came as soon as I received your message. I hope you were right when you said you could solve all my problems."

"Before we proceed, I have to know what your intentions are, your course of action. Are you planning on giving up your congressional seat and stepping aside from your bid to be the VP?"

"I'm not giving up anything!" he said indignantly. "I have friends in high places. This will all blow over. The question is, what are you going to do for me?"

"I would advise you to step down. You may be right. This may all blow over, but maybe it won't. Every story has to have a bad guy, a scapegoat, someone the public can blame and vent their distain and anger on, and right now, that villain is you."

"That person is certainly not going to be me! There were others involved. If I go down, I'll name names and take a lot of people down with me," he said, with a forced grin to hide his nervousness. "I'm not going to be the only one without a chair when the music stops."

The Prince of Darkness thought for a moment. The senator's last response had sealed his decision and course of action. "Don't worry, Senator. That's why I'm here. The board asked me to solve all your problems. We don't have much time. The Justice Department will get a warrant and take all your records. Open your wall safe, and we'll go through your documents and remove any incriminating evidence."

Senator Bryant swung open a painting that was on hinges, twisted the dial on his safe, and opened it. "You want me to take out everything now?" he asked.

"Not right now. First I want to go over the official storyline and how we're going to make all your problems vanish."

Bryant sat back down behind his desk. "If this doesn't work, I'm finished. My career is over. I hope you're not going to renege on our deal. The deal was, I was to be your guy in the White House, and you were going to protect me."

The Prince of Darkness gave Bryant a devious, omniscient smile, which disconcerted him. "I know what we agreed upon, Senator, and you didn't listen to my advice. You thought you were above it all and could get away with just about anything. In all the years I've known you, with all the skims and scams you were behind, with all the people you bought and sold, with all the lives you've ruined, you didn't hold up your part of the bargain. There are some pacts that must be honored, and the most important one…is the one you made with me."

A buzzer rang on Senator Bryant's Rolex. "Excuse me for a moment," he said, picking up a pen with his left hand. "That was a reminder for me to jot down a date in my appointment calendar. I have a fundraiser to attend in DC next week."

"I see you're left-handed," the Prince of Darkness said matter-of-factly.

Bryant turned and gave him an odd look. "What does that have to do with anything?"

"It's just that I'm a lefty too," he replied, calculating his next move. "Well, look at that," he said, turning toward a framed picture on the wall. "Is that you with Nelson Mandela?"

As Bryant turned to look, a single shot rang out from a small silver-plated pistol that had been presented to the Senator as a commemorative gift from his constituents. As he slumped forward, blood poured from a small hole in his left temple, covering his appointment calendar.

"Looks like you won't be making that fundraiser next week, Senator," the Prince of Darkness said as he took out his handkerchief, wiped his prints off the pistol, and placed it into Bryant's limp left hand. Then he took a puff ball from his valise and sprayed gunpowder fragments on Bryant's left hand that would confirm to forensic investigators that Bryant had self-inflicted the lethal round.

The Prince of Darkness removed the SIM card from Bryant's cell phone and replaced it with a new card that contained incriminating phone numbers. Then he went through his wall safe, removing various documents and replacing them with damaging evidence, and closed the safe.

Just before he left the office, he turned and looked at Bryant's corpse. "I never reneged on my part of a bargain, Senator. I told you that after today you'd never have anything to worry about again. I have fulfilled my oath and promise: to protect the party and country from you and to protect you from certain disgrace and from having to serve a lengthy prison sentence. This story has to have a bad guy, and it's going to be you! When you sell your soul to the devil, that's exactly what he's taking."

When the Prince of Darkness returned to his vehicle, his laptop was flashing an EAC. The details were preliminary and brief. He took off quickly and headed down the interstate highway toward Silver Verde.

Legacy

JUST AS THE Prince of Darkness had predicted, when the citizens embraced and understood what happened in Silver Verde, the last domino fell, and all those small fires of rebellion grew into a firestorm of protest. At first, the demonstrations were vocal but orderly, but as the sheer magnitude of the protesters overwhelmed the local and state police, the government made their greatest and fatal mistake, adding fuel to the fire.

In an attempt to restore order, martial law was declared and the Constitutional right of habeas corpus was suspended. It had the opposite effect the government intended. The protests grew violent, and anarchy and civil disobedience became rampant.

It was similar to what happened in Europe and with the Wall Street protesters many years before, only with more fervor, better organization, and widespread participation. Unlike those protests, each group had authoritative spokesmen with unified and definitive goals and demands. Their creed was to restore individual rights and freedoms, rescind unconstitutional mandates, reduce the deficit, and upstart the economy that had collapsed; in short, to revitalize and restore the American dream.

Billy Ray was regarded as a hero. In the public's mind, his act of defiance solidified and justified their acts of defiance. Most felt that if the government and sinister military men could conspire and perpetrate this type of injustice upon one man, it could happen to any one of them. His fate could easily have become their fate.

His actions meant many different things to many diverse people, crossing political, racial, and ethnic lines. He had fulfilled his promise to clear his name and to take back everything that had been taken from him, and now the common man wanted the same.

Not every citizen or those in the government or military condoned what Billy Ray had done. Some viewed him as a terrorist and his act as one of domestic terrorism. But in light of the circumstances surrounding his motivations and the fact that the majority of the people believed his actions were justified, none of his detractors would publically criticize or condemn him.

The board had devised and implemented a plan to restore order. They used their influence with key congressmen to hold hearings and to rescind the order of martial law and restore the right to habeas corpus. They persuaded local and state authorities to release all the protesters without charging them with any offenses. At the heart of their plan was to shift the blame from the government and military to individual villains against whom the public could vet and vent their outrage, and thus disarm the volatile situation.

The board started with Governor Maxwell, who was impeached; Judge Tores, who was removed from the bench; and Billy Ray's attorney, William Coyle, who was disbarred. They all accepted plea agreements and received various prison terms. Warden Van Leeston and Lieutenant O'Rourke were indicted on conspiracy charges to have Billy Ray killed. O'Rourke cut a deal with the state prosecutors for a lesser charge and became a star witness against the warden in a televised trial. They were both remanded to separate prisons and placed in solitary confinement for their own protection.

The blame for the deaths of the ISS soldiers was attributed to the incompetence of General Bishop and the vendetta he had against Billy Ray. He was portrayed as a rogue general with fascist principles, acting alone, without authority, and outside of the boundaries of common decency. He was vilified by the press and the public for his role in the death of Father Pat.

The board believed that this still would not be enough to placate the citizenry, so they saved their coup de grace for last. They had the California US attorney general release the damaging evidence gathered from Senator Bryant's wall safe. The evidence showed that he was the chief architect behind the conspiracy and cover-up against Billy Ray. He was portrayed as an out-of-control senator, intoxicated with power and privilege. He would be the villain fed to the rabid wolves of public opinion that the board hoped would satiate and appease their taste for blood and quell the outrage and chaos.

Just as the board had hoped, the disturbances diminished, and order was slowly restored. In the aftermath, there was endless debate as politicians, talk-show hosts, and pundits jousted and bandied their various opinions about what had happened, why it happened, and how it was going to affect public policy and politics going forward.

Prodded by the constant urging from his constituents, Mayor White ran for the seat vacated by Senator Bryant's apparent suicide and won by an overwhelming majority. Most of the old guard in congress had been kicked out and replaced by a new breed of politician. For the time being, they were more concerned with the welfare of the nation than they were with partisan "to get along you go along" politics, self-interests, or lining their own pockets. In concert with the new Congress, Senator White's first order of business was to pass legislation to restore the liberties and freedoms that had eroded over the years, without compromising the security of the nation.

In spite of the significant loss of the electorate because of his association with Bryant, Senator Morton was elected to the presidency by a narrow margin. With the leadership of his conservative policies, the economy was improving, and the general consensus was that public confidence was restored and the country seemed to be headed in the right direction. Even though the $20 trillion deficit was slowly being reduced, economists were not convinced that the collapse had been averted but merely delayed.

Using his influence with President Morton, Senator White persuaded him to award Billy Ray the Congressional Medal of Honor posthumously, for conspicuous bravery and valor for his actions in Afghanistan.

Jenny had waited in Alberta for the bluebird that never arrived. She returned home when she realized that Billy Ray was not coming and that she was pregnant. It was the source of her greatest joy, and yet one of sadness and anguish as she remembered what Billy Ray had written in his letter, and she wondered if the father of her child was still alive.

Twins had always run in the Blu family. Almost nine months to the very night she had spent with him, she gave birth to twins, a girl that she named after the boys' mother, Adeline, and a boy that she named after his father, William Raymond Blu, Jr.

Months slowly turned into years. Websites were dedicated to exploring every Billy Ray sighting. There were people who positively identified seeing him in Alberta, Canada. Others filled out affidavits swearing that he was at a wine symposium in Burgundy, France. After a while the sightings diminished, but occasionally reports surfaced that he was seen on almost every continent. There were those who believed that he had died in Silver Verde. Others believed, or at least hoped, that he was still out there waiting, watching, only to surface if things ever got out of control again, and so the myth grew.

Senator White kept the promise he made with Billy Ray that night in St. Mary's Church. He looked in on Jenny from time to time and asked her out to dinner many times, which she always gracefully declined. At first she resisted his affections, but after a while their mutual respect turned into something more. As their relationship grew, he asked her to marry him. She finally accepted when her heart told her that Billy Ray was never coming back and remembering what he had said in his letter, for her to move on with her life, as she had done once before.

⇥⊙ ⊙⇤

July 4, four years later

It was celebration day for the dedication of Patriots Park and the unveiling of the monument for all those who had lost their lives for liberty, freedom, and restoring the American way of life. It was the day Billy Ray had envisioned when he had his epiphany in the basement of St. Mary's Church.

Patriot's Park was constructed from private donations in the area that used to be known as Blu's Bluff, and it overlooked a cascading waterfall that flowed over the remnants of the dam. The ten-acre park was landscaped with many ornamental trees and shrubs and flowering annuals that had been planted for the occasion. It was framed by a cobblestone walking path and an expansive dark-green lawn, picnic tables, and a large gazebo in the center of the park.

Restaurants, caterers, and bakeries from all over the state had donated wait-staff and delicacies of roasted meats, grilled vegetables, freshly prepared seafood, and baked goods.

Thousands of people from all walks of life had gathered for the occasion. Dignitaries, politicians, and movie stars were in attendance, posing for pictures and giving sound bites for the camera crews of every major network. Veterans, many of them wearing their old uniforms, and wounded warriors, some missing limbs, others in wheel chairs or on crutches, gathered near the monument for the dedication.

Governor Walcott, who replaced Maxwell in a special election, gave a short speech for the dedication. Everyone stood in silence as Father John Admiral, the new young pastor of St. Mary's Church, gave the invocation. He knew he had large shoes to fill, but he was pious, well liked by the parishioners, and seemed up to the task.

The steps leading up to the monument were light-gray flamed granite. Two towering flagpoles were behind the monument, one with the California state flag and the other with a sprawling US flag. Standing tall in the middle of the monument on top of a large gray granite pedestal was a bronze statue that was cast in Billy Ray's image, with both his hands extending upward. Under the statue, deeply carved into the granite was: Sergeant William "Billy Ray" Blu, USMC, Congressional Medal of Honor Recipient, Our Hero, Ever Vigilant, Lest We Ever Forget. Next to the center monument was a smaller one dedicated to Father Patrick O'Keefe, DOD, USMC, and Congressional Medal of Honor Recipient.

To the left were two monuments, one for Colonel Alexander Clay and one for Captain Aloysius "Midnight" Smith. To the right was a monument for Raymond "Junior" Blu, and the final monument was dedicated to all those American patriots, soldiers, who had given their lives or served to preserve and safeguard the freedom and security of the United States.

Jenny stood alongside her husband. They were wearing aprons and serving food to the crowd from inside one of the several large tents. Mayor Roy entered the tent. He had gained weight over the past four years and was now a portly man. He shook Senator White's hand and gave Jenny a hug and a kiss. Then he helped himself to a generous portion of barbeque spare ribs. Next to him was his daughter-in-law and his eldest son, who had been elected to his former position as town sheriff. A few minutes later, Carla came walking through the line, pushing a baby stroller.

"He looks just like his father," Jenny said, handing her a piece of warm corn bread. "Where's Robert?"

"You know BB," she said, leaning over to give a piece of the cornbread to her son. "He's with the guys near the monument, probably telling war stories."

After BB had taken Jenny to Canada, he went to the county hospital to give Carla the money as Billy Ray had told him to for "someday." They spent some time together while she was convalescing. When he returned home, they carried on a long-distance relationship. He finally returned to Silver Verde and with the stake that Billy Ray had given him, bought Handsome Butch's Firework Factory. In little time he built up his business, exporting his brand of East Coast pyrotechnics and artistry to the West Coast, even shooting shows for the opening of casinos in Las Vegas. Since Carla knew that "someday" for people like her usually meant "never," when BB asked her to marry him, she accepted, knowing it would probably be her last chance for a stable life and happiness. A year later Robert Brazoli Junior was born.

In the middle of the afternoon, Jenny and Senator White sat with Warden Curtis and his wife of two years, Dr. Catalina Vibes. Most of their conversation revolved around the events of the day, but it always gravitated to stories about Billy Ray. Throughout the day, everyone who knew him told their favorite Billy Ray stories. Even the McFarlane brothers, who came with their wives and children, were telling anyone who would listen about the "good old days" and how they had been the best of friends with him since childhood.

The Wiz, BB, and Big John Rollins were sitting at a picnic table near the monument, drinking coffee from paper cups and eating from a tray of Italian pastries consisting of zepoles, cannolis, and sfogliatellas. Rollins had come with his wife and children. He had just finished telling the men about how his sons had made all-state on their state-champion baseball team and that college and pro scouts were already recruiting them as future prospects.

The sun was low in the sky. BB had strung up large canisters of pyrotechnics across the waterfall that would cascade red, white, and blue sparks over the water during the finale. "Mar-done! It's almost show time. Wait till they get a load of the fireworks I set up." He picked up the last cannoli, and as he ate it, the powdered sugar fell on his shirt and surrounded his lips. He dusted off his shirt and face using his hand as a napkin.

"Hey slob," the Wiz said. "I think you missed a spot."

BB lit up his cigar and hit the Wiz on the back of his head. "You can take the boy out of Brooklyn, but you can't take the Brooklyn out of the boy...at least that what my wife keeps telling me."

"How's that working out?" Rollins asked.

"Great," BB said. "If there's an ass for every seat and a seat for every ass, we were made for each other."

"Wow!" the Wiz said. "What a philosophy."

BB tapped the Wiz on the backside of his head once again, only this time a little harder.

Rollins laughed. "You guys never give it a rest, do you?" Then Rollins looked up at the statue of Billy Ray and became introspective. "Hey BB, what do you really think happened to the colonel, Midnight, and Billy?"

"I'm pretty sure the colonel bought it when his Black Hawk crashed, and God only knows what happened to Midnight. As for Billy, I don't think we'll ever know, and maybe that's the way he wanted it."

The Wiz finished his cup of coffee. "With all the fake IDs and passports, if he's still alive, he could be just about anywhere."

Rollins looked up at the statue again. "My wife really wanted to meet him. Did you ever think that maybe the ultimate sacrifice he made was not sacrificing his life for what he believed but giving up the life he had—forever—to protect us and the woman he loved?" he said, nodding in Jenny's direction.

"Maybe," BB said. "It's just the kind of thing a noble man like Billy would do. Maybe he figured that if Standz and the other G-men couldn't confirm if he was dead or alive, it would keep them in line. The last thing they would want to do is light a fire under his ass...twice."

Suddenly, BB nudged the Wiz. "Speak of the devil. What the fuck's he doing here?"

Rollins looked into the crowd. "Is that him? Really him?"

"Sure is," the Wiz said. "Probably on a fishing expedition, along with the other spooks I saw in the crowd. They took our pictures, but I also took pictures of them."

A devious smile appeared on BB's face. "I'll be right back. There's just something I have to do," he said, biting the side of his hand in defiance.

BB and the Wiz recognized him at once, but Rollins had never seen him before. He was wearing a black pinstriped Armani suit, a gray open-collar shirt, highly polished black Cordovan leather shoes, and a darkly tinted pair of tear-drop sunglasses. He was walking casually through the crowd toward the monument, sipping a cup of coffee as he took in the panoramic view. He had retired from the CIA and was now a member of the board, having replaced the deceased chairman.

Ocho stood with his wife, looking up at the monument, his hands folded in front of him as if in prayer. Ocho missed his old friend and was reminiscing about the good times he and Billy Ray had growing up together and working in the vineyard.

BB returned and sat down with a cat-that-ate-the-canary look on his face.

"I know that look, BB," Rollins said. "What did you do?"

"I'll tell you about it later."

It was late afternoon. Jenny's son came running over, dangling something in his hand, spinning it around his finger. Warden Curtis and Dr. Vibes were leaving and thanked Jenny for a wonderful day.

"Mommy, Mommy," Billy Ray Jr. said. "Look what the man gave me."

At first, Jenny didn't pay attention to what he was saying. Then she glanced over and saw that he was twirling a bluebird keychain. As she remembered what Billy Ray had told her in his letter, her face became flushed, and her heart raced. "I'll be right back," she said to her husband.

As she walked with her son in tow in the direction of where he said he had received the keychain, her heart began beating faster. "Show me, Billy. Show me the man who gave you that."

Her son pointed in the direction of a group of well-dressed men and several veterans in uniform mulling around the base of the monument. She walked up to one of the well-dressed men and stood beside him, wondering what she would say if it was him. The man turned and smiled. It was Phillip Renard, from the Wine Consortium. Upon seeing who it was, she was saddened and yet relieved. It must have been him who gave her son the key chain, she thought.

"Mrs. Blu, or shall I say Mrs. White," Renard said, with a thick French accent, extending his hand.

"It's Mrs. Blu, Mr. Renard. I kept my first married name."

"With all the activities, we haven't had time to talk on such a magnificent day. I would never be so crass to talk business on a day such as this, but I thought you should know the good news. Even though you have increased production tenfold, in light of Blu Select winning best of show for the past several years and with William's notoriety, demand is still ahead of supply."

"Several years ago, we planted the entire acreage of the Kramer farm with the pinot noir stock. In the fall those fields will be ready for harvest, and then I think we will be able to keep up with the demand."

"Excellent news. Sorry to say, I must depart before the festivities are concluded, or I'll miss my flight. I look forward to seeing you again at harvest time." And with those words, he shook her hand and left.

Her son ran over and began walking up the steps to the monument. "Stay close to Mommy," she said. "It's getting dark, and the fireworks will be beginning soon." As usual, her son wasn't paying attention to her. "Billy Ray, did you hear me?"

As soon as she mentioned her son's name, another well-dressed man glanced over, smiled, and then looked away.

Jenny became paralyzed as she looked at his profile, build, and height. She could feel her heart racing once again. "Could it be him?" she thought. As she looked back, he was gone. As she turned to look for him, they bumped into each other.

"Excuse me," Jenny said, not looking up.

"That's quite all right, Jenifer."

Jenny looked up into his bright-blue eyes. The Prince of Darkness could see that as she was studying his facial features, her mind elsewhere. Finally, she was back to the moment.

"Pardon me for staring. You look so familiar. Have we met before?"

"Maybe that's because some people think I resemble William. Yes, we have met before."

Jenny was looking out into the abyss, trying to remember.

"In the library. You helped me find some books by Milton. I'm Richard Standz," he said, extending his hand.

As she shook his hand, she noticed that he caressed it. "I remember now. *Paradise Lost*. Did you know Billy?"

"As well as anyone, except maybe for you. William was an extraordinary man. He accomplished so many great things in his short life. I know it may not be any consolation to you when I say that sometimes the candle that burns twice as bright burns half as long. He left a great legacy, one to be admired and emulated. And this," he said, waving his hand toward the monument, "is a fitting testimony to him."

Her daughter came running up to her, and her son came down from the granite steps. They both looked up at the Prince of Darkness with their piercing bright-blue eyes. The Prince of Darkness smiled to himself with the knowledge that he knew these two children were also a part of his legacy.

"It was nice to meet you, Mr. Standz," Jenny said.

"I wish you, Senator White, and your children all the happiness. I know William would have been proud of this day."

As Jenny walked away with her son and daughter, the Prince of Darkness stared up at the statue, took a chess piece out of his pocket, and laid it on the first step of the monument. It was a black knight.

The Prince of Darkness walked over to where the men were sitting. As he began talking, he looked straight forward and did not make eye contact with them. "Mr. Castle, Mr. Brazoli, and," he said, looking briefly toward Big John, "Mr. Rollins. We were not aware that you were part of this motley crew."

"Well, I guess you don't know everything."

"I guess, Mr. Rollins, I know more now than I did before I arrived. Have you men been behaving?"

"No more or no less than you, Standz," the Wiz said with a sarcastic tone.

"Hey, Standz," BB said. "You see Billy? I think he's over there with Colonel Clay."

As Prince of Darkness looked into the crowd, he noticed BB smiling to the other men and knew he was pulling his leg. "I saw William die in Afghanistan. Most assumed he died after the prison break. This time, I'm sure Captain 'Midnight' Smith, Colonel Clay, and William didn't make it out."

"Didn't you play chess with Billy?" the Wiz asked. "Maybe that was his best move ever!"

"Maybe," the Prince of Darkness said. "Maybe."

"Next time I talk to Billy," BB said, "I'll give him your regards."

The Prince of Darkness smiled. He turned toward the men; gave them a cold, ominous stare; and then walked away. "Good evening, men. Catch you later," he said, without turning around.

When he was out of hearing distance, BB nudged the Wiz. "Wait till he gets into his Crown Victoria," he said with a wide grin.

"What did you do, BB?"

"Just something to keep that asshole looking over his shoulder the rest of his miserable life!"

It was twilight. The last gleaming shreds of pale-amber and orange light filtered through the waves of dark purple clouds on the horizon. Roscoe Clements was standing in front of the monument with his sons, their wives, and his grandchildren. He had received an out-of-court settlement from the remaining partners of the village of Silver Verde for $12 million, and another $3 million from the State of California for wrongful prosecution and imprisonment. He purchased a one-hundred-acre farm just outside of Silver Verde and, with his entire family, resumed the simple life of a farmer.

He looked up at the statue and silently said a prayer, thanking his friend for what he had done for him. "We'll meet again and continue our game where we left off, old friend, if not here, in the hereafter."

Then he sat down on the granite steps and took out his guitar from an old brown leather case. It was a small, high-pitched guitar that sounded more like a ukulele. As he began playing and singing—with his distinctive low, raspy voice—the Woody Guthrie song "This Land Is My Land," a crowd formed and began singing along with him.

The Prince of Darkness got into his Crown Victoria and took off his sunglasses. As he put the car into reverse, he was startled when he thought he saw Billy Ray sitting in the backseat. He turned around quickly and realized that his rearview mirror was tilted and that what he saw was his own reflection. When he went to adjust the mirror, he saw a bluebird key chain dangling from it. A sense of fear and paranoia enveloped him, emotions he was not accustomed to having. At the exact moment he tried to adjust the mirror, the first volley of fireworks exploded in the air behind him. He ducked and nearly slid off his seat. He adjusted the mirror, locked the doors, and sped off into the darkness.

Just as BB had promised, the display and artistry of the fireworks was like nothing anyone had ever seen in the region. They went off in rapid succession over the waterfall, with the monument in the foreground, filling the sky with brilliant color and sound. Jenny looked back in the direction of Blu's Bluff and thought she saw a figure looking down over the crowd. When another series of fireworks exploded, she could see that it was just the illumination of the fireworks casting long, colorful shadows over the area. She thought about all the things she was grateful for and all the things she missed. She had a husband who loved her and the children she always wanted. If all but one of her dreams came true, she knew she was more fortunate than most.

As the finale began, the canisters BB had strung over the waterfall cascaded red, white, and blue sparks over the water. She looked up at the monument and was transported to another time and place. She was sitting on a picnic blanket with Billy Ray on the banks of Silver Verde Lake. The late afternoon sun was shimmering off the calm, blue water. Her CD player was playing her favorite rendition of "Four Strong Winds," by Neil Young and Emmylou Harris.

That was the day, that perfect day Billy Ray said he would love her forever and sealed his promise with their first kiss. He lived now, only in her memory.

Intermittent Light

July 5

HE SAT ON a lawn chair on the veranda outside D-Ward Psychiatric Center in a VA hospital on Chalkstone Avenue in Providence, Rhode Island. A small battery-powered TV was on a table next to him, playing reruns of *The Family Feud*. He took a small role of transparent tape from his pocket and taped two cigarettes together.

Every now and then, a lucid thought would break through the clouds of Thorazine, just like the morning sun was filtering through the hazy sky to the east, warming him. He wondered how many people were in the same condition as him, without the hindrance of perception-numbing drugs. He knew that for those who understood the ramifications of what had transpired, no explanation was necessary, and for those who did not, no explanation would ever suffice.

The only memory that gave him solace was the last words he said to Billy Ray and the privileged knowledge of what they meant. He lit up the two cigarettes, took in a deep drag, and smiled. "Who's your daddy?" he said to himself. "Who's your daddy now?"

61844331R00167

Made in the USA
Charleston, SC
26 September 2016